PRAISE FOR

The Lady Sherlock Se...

"These books, which recast Sherlock Holmes as Charlotte Holmes, are perfect for those who adore layered stories. Unignorable questions of gender, expectation and privilege lurk beneath complex mysteries and a slowly scorching romance." —*The Washington Post*

"Loaded with suspense . . . a riveting and absorbing read . . . a beautifully written novel; you'll savor the unraveling of the mystery and the brilliance of its heroine." —NPR

"Sherry Thomas has done the impossible and crafted a fresh, exciting new version of Sherlock Holmes." —Deanna Raybourn, *New York Times* bestselling author of *A Perilous Undertaking*

"Sherry Thomas is a master of her craft, and *A Study in Scarlet Women* is an unqualified success: brilliantly executed, beautifully written, and magnificently original—I want the next volume now!" —Tasha Alexander, *New York Times* bestselling author

"Readers will wait with bated breath to discover how Thomas will skillfully weave in each aspect of the Sherlockian canon and devour the pages to learn how the mystery unfolds." —Anna Lee Huber, national bestselling author of the Lady Darby Mysteries

"Clever historical details and a top-shelf mystery add to the winning appeal of this first volume in the Lady Sherlock series. A must-read for fans of historical mysteries." —*Library Journal* (starred review)

"A completely new, brilliantly conceived take on the iconic detective . . . A plot worthy of [Sir Arthur Conan Doyle] at his best." —*Booklist*

"Readers will revel in seeing Charlotte and her dearest companions at the top of their game in this eventful and pivotal entry in the formidable series." —*BookPage* on *Miss Moriarty, I Presume?*

"Settle in for a delightful read, full of red herrings and memorable set pieces and above all, let the talented Sherry Thomas dazzle you as she performs literary sleights of hand at every turn. Brava!"
—Criminal Element on *Miss Moriarty, I Presume?*

"Fast-paced storytelling and witty prose add further appeal for those who like their historical mysteries playful."
—*Publishers Weekly* on *The Art of Theft*

"Quick-witted and swashbuckling, Thomas's novel is a feminist Victorian delight. Perfect for fans of Deanna Raybourn, Elizabeth Peters or C. S. Harris, *The Art of Theft* is an excellent entry in a wonderful historical series. Its deft pacing, quirky heroine and intriguing cast of characters make it a mysterious tour de force."
—Shelf Awareness on *The Art of Theft*

"With an increasingly beloved detective crew, this Victorian mystery offers thrills and sharp insights into human behavior."
—*Kirkus Reviews* (starred review) on *Murder on Cold Street*

A
RUSE OF
SHADOWS

SHERRY THOMAS

BERKLEY
New York

BERKLEY
An imprint of Penguin Random House LLC
penguinrandomhouse.com

Copyright © 2024 by Sherry Thomas

BERKLEY and the BERKLEY & B colophon are registered trademarks of
Penguin Random House LLC.

Library of Congress Cataloging-in-Publication Data

Names: Thomas, Sherry (Sherry M.) author.
Title: A ruse of shadows / Sherry Thomas.
Description: First edition. | New York: Berkley, 2024. |
Series: The Lady Sherlock series
Identifiers: LCCN 2023050042 (print) | LCCN 2023050043 (ebook) |
ISBN 9780593640432 (paperback) | ISBN 9780593640449 (e-pub)
Subjects: LCGFT: Detective and mystery fiction. | Novels.
Classification: LCC PS3620.H6426 R87 2024 (print) |
LCC PS3620.H6426 (ebook) | DDC 813/.6—dc23/eng/20231106
LC record available at https://lccn.loc.gov/2023050042
LC ebook record available at https://lccn.loc.gov/2023050043

First Edition: June 2024

Printed in the United States of America
1st Printing

To J

What a pleasure to geek out with a story buddy right at home

Cast of Characters

CHARLOTTE HOLMES: *Solves crimes as sister of and oracle to the nonexistent Sherlock Holmes*

MRS. WATSON: *Charlotte's dear friend and business partner*

LORD INGRAM ASHBURTON: *Aka Ash; Charlotte's longtime friend and newish lover*

LIVIA HOLMES: *Charlotte's third-eldest sister; creator of Sherlock Holmes stories*

PENELOPE REDMAYNE: *Mrs. Watson's niece (daughter)*

BERNADINE HOLMES: *Charlotte's second-eldest sister; cannot look after herself*

MISS LONGSTEAD: *Charlotte's friend; a chemist by training*

LEIGHTON ATWOOD: *Lord Ingram's cousin; recruited to help Charlotte*

STEPHEN MARBLETON: *Moriarty's natural son; the man Livia loves*

LAWSON: *Mrs. Watson's groom and coachman*

LORD BANCROFT ASHBURTON: *Lord Ingram's recently deceased older brother; formerly in charge of secret portfolios for the crown*

UNDERWOOD: *Lord Bancroft's chief lieutenant*

MRS. CLAIBORNE: *Lord Bancroft's former mistress; Underwood's former mistress and current fiancée*

LORD REMINGTON ASHBURTON: *Lord Ingram's older brother; in charge of certain overseas security matters for the crown*

INSPECTOR TREADLES: *Scotland Yard officer; Lord Ingram's friend and Charlotte's sometime collaborator*

CHIEF INSPECTOR TALBOT: *Retired Scotland Yard officer*

SERGEANT MACDONALD: *Inspector Treadles's protégé*

VICTOR MEADOWS: *Victim in the Christmas Eve Murder of 1871*

MRS. MEADOWS: *Victor Meadows's wife*

MIRIAM TIPTON: *Mrs. Meadows's sister*

MRS. HARCOURT: *Victor Meadows's sister*

MISS HARCOURT: *Mrs. Harcourt's daughter; Victor Meadows's niece*

EPHRAIM MEADOWS: *Victor Meadows's and Mrs. Harcourt's older half brother*

DANNY STOW: *Gardener who discovered Victor Meadows's body*

MRS. FARR: *Charlotte's former client who requested assistance in search of a missing sister*

JOHNNY, MUMBLE, AND JESSIE: *Young boxers sponsored by Underwood*

MRS. CALDER: *Old woman enjoying a seaside holiday*

DE LACEY: *Moriarty's chief lieutenant in Britain*

A
Ruse of
Shadows

One

Before Inspector Robert Treadles had wanted to be Sherlock Holmes, he had wanted to be Chief Inspector John Talbot.

The chief inspector had retired the year after Treadles had been promoted to detective sergeant, but Treadles had worked with him once. The senior officer had been patient and fair, interested not in producing likely seeming culprits to prosecute but in chiseling away at a case until he had revealed everything about the crime and its participants.

Under any other circumstances, Treadles would have been delighted to welcome the chief inspector out of retirement—and to observe the wise old policeman again in a professional capacity.

Under any other circumstances.

The parlor of the hotel suite in which he found himself boasted dark varnished wainscoting, scarlet velvet curtains, and a deep pile blue-and-gold Turkish carpet underfoot. The décor had been conceived to provide luxurious warmth during London's long and gloomy winter. But on this sultry day, the room closed in.

Chief Inspector Talbot, his thick head of white hair combed back, his gaze kind yet penetrating, asked, "Young lady, may I inquire as to the nature of your association with the deceased?"

The young lady in question, a woman in her mid-twenties, was attired in a full English garden. So many roses, foxgloves, and hydrangeas flourished upon her dress that it had taken a while for Treadles to discern that the garment was made of a light green muslin. And, of course, embroidered sprigs of lavender proliferated across the circumference of the hem.

In contrast to the gaudy botanical excesses of her frock, her expression was solemn and blank.

"Lord Bancroft Ashburton was the brother of my friend Lord Ingram Ashburton. Several years ago, Lord Bancroft asked for my hand in marriage. I did not believe we would suit and declined his proposal."

She spoke with a calm detachment, as if she were fielding slightly intrusive questions at a tea party rather than inquiries stemming from a murder investigation.

"And was that the extent of your acquaintance?"

"Not quite. Due to certain events, I am now no longer welcome in polite circles. After I became an exile from Society, much to my surprise, Lord Bancroft proposed again."

Treadles, who had been in the middle of tugging on his collar, stilled.

He had learned some time ago that Miss Charlotte Holmes had been highly successful on the Marriage Mart: Several of the proposals she'd received had been considered not just good but spectacular.

Even so, to number Lord Bancroft as a suitor not once but twice.

"And I surmise that, once again, you turned him down?" murmured Chief Inspector Talbot.

"He withdrew his offer, rather," said Miss Holmes. "But you are correct, Chief Inspector, in that after much consideration, I still did not wish to marry him."

"And yet lately you have visited him—repeatedly."

She was, in fact, the only person Lord Bancroft had met with in the weeks preceding his death.

The grandfather clock in the corner gonged. Treadles glanced at it. Half past three in the afternoon.

Miss Holmes cast her gaze in the same direction. "Our tea should be here."

As if on cue, a knock came. Miss Holmes excused herself, went to answer it, and returned with a laden tea tray. She poured for her callers and handed around a plate of baked delicacies. "The hotel provides an excellent Madeira cake. The tea cakes are very decent, too."

The hotel also provided suites that functioned much as residences, with private entrances from the street. That Miss Holmes had chosen to lodge at a hotel, rather than opening up 18 Upper Baker Street or Mrs. Watson's house, had signaled to Treadles her intention of only a brief stay in London.

Surely she hadn't planned on becoming a murder suspect in so short a time?

Miss Holmes took a bite of the tea cake she had recommended. "Lately I *have* called on Lord Bancroft a little more than is my wont."

She glanced at Treadles. "Are you sure you wouldn't care for a tea cake, Inspector?"

Treadles's innards, wound tight, rebelled at the thought of sugar and butter. He didn't know how she managed to enjoy—or at least appear to enjoy—the rich assortment on her plate. "I'm quite all right, thank you."

Chief Inspector Talbot, in his dove grey Newmarket coat, sipped his tea and studied Miss Holmes. He seemed very much a benevolent if youngish great-uncle, inquiring after the latest doings of his favorite grandniece.

"And what would be the reason, Miss Holmes, for your more frequent visits to Lord Bancroft?"

Wildebeests rampaged inside Treadles's stomach. Talbot could control an interview as well as anyone. But unlike some other investigators from Scotland Yard that Miss Holmes had dealt with, including

Treadles himself at one point, Chief Inspector Talbot never underestimated women.

"I received a letter from Lord Bancroft," answered Miss Holmes, who consumed her tea cake at a steady pace. "He expressed a desire to see me. The missive was unexpected, as were his sentiments. He had retired from public life under occluded circumstances, and I was curious as to why he wished to meet again."

"Did you find out why?"

"He told me that he feared for his life."

Treadles hadn't expected the lies to start flying so soon. When they'd met earlier in the month, Miss Holmes had said nothing to him about Lord Bancroft cowering in mortal dread. He tugged at his collar again, wishing for a draught of fresh air.

"And it appears now," mused Chief Inspector Talbot, "that his lordship was right in his apprehension. But if you will forgive my question, Miss Holmes, why did he wish to burden you of all people with the knowledge that he might be in danger?"

"Do you believe, Chief Inspector, that there is any reason why he shouldn't have?"

"I can play games with you, Miss Holmes, but I won't." Chief Inspector Talbot set down his teacup and leaned back in his chair. "Part of the reason that I am investigating this case is a matter of personnel: Chief Inspector Fowler, who most likely would have been given the portfolio, is otherwise occupied.

"But in truth, that is only a convenient excuse. The real reason is that in the past I have worked with certain more obscure bureaus of the government and have become trusted for my discretion. For example, I have long known that Ravensmere, where Lord Bancroft dwelt for the better part of a year, is no ordinary lodging house for gentlemen but a cushioned facility for sensitive prisoners.

"I have also been informed, though much more recently, that you, Miss Holmes, far from languishing in your exile, have in fact become the celebrated-but-reclusive consulting detective Sherlock Holmes, who has, among other great deeds, cleared my young colleague here of suspicion of murder last December."

Treadles could only hope that Miss Holmes would not think *he* had been the informer. It had been discomfiting to learn from Chief Inspector Talbot that the senior officer already knew of Sherlock Holmes's true identity. But at the same time, that had been nothing compared to the shocking revelations concerning Lord Bancroft.

The previous autumn, during the investigation of a murder for which Lord Ingram had been—briefly—the chief suspect, Treadles had met Lord Bancroft. It had seemed natural enough that with his youngest brother in trouble, Lord Bancroft had come to Stern Hollow, Lord Ingram's estate, to lend moral and practical support. It had seemed equally natural that after the case was resolved, Treadles had never heard from or about Lord Bancroft again.

The police and the public had eventually learned that Lady Ingram, Lord Ingram's then wife, had run away with a man named Moriarty. And that the body found in Stern Hollow's icehouse had been not that of Lady Ingram but that of her twin sister, killed by Moriarty to frame Lord Ingram.

In private, however, Lord Ingram had informed Treadles that no, Lady Ingram had never formed a romantic liaison with Moriarty. She had done something far worse: She had worked for Moriarty and used her proximity to Lord Ingram, and therefore Lord Bancroft, who handled highly sensitive portfolios for the crown, to ferret out bits of intelligence to pass on to Moriarty's organization.

Treadles had been chosen to assist Chief Inspector Talbot because he was already acquainted with Miss Charlotte Holmes, the current case's—as of now—sole suspect. And because he had at least met the victim and knew something of his general background.

Only to then learn that he'd known nothing of the dead man when Chief Inspector Talbot notified him that Lord Bancroft had not stopped by Stern Hollow last autumn as a concerned brother but as a perturbed perpetrator. *He* had placed a body in the estate's ice well, hoping to frame his brother. Moriarty had played the spoiler and swapped one body for another, but the scheme had begun with Lord Bancroft.

As for why Lord Bancroft had done something so nefarious? In the end, it had been to protect himself: He had been living a secretly lavish lifestyle, which he had financed by selling state secrets in his keeping.

"You need not worry that the knowledge of your secret profession will travel beyond this parlor," continued Chief Inspector Talbot to a Miss Holmes who, on the surface of it, did not appear remotely concerned.

Once Treadles had believed her unfeeling. But now that he knew her—and himself—better, he saw that in the past he'd missed a number of clues with regard to her state of mind. For someone who delighted in food, last autumn she'd scarcely touched the myriad delicacies served at Stern Hollow.

And now, despite her matter-of-fact praise for the hotel's baked goods, she ate not with the savor of a gourmet, or even the gluttony of a gourmand, but the resolve of a ditchdigger, one with a great deal of cold, hard ground to bore through.

"Even if I weren't required to keep everything concerning this investigation in the strictest confidence, I still wouldn't have interfered with your livelihood," Chief Inspector Talbot went on. "But I will need you to answer my questions honestly and completely, because I also happen to know that it was as a result of Sherlock Holmes's inquiries at Stern Hollow that Lord Bancroft's misdeeds came to light.

"You tumbled him off his pedestal—into infamy among a select few, and into obscurity in the eyes of the public. You made him an inmate. I did not know the late Lord Bancroft very well, but I cannot imagine that he would have wished to entrust the matter of his personal safety to the one who had deprived him of his freedom in the first place."

Miss Holmes, having finished the small tea cake on her plate, set it aside and took a sip of tea. "The crown deprived Lord Bancroft of his freedom, Chief Inspector," she pointed out, with the sort of perfect logic that worked only for a very few. "But yes, I see what you mean. The immediate assumption would be that Lord Bancroft would want nothing to do with me and vice versa.

"To a certain extent, that is correct. For the past few months, my patroness, Mrs. Watson, and I have been living in Paris, where her niece studies medicine. Upon receiving Lord Bancroft's letter, I was not moved to travel across the Channel solely for his sake.

"But recently we visited England for a different reason, and I thought I might as well look in on Lord Bancroft before I left again. A man such as he is hardly neutered when kept behind bars. It would be wiser, I felt, to find out his purpose."

"But once you found out his purpose, what compelled you to care whether his lordship's life was in danger? If you will pardon the observation, Miss Holmes, you are of a cool disposition and not given to sentiments another young woman might feel toward a man who has twice proposed to her. I can easily envisage you brushing aside Lord Bancroft and his sense of impending doom."

This was very blunt but . . . not wrong. Indeed, sometimes Treadles worried about his friend Lord Ingram, so in love with this woman who, by temperament, might not be able to return his affection in equal measure.

Miss Holmes took no offense at Talbot's remark. If anything, she seemed to warm up a bit toward the older man. "True, Chief Inspector. It would have troubled me had Lord Bancroft escaped. But his destruction at the hands of his enemies? That would not have affected either my daily appetite or my nightly rest.

"Lord Bancroft understood that. He offered me five hundred pounds sterling to find his faithful acolytes, who had scattered in the wake of his arrest, so that they could come to his aid. I told him that I would not bestir myself—not for him, in any case—for less than two thousand."

"I applaud your astute negotiation, Miss Holmes, but may I

remind you that Lord Bancroft's crimes came to light largely because of his very unkind act toward Lord Ingram. Your friend Lord Ingram. Yet you still took him on as a client, this man who betrayed your friend?"

Chief Inspector Talbot appeared distressed at this line of questioning; Miss Holmes, not so. She had been about to go out when the policemen had arrived. Now, as if realizing she would not be going anywhere in a hurry, she removed her hat and placed it on her knees.

"Chief Inspector, I took on Lord Ingram's estranged wife as a client, too, when they were still married—and for far less than two thousand pounds. Also, do you believe Lord Ingram would have advised me differently, had he accompanied me to my initial meeting with Lord Bancroft?

"His lordship, as Inspector Treadles can tell you, has a truly noble soul. As disappointed as he was in his brother, he would not have wanted Lord Bancroft to die. Had I been able to save the latter's life and win myself two thousand pounds in the bargain, he would not have questioned my loyalty to him but only said, 'Well done, Holmes.'"

Chief Inspector Talbot cleared his throat. "That is, of course, between you and Lord Ingram, Miss Holmes. But did you also feel no compunction about the provenance of Lord Bancroft's funds? He would have paid you with money derived from the illicit sale of crown secrets, would he not?"

The wide brim of the hat in her lap featured an abundance of flowers, a circular boulevard of yellow silk petals. She smoothed the trio of ostrich plumes that erupted from its crown, dyed a matching, eye-jabbing yellow. "Are you trying to persuade me, Chief Inspector, that Lord Bancroft, a son of a noble family, and a man gainfully employed for many years in a position of high trust, did not possess two thousand pounds that he had procured by honest means?"

"That I cannot say, without a thorough auditing of Lord Bancroft's personal finances."

"Then you can see how I easily convinced myself that my remuneration would consist entirely of funds from legitimate sources."

Chief Inspector Talbot shook his head. "I must say, Miss Holmes, even after learning how you came to be Sherlock Holmes, I still thought that the person behind the great detective's façade would be of a more heroic character."

The gentle reproach, which would have stung Treadles to his soul, fell off Miss Holmes like raindrops from a mackintosh. She gave a small flick to the tip of one ostrich plume; its buoyant barbs undulated. "People come to Sherlock Holmes not for his character but for his detection. Men who are capable enough are rarely taken to task for personal flaws. Therefore I do not ask more of myself than the world would have were I a man.

"But we digress, Chief Inspector. Surely Sherlock Holmes's qualms or lack thereof isn't your primary concern?"

A change came over Chief Inspector Talbot. There was no clenching of jaw or narrowing of eyes, yet Treadles felt the hardening of his attitude: Upon meeting Miss Holmes, the senior policeman had viewed her as an unusual young woman; now he considered her only an adversary.

Or perhaps he had always seen her as purely an opponent, and Miss Holmes had known from the first that she faced an interrogator unlike any she had encountered before. Perhaps that was the reason for her dogged consumption of the tea cake—the reason for the fidgeting of her fingers, climbing and descending the central rachis of a plume, when she could otherwise remain effortlessly still.

"Indeed, I am here not only because you were a frequent visitor to Lord Bancroft in the final days of his life but because he himself declared, in a handwritten note, and I quote"—Chief Inspector Talbot set a pair of eyeglasses on his nose, pulled an envelope from his pocket, and extracted a piece of paper—"'Should anything happen to me, I have no doubt that Miss Charlotte Holmes would bear the preponderance of blame.'"

To this direct accusation, Miss Holmes's response was a tight smile. "Surely you must see, Chief Inspector, that as a professional who has unraveled a number of murders, if I were to take justice into my own hands, so to speak, I would not choose to call on my alleged victim several times in a short span *and* allow him to leave behind such a message."

"Well said, Miss Holmes," replied Chief Inspector Talbot. "However, it remains that, of late, you are the main vector of change in Lord Bancroft's life. Would you, as an investigator yourself, choose to leave your doings and whereabouts unexamined?"

"Certainly not," said Miss Holmes. She set aside her hat and laced her fingers in her lap. "Please go ahead with your questions."

Her knuckles were pale with tension. Treadles's pulse accelerated.

"I should like a detailed account of your doings since your return to England," said Talbot. "And a thorough report of all your dealings with Lord Bancroft."

Treadles's heart now thumped. In the softness of the chief inspector's tone, he heard a new conviction: This woman made for a brilliant murderer.

Charlotte Holmes inclined her head. "I shall furnish a complete narrative."

Two

My dear Mrs. Watson, Miss Holmes, and Miss Redmayne,

I write with less than joyful news.

No, do not fear. Nothing is terribly wrong, only that I have sustained an inconvenient injury.

From London, the children had gone with their cousins to Eastleigh Park. Home by myself in an echoing manor, I became a little restless, decided on a long walk, and got carried away.

By the time I realized that the day had waned, it was nearly eight, with a storm rolling in. The abrupt darkness made me choose a shortcut. Alas, chancing an unfamiliar footpath in pouring rain led to an unfortunate slip down a small ravine that fractured my left limb.

The trek back nearly bested me, even with the lucky find of a suitable branch for a makeshift crutch. But I was spared the worst, as I was found half a mile from home and carried the rest of the way.

I have since been fitted with a plaster cast and two proper crutches. The pain has become tolerable even without morphine. Instead, I take a few tablets daily of a new synthetic substance called phenacetin, and I must say its effects are remarkable. I am in no particular discomfort, and my mind is unclouded.

Pray do not worry about me. My overall health remains robust, and the physician expects the limb to be good as new in due time.

Your faithful if hobbling servant,
Ash

P.S. You are probably wondering why I chose not to keep this news to myself. Indeed, I would have, but I was to attend a dinner at a neighbor's estate, where a gaggle of houseguests had just come from London, on their way to Cowes. My staff, in conveying my regrets, let slip the truth, and now there is no point concealing it from you.

—⚬—

The day was fading, the sun dropping below the tops of the trees. Yet the gentler illumination of early evening saturated every vista with a rich golden tint—a wall of pink and white rhododendrons, a slope of lavender in bloom, a family of swans gliding across a small lake, passing in front of a slender marble pavilion that seemed to float above its own reflection.

The last time Mrs. Watson had visited the grounds of Stern Hollow, she had been in raptures. Today, however, its beauty failed to ease her apprehension. The solitude and vastness of the estate did not feel sanctuary-like, only faintly sinister, an area too large to patrol and too easy to infiltrate.

The silence also did not help. Who knew that birdsong, the rustling of leaves, and the rotation of steel wheels upon well-packed gravel could produce, after a while, a palpitation in the heart, a tense expectation that this tranquillity would be brutally shattered?

All this uneasiness, with Lord Ingram perfectly sound and whole!

Yes, his letter was a ruse. Mrs. Watson, Miss Charlotte, and Penelope's hasty trip, traveling overnight from Paris to England, so that they could see this beloved young man with their own eyes and make sure that he was all right—that, too, was part of the ruse.

But ruses would not be necessary if they didn't find themselves in perilous circumstances. They already had their hands full with Moriarty and his minions. This new wrinkle from Lord Bancroft—what in the world did *he* want?

"I, for one, am looking forward to an excellent dinner," said Miss Charlotte.

She was dressed as Mr. Sherrinford Holmes, brother to the fictional Sherlock Holmes. Her seafoam-colored jacket was cut to show a large expanse of anchor-printed waistcoat. Instead of a tie, she wore an elaborate cravat, secured by a jeweled shell brooch below the knot. And to complete the nautical theme, for her boutonniere, an actual—if deceased and long-desiccated—starfish, three inches across in diameter, which remarkably looked not *too* out of place on the lapel.

"I volunteer to brush your beard afterwards!" said Penelope.

Overly enthusiastic combing might damage the costly hairpiece, but the last thing they wanted was to put a prosthetic beard into storage with food crumbs trapped inside.

"Thank you," said Miss Charlotte in all seriousness. "It would have been better if Sherrinford Holmes had no stomach. Alas, mine is always in need of sustenance. I wonder what marvels Stern Hollow's pastry sous-chef has prepared for us—I hope there will be a charlotte russe."

The carriage emerged from a tunnel of green bough, and before them unfurled acres upon acres of gardens in lavish bloom, as if all the annuals knew that the peak of summer was about to pass them by and there was no time to waste in luring one more honeybee into that eternal dance of pollination.

Beyond the gardens, a reflecting pool glittered. The plume of water at its center, jetting up twenty feet in the air, glittered. The windows of the house, lit just so by the setting sun, also glittered. So beautiful, so serene, so normal—when what they were about to attempt was anything but.

The majordomo himself, the stately Mr. Walsh, awaited by the granite steps that led up to the house. He seemed especially glad to see Sherrinford Holmes—that gentleman had been, after all, instrumental in clearing Lord Ingram's name following a particularly unfortunate turn of events at the estate—but he was also highly solicitous of Mrs. Watson and Penelope. "Had you arrived under different circumstances, ladies, I would have arranged for a tour of the house. But I imagine today you will wish to see his lordship first?"

"Indeed, that is so," answered Mrs. Watson gravely. "His lordship first, everything else later."

She had visited the grounds of Stern Hollow but never the manor, and she had long wished to wallow in its spectacular interior. But as Mr. Walsh led them down the avenue of statues at the center of the grand entrance hall and up the double-returned staircase to his lordship's apartment, she did not need to pretend that she was too worried to gawk.

She sincerely paid little mind to the old-master paintings that littered halls and galleries. All she wanted was to see her dear boy.

Yet his brilliant, delighted smiles weren't enough to put her mind at ease. Or even his whispered reassurances that everything had gone according to plan. With the footmen off to fetch tea, all the curtains drawn, and his valet, Cummings, guarding the door—Cummings, along with Mr. Walsh and the housekeeper, Mrs. Sanborn, took part in the ruse—Lord Ingram rose and hopped a few times on his "broken" limb to show Mrs. Watson that indeed all was well.

They returned him to his chair, his plaster-entombed left limb placed in the exact same spot on the leather ottoman, just in time for the staff to parade in with enough tea things to host a garden party.

"I am very sorry to have put you to so much trouble with my carelessness," he said for the benefit of their audience with a perfect degree of ruefulness. "Could I at least propose tea and jam tarts? We've some excellent strawberry and raspberry jams made only days ago."

His eyes were on Sherrinford Holmes as he made his offer, his lips softening into the beginning of another smile.

"Sir, our haste was assuredly motivated by concern for your well-being," replied Sherrinford Holmes. "But I cannot deny that my mad dash to Stern Hollow was also spurred on by the anticipation of your legendary hospitality. I am ready for jam tarts—and all other acts of generosity you choose to bestow upon us."

———※———

"Now this is an act of generosity I had not anticipated," said Holmes.

Following dinner, also in Lord Ingram's apartment, Mrs. Watson and Miss Redmayne, citing fatigue, had left, leaving the "gentlemen" to their glass of postprandial port. And Holmes had wasted no time in ripping off her beard and climbing atop Lord Ingram.

Even men with actual broken limbs could probably cope with the amatory act just fine, and Lord Ingram was only somewhat inconvenienced by the large cast.

He managed splendidly.

Afterward, he expected that they would discuss the situation at hand, what with Bancroft's abrupt and unwelcome insertion. But she wanted to look at a pair of letters he'd penned during his "convalescence" largely to amuse himself.

"How nice that I don't need to write this performative letter—that you've done it for me," she murmured.

He looked down at her, lying across his bed, using his "uninjured" leg as a pillow. This also surprised him. As much as she enjoyed lovemaking, outside of it, she was not one to linger in a cuddle or to engage in any kind of prolonged touching. He supposed that putting her head on his thigh suited her, as she could change her position or cease contact at any moment.

But a small part of him—no, a large part of him; all of him, in fact—wanted this semi-embrace to be a harbinger of things to come.

Except he couldn't quite conceive what a future might look like for them—or how it might differ from the status quo of occasional meetings followed by long separations.

She read aloud. The first letter purported to be from her to him.

Dear Ash,

I know I already thanked you for the gift of the hamper, but now that I've at last plumbed its great depths, I am beyond delighted at this vast stockpile of foodstuff at my disposal.

She glanced up. "I can't say I've ever been informed in so agreeable a manner that I am about to receive a heroic quantity of delicious things."

"You are most welcome, Holmes."

"I look forward to discovering the contents of this fabled hamper. And by the way, thank you for the scrumptious charlotte russe at dinner."

The last time she'd visited Stern Hollow, her appetite had suffered a rare collapse, and she'd picked apart, rather than enjoyed, a beautiful slice of charlotte russe. Tonight, she'd relished it, and he had been most gratified by the sight of her empty plate.

In fact, when Inspector Treadles called at my hotel this afternoon, I treated him to some excellent plum cake from the hoard.

"Ah, so I'm to expect a visit from our Scotland Yard connection. You are beginning to sound clairvoyant, my lord."

Her golden hair had been dyed grey to play an old lady on the RMS *Provence*. Since then it had been shorn and was now just long enough to hold a curl again.

"I *have* been working on my ability to control the future," he said modestly, taking hold of a strand of her hair and feeling its fine, weightless texture against his skin.

The good police officer was saddened that the trip you two had planned for the Isles of Scilly must now be postponed. But he was far more concerned that your injury might not have been a result of pure bad luck. I tried, but he left still fixated on the absence of kerosene at your children's play cottage, which would have provided illumination for you on the way back.

It is possible that I could not convince him otherwise because I myself do not entirely believe that there were no other forces at work that night, lack of evidence notwithstanding.

"I like this bit," she declared. "If you had truly been hurt, everyone would have been highly suspicious of foul play."

Inspector Treadles then asked whether I would be leaving directly. You know I do not wish to be away from France for too long, but I could not bring myself to cross the Channel right away. The odd timing and serious nature of your injury—I told the inspector that I planned to remain in Britain until I felt better assured.

Upon hearing that, he replied that he would like me to look into something for him, if I happened to be idle in the near future. This surprised me, but I accepted the commission, with the understanding that other demands may preclude me from finishing the investigation in a timely manner.

"Have I mentioned yet, my lord, that I am somewhat alarmed by your extraordinary imitation of my handwriting? I can scarcely tell that I haven't penned this myself."

She could indeed post the letter to him from London, if she so wished. He let go of her hair and briefly touched her soft, cool earlobe. "Why, thank you, Holmes."

So there you have it, my itinerary for the days immediately ahead. Keep me apprised of your recovery. If circumstances are favorable, perhaps I'll travel to Stern Hollow again before I return to Paris.

Yours,
Holmes

P.S. Have I mentioned how grateful I am for the lovely hamper, one of the best gifts I've ever received? So grateful that I have decided to write the next installment in the very sedate little story that you found so relaxing.

At this, Holmes sat up.

Six months ago, he had sent her a pair of fuchsia silk stockings and she, in return, had penned an erotic vignette of a man watching a woman undress. And she had enjoyed his deliberately overwrought response so much that she asserted more than once her intention to continue the tale. Well, now he had done so for her.

She scanned the next few lines, which had been set down in a simple Caesar cipher.

He, of course, knew exactly what it said.

Her clothes lay discarded at the foot of the bed. Firelight caressed her smooth, supple skin. She made no attempt to cover herself, though occasionally she adjusted the pillows underneath her head.

He stared at her. His hands were busy, but his feet had been nailed in place since she had removed her garments and lain down on the rumpled bed. Light refracted from the folds of black satin sheets. Her lips were red, her calves shapely.

He swallowed.

His alarm clock clanged. He swore under his breath and silenced it. The woman rose, dressed quickly, came forward, and took her payment from him.

"Thank you," she said softly. "Will the painting be finished soon?"

"Yes, soon," he mumbled.

"Ah, I'm almost sorry," she said as she walked out the door. "Your studio is the only one that's remotely warm in winter."

"You made my tale of torrid seduction into one of a professional relationship, and a platonic one at that? Ah, but wait, you wrote a reply to this letter, too, didn't you?"

Dear Holmes,

The hours have been long since your departure.

To answer your question, my recovery continues apace. My staff aim to build the best wheelchair known to man so that I can move about outside.

But they have had to admit that even if they fitted pneumatic tires to this wheelchair, without a spring suspension, my broken limb would still be badly jostled along the garden paths, which was not designed with invalids in mind.

So, for now, I remain confined to my apartment. There are also plans to have me carried, like a pharaoh upon a palanquin, on the shoulders of four footmen, for me to visit other parts of the house. I have thus far demurred, not only out of hidden egalitarian principles deep in my heart but also out of fear that my inexperienced footmen might drop me while descending the grand staircase and give me a concussion and a dislocated shoulder to go with my fractured femur.

Do please convey my regards to Inspector Treadles next time you see him. I am sure he is grateful to receive your help, and I have no doubt you will be of great assistance to him.

I do not know how else to reassure you that the accident was indeed a result of my own misadventure, so I will simply let time bear witness to that. Please do not worry about me.

> *Yours,*
> *Ash*

P.S. While I am relieved for your immortal soul that your story has taken on a, well, not exactly wholesome but at least less lubricious bent, I must say the part of me that was looking forward to a bit of outrage was rather disappointed. Ah, Holmes, how you have corrupted your old friend.

P.P.S. However, I cannot help but think that the story would benefit from the addition of a few more lines. May I suggest the following?

The man stared at the closing door.

The painting was finished some time ago, and he suspected that she knew it. Where did that leave him then?

Holmes did not say anything, even after enough time had passed for her to have read the letter five times over.

Pinpricks of sensation stung Lord Ingram's fingertips—and the inside of his chest. It had not occurred to him when he wrote his "reply," but now it was blazingly obvious that he had revealed everything of himself in the little addendum to "her" story.

What did it say about them that her naughty and lighthearted tale, when he took over its authorship, immediately became a narrative of suppressed yearning, even though he had intended only a humorous rebuttal?

Perhaps it was a sign of how much more relaxed he had become around her that at this realization, he felt not a soul-crushing angst but only a bout of acute self-consciousness, which caused him to say, "I noticed that Mrs. Watson was tense—far more tense than she had reason to be. Did anything happen?"

The answer occurred to him as the question left his lips. "My goodness, did Bancroft write again?"

Holmes had informed him of Bancroft's first letter as soon as she'd received it, and he had been waiting, on tenterhooks, to see what his brother would do next.

She glanced at him, but chose not to question the abrupt change in their topic of discussion. "He did. His latest missive reached us just as we were about to begin our trip here to see you. The first letter had been addressed to Sherlock Holmes and sent to the General Post Office in London. This second note was delivered directly to the front door of Mrs. Watson's hired house in Paris."

The windows of Lord Ingram's apartment had been closed for hours. But now the air became too still, too thick to flow into his windpipe. "Did he say this time what he wanted?"

"No, he only chided me for not yet replying to his previous note and neglecting our long-standing friendship." Holmes was silent for a moment. "*You* and I are lifelong friends. Lord Bancroft and I, his two proposals notwithstanding, are only acquaintances. And my lord Bancroft, as you know, never does anything without calculation."

His hand gripped the cast on his limb. He had the irrational desire to claw at the plaster. "What about the situation in Aix-en-Provence?"

In the struggle against Moriarty, they were not without allies, one of whom was none other than Moriarty's daughter, Miss Marguerite Moriarty. Above all else, Miss Moriarty wanted to be reunited with her son—and Holmes had discovered the boy's whereabouts aboard the RMS *Provence* earlier in the year.

Now Miss Moriarty was ready to strike, which meant that they, if they wished to pry their friend Stephen Marbleton from Moriarty's grip, must act at the same time. Otherwise, once Miss Moriarty's actions became known to her father, Mr. Marbleton's chances of a successful escape would tumble precipitously.

"The situation in Aix-en-Provence is manageable," answered Holmes. "For now, at least, we have enough personnel."

Thanks to her bargain with his brother Remington, which allowed her to borrow some of his agents, with the understanding that they were officially on loan not to her but to Lord Ingram.

Slowly she folded the letters in her hands, as if she were reading them again as she did so. "As for my lord Bancroft, we will learn soon enough what he wants."

"I suppose that's the reason I only wrote a single exchange of correspondence for us ahead of time. After tomorrow, I have no idea what will happen."

And compared to the difficulties ahead, that she didn't read his letters and immediately offer reassurances of love and regard barely counted as a vexation, let alone a problem.

"But these are lovely letters." She kissed the edge of the letters and looked him in the eye, her gaze deep and clear. "One of the best I've ever received, and certainly one of the best I've never sent."

Three

True to Lord Ingram's "prediction," Inspector Treadles called on Charlotte at her London hotel the next afternoon.

He was attired in a stylish fawn jacket in a lightweight summer wool. His wife saw to his clothes, and it appeared that Mrs. Treadles still took great pleasure in dressing her husband well.

"Lord Ingram and I met regularly this summer," said the policeman. "I trust you know that, Miss Holmes?"

Charlotte nodded. After she and Lord Ingram had parted ways in Gibraltar, roughly three months ago, he had sailed on to Malta and Brindisi, then returned to England via the overland route and spent the summer in London. He typically took part in the Season, so that in itself was not unusual. But the Upper Ten Thousand was not accustomed to recently divorced men at their social functions, and his presence had caused some tongues to wag.

On the other hand, he was young, wealthy, and physically striking. No one blamed him for the dissolution of his marriage. And as he had limited himself to lectures and a few dinners hosted by old friends, the gossip had soon died down, replaced by renewed interest in him as a marital prospect.

None of this had been related to Charlotte by Lord Ingram but by Lady Avery, Society gossip extraordinaire, who occasionally wrote Mrs. Watson, whom she knew as Sherlock Holmes's collaborator

Mrs. Hudson, with the latest on-dits. Lord Ingram, conversely, had been curiously silent about life in the relative thick of things.

"His lordship and I had planned a trip to the Isles of Scilly in mid-August, after the end of the Season," continued Inspector Treadles. "When we last saw each other, he let me know that chances were those plans would not come to pass. Still, I hadn't expected *this*."

"We are anticipating some problems," said Charlotte. "To head them off, I prefer to be in London. But I had no ostensibly compelling reason to leave France. Ergo, this ruse."

It was always a struggle, how much she ought to tell someone not yet deeply involved in everything. Would that knowledge illuminate their choices or merely make them huddle in fear?

"But pretending to have broken a limb—won't his lordship need to remain immobile for months on end?"

"True. But there is no reason that after, say, a fortnight or so, his lordship couldn't travel somewhere out of sight and move more freely."

Inspector Treadles exhaled. "I would ask how I can help, but I already did at our previous meeting, and Lord Ingram said that he would greatly appreciate it if I would find a case for Sherlock Holmes."

"Correct. Lord Ingram's 'injury' handed me a reason to come to England. A good case from you would provide an excellent excuse for me to stay for a week or two." Charlotte handed Inspector Treadles a cup of tea. "I hope you didn't need to fish too hard for a suitable conundrum."

"As a matter of fact, as soon as Lord Ingram mentioned this need, I thought of something that had been on my mind of late. The only problem is that, for the moment, it is an internal matter for Scotland Yard."

"Oh?" She added a cube of sugar to his cup.

In response, Inspector Treadles stirred his tea, but rather mechanically. "Miss Holmes, you recall Inspector Brighton, who investigated the Longstead-Sullivan murders last December?"

Charlotte, loading onto her plate a slice of plum cake—from the magnificent hamper Lord Ingram had gifted her, of course—nodded.

Inspector Brighton, who had been beastly toward the inspector and Mrs. Treadles during the investigation, had boarded the RMS *Provence* this past spring to travel to Malta, where he was to train the local constabulary in modern detection methods on behalf of Scotland Yard.

Charlotte, unbeknownst to Inspector Brighton—and Inspector Treadles—had also boarded the sleek oceangoing steamer in disguise, for her own purposes, and had therefore witnessed certain fateful events for Inspector Brighton.

"I was relieved to see Inspector Brighton set off for Malta—it was not easy to be collegial with a man who had attempted to send me to the gallows. And perhaps Inspector Brighton was also relieved to be away on official business for a while—I was not without allies at work, and many of them considered him much too eager to see a fellow policeman come to an ignominious end."

Did this mean that had Inspector Brighton not been so determined to charge Inspector Treadles with two counts of murder, today he might still be a trusted and feared officer of the law?

"Apparently, before he left, Inspector Brighton submitted an unsolved case for review. Knowing him, he must have seen something in the case that could rehabilitate his reputation within Scotland Yard. Of course, after the events aboard the RMS *Provence*, his reputation is beyond repair, but still I am wary about the case.

"Fortunately, we've been shorthanded these past few months, what with Chief Inspector Fowler's injury and Inspector Brighton's . . . misadventure. And when Chief Inspector Fowler returned to work, *he* had to set out for Malta, because the constables there still hadn't received their promised training.

"When he comes back, I believe he will assign the case to a junior officer so as to satisfy procedural requirements. Chances are the junior officer will encounter decade-old clues that lead nowhere and give up. However, we do have several talented and ambitious newcomers, and the one who receives the dossier might very well dig up something significant."

Inspector Treadles paused to drink from his teacup. He had arrived a little tense, no doubt worried for Lord Ingram—and discomfited by the puzzling ruse of which he had only the most superficial grasp. But that uneasiness of knowing too little had by now transmuted into the distress of possibly knowing too much.

Charlotte took a bite of her plum cake—highly toothsome, with a moist crumb and perfectly macerated raisins. "May I ask the nature of *your* interest in this case, Inspector?"

"Inspector Brighton wasn't subtle about his desire to see me charged for murder. Had he succeeded, it would have made his reputation. But he didn't. When you proved my innocence, it not only exposed his ruthlessness but also left his judgment open to question. Why had he not asked for the same accounts and documents from Cousins Manufacturing? Why had he not bothered to trace misallocated funds?"

The policeman turned his teacup on its gold-rimmed saucer a few degrees—clockwise, counterclockwise, then clockwise again—producing faintly audible scratches of porcelain on porcelain. "I doubt that Inspector Brighton cared greatly what others thought of his character, but it agitated him that his much-vaunted competence became a subject of debate. He meant to prove that while he might have stumbled on one highly visible case, his ability to sniff out guilt remained intact. And to do that, he sought to bring down a different officer at the Yard."

"The officer responsible for the unsolved case?"

"Correct. I was lucky to escape Inspector Brighton's malice, but I do not want anyone to pay for my good fortune with their reputation." He looked up and hastened to add, "Please don't understand this to mean that I have come to you to prevent any facts from coming to light—not at all. What I have is a slight advantage of time—Chief Inspector Fowler won't be back for a few days, and even then it will likely be another fortnight before he officially assigns the dossier.

In the meanwhile, I hope to learn the truth before anyone else at Scotland Yard does—the whole truth or whatever nuggets you can discover."

Charlotte sipped her tea. She drank Ceylon in Paris, too, but in London the same tea tasted smokier and more full-bodied. "Inspector Brighton wasn't completely without cause in trying to pin the Longstead-Sullivan murders on you: Both you and Mrs. Treadles tried to hide evidence. And he might be right about this unsolved case as well. What will you do should I discover misconduct on the part of the investigating officer?"

Inspector Treadles grimaced and reached for a slice of cake. "I don't know, Miss Holmes—the possibility unnerves me. But if we cannot escape the truth, we might as well learn it sooner."

———※———

Inspector Treadles had not handed over the actual Scotland Yard dossier; instead he had given Sherlock Holmes an excellent summary, a nearly word-for-word copy of the original investigator's report. He had also informed Miss Charlotte that Garwood Hall, where the so-called Christmas Eve Murder had taken place, was currently up for let.

Garwood Hall was located not in the environs of London but in Lancashire. After a brief discussion, Mrs. Watson and Miss Charlotte set out that very evening for Manchester.

During the journey, Mrs. Watson needed a dozen attempts before she managed to read the police summary to the end—only to realize, an hour later, that with her mind still full of Lord Bancroft's letters, she'd failed to retain names and crucial details.

Starting with Lord Ingram's "injury," the ruse was all about misdirection, to make their enemies think that they were otherwise occupied. Given that assisting Inspector Treadles was very much part of the overarching plan, she had trouble thinking of the Christmas Eve Murder as a real commission for Sherlock Holmes.

And this was before one considered Inspector Treadles's ambivalence toward the case. From speaking to Miss Charlotte, Mrs. Watson had come away with the impression that while the inspector had steeled himself for the truth, he would much rather be told that despite Sherlock Holmes's best effort, absolutely nothing else could be unearthed about this long-ago crime.

At the railway station nearest Garwood Hall, an estate agent named Mr. Elstree collected them. After an enthusiastic greeting, he guided them to his dogcart, that most useful country vehicle.

The drive was lovely. The landscape bore no marks of industry, and every bend in the road yielded only more unspoiled greenery, fields, orchards, and pastures bordered by stacked stone walls.

Mrs. Watson imagined this vista at Christmas: wreaths of holly on farmhouse gates, the berries red and festive against waxy green leaves, an aroma of freshly baked mince pies in the air, and upon every brightly lit window, silhouettes of families gathered around laden tables.

At Garwood Hall, too, there had been a family. Mr. Victor Meadows had acquired the manor only months prior to his death, with wealth inherited from his industrialist grandfather. Mrs. Meadows, his much-younger wife of eight years, had been on hand, as well as her sister, still a child then; Mr. Meadows's older half brother, Mr. Ephraim Meadows; and a dozen indoor servants.

No doubt the house had been Christmas-card perfect, pine garlands over the mantelpieces, a cornucopia on every table, and in the kitchen, the Christmas goose slowly roasting in the oven.

Yet underneath, ill will had festered.

But whose ill will? A mistreated member of the staff? A disgruntled worker from one of Victor Meadows's factories? His wife, who had married him at sixteen, after the bankruptcy and death of her parents? Or his much poorer half brother, who'd seethed with jealousy and discontent his entire life, because his younger sibling had been born with not only a silver spoon in his mouth but gold rings on every finger?

"Here we are!" chirped Mr. Elstree as he reined the dogcart to a gentle stop.

Garwood Hall did not have a gatehouse. Mr. Elstree simply unlocked the gate, drove the dogcart through, and locked it again.

The gate itself might be difficult to climb, all bare wrought-iron pickets topped with stabbing finials, but the estate wall that ran along the country lane was only five feet high and posed little challenge to a nimble evildoer. With a ladder, even a clumsy one could scale it.

"Was that not a quick, easy trip from the railway station?" extolled Mr. Elstree. "And such a pretty drive ahead of us."

The drive couldn't compare with that at Stern Hollow—what could? For one thing, with the grounds as flat as a cricket pitch, there was no topographical variety. For another, the house became visible after only a minute or two. And in five more minutes, they were pulling up to the front door.

To be fair, the approach *was* nice—the lane swerved just so, to give the visitor a glimpse of the small man-made lake behind the house, with its picturesque jetty and a blue rowboat tied to a post.

The house itself, however, made Mrs. Watson shake her head. Elizabethan timbers, Gothic turrets, Palladian columns, and an Italianate belvedere—was there a single notable feature from the last few centuries of manor construction that Garwood Hall had failed to reference?

She leaned closer to Miss Charlotte. "My dear, I take it you approve?"

For this occasion, Mrs. Watson was Miss Charlotte's mother. Or rather, she was Mr. Yardley's mother, Mr. Yardley being the role Miss Charlotte had taken on for the day.

From behind a pair of wire-rimmed spectacles, Owen Yardley's blue eyes twinkled. "I have no complaints about an architectural buffet, Mother."

The dutiful "son" descended first and held out his hand for Mrs. Watson. Other than his portly build, there was little else to make him stand out in a crowd. Besides the reddish hair and beard, that is.

"Oh, you men. You are all the same—blind to such glaring defects."

"I will admit that the house is a bit of a mishmash, stylistically, but it grows on one. It most certainly does," Mr. Elstree hastened to reassure them. "And it is perfect for a busy man of business in need of a haven away from the cities: easy access on bank holidays, no tenants to deal with, very little wear and tear, and plumbing as advanced as any in the finest town houses."

In other words, this was not a great house, with its attendant land, myriad outbuildings, and equally burdensome responsibilities, but merely a holiday lodge of recent fabrication that boasted certain modern amenities.

Mrs. Watson anticipated a similar hodgepodge inside: medieval weaponry next to Renaissance marble statues, maybe, and Louis XIV chairs backed by Japanese print screens. But on that front, she was pleasantly surprised. The interior decoration was thematically unified by an abundance of floral patterns, from almost imperceptible Egyptian lotus motifs on the wallpapers, to ornate swirling vines on the curtains and upholstery.

Although she did chortle a little to herself at the acreage of ancestral portraits on the walls, likely acquired at auctions and meant to make prospective tenants forget that they were not, in fact, visiting the manorial home of a landowning family that had earned its first royal patent before the Wars of the Roses.

The tour wended through the public rooms and then proceeded upstairs. Mrs. Watson tensed as Mr. Elstree showed them into the master's apartment: It was in this bedroom that Victor Meadows had been found slain on Christmas morning, 1871. But here the décor carried on its botanical cheerfulness. Even the bed, which was said to have been blood-soaked, did not exude any sinister airs. It appeared to be simply another bedstead, solidly built, the top mattress so far above the floor that a step stool had been put in place to help with the ascent.

Mrs. Watson couldn't help herself—she went to the adjoining

door. It opened easily—too easily, almost—to reveal the mistress's bedroom on the other side, bathed in daylight.

On that fateful Christmas Day, the housemaid who came around every morning to sweep out grates and lay new fires had found Victor Meadows's door locked. When she returned some time later, the door remained locked.

Perplexed, she'd knocked at the mistress's apartment. Mrs. Meadows, in her dressing gown, was writing her to-do list for the day. The maid described the problem. Mrs. Meadows approached the adjoining door, only to find that it, too, had been barred from the other side.

Do you feel a draught? said Mrs. Meadows to the maid.

Icy cold air was rushing into the mistress's room from underneath the adjoining door. Mrs. Meadows, who until then had only tried the door, now knocked and called to her husband.

Receiving no answer, they were puzzled but not alarmed. Perhaps Mr. Meadows had locked the adjoining door by mistake the night before. And it was possible he had gone for a long walk and locked the apartment door behind him when he'd left.

Mrs. Meadows instructed the maid to go on with her duties. She herself descended and spoke to the housekeeper. The housekeeper had been up early but had not seen the master come down.

At this point Mrs. Meadows's brother-in-law, Mr. Ephraim Meadows, arrived for breakfast. Upon learning of the problem, he, too, knocked on his brother's door. When he likewise received no response, he ventured outside and saw that one of the bedroom's windows was wide open.

Mrs. Watson let go of the door handle still in her grip and glanced toward the windows. Her "son" stood before one.

"Sterling view, is it not?" said Mr. Elstree. "You will find the foliage very pleasing in autumn, too, my good sir."

Mrs. Watson joined them at the windows. Instead of the scenery, Miss Charlotte seemed more interested in the architrave that ran beneath the windows. Or was "he" examining the paths on the lawn below, leading toward the front of the house in one direction and the jetty in the other?

The paths had been clear on that Christmas Eve, but snow had fallen overnight. Footprints on the paths would have been lost after the snow finally melted. Marks left below the window itself would have been trampled on Christmas morning by the entire household, which gathered to watch the gardener climb up into the open window.

"The panorama is impeccable," said Owen Yardley. His voice was higher than Sherrinford Holmes's. In fact, he was at least two inches taller than that other character in Miss Charlotte's repertoire—those shoe lifts were working as advertised. "A remarkably agreeable place, Garwood Hall."

It should have been an excellent opening for Mr. Elstree to sing more of the house's praises. But the estate agent probably heard something in Owen Yardley's tone, for his smile dimmed.

"My mother and I were both highly enthused about Garwood Hall," continued Owen Yardley. "It is conveniently located and reasonably priced. We were willing to sign the lease if the property itself was halfway decent.

"On the train today we were talking about our prospects—how likely we were to find the estate in reasonable repair. Alas, a fellow passenger overheard our conversation and hastened to tell us that a former owner had been brutally murdered in this very house, in his own bed."

All eyes darted to the bed. The bed curtains, ample yards of blue damask, fluttered with an influx of summer air. It was a handsome bed, dignified in every way.

Mr. Elstree must have taken heart from how pretty and peaceful everything looked, even in the face of a direct reference to the murder. "I would have told you about the murder myself, Mr. Yardley, had you expressed a serious interest. I still think, sir, that you should not let one instance of isolated misfortune deter you from considering this lovely house for your future residence."

"But my son is about to win the hand of a wonderful young lady!"

exclaimed Mrs. Watson. "He himself can perhaps overlook this tragic incident. What about her? I don't think we can hide it from her."

"But we've had any number of ladies live and thrive in this house, ma'am. Of the four sets of tenants since the tragic incident, except for an old brigadier general who lived by himself, all the others were families with ladies and children. They all left letters of recommendation for Garwood Hall as a delightful and salutary place to live—I shall be happy to show them to you. And while these tenants have been, without any exception, wonderful people, they were also quite ordinary—truly no superhuman courage is required to live here."

As if to underscore his words, a sparrow landed on the window ledge, looked around for a bit, and flew away—a messenger of unimpeachable normalcy, surely, if one were at all inclined toward omens and metaphors.

Mrs. Watson grew more optimistic: She hadn't been certain that the estate agent would know much about the murder, but it appeared that he'd had to routinely defend the place against whispers of infelicity. Perhaps he'd educated himself on the subject.

Owen Yardley obviously came to the same conclusion. "I'm relieved to hear that the instance of singular unhappiness has proved the exception rather than the rule. You wouldn't happen to know anything about what happened to the people involved in the ill-fated incident, would you, Mr. Elstree?"

"I've made inquiries," answered Mr. Elstree, both proudly and unwillingly. He no doubt viewed the murder as history as ancient as the signing of the Magna Carta, only far less relevant. "I accepted this post eight years ago. It quickly became obvious that I would need to be able to answer questions about the Christmas Eve Murder. I decided I might as well learn from those who knew the most. But by that time the only member of the family I could locate was Mrs. Harcourt, the two Meadows gentlemen's sister. And she told me that her widowed sister-in-law lived for some time in Manchester with her young sister, after the murder, but later moved away without notice. Mr. Ephraim Meadows likely emigrated to Australia."

"Likely?"

"That was what Mrs. Harcourt said—she told me that she hadn't heard from him in years and could only assume he had gone abroad."

"So she wasn't close to this brother?"

"Half brother—she and Mr. Victor Meadows were full siblings, while Mr. Ephraim Meadows was born to old Mr. Meadows's first wife. And no, they weren't close. I daresay Mr. Victor Meadows didn't much care for this half brother either. In his will, he bequeathed all of fifty pounds to Mr. Ephraim Meadows."

Mr. Elstree lowered his voice. "I know that's no pittance. But for a man with houses in the city and in the country, not to mention a number of factories, to leave a final parting gift of fifty pounds to his only brother? That was more than an insult—that was a slap in the face, if you asked me."

And then, perhaps realizing that no one had asked him to pass so decisive a judgment, the estate agent reddened and cleared his throat.

"I'm sure Mr. Ephraim Meadows is living an exemplary life in the Antipodes, a burden to no one and a credit to himself."

Four

The tour of the house continued.

Mr. Elstree made sure to point out that after the murder, the master's and the mistress's apartments had been stripped and refurnished entirely. Miss Charlotte asked several times to ascertain that the rest of the house had *not* been substantially altered or refitted, except for new wallpapers put up ahead of its sale to a family of nabobs who still had not returned from the Subcontinent.

The staff at the time of the murder had since scattered and Mr. Elstree didn't know their current whereabouts, with one notable exception: The gardener who had discovered Victor Meadows's body had left domestic service and now owned a newsagent's shop three railway stops away, in the direction farther away from London.

Which deterred the ladies not at all from heading there as soon as they were finished with Garwood Hall.

Mr. Elstree had mentioned that Danny Stow, the former gardener turned newsagent, had married a woman who made locally famous pies. As the train pulled into the station, a mouthwatering aroma of hot water crust pies cooking to a bubbling finish wafted in through the windows.

Danny Stow handled the rush of customers with aplomb and sent them back to the train laden with not just pies but newspapers, magazines, and small packs of homemade boiled sweets.

The Yardley "mother and son" waited until the train had departed the station. Danny Stow, now a man in his mid-thirties, wiped his brow with a sleeve, took out a broom, and swept up the detritus from around his shop. Then he washed his hands with water from a pitcher.

"Mr. Stow? One each of the missus's marvelous pies, please," said Owen Yardley.

Danny Stow showed little surprise at being addressed by name by a stranger. He only said, "Indeed, sir. Excellent choices. The missus recommends them one and all."

His straw-colored hair was thinning and his otherwise lean build beginning to pad out in the middle—nothing yet, compared to Owen Yardley's proud girth. But he had a boyish face, and it was easy for Mrs. Watson to imagine him as a much younger man, climbing up that ladder, self-conscious under the gaze of the entire Meadows household, apprehensive yet anticipating not at all the bloodbath that he would find.

According to the police report, the ladder from the garden had been slightly short, and Danny Stow had pulled on the ivy on the exterior wall and hung by his fingernails in order to get up to the open window. And once he was inside the chamber, he'd taken a look, turned around, and called to the crowd below, *There's—there's blood next to the bed!*

But where is my brother? Ephraim Meadows had shouted back. Mrs. Meadows, still unaware of her new widowhood, swayed and murmured, *No, surely not. Surely* not!

I—I think the master might be under the—the covers, had been Danny Stow's halting answer.

Urged to pull back the covers, he had disappeared from the window. When he reappeared, he had been unable to speak for a minute, and then said, *I'll open the door. You'd best come see yourselves!*

The crowd, rushing back in, had found him standing outside the now-open door of the master's bedroom, trembling, after having pulled back the bedcover to reveal Victor Meadows with his throat cut.

Present-day Danny Stow wrapped up Miss Charlotte's purchases in brown paper and took out a spool of twine. "Dare I presume, sir, ma'am, that you've just come from Garwood Hall?"

A good number of visitors Mr. Elstree squired about Garwood Hall must not be serious prospective tenants at all, but those looking for a shiver down the spine by touring a former murder scene. Did Danny Stow think that was what they were, too? Mrs. Watson's cheeks prickled with embarrassment.

Miss Charlotte was beyond such minor chagrins. "Indeed, that is so. We had heard some unfortunate rumors concerning the estate on our rail journey this morning. Mr. Elstree, after offering his reassurances, said we could speak to you, if we still felt in need of a greater understanding," she said, sounding just like an earnest, prudent Manchester linendraper who had no idea that he might be deemed a seeker of unseemly titillations.

Danny Stow paused in the unraveling of the spool of twine. "Greater understanding, sir? I'm afraid all I can give you is a description of what I saw on that Christmas Day."

"Good gracious, my dear fellow, why would we make you relive that harrowing memory? No, I wanted to ask if you know whether Mr. Meadows had the habit of sleeping with his windows open in winter."

The shopkeeper blinked, taken aback by the query. "I had a pint with a footman from that time a few years ago. He mentioned that Mr. Meadows himself must have kept the window ajar. He didn't like a room too warm, Mr. Meadows, and the house was new back then, everything flush and plumb. Maybe if he didn't open a window, the room would've been too stuffy."

"You think the murderer gained access to the room from the window?" asked Miss Charlotte.

"The house was locked up every night, and those locks weren't disturbed." The former gardener, deep in thought, slowly wove a net of twine around the wrapped-up pies. "It had to have been the window."

"But getting in through the window would still have been the easy part," mused Miss Charlotte. "From what I understand, the duvet had absorbed almost all the arterial spray from the cutting of Mr. Meadows's throat. This meant that the murderer had climbed onto the bed, pulled the covers above Mr. Meadows's head, and then reached a blade under to do the evil deed. Odd that Mr. Meadows didn't wake—I understand there was no sign of any struggle."

Stow shrugged. "His older brother said that after dinner on Christmas Eve, the two of them finished off a bottle of brandy, reminiscing over old times. Mr. Meadows could have been in a bit of a stupor going to bed."

That had been the police inspector's opinion also, that the victim had been too inebriated to respond to mortal threat.

"Do you think it was an outsider?" Miss Charlotte continued her unhurried questioning.

"I do," answered her interviewee without a moment of hesitation. "The ladder that I used? It wasn't where it should have been. It was moved during the night and tossed back somewhere in the garden. And the ivy around the window was loose—someone used that to help pull themselves up from the top of the ladder, the same way I had to."

"Oh my," said Mrs. Watson, rubbing a hand over her sleeve as if she felt chilled by the prospect. "But in a place as isolated as Garwood Hall, wouldn't strangers in the neighborhood have been noticed?"

"If they'd come off the train at the village station, maybe. But we were only twenty miles north of Bolton—and that was no small place even fifteen years ago. If someone hired a carriage there, they could have easily covered the distance to Garwood Hall at night and been gone before morning."

"But to accomplish that," mused Miss Charlotte, "the so-called rabble-rousers from the factories would have needed to be fairly organized."

Stow completed the twine netting he'd made around the paper-wrapped pies with two loops that served as a pair of handles. A few travelers had arrived and were milling around the platform, waiting for the next train. He glanced around and lowered his voice. "I don't know more about the murder than anyone else, Mr. Yardley, but I don't think it was perpetrated by rabble-rousers. For one, the timing was perfect: Christmas Eve might be the only time when nobody pays attention to a carriage careening down a country road—folks would think that's just other folks rushing home for Christmas.

"For another, look at the way the murder was carried off. Well, I suppose the snow that night was pure luck—those several inches covered up all the tracks any outsider might have made coming to and leaving the house. But other than that, it was all planning and skill. The deed was done so fast Mr. Meadows was probably dead before he knew what was happening. And other than the blood that dripped to the floor, there was no splatter anywhere else.

"At that point it would have been easier for the murderer to leave by going through the house. But did he do that? No, he left via the ladder again. True, he didn't put the ladder back exactly as he ought to have—his one oversight—but by locking Mr. Meadows's doors and leaving the window open, he had us, everybody in the household, do the work of trampling the area under the window for him, destroying any signs he might have left behind. Not to mention, no murder weapon was ever found."

He shook his head. "The police inspector, I remember him, he was patient and conscientious, but he could find no clues, absolutely nothing to go on."

"I see you have done some serious thinking on the matter, Mr. Stow."

Stow gave a bitter smile. "Believe me, Mr. Yardley, the last thing I wanted, all those years ago, was to ever think about the murder again. I didn't even care who did it—I just wanted to stop seeing Mr. Meadows in my sleep. Thankfully that did stop, after a while. But because I'm linked to the murder, people asked me about it. By and by I found myself turning it over in my head. I even brought it up with other members of the staff, when we were at the housekeeper's funeral a few years ago."

"Did you learn anything?"

"Not really, except the bit about Mr. Meadows not liking his room too warm, from the footman I mentioned."

Miss Charlotte, as Owen Yardley, stroked the beard on her face. "Mr. Stow, judging by everything you've said, you must believe the murderer to be a professional criminal—an assassin for hire, even. But such a person would have harbored no personal enmity toward the late Mr. Meadows and would have been acting only at the express desire of his paymaster. Do you have any opinion on the identity of *that* shadowy character?"

Stow expelled a breath. "The missus would be cross if she knew the direction of our conversation. And she's right—the purpose of my life isn't to speculate on Mr. Meadows's murder. We've got each other, we've got the boys, and we've got plans to expand the pie business so we can give the boys a proper education.

"Mind you, she knows there's no stopping people coming up to me asking about the murder—just make sure they buy enough of everything to make it worth your time, she always says. And most of the time, the folks who are interested, they only want the gory details. Or they want to tell me what *they* think happened—and I only need to listen and nod.

"It's hardly ever that I'm asked about my theories. So I must beg you, Mr. Yardley, Mrs. Yardley, to please let this go no further than the three of us."

Mr. Yardley raised a hand. "You have our solemn promise."

Stow looked around again. More travelers had arrived on the platform—some were even eyeing the pies from not too far away. He lowered his voice further. "I think the person who did the hiring was most likely Mrs. Harcourt, Mr. Meadows's sister, the one he gave everything to."

With a soft gasp, Mrs. Watson's hand came up to her lips. She herself had raised that possibility to Miss Charlotte on the rail journey this morning, but Owen Yardley's mother could scarcely be unmoved by such a sensational scenario. Her "son" gripped her by the shoulder even as he placed a hand over his own heart.

"I'm from hereabouts," Stow went on. "But some of the indoor staff, they worked for Mr. Meadows in his Manchester town house and they knew more about his business. Before he died, I heard a good deal about troubles at his factories. But afterwards, those troubles went away, which tells me they could have been ginned up to pin the murder on labor agitators and whatnot."

Mrs. Watson, obligingly, gasped again.

Stow shook his head and chortled. "But you know what the missus said? She said maybe the sister raised wages and improved conditions and the workers simply had far fewer causes to protest. And who is to say she isn't as likely to be right about it?"

They thanked Danny Stow profusely and left on the next train out. In Manchester, the ladies parted ways temporarily. Mrs. Watson, having sent a cable the day before, visited the archives of the *Manchester Guardian* to see what the local newspaper had to say about the Christmas Eve Murder. Charlotte had the more pleasant task of calling on Miss Longstead in Berkshire.

The previous winter, Miss Longstead's uncle had been shot dead, and Charlotte had worked to clear Inspector Treadles of suspicion for that crime. Despite, or perhaps due to, the inauspicious circumstances of their meeting, the two young women had forged a strong trust.

Since then, Charlotte and Mrs. Watson had come to rely on Miss Longstead, a talented chemist, to supply them with formulations that imitated the texture of skin, essential for more involved disguises.

Because Charlotte still had on her masculine veneer, to avoid causing unnecessary gossip she did not ask the trap driver to deliver her to the estate Miss Longstead inherited from her uncle but to a nearby church of some renown.

From the church it was only fifteen minutes on foot along a secluded path to reach the side gate of an unoccupied property that belonged to Miss Johansson, Miss Longstead's neighbor and mentor in chemistry.

Miss Longstead was already waiting and quickly admitted Charlotte.

Earlier in the year, before her voyage on the RMS *Provence*, during the months when she'd kept out of sight following her "death" in Cornwall, Charlotte had already visited Miss Longstead dressed as a man. So her appearance today earned only a small chuckle from her hostess.

Miss Longstead had a well-sprung dogcart waiting. They climbed up, and Miss Longstead shook the reins.

"I am both envious that you get to wear disguises and worried about the necessity that drives you to it. Have you been all right, Miss Holmes?"

Her gold-flecked green eyes peered at Charlotte. The afternoon sun shone on her wide-brimmed hat, which protected her gleaming light brown skin and lovely features from the elements.

Charlotte nodded slowly. "I'm all right. More tired than anything else—there has just been so much to do."

"At least after you see the laboratory, it will be one less task on your list."

The laboratory, too, belonged to Miss Johansson, who was currently teaching at a women's college in America. In her absence, Miss Longstead kept an eye on her small estate.

Prudently enough, the laboratory was in a separate building from the converted farmhouse that served as the main dwelling. Inside, it teemed with beakers, test tubes, flasks, and more Bunsen burners than any one person could possibly need. A strong smell shot up Charlotte's nostrils, at once metallic and acidic.

Miss Longstead took out a key ring and unlocked a glass-front cabinet. "You see? There used to be four bottles of the stuff in here. Now there are only two."

"You should put the last two bottles somewhere safer," said Charlotte. "And just in case, it might be better for you not to come near this laboratory for some time, until you hear otherwise from me."

Miss Longstead bit her lower lip. "Are you sure everything will be all right?"

Charlotte took a deep breath—the odor of chemicals grew harsher, more pervasive. She glanced around at the breached laboratory. Uncharacteristically, her heart thumped a few times, with a sudden surge of nerve.

"I hope so," she said. "But there is more uncertainty than ever, and only time will tell whether our work will bear fruit."

———❉———

Miss Longstead's place in Berkshire, and Ravensmere, the estate that served as Lord Bancroft's prison, were about the same distance from London. But the former was situated due west of the great metropolis, the latter north-northwest. To call on Lord Bancroft after her meeting with Miss Longstead, Charlotte had to take the train into London and then head back out.

A generation ago, Ravensmere would have been entirely outside London, a house in the country that was convenient for a well-to-do man of the city to repair to at the end of his working week. But London's inexorable growth had devoured most of the fields and pastures that had once formed a green barrier between the estate and the capital.

The present-day villa was not exactly on the doorstep of industry—it was far from any major bodies of water that could effectively carry away effluvia. But the tiny hamlets that used to be its nearest neighbors had sprouted tracts of development that encroached in its direction, some of those tentacles almost near enough to brush up against the villa's boundaries.

Charlotte detrained at one such hamlet and hired a trap to take her the rest of the way. When she arrived, the last of twilight had faded. The high-walled estate was eerily silent; not even a cricket chirped.

The path that would allow her inside passed directly under the arch at the center of a slate-roofed gatehouse. Unlike the usual ornamental gates meant to show off the beauty of the grounds, this gate was solid metal and fitted close to the limestone of the arch, giving no glimpse of the landscape beyond.

As she alit, a small window on the gate slid open, revealing a pair of eyes under bushy brows and an unfriendly gaze.

Charlotte stopped several feet away. "Evening. Sherrinford Holmes at your service. I'm here to see his lordship."

The face glanced down. "Yer name isn't on the list."

This was not the answer Charlotte had anticipated. The previous day, before she boarded the train for Manchester, she'd sent word informing Lord Bancroft that she had received his letters and would be calling this evening. "What about Charlotte Holmes?"

The permission she had been granted applied to both Sherrinford and Charlotte Holmes.

"Not on the list either, and you are no Charlotte Holmes."

"Indeed not. Did his lordship perhaps make a mistake and think I would be visiting on the morrow?"

"Tomorrow's list will be given to us tomorrow. Now, since you've no business here, sir, you'd best be on your way."

—◈—

Lord Ingram, due to his service to the crown, could have compelled Lord Bancroft to receive him. Charlotte had no such powers—yet. She had no choice but to go back to the village railway station and take the next train to London.

It was past dinnertime, yet she was not hungry. True, she dined so regularly that she rarely experienced true hunger, merely a sweet anticipation for her next meal. Still, to stare at Mrs. Stow's curried chicken pie *and* her rhubarb-mulberry tart and not be tempted?

Charlotte looked out of the window of her compartment. A gas lamp–dotted landscape slid backward as the train trundled toward Euston Station. On the way to Ravensmere, the man who had shared her compartment had barely refrained from offering dermatological advice as Charlotte had scratched and scratched at her beard. She was sure that her face still itched from the glue used to hold the beard in place, but now she barely felt it.

What was Lord Bancroft up to?

He was the one who had repeatedly written her, expressing a

desire to renew their acquaintance. He knew that Sherrinford Holmes was none other than Charlotte Holmes. Why had he not received her tonight?

From Euston Station she took a hansom cab. The cab drove past a hole-in-the-wall that sold fried pies. The smell of pastry dunked in hot oil should have made her peckish even if she'd just eaten a full meal, but tonight she remained indifferent.

No, she grew slightly repulsed.

The last time she'd lost her appetite outright had to do with Lord Bancroft. Was her stomach trying to tell her something? That it sensed—and was bracing for—imminent danger?

She asked to be deposited some distance from her hotel. There had been no time to ready Mrs. Watson's house, which had sat empty for nearly half a year, for habitation. Fortunately, with most of the Upper Ten Thousand having already decamped for the countryside, it had been easy to secure a suite of rooms with its own street entrance, so that they did not need to pass through the hotel's sometimes still-crowded foyer.

That street entrance flew open before Charlotte was even close enough to take her keys out from her pocket. A wild-looking Mrs. Watson bridged the fifteen feet or so that separated them, grabbed Charlotte by the elbow, and dragged her inside.

Charlotte nearly tripped on the threshold.

Mrs. Watson shut the door hard, throwing her shoulder against it as if a battering ram had been deployed on the other side. She opened her mouth, but no words emerged.

It was Miss Redmayne, standing at the door that connected the vestibule to the parlor, her silhouette backlit, her face in shadows, who said, her voice shaking only a little, "Miss Charlotte, they have Miss Bernadine. Lord Bancroft's men have your sister."

Five

THE INTERROGATION

"Jf you'll excuse me for a moment, gentlemen," said Miss Charlotte
Holmes.

She rose, disappeared into an adjacent room, and returned a minute later with a small stack of papers, from which she presented two
items to Chief Inspector Talbot. "You asked for a full account of my
recent dealings with Lord Bancroft. These are the initial missives I
received from him."

Thoughtfully, she went to the window and pulled back the curtains. Light flooded in. As she retook her seat, Treadles noticed the
shadows under her eyes, and the bloodshot vessels across the sclera of
those eyes. Even her skin lacked its usual firm youthfulness.

Had she not slept last night? What had she been doing?

Chief Inspector Talbot examined the sheets of paper before hand-
ing them to Treadles. "It would be difficult to prove their authen-
ticity."

"Indeed, it might be," Miss Holmes concurred about the typed
and unsigned notes.

"We were told by the gatehouse at Ravensmere that a certain Mr.
Sherrinford Holmes was refused entry twelve days ago," pointed out
Talbot. "Lord Bancroft knew that you are, in fact, Sherlock Holmes,

consulting detective. He also knew that Sherrinford Holmes, brother to this fictional character, is but another one of your alter egos.

"If he was truly intent on securing your help, why did he decline to see you, Miss Holmes? You were already on his doorstep."

Treadles's stomach pitched. Miss Holmes would have a ready story, certainly, but Chief Inspector Talbot would find all its weaknesses.

"That puzzled me greatly, too, Inspector Talbot." Something that felt very much like genuine bafflement radiated from Miss Holmes's large blue eyes. "But the gatehouse at Ravensmere was not where one obtained detailed explanations, or any explanations at all. I had no choice but to leave, my perplexity in tow."

"Leaving all the way to Paris the same night?"

"We received a cable from my patroness's butler that my sister was not well."

Treadles felt as if he'd been kicked in the shin. Memories rushed back of Miss Olivia Holmes giving him the cut direct for insulting Charlotte Holmes. Her conduct had made no sense to him then, but now he not only understood but shared that staunch loyalty. His nape heated with mortification at the recollection, but he prayed that what Charlotte Holmes stated so plainly was not true.

He did not want anything unhappy to have befallen her proud, lonely, and desperately caring sister.

Charlotte Holmes handed over a telegram.

Chief Inspector Talbot scanned the cable. "This says only, 'Miss B won't eat eggs anymore.'"

"My sister, Miss Bernadine Holmes, has a delicate constitution. Her digestion cannot tolerate anything made with dairy or wheat products. She also does not chew meat very well. Eggs, then, constitute an important part of her diet, and her refusal to eat eggs was nothing short of a crisis."

Treadles vaguely recalled that the Holmes ladies had an older married sister, now known as Mrs. Cumberland. Who was Miss Bernadine Holmes then? And why was she living with Charlotte Holmes and Mrs. Watson?

"We left as soon as we could," continued Miss Holmes. "But when we reached Paris, after an anxious journey, we discovered that the situation was not as dire as we'd originally supposed. My patroness's cook had devised a way to grind meat and poultry extremely fine and mix the cooked puree with mashed potatoes. And my sister did not object to that."

Food? They were talking about food?

Yet Treadles could detect no flippancy in her narrative. She approached her sister's diet with the solemnity others reserved for horse racing and affairs of state.

"Still we debated her abrupt rejection of eggs. If she could stop eating eggs at the drop of a hat, she could spurn other foods that we rely on for her nourishment. But in the end, it was not a problem that could be solved speedily. We would need to wait and observe. My patroness's niece stayed behind—she is a student of medicine and better qualified than us to judge matters of health and nutrition. My patroness and I returned to England."

"Why did you not stay on in Paris as well, Miss Holmes, you and your patroness?"

"For the reason we made the trip to England in the first place. My friend, Lord Ingram Ashburton, had suffered a broken limb, and we wanted to make sure that it hadn't been the work of malevolent forces."

"You didn't suspect Lord Bancroft?"

Treadles clenched his hand.

Miss Holmes's chaotically summery dress glared in the now brilliantly lit parlor. "If I hadn't suspected him at all, Chief Inspector, I wouldn't have attempted to call on him. But that he didn't receive me then, I will say, lessened the chance that he was the culprit behind my lord Ingram's injury."

She passed over yet another slip of paper. "When we returned here, after seeing to my sister in Paris, we found this note waiting for us."

The typed note said,

Dear Miss Holmes,

My profound apologies for missing your visit the other day. I shall be delighted to receive you tomorrow morning at an hour of your choosing.

Yours truly,
Bancroft Ashburton

Treadles, who had become the repository for all the evidence Miss Holmes presented, compared the note to the other two purportedly from Lord Bancroft. The slips of paper, identical in size, were also exactly the same in color, thickness, and texture.

He would wager that the typewriter used to tap out the messages had been the same one, too. The notes shared a notch in the bowl of the lowercase *g*, and an ever so slightly misaligned lowercase *a*, which sat a fraction of an inch higher on the baseline than the other letters.

When Miss Holmes was satisfied that the policemen had absorbed the contents of the third note, she said, "This time, when I called on Ravensmere, Lord Bancroft met with me."

Chief Inspector Talbot was silent for some time. "Miss Holmes, I find your account questionable. It seems much more likely that you were coerced into cooperating with Lord Bancroft. What did he do? Did he, for example, threaten the safety of your sister Miss Bernadine Holmes?"

Six

TWELVE DAYS AGO

Miss Charlotte had yet to change out of her disguise, so it was a portly, redheaded young man who stood in the middle of the parlor, two slips of paper in his hands.

Mrs. Watson, still wearing her own traveling dress, as she'd returned from Manchester only a quarter hour ago, knew exactly what the cables said.

Miss B won't eat eggs anymore.

Lord Bancroft sends his regards.

Even before she had opened the cables, a chill had pooled in the soles of Mrs. Watson's feet. Mr. Mears, her butler, was highly competent. Had anything less than catastrophic taken place in Paris, he would not have sent a telegram, let alone two.

Her hands had clutched so tightly around those slips of paper that Penelope had had to pry them loose from her grip. And then she'd brought Mrs. Watson a large draught of whisky, which Mrs. Watson had tossed back as if it were so much room-temperature tea.

Miss Charlotte exhibited no such signs of agitation. From where

Mrs. Watson sat, she could see the girl reflected in two different gold-framed mirrors. Every iteration of her was perfectly still, her expression, under the proliferation of false facial hair, as tranquil and bland as it had ever been. Yet something rippled and burned in the air. Mrs. Watson shivered.

Anger. She'd known Miss Charlotte an entire year and she had never once seen the girl angry.

Penelope glanced at Mrs. Watson. Had she felt the same tidal surge of wrath?

"I was just at Ravensmere, and Lord Bancroft did not meet with me. I guess he knew that until I learned about Bernadine, there was no point in seeing me, as I would not have agreed to anything he proposed."

This made Mrs. Watson seethe.

"You missed dinner, Miss Charlotte," said Penelope. "Are you hungry?"

"I wasn't earlier," answered Miss Charlotte slowly, "but now that I have some idea what Lord Bancroft wants, I believe I can have a nibble or two."

She sat down, dropped the telegrams on an occasion table, and unwrapped the two hand-raised pies she'd bought at that little railway station as they inquired into the Christmas Eve Murder.

How long ago that seemed—and how utterly immaterial.

Miss Charlotte sliced open a cylindrical curry pie and ate one half methodically. She then did the same to a three-inch-across fruit tart, and similarly consumed one half, her motions smooth, her face serene.

It was not easy to read the young woman's expression, but usually at mealtimes it was possible to detect a glow of pleasure upon Miss Charlotte's countenance, especially when dessert courses were brought around.

Tonight that glow was absent.

Mrs. Watson's heart pinched.

Miss Charlotte finished her supper, drained her travel canteen, and said quietly, "I must go back to Paris and take stock of the situation."

She was no longer incensed. Not in the sense that she had leashed her anger but as if for her, anger was not a dark vine that hooked its barbed tentacles into the heart and refused to ever let go but as much of a soap-bubble emotion as surprise, something that existed only in the moment of reaction.

"We'll come with you," Mrs. Watson said immediately.

Her staff, too, were in that house.

Penelope leaped up. "I already checked. If we leave by the late train from Charing Cross, we should make Folkestone Harbour in time to take the first tidal boat across the Channel. We could be in Paris before ten in the morning."

After Penelope left to secure tickets, Mrs. Watson said to Miss Charlotte, "My dear, I don't question your decision at all—in fact, I think it's the only right and proper thing to do. But surely Lord Bancroft, by his barbarous act, means for you to go to him this instant. Are you not worried that he might make things more difficult for you later on if you choose to make him wait?"

"I went to see him tonight, and he chose to make me wait," countered Miss Charlotte.

But Lord Bancroft held the upper hand and could afford to antagonize them; the reverse was not true.

The mother hen in Mrs. Watson wanted desperately to explain that to Miss Charlotte. She had to remind herself that the girl, with her extraordinarily capacious mind, would have already considered the point before making her choice.

Instead, she murmured, "Can I just say how glad I am that you refused that man not once but twice?"

Miss Charlotte had been obliged to consider his second offer, which came after her exile from Society, with utmost seriousness. Marriage would have restored some of her former respectability, and that would have helped her family, especially her sister Miss Olivia.

"There was always something about him, wasn't there," Mrs. Watson went on, "that made you feel that he couldn't be entirely trusted? Now I know it's an emptiness of the soul. No wonder I never could bring myself to like him—and you know it's in my nature to like everyone."

"I always knew it would be only a matter of time before he made his vengeance felt," said Miss Charlotte, wiping her fingers one by one with a napkin. She threw aside the napkin abruptly. "I didn't think, however, that it would be at this moment."

This moment when they needed all their energy and attention on Moriarty.

— ❧ —

Miss Olivia Holmes was unexpectedly enchanted by Aix-en-Provence.

For all that she had always wished to visit the South of France, she had largely aspired to the Côte d'Azur, sunny and mild even in the deepest winter, its towns and seaside villages fashionable retreats for those who could afford to get away from England in cold, damp January.

Charlotte, however, had not asked Livia to meet with her in Cannes, Antibes, Saint-Tropez—or even the little principality of Monaco—but in Aix-en-Provence.

We have visited Aix a time or two, and it charms Mrs. Watson greatly—perhaps it will have the same captivating effect on you.

Once Aix had been the seat of the Counts of Provence, a nexus of both power and culture. Now it was but a quiet provincial town. Why had Charlotte and Mrs. Watson journeyed more than once from Paris to visit the place, and then proposed it for their reunion?

A few months ago on the RMS *Provence*, Mrs. Watson had told Livia, *We have news of Mr. Marbleton's whereabouts. And we plan to take advantage of that.*

Livia, when she'd recovered from her astonishment, had promptly offered her assistance, such as it was. But Mrs. Watson had smiled and said, *You go on with your travels, my dear. Enjoy yourself. Enjoy your hard-won freedom. Write more tales of Sherlock Holmes, if you wish. We will ask for your help when the time comes.*

The time was nigh, Livia was sure. Mrs. Watson had not disclosed Mr. Marbleton's location, but dared Livia presume that he was being held right here?

Charlotte's letter, inviting Livia to come to Aix, had reached Livia in Athens, as she and Mrs. Newell returned from Constantinople. Livia's heart had not stopped hammering since, with both dread and wild hope. Aix-en-Provence had loomed large in her mind, a vaguely sinister locale full of locked doors and closed shutters, its public squares deserted, its very air heavy and oppressive.

When she arrived, however, she'd found the town lovely, full of edifices the colors of sunshine and warm butter. The sidewalk cafés, cool in the dappled green shade of tall elm trees, brimmed with patrons reading books and newspapers, and children looking about curiously as they drank their syrupy soda water. Fountains burbled everywhere, from splashy congregations of mythological creatures to some that were little more than a spigot on a wall spouting into a plain stone basin, yet somehow that little stream of water sparkled in the sun and made music as it fell.

She prayed that Mr. Marbleton, so talented at taking pleasure in small things, managed to enjoy the unspooling of daily life here: the vibrant produce on market days; the scent of thyme, aniseed, and good bread in the air; the soft thuds of coffee cups on marble-top café tables giving way to the clinking of wineglasses and silverware as day drifted into evening.

Was there—was there any chance at all that he had already spied her, walking about? Had he perhaps seen Charlotte and Mrs. Watson, too, on their earlier jaunts? Had he begun his own preparations, sensing that his escape was near—that maybe now, with her appearance, it was imminent?

He loved life; she never loved life so much as when she saw it through his eyes. But by that same token, as long as he remained a prisoner, her own freedom would be incomplete.

"Mademoiselle Holmes?" called out the clerk at the reception desk as she came through the hotel's front door with enough patisserie for three Charlottes. "Mademoiselle, we have a letter for you."

Charlotte!

Livia took the letter from the clerk, thanked him, and made sure that she walked normally out of the foyer and up the curving staircase to her bright, high-ceilinged room on the next floor. There she carefully set down the packages in her hands and sliced open the envelope.

Dear Livia,

I hope this letter finds you well and that you have been pleasantly situated in Aix-en-Provence.

I'm afraid I write with unhappy news.

Don't worry, no one is in danger—at least not at the moment.

I have not told you this earlier, but in the past several weeks, I have received two notes from Lord Bancroft, each expressing a desire for greater understanding and friendship. It was obvious Lord Bancroft harbored ulterior motives, but it was not obvious what exactly he wanted.

The second of these notes arrived just as Mrs. Watson, Miss Redmayne, and I began our recent journey to England to call on Lord Ingram, who fractured his limb in an accident at Stern Hollow.

Livia sucked in a breath. Lord Ingram was the last person to break a bone while proceeding under his own power.

Instead of starting immediately for Paris after the visit—Lord Ingram appeared in decent form and I could discern no signs of foul play—we headed to London, so that I might call on Lord Bancroft and uncover his purpose in writing to me.

I did just that yesterday, but was not granted an audience. Upon reaching the hotel, however, I learned that henchmen under orders from Lord Bancroft had overrun Mrs. Watson's house in Paris and taken its residents hostage.

Livia cried out, "What?"

Our return journey began within hours. We reached Paris this morning and found the house indeed occupied by four armed individuals, three men and one woman.

They have an air of mercenaries about them—the sort to do evil mechanically, rather than with personal relish. But they let Mrs. Watson, Miss Redmayne, and myself into the house without raising a fuss: My lord Bancroft, it would seem, understands that I will do nothing for him unless first assured of the well-being of everyone in the household.

The mercenaries have not mistreated anyone but hand down strict orders that they expect to be meekly and swiftly obeyed. Mr. Mears, the only man in the household, has been locked in his own room. Madame Gascoigne has to cook for everyone, Polly and Rosie Banning waiting on the mercenaries hand and foot.

Thankfully they let Mademoiselle Robineau remain with Bernadine in her room at all times.

When I saw her, Bernadine was not too badly off. Fortunately, at this point, Mademoiselle Robineau has been a part of the household for months. And she has an innate calm and a cheerful presence. So even though Bernadine must feel, to some extent, the fear and tension of the situation, within her own room, with the invaders out of sight, she seemed to be carrying on more or less normally except for a reduced appetite.

We were not allowed to remain long. After a quick visit with everyone and a few words spoken across Mr. Mears's door, we were booted out. Miss Redmayne kindly put us up in her place, where I may compose letters and telegrams. She and Mrs. Watson are out now, purchasing enough ready-to-eat foods to supply a platoon. We will deliver all that, plus a large hamper of foodstuff from Lord Ingram, to the house this evening. It should make life easier for the staff. And, we hope, allow us another chance to see Bernadine.

By the time you receive this letter, on the morrow, I should be getting ready for the railway trip to Boulogne, there to cross the Channel back to England again.

To confront Lord Bancroft.

At this point the letter switched to a jumble of letters, which Livia recognized as the Cdaq Khuha code that she and Charlotte had devised to use with each other when they were children.

Deciphered, it read,

No doubt you feel anxious and likely wish that you could either journey to Paris to keep an eye on the situation or join me in England. But I must ask you to remain in Aix. Since I cannot be there, you must be my eyes and ears. I am counting on you.

Love,
Charlotte

———※———

For most of her life, Livia had felt insufficiently heated. At the height of the English summer, she often needed a shawl. And even then, she would have preferred a fire laid in her room morning and evening, to dispel the chill brought in by a damp draught.

During the past few months, however, she had been gloriously, sensationally warm. Malta. Egypt. The Aegean Sea. Everywhere she'd broiled luxuriously, wallowing in the sensation of fingers and toes that didn't feel the least bit cold. Why, Provence itself was prodigiously sultry.

She'd thought that somehow, with all the heat she'd soaked up, she would be like a sunbaked stone and remain warm for a while, even after day turned into night. How naïve she had been. In a single moment, she felt herself transported back to that drafty bedroom at home, cold all over and dead certain she'd never again be warm enough.

Carefully she read the letter again, especially the part originally in cipher. Then she went down to the reception and said to the clerk, "Alas, I have some unwelcome news. My friends will not be able to join me as scheduled."

"We are sorry to hear that, mademoiselle."

"Thank you. I will let you know if anything changes."

She began to walk away, then turned around, as if in afterthought. "In Paris I knew a Swiss manufacturer named Herr Albrecht. I've heard that he has a house in Aix. Would you happen to know anything about it?"

"Herr Albrecht? *Mais oui, mademoiselle.* He bought an *hôtel particulier* seven or eight doors further east on the Cours Mirabeau, on this side of course—this is the superior side. But I don't believe he visits much."

So Charlotte's information was correct.

Livia walked out of the hotel onto the Cours Mirabeau. Charlotte had never said that Mr. Marbleton was here, only that Miss Moriarty had become convinced that das Phantomschloss, the rumored castle where Moriarty kept his treasures, secrets, and prisoners, did not exist. That instead he made use of a loose network of locations, the house in Aix-en-Provence under the name of Albrecht—one of his aliases—among them.

Livia crossed the boulevard to the less superior side of the Cours Mirabeau, which faced north and would be in the shadows for much of the day as the sun rounded toward the south.

She passed a bank, an elegant patisserie, and an office for some sort of agricultural cooperative. Another bank. A school that was empty of students at the height of summer.

Her heart pounding, she cast a quick glance across the street.

That house. Yes, that particular house. She risked another peek from underneath the tassel fringes of her parasol. Four floors up, did a curtain flutter?

Her beloved Mr. Marbleton—her Stephen—looking down at her?

Yesterday, when she'd walked the same route, that thought and that thought alone had consumed her. Now the chaos inside her head was a sustained wail, a cry for help in the middle of an infinite wasteland.

Would Bernadine be all right? Would Charlotte be all right? Would any of them, in the end, be all right?

The unmarked carriage was parked two streets away from the headquarters of Credit Lyonnais, where a cache of secrets that Charlotte had stolen from Moriarty the previous December sat undisturbed in an underground safe-deposit box. The inside of the carriage, with its curtains drawn, was dim—and a bit warm. Charlotte studied her slightly hazy reflection in the mirror.

She was disguised as an old woman this morning, but not an old woman who bore any resemblance to Mrs. Ramsay, the character she'd played on the RMS *Provence*. This old woman, with her fully grey hair, her plain black attire, and her hunched posture, would attract little notice but for the headscarf suggesting that she might be an adherent of the Eastern Orthodox church.

She put away the mirror and nibbled, in a most genteel manner, on a cream puff held in an embroidered handkerchief—and started only a little when a knock came at the carriage door.

"*C'est moi, madame, votre seigneur et maître,*" announced a reedy and somewhat crackly voice.

Charlotte almost choked on her cream puff—and hastened to admit her "lord and master." A man as old as she must currently appear hooked his walking stick over his arm, grabbed the side of the open door, made a feeble attempt to climb up—and promptly planted himself face-first in the interior of the carriage.

This heavenly creature, clad in fashion from at least three decades ago, his cologne overpowering, his face spotted with age, squinted at her in indignation as he finally managed to raise himself to the seat opposite hers.

"Will you never learn to dress with discretion, woman? Why, every man in Paris would look twice at your headscarf," he sputtered.

After that huffy commentary, he took a moment to catch his breath before pulling the carriage door shut with a shaky hand.

Catching her gaze on his hand, he pointed an equally shaky finger at her. "This is all your fault, woman. How many times have I told you, at our age, you can't keep me up at night like that?"

"So . . ." Charlotte said meekly, "no more games of draughts before bed?"

The man coughed. "And no more waking me up to massage your calves."

Charlotte sat up straighter. "Does that mean that when my calves cramp up in the future, I can call on our new footman for it? You know, Pierre, the one with biceps the size of hams?"

The man coughed some more. "Well, Pierre must work during the day, too. I'll buy you a Granville hammer that you can use to percuss your limbs at night."

Charlotte's eyes widened. "A vibrator?"

She leaped across the carriage and wrapped her arms around him. "You would buy a vibrator, sir? For me? Oh, my decrepit angel!"

The man burst out laughing. "Vibrator, what a word. Makes those clunky devices sound absolutely deviant."

He kissed her on the lips. "Hullo, Holmes."

She drew back a few inches—that perfume indeed overwhelmed. "Hullo, Ash. Thanks for coming to my aid."

"Speak nothing of it—what's an English Channel crossing or two between friends?" But his expression sobered. "I'm sorry for what happened, and I'm incensed on Miss Bernadine's behalf."

She flattened her lips. "As am I."

She felt another flare of anger, that unfamiliar emotion, before it was superseded by a stab of fear, a sensation that she was coming to know more than she wished to.

"Don't worry," said her lover quietly. "He might laugh now, but he won't laugh long, not if I have anything to say about it."

Seven

This time, when Charlotte arrived at Ravensmere, a woman searched her to make sure that she wasn't carrying weapons or contraband and then escorted her inside.

The entirety of the estate was enclosed by a high wall. But inside that, another set of walls sealed off a sizable garden. From the gatehouse, the ground sloped down. At the garden wall, it sloped up again toward the manor. As a result, visually, this second wall did not constitute much of an obstruction—a great many of the garden's geometric parterres remained visible during the approach. Yet up close, the wall formed an effective barrier, seven feet tall, plastered smooth, and topped with shards of glass that glittered in the sun.

Charlotte passed through another gate, this time in a wrought iron fence that isolated the house and a small portion of the grounds from the rest of the garden.

The house featured a limestone exterior and a slate roof. It was handsome enough but not remarkable, certainly not the kind of great house that typically spawned extended acreage of formal French landscaping. But if one considered the barely knee-high patterned hedges as yet another measure of escape prevention—there was nowhere to hide in this very large garden—then everything made more sense.

Charlotte was conducted not into the house but into a side garden delineated by three-foot-high pickets, where Lord Bancroft Ashburton ambled by himself on a smooth stone path.

She almost didn't recognize him. True, he now sported a scraggly beard and his hair hung lank around his nape, but that was to be expected.

She had not anticipated his new ampleness.

The last time they'd met, he'd been gaunt, almost haggardly, living in fear of his crimes coming to light. Now the worst had already happened; now he had lost his stature, his power, and his prestige. A man who thought strategically would use the time to recuperate, and it was obvious he had.

Still, the gain of two stones struck her. He was not fat. He could not even be considered stout. But for a perpetually slender man, this plumping-up was drastic. And his sack suit, made of a strange orange-brown fabric and cut far too loose, was something his former self would never have glanced at, let alone donned.

Yet this man, who bore little resemblance to his sleek, fashionable former self, had managed to organize a successful invasion of Mrs. Watson's household.

There was no welcome in his gaze. "Will you join me for a walk, Miss Holmes?"

She did. "How do you do, my lord Bancroft?"

"A rhetorical question, I presume, as my circumstances are hardly ideal," he replied, his tone as devoid of warmth as hers.

"That you can now take walks outside would indicate that your circumstances have improved markedly."

When Lord Ingram last visited Ravensmere in February, he'd reported that his brother remained confined to his rooms.

"Half an hour a day outside does not make me content with my lot."

"Interesting. Your dissatisfaction with your lot was what led to your downfall in the first place."

Her host snorted without humor and made no reply. They walked twice along the periphery of the diminutive side garden in silence. There was no rustle of trees—there were no trees nearby—but an occasional bird trilled.

"Tea?" he offered at last, indicating a pair of wicker chairs.

She took a seat.

Two plainclothes guards had followed in their wake during their promenade. Lord Bancroft spoke to one. The man left, returned a few minutes later with a tea tray, and set it on the wicker table between the chairs.

It was the first time Charlotte had ever seen tea served in wooden cups. She picked one up and examined the handleless, rustic-looking container.

"Height of elegance, is it not?" murmured Lord Bancroft.

A year ago he had treated her to the best Victoria sandwich she'd ever enjoyed—at a murder site, no less, with a body in the next room. Mostly she remembered the perfection of the cake itself, but the presentation, too, had been flawless: etched-glass cake stand, hand-painted plates, and monogrammed linen napkins.

The guards were now stationed out of earshot. Did they think that a dialogue of delicate sentimentality might be taking place? "What is it you want Sherlock Holmes to do for you, my lord?"

"Underwood is missing. I want you to find him, if he is alive. Otherwise, find out what happened to him."

When Lord Bancroft had been in charge of certain clandestine operations for the crown, Mr. Underwood had been his right-hand man.

He was the reason Bernadine became a hostage?

"I thought Mr. Underwood was in Paris, overseeing the occupation of Mrs. Watson's house."

Lord Bancroft bit into a biscuit that had come with the tea and frowned, an expression of profound disdain. "It would be wholly unnecessary, would it not, to secure your assistance for a problem I didn't have?

"Besides, you might be an excellent investigator, but you've been no lucky charm to those who have come to you in search of missing persons. The matter ended badly for Lady Ingram; it did not prove much better for Moriarty. I would have hesitated to use you at all, but I need Underwood found and you are good at the hunt."

Charlotte took a sip of her tea. The water used for steeping the leaves hadn't been hot enough, and the brew was anemic. "How do you know that Mr. Underwood hasn't been found and arrested by the crown?"

"Because the crown would have told me. You believe that I've been punished very lightly for my supposed crimes, I imagine?"

"Yes."

Her unembellished answer seemed to surprise him. He stared at her a moment, his gaze flat and cold. "You might have guessed—or certainly Ash would have—that my life has been spared because I know enough secrets about enough people. I've let it be known that those secrets would become common knowledge should anything untoward happen to me—and, well, thus far I have been safe.

"But my former superiors have been urging me, with much greater frequency and impatience, to give up what they consider to be my ill-begotten gains. Had they caught Mr. Underwood, they would have informed me straightaway, in the belief that it would make me more pliant to their demands."

True, an underling such as Mr. Underwood had no value on his own. He was only important as an appendage to his master. "Fair enough. Tell me what you can of Mr. Underwood. I know what he looks like, but beyond that, nothing else."

"He is forty-three years of age and hails from the countryside surrounding Eastleigh Park. He was orphaned early in life. His cousin was an under-housekeeper at Eastleigh Park, and so he became a hallboy there at age ten."

Eastleigh Park, the country seat of the Dukes of Wycliff, was also Lord Bancroft's—and Lord Ingram's—childhood home.

"Underwood rose rapidly through the ranks," continued Lord

Bancroft. "But twenty years ago he left Eastleigh Park to work for me."

Charlotte waited. He said nothing more. Was that all he was going to tell her about Mr. Underwood? "How did you learn that he was missing?"

Lord Bancroft tossed the biscuit that had so displeased him back onto the plate, also made of wood. "I had a mistress. Once we parted ways, she took up with Underwood—and became engaged to him in time. After my imprisonment, he had her act as a go-between, and she came on regular conjugal visits."

This was more gossip than Charlotte had anticipated. Had she been playing any kind of role, her brows would have shot up to her hairline.

Strictly speaking, we are not allowed conjugal visits. But when palms are sufficiently greased, eyes look elsewhere. Those had been Lord Bancroft's words, as relayed to Charlotte by Lord Ingram the previous February.

She was curious as to whether the woman came only to deliver and fetch messages or whether hers functioned as true conjugal visits—but not so curious that she asked the question aloud.

Lord Bancroft seemed equally disinclined to discuss the matter. "She was here a fortnight ago, distressed, because Underwood hadn't visited or sent a message for some time."

A cloud occluded the face of the sun; with the shade came an abrupt drop in temperature. "And it's unlike Mr. Underwood to disappear in this manner?"

"Extremely unlike him."

"So most likely he is already dead."

"I'd put his chance of survival at no more than twenty percent. But these are not impossible odds."

It was usually harsher illumination that revealed flaws in a person's appearance, but in the relative dimness, the lines on Lord Bancroft's face stood out more starkly. "Any enemies of his—and yours—that I should know about?"

Another look of distaste passed over Lord Bancroft's countenance before he took a sip of his tea. "I have asked myself the same. We and the work we did for the crown were not known to the public. We collected information. Others, not I and certainly not Underwood, made decisions based on what we learned. If any ramifications of those decisions provoked anyone into retaliation, I should think their wrath would first fall on the decision-makers, and not on those of us who were mere intelligence gatherers."

Charlotte knew something of his official responsibilities because of Lord Ingram, but it had always been evident that she knew only a fraction of what Lord Ingram did and that he in turn had known only a fraction of everything under Lord Bancroft's purview.

No doubt Lord Bancroft's subordinates had gathered intelligence. But had that been their sole activity? What else had he—and Mr. Underwood—done during those years when he had been entrusted with many of the empire's secret portfolios?

"Ash once said to me, 'Empires are not built with clean hands.' Surely you have staged less benign schemes during your tenure."

"And surely, had I done that, I'd have been careful to leave no calling cards. Underwood likewise."

In other words, Mr. Underwood's disappearance was not related to their work on behalf of the crown. "Then what about activities that were not sanctioned by the crown? Could they have caused someone to harm Mr. Underwood?"

Lord Bancroft gave her a thin smile. "I have never participated in or condoned any activities that were not sanctioned by the crown. And neither has Underwood."

Of course, Lord Bancroft had never officially admitted to any wrongdoing. The parties who had purchased state secrets from him were not going to step forth to help with his prosecution. And the properties that the crown had confiscated, in the wake of the discovery of his treachery, could still, if barely, be explained away as having been paid for by some long-ago parental largesse combined with subsequent gains on the stock market.

But why this insistence of blamelessness? It was not going to convince her, the discoverer of his guilt, otherwise. And incomplete knowledge would only hamper her search for Mr. Underwood.

"If Mr. Underwood's disappearance had nothing to do with his professional life—or yours—then what could have caused it?"

Lord Bancroft ran his fingers down his sparse beard. "He might have made enemies in boxing gymnasiums."

"He boxed?"

Boxing was a sport beloved by gentlemen and ruffians alike. But the kind of gymnasiums Lord Bancroft referred to, which seemed to exist on every other street in London, were not genteel establishments. They used the upper floors or back parlors of pubs, ran matches that didn't follow the Marquis of Queensberry rules, and engaged in prizefighting, which was not precisely legal.

"Why, hello, young lady!"

Charlotte glanced over her shoulder at the man who stood at an upper-story window, waving at her from behind bars.

"My goodness!" the man exclaimed further. "I thought I was hallucinating. But you are real and you are a vision, miss!"

"Thank you," said Charlotte, squinting.

"Very kind of you to call on my housemate—and good day to you, too, sir! What brought you here? What were you discussing?"

"Your housemate was assuring me of his innocence."

"Well, I believe him!" cried the man whose voice seemed to belong to someone middle-aged. Late middle age, perhaps. "And please, you must believe me, miss, when I say that I, too, have done nothing to deserve this prolonged internment. It must be extrajudicial and highly illegal to hold me here, and if you would please contact the newspapers for me, I would be most grateful. The reporter who speaks truth on my behalf will surely be rewarded with readership beyond his dreams!"

His face was now pressed into the bars, an ordinary face, its enthusiasm belied by a lack of true goodwill. A guard appeared and pulled him away from the barred window, which was then closed and shuttered from the inside, firmly cutting off Charlotte's line of sight.

Lord Bancroft narrowed his eyes, then said, as if the interruption hadn't taken place, "No, Underwood didn't box—at least I never saw cuts and bruises on him. He sponsored boxers, and his boxers were successful, from what I understand."

That *could* lead to retaliations, if those boxers' successes were due to underhanded methods, although a knife between Mr. Underwood's ribs seemed a more likely outcome than his wholesale disappearance.

"I will speak to Mr. Underwood's lady and find his boxers. What about his subordinates? Any of them at large?"

"Not all have been arrested, but I do not know their precise whereabouts, just as I didn't know Underwood's."

Charlotte rubbed her thumb across the side of her wooden cup. It was smooth and just a little bit warm. "Any helpful advice on how I can best locate Mr. Underwood?"

For all that Lord Bancroft had gone through a great deal of trouble—and illegality and heartlessness—to secure her help, he had not given her much useful information.

As if he'd heard her thought, Lord Bancroft said, "It has occurred to me before that I did not know Underwood very well as a man, but at the time our lack of greater intimacy had struck me as both correct and seemly. He discharged his duties by being useful and efficient, and I rewarded him with income and opportunities far beyond what he could have achieved in domestic service.

"Now, that once highly appropriate distance has turned out to be a disadvantage. Even the bit about boxing I learned by chance. After that, I did ask him whether he boxed personally. When he assured me that he didn't, I told him to beware the unsavory elements found ringside. I did not inquire after the identity of the boxers he sponsored, where they trained and fought, or how much money exchanged hands."

He chuckled without mirth. "Let that be a lesson to me, a man who has spent his life in the acquisition of particulars: Knowledge I disdain to acquire today might prove to be the vital intelligence I lack tomorrow."

———❖———

Charlotte glanced at the guards. One studied the sky; the other had his eyes on them but in truth might be looking *through* them, busy with his own thoughts. Both remained safely out of earshot.

She returned her attention to Lord Bancroft. "If I may speak frankly, my lord, I find it difficult to believe that you are so generously disposed toward a subordinate, even Mr. Underwood. I thought at the very least you would demand my help freeing you from Ravensmere."

Lord Bancroft snorted. "So now Sherlock Holmes also engages in jailbreaking? Look at this place, all the windows are barred. The single entry into and out of my rooms is guarded by two sets of reinforced doors. As a further precaution, there is a security cabin in my parlor, bolted to the floor. Before any guards or charwomen come inside, or even unlock the swinging tray to deliver my meal, I must lock myself into this security cabin.

"The front door of the manor is barred from both inside and outside. The back door has been bricked over. Stairs are barred at each landing. There are two guards on each floor and four in the garden, one by the front door, three patrolling the expanse.

"Moreover, all my meals are cut into bite-sized pieces, and I am only given a single wooden spoon, which must be surrendered at the end of every repast. As you can see, I haven't shaved in months—or had my hair cut. I do not even have proper suspenders these days. What approximations I'm allowed are of such flimsy construction that if I attempted to asphyxiate anyone with it—or even to tie him up—the whole thing would disintegrate into segments too short to be of any use."

In disgust, he picked up his discarded biscuit and bit into it again. In even greater disgust, he hurled the rest beyond the wrought iron fence into the larger garden. "Now, given all that, could Sherlock Holmes have succeeded in getting me out?"

———※———

Lord Bancroft's voice remained low, but his action constituted an outburst. One guard took a step forward, the other reached inside his jacket, presumably for a firearm.

Charlotte drank her tepid tea. After a moment, Lord Bancroft picked up his teacup and joined her, sipping in silence. When it became apparent that nothing else was going to happen, the guards relaxed somewhat but kept their eyes on Lord Bancroft.

Charlotte reviewed what he had said about the security measures in and around Ravensmere. They accorded with what Lord Ingram had told her about the place. She did not believe in the impossibility of getting out of a place that had doors and windows. All the same, Lord Bancroft was correct that it would not be easy.

"All right, so it is only the disappearance of Mr. Underwood for which you have engaged me. And now that I understand my task, I have some conditions about the house in Paris."

Lord Bancroft raised a brow.

"Your people are not to enter Miss Bernadine's room under any circumstances. Miss Redmayne is allowed access to the house at least once a day, twice if she so wishes, and no part of the house will be forbidden to her. You may limit the amount of time she spends in the house, but on any given visit, she cannot be ejected before half an hour has passed."

Lord Bancroft flicked nonexistent biscuit crumbs from his fingertips. "Very well. You may send a cable to the house, starting with the words '*Corvus dicit*.' They will know it's from me."

"And you had best inform the gatehouse that Sherrinford and Charlotte Holmes should be on the guest list for the foreseeable future."

Her adversary rose. "Anything else? I will be escorted back inside in a minute or so."

Under normal circumstances, this would be when Mrs. Watson,

while accompanying a client out of 18 Upper Baker Street, discreetly broached the topic of remuneration. But Mrs. Watson was waiting outside many walls, and it was highly unlikely that Lord Bancroft intended to compensate Charlotte for her work.

"The man who interrupted us," she asked, "do you believe in his assertion of innocence?"

A brief beam of sunlight struck Lord Bancroft's startlingly pale face before shadows took over again, limning the spreading web of fine lines on his no-longer-supple skin. "I do not," he answered with a sneer. "I believe only in my own assertion of innocence."

Eight

Mr. Underwood's mistress, Mrs. Claiborne, had an address in St. John's Wood.

It was an excellent neighborhood in which to keep one's mistress, especially if one wished to be discreet. The area was not too fashionable, yet not too remote. The rent was affordable. Freestanding houses on larger lots, called villas, rare in Mayfair and Belgravia, were more plentiful in these parts. With spacious gardens, and driveways that curved under large porticos, a man could visit his paramour regularly without ever being seen by nosy neighbors.

Mrs. Claiborne, however, lived in a row of town houses packed as tight as matches in a box.

Lord Bancroft had cautioned Miss Charlotte that Mrs. Claiborne, concerned for her safety, no longer answered the front door. Miss Charlotte and Mrs. Watson therefore approached from the back.

The alley behind a row of town houses, at the best of times, smelled of horses. In the heat of August, all the uncollected droppings in all the mews had aged to a fine stench. The onslaught of odors made Mrs. Watson's head throb.

Miss Charlotte had given her an account of the meeting with Lord Bancroft, and Mrs. Watson didn't believe a single word the man had said. She could only hope that this whole rigmarole wasn't some horrible trap. No, she knew it to be a horrible trap; she simply didn't know yet what would trigger its razor-sharp steel maw to snap shut around them.

But for the sake of everyone in Paris, they had to keep Lord Bancroft happy. And if that meant finding Mr. Underwood—or his corpse—then so be it.

Mrs. Claiborne's mews was empty, neither horse nor carriage stowed therein. The ladies sidestepped fresh knolls of equine excreta, entered Mrs. Claiborne's tiny back garden on the other side of the alley, and rang the bell.

The curtain on the window next to the door fluttered. "Who is it?" called out a voice speaking with a soft but noticeable French accent.

"Miss Holmes and Mrs. Hudson," answered Miss Charlotte. "We are here to see Mrs. Claiborne on behalf of Mr. Sherlock Holmes, at Lord Bancroft Ashburton's request."

The door opened immediately.

Most men chose mistresses on the basis of physical attractiveness. Even so, Mrs. Claiborne was exceptionally lovely—her eyes made Mrs. Watson think of a starlit sky, and her figure was superb. She wore a white blouse and a skirt in the same shade of sky blue as the ribbons that trimmed her lacy sleeves.

A very pretty ensemble that might have been a bit too pastel for a woman in her early thirties were it not for the crispness of the fabric and the simplicity of the cut.

"Thank goodness you're here!" she cried. "When Lord Bancroft said that he'd have Mr. Sherlock Holmes help me, I thought he meant only to keep me from losing my mind. Do please come in!"

The visitors folded their parasols and entered the house. The ground floor felt dim and smelled a little stale. The upstairs parlor Mrs. Claiborne ushered them into, its drapes completely drawn, turned out to be gloomier and even more airless.

"My apologies—I wasn't expecting callers."

But instead of pulling back the curtains, Mrs. Claiborne turned on all the lamps in the room, revealing a profusion of red velvet and golden fringes. The curtains, the upholstery, and even the piano cover used the same fabric and trimming—Mrs. Watson had visited less exaggerated theaters.

Their hostess plumped seat cushions, offered chairs to her visitors, put water to boil, and set out plates of cake. "Please allow me to thank you again, ladies, for coming to my aid."

Relief and gratitude shone in her eyes—yet they couldn't quite hide the panic simmering underneath. Mrs. Watson felt an involuntary twinge of sympathy. Sternly, she warned herself not to get carried away. She'd heard this story before—a lonely woman desperately seeking her lost beloved—and this time around she refused to be deceived.

Miss Charlotte, her purple-and-white-striped day dress clashing overwhelmingly with the décor, said, after they'd spent a few minutes on small talk, "I understand that you began to worry when letters and visits from Mr. Underwood ceased. Can you elaborate a little, beginning with how he became a . . . regular member of your household?"

Mrs. Claiborne perched at the edge of her chair. There had been a magazine lying there, which she'd picked up and set on her lap. Her thumb rubbed against the edge of the publication. "Well, um, I was under Lord Bancroft's protection for three years. Then one day he told me that it was time to let me go, because he wished to court a young lady and his brother advised him not to keep a mistress at the same time, if he wished his suit to succeed."

Mrs. Watson barely managed not to glance at Miss Charlotte. So Mrs. Claiborne had lost her livelihood because Lord Bancroft decided to pursue Miss Charlotte's hand in marriage?

"He was generous," Mrs. Claiborne carried on, "and made me a gift of the house I was living in—not this town house but a villa on Prince's Grove Close. The villa, as it turned out, became a contributing factor in Mr. Underwood's decision to approach me.

"He was very straightforward. Were it not for the fact that I already had my own place thanks to Lord Bancroft, he said, he would not be able to maintain me in a similar style. But since I did have the house, would I be amenable if he footed the bill for my staff, carriage, and cattle, and a certain number of new garments each season?

"His frankness . . . had an unexpected effect on me. I confessed that over the years, in my boredom, I'd frittered away too much pin money—and must now save in earnest for the future." Color crept into Mrs. Claiborne's cheeks. She lowered her face to warm a teapot with freshly boiled water. "I meant to reduce my staff, get rid of my horse and carriage, and not invest in new frocks for at least three years. But if he would hand me in cash what he would have paid for those luxuries, I'd consider having him as my protector."

Mrs. Watson was fascinated. She herself had been in the same profession but had never negotiated face-to-face with prospective protectors. Instead, she had brokered deals with their men of business to translate *whatever your heart desires, darling* into exact, transferable amounts.

She was also intrigued by Mrs. Claiborne's tendency to blush, surely a rarity among kept women. But perhaps this was precisely what her protectors liked, that someone who sold her favors for a living could still appear maidenly and easily flustered.

"Mr. Underwood was amenable to my idea," Mrs. Claiborne went on. "Lord Bancroft gave his blessing. I made my domestic reductions, Mr. Underwood deposited money into my bank account, and . . . well, to answer your question, Miss Holmes, that was how he came to be a member of my household."

Miss Charlotte took a slice of cake. "The two of you got along well then, I take it?"

"We did." Mrs. Claiborne had not looked anyone in the eye while she made confessions about her personal finance, but now she slowly raised her face, her expression dreamy. "With Lord Bancroft, I was always nervous. He wanted the best in everything, and I was convinced that I didn't measure up. But Mr. Underwood wasn't shy in telling me that he felt downright fortunate that I accepted him.

"Otherwise, he didn't talk much, which suited me just fine. He was happy to study the papers while I played the pianoforte. And he liked to hear me read aloud from books and magazines while he nursed a drink."

She patted her blouse, near the third closely spaced button from the top. Mrs. Watson, who had once worn a locket with her wedding photograph inside, wondered whether Mrs. Claiborne didn't have a locket, too, under the blouse.

"Last September, he asked me to marry him. I said yes. I wanted to post banns, but he said a special license would be better—he didn't want it known to people who might not be kindly disposed toward him that he would soon have a wife. He thought it could be dangerous for me, and that, in turn, would be dangerous for him, too."

"Did that concern you, his fear?"

Mrs. Claiborne covered the diamond ring on her left hand—her engagement ring, probably—as if to protect it. "Miss Holmes, Mrs. Hudson, you must understand, my mother, she, too, was a courtesan. That's what we are sometimes called in Paris, women destined to be wealthy men's mistresses. And that was what she trained me to be, except I was never that good at it.

"Marriage would at last halt my progress toward life as a failed old cyprian—I was jubilant about never having to reel in another protector. That relief was real, whereas the danger Mr. Underwood mentioned seemed hypothetical.

"But I was wrong, of course. One dreadful day, Mr. Underwood didn't come home. Instead, he sent a message saying that Lord Bancroft had been arrested and he himself must go into hiding for a while."

Mrs. Claiborne riffled the edges of the magazine's pages, deaf to the sibilant susurration produced by her nervous tic. "He had always instructed me not to keep any correspondence from him, but I'd kept them in secret. That night I burned everything—letters, bills, photographs, anything with his name or face on it. The next day I dismissed everyone from my already-reduced household staff.

"Mr. Underwood slipped into the house one night and told me

that he might flee to America or Australia at some point but he couldn't abandon Lord Bancroft just yet. From that point onward, he wrote me twice a week. Sometimes he didn't send letters, only an empty envelope, so that I could tell by the postmark where he'd been. But I burned even those.

"The regularity of those letters lulled me into a false sense of security. I began to dream of our future in a distant land, where no one would know anything about us and we'd have that ordinary life I'd always wished for. And then his letters stopped."

Abruptly Mrs. Claiborne rose, went to the window, and peered around the edge of the curtain. Mrs. Watson came half out of her own chair.

Mrs. Claiborne turned around. "I'm sorry. There was nothing, but I'm jumpy these days."

Mrs. Watson slowly sat back down, the room's stuffy warmth an abrading heat just inside her collar.

"You are sure everything is all right?" asked Miss Charlotte.

"Yes, I'm sure." Mrs. Claiborne smiled tightly. She tugged at a few tassels on the fringe of the red velvet curtain. "When Mr. Underwood's letters stopped, I tried to bide my time, because he'd asked me not to panic if a single letter went astray. But after a week went by, I couldn't wait any longer.

"I went to see Lord Bancroft, worried sick that he would tell me it was nothing to lose sleep over. Fortunately his lordship was as alarmed as I was—I mean, he was calm and not in tears, but you could tell the news did not please him at all.

"He said he'd get me help. I wasn't sure I believed him, but here you are, beyond all expectations." She gazed at Miss Charlotte, her expression that of a believer near the end of her pilgrimage, desperate to witness a miracle. "Miss Holmes, your brother is a legend in the making—I read all about the double murder last December. I'm thrilled to have his assistance, especially since Lord Bancroft told me that he excels at finding missing persons."

Did she not know that one such missing person had been killed by perhaps none other than Mr. Underwood himself, on Lord Bancroft's orders? And had no one told her that Sherlock Holmes was responsible for Lord Bancroft's current incarceration, however bucolic and genteel?

But perhaps Mrs. Claiborne, with her ardent desire for a calm and stable domestic life, was the kind of woman from whom men who did awful things kept those things hidden, so that they, too, could enjoy a pretense of normalcy, a cocoon in which their hands did not drip with blood.

After all, did Mrs. Watson not sense a desire in herself to shield Mrs. Claiborne from the knowledge that representatives of Sherlock Holmes were here against their will, their "assistance" secured by loathsome means?

Mrs. Claiborne must not have expected a profound silence to greet her account of events. She glanced uneasily from Miss Holmes to Mrs. Watson, then back again.

Miss Charlotte set down her biscuit plate and rearranged her already beautifully draped skirt. "Lord Bancroft seems to think that Mr. Underwood might have enemies stemming from his sponsorship of some boxers who compete in fights that are not precisely legal."

"I suppose that's possible," said Mrs. Claiborne hesitantly. "Mr. Underwood spoke very little about boxing—he was glad that I didn't like the sport."

"Did he say anything about the boxers he sponsored?"

"Only that there were three of them, somewhere near New Cross—I think, but I'm not sure. I rarely venture farther afield than Oxford Street."

"Anything else you can tell us that might lead us to find Mr. Underwood?"

"But I know so little of the rest of Mr. Underwood's life." Mrs. Claiborne blinked rapidly. Judging by the sudden brilliance of her eyes, she was trying to hold back tears.

Miss Charlotte folded her hands in her lap and leveled her inscrutable regard at Mrs. Claiborne. "Is this really all that you can tell me?"

Mrs. Claiborne swallowed. Possibly in an unconscious imitation of Miss Charlotte, who radiated composure, she, too, clasped her hands in front of her. But her new posture only made Mrs. Watson feel tense from shoulder to wrist.

"Ladies, will you promise never to tell Mr. Underwood what I'm about to tell you?"

"We take client confidentiality very seriously," answered Miss Charlotte.

This was no promise at all, yet Mrs. Claiborne exhaled. She crossed to the sideboard and drank from a silver flask. With her fingertips, she flicked at the corner of her lips. "The last time Mr. Underwood visited me in person, six weeks ago, I woke up at night to the sound of men in a heated conversation. I recognized Mr. Underwood's voice but not the other person's.

"They were downstairs in the entry, and Mr. Underwood was warning the man not to come to the villa again. Shortly after that he showed the man the door. And the very next day, he found this town house and I moved."

Mrs. Watson did think that the town house had all the signs of having been leased fully furnished and in a great hurry, as the décor was completely at odds with the soft-hued elegance of Mrs. Claiborne's attire.

"Describe the man who argued with Mr. Underwood that night."

"Mr. Underwood didn't call him by name, only 'you swine.' As he was leaving, I saw a large scar on his face, running down the entire left side of his cheek. I assumed that he was someone Mr. Underwood knew from boxing—so many of them had that hard, battered look, and so many of them go from incarcerated criminals to feted boxers and then back again."

She panted, as if the account had drained her of all her strength. Incongruously, a peal of laughter erupted outside, muffled by the closed window.

Mrs. Watson stared a moment at the drawn drapes and longed for fresh air.

Miss Charlotte did not reply, even after the last echo of mirth had died down. The silence dragged. Mrs. Watson's breaths began to whoosh in her own ears.

"Have you decided against telling us the rest, Mrs. Claiborne?" said Miss Charlotte at last.

Mrs. Claiborne jerked, then keened in the back of her throat, a sound of torment.

"Sherlock Holmes's effectiveness depends on knowing as much as he can, going into a case," said Miss Charlotte, her tone inexorable. "What do you want more, Mrs. Claiborne, to find Mr. Underwood or to keep your secret?"

Mrs. Claiborne covered her face with her hand. It was another minute before she let that hand fall limply to her side. "Mr. Underwood and I have dealt favorably with each other from the beginning. And I believe we will be happy in the future, too. But after he went missing, I've had too much time to think. As good as I am at not thinking about what I do not wish to, sometimes I can't help but remember that at times . . . at times . . ."

"Yes?" came Miss Charlotte's implacable prompting.

Mrs. Claiborne squeezed her eyes shut. "At times I've smelled perfume on him—and I don't use fragrance."

Mrs. Watson sighed. She herself would have never expected a protector to be faithful. But an expectation to marry changed things. In her longing for a traditional life, Mrs. Claiborne had turned a blind eye. Until she could deceive herself no longer.

Mrs. Claiborne opened her eyes again; she looked nauseated. "In the past I told myself that it must have been a female relation he found after he'd come of age, or the widow of a colleague he was kind enough to visit. But now that he's gone without an explanation to anyone, and Lord Bancroft is sure that he hasn't been caught by the crown . . .

"Maybe someone in the boxing circles wished him ill. Maybe he went away with that other woman instead. Or maybe he has left us both behind. After all, women are everywhere to be had. It would be more convenient for him to find a new mistress or two in the New World, wouldn't it, rather than taking the trouble to export one from here?"

Silence fell again. Mrs. Claiborne returned to her seat and dropped into it.

Her motion felt like a collapse, her unhappiness a great numbness in the air.

"If I may ask, Mrs. Claiborne," said Miss Charlotte, her bland expression unchanged, "what have you done with the villa, the one Lord Bancroft gifted you?"

She did not ignore Mrs. Claiborne's distress but cut through it like a fast, sharp-hulled vessel parted the waves.

Mrs. Claiborne appeared bewildered. "The villa? It—it's still there. But I don't think you'll find anything useful inside."

"Nevertheless, I'd like to take a look."

"Of course. One moment, please."

Mrs. Claiborne returned two minutes later with a set of keys— and red-rimmed eyes.

She handed the keys to Miss Charlotte, her eyes swimming again. "Miss Holmes, in case—in case you find out that Mr. Underwood left the country with that other woman, please don't let me know. Just tell me that he emigrated by himself."

"I'm sure it won't come to that, Mrs. Claiborne," said Miss Charlotte, rising from her chair, looking as serene as the Madonna of Bruges. "I'm sure of it."

Nine

Leaving Mrs. Claiborne's town house, the two women went in separate directions. Mrs. Watson would join forces with Lawson, her groom and coachman who had not moved to Paris with the rest of the household, to look for Mr. Underwood's boxing connections. Charlotte, newly acquired keys in hand, headed for Mrs. Claiborne's original house, the villa on Prince's Grove Close.

The location was suitably private, the last dwelling on a secluded cul-de-sac. The front gate opened to a rose garden in furious bloom, every single flower a perfect shade of sugarplum. The view was lovely, but Charlotte noticed the weeds pushing up everywhere, as well as the plethora of faded blossoms that hadn't been trimmed.

The interior of the villa was dark—the windows had been shuttered and the gas lamps no longer supplied with fuel. Charlotte managed to find a candlestick and lit the taper.

Candlelight shone on muted gold wallpaper of Japanese six-point-star patterns. The upholstery was an ivory chintz printed with birds and stylized cherry trees. Had the windows been open and light flooding in, the room would have been airy and pretty.

Out of curiosity, Charlotte drew close to a wall and lifted the candlestick high to inspect the area above a sconce—near gas flames, it would have been difficult to keep such light wallpaper from discoloration. But Mrs. Claiborne had anticipated the problem and installed a miniature shelf that held a blue ceramic plate with Japanese wave patterns—much easier to clean than silk wallpaper.

Charlotte descended to the basement and began her inspection there.

The domestic offices, completely emptied of all papers, did not yield so much as a receipt for coal.

In the kitchen, all the food had been disposed of, not a scrap of bread or potato peel left to collect mold. The stove, the inside of which had not been similarly cleaned out, showed an inch of ash mingled with charred bits of wood.

Charlotte climbed up one story to the ground floor and looked in on the morning room, the dining room, and the study. Unlike most studies Charlotte had encountered in her time, this one contained only sixty or so volumes that barely filled one lonely bookshelf to half capacity. She didn't know about Mr. Underwood's or Mrs. Claiborne's tastes in written material, but once upon a time Lord Bancroft had mentioned in Charlotte's hearing that he read deeply on the history of art and was fascinated by the development of the Italian city-states from the tenth to the fifteenth century.

Most of the books on hand appeared to have been acquired for his benefit.

She had already examined the table in the dining room and the mantelpiece in the morning room, and those surfaces held six weeks' worth of accumulated dust.

The bookshelf, upon first glance, had collected dust for much longer, months rather than weeks. Presumably Mrs. Claiborne, shorn of all staff since the previous autumn and faced with a house that was too much for one person to maintain, had retreated from the study early on.

Charlotte stared at the rows of books for a while, then loosened a bookend and picked up a tome.

The dust *under* that book told a different story. The first half inch or so of the narrow strip of shelf surface exposed by the removal of the book, the part that had lain beneath the spine, bore noticeably thicker dust than the surface near the rear of the shelf. She lifted another book; the same pattern held. Another, still the same.

The books had once stood farther back on the shelf. But someone had moved them—possibly recently—and had set them down closer to the edge, so as to hide a disturbance in the dust.

She checked each volume but came across nothing unusual. Whoever had been here before her, a thorough soul, would have gone through all the books. The only question was whether the intruder had found anything worthwhile.

The study's desk drawers did not seem to have been disturbed—if one looked only at the drawer pulls. But Charlotte, with a pencil from her handbag, was able to open and close those drawers without touching the dust on the drawer pulls or leaving fingermarks behind.

On the next floor she at last came across signs of a hasty departure: In Mrs. Claiborne's bedroom, the wardrobe doors hung ajar; half of the drawers in her dressing room remained pulled out. Charlotte assumed, given the care the clandestine visitor had taken, that this part of the house had appeared just so in the wake of Mrs. Claiborne's flight.

Up in the attic, however, that care flagged. Or perhaps it would be fairer to say that here it was nigh on impossible to conceal all traces of one's presence.

The door to the attic was secured with a padlock that had been wiped clean—about three days ago, Charlotte would say. The clandestine visitor, who had not come equipped with keys, had picked the lock, and he or she could not have accomplished that without disturbing the dust on the padlock.

The corridor in the attic, uncarpeted, was so dusty that footmarks could not be concealed. Still, the secret explorer had not been willing to leave actual shoe prints. The dust had been—not swept but rearranged, possibly with a piece of cloth or an outer garment the intruder had dragged behind as he or she left.

The attic, with its cramped quarters for servants, held no other revelations. Charlotte relocked the door, descended, and took one more round on each floor, making sure that she hadn't overlooked anything.

After that, she opened the back door and went out into the rear garden.

And there she found something interesting.

—❊—

As Charlotte approached the street entrance of her hotel suite, she spied an old man striding in her direction.

When she last saw him, the old man had been deeply unstylish, liver-spotted, and reeking of too much eau de cologne. As he marched past her today, the overpowering miasma was gone, the liver spots nowhere to be seen, and the garments only a few years, instead of a few decades, behind the forefront of fashion. He was still an old man but a spry one, with a thick head of salt-and-pepper hair and spectacles that gave him an air of quiet authority.

"Oh, sir! Sir, one moment, please!" she called out.

The most tempting old man this side of the English Channel stopped and turned around. He looked vaguely perplexed. "Yes?"

"I do apologize, but I found these on the pavement. They wouldn't happen to belong to you, would they?" asked Charlotte, her eyes wide as she held out the pair of wire-rimmed glasses she used for her gentlemen characters.

He made a show of looking them over carefully. "Thank you, miss, but these are not mine."

"Oh." She made her best crestfallen face. "I will leave them at the reception then."

"I wish you a good evening, miss." He inclined his head and left without a moment's hesitation.

Always playing hard to get, her lover.

It was too late for tea and too early for dinner. So Charlotte, back in her hotel suite, rang for both.

She had just changed into a home dress when a knock came.

Taking advantage of Society's exit from London, Charlotte and her friends had booked three side-by-side suites at the hotel, each with a private entrance. Between Lord Ingram's suite and the one occupied by the ladies was an even larger one, the only one at the hotel that connected to the suites on both sides, meant to host a very large family or dignitaries who simply demanded more space.

This suite was currently taken by none other than Lawson, who played the part of a Manchester man of business. But as Lawson preferred his own lodgings behind Mrs. Watson's house near Regent's Park, this very nice suite mostly served as a corridor between Lord Ingram's and the ladies' quarters.

"Do excuse me, miss," said an elderly voice on the other side of the connecting door. "I hope I am not too previous in calling on you. But perhaps I should take one more look at the glasses you found. You haven't placed them with the reception yet, I take it?"

Charlotte sauntered to the door, unlatched it, and admitted her lover. "My, what a proper old gentleman you are."

He snorted, an incongruous sound coming from such an ancient paragon. "Would you prefer if I were the sort of old man who leered at young women? No, never mind that, I remember now: You prefer great beauties such as Mr. Gregory."

Mr. Gregory, a fellow traveler on the RMS *Provence*, had indeed been a great beauty. Charlotte batted her eyelashes. "Do I detect a note of jealousy, my lord?"

"A note?" He scoffed. "I have composed an entire symphony of jealousy. This is merely the overture. In fact, this might be only the orchestra tuning up."

She held back a smile. She was not the liveliest or most responsive woman, but he moved her to mirth rather easily. "Oh my. How wrong you are. I am not interested in the lovely Mr. Gregorys of the world. It has always been the prim, repressed Lord Ingrams of the world for me."

"Huh," he said, walking to the sideboard to pour himself a glass of water from a carafe.

"However, that old gentleman in Paris that I encountered in a carriage . . . I am fascinated by him, too. I wonder if Monsieur Lord and Master secretly enjoys being tied up in bed."

Lord Ingram spat out his water. Then he thought for a moment. "He might. That could be why he's so grumpy. He's always felt as if something has been missing in his life, but didn't know what. And his lady wife, instead of understanding him better than he understands himself—and sourcing the best silken cords in Paris—is too busy ogling Footman Pierre of the ham-sized biceps."

The smile that had been threatening to erupt upon Charlotte's face did so at last. "I see the orchestra has finished tuning up and now we are in the opening bars of *La Grande Symphonie de la Jalousie*."

He set down his glass, closed the distance between them, and embraced her. "Are you all right, Holmes?"

She hugged him back. "I would prefer a case in which I had no personal stake—the little conundrum from Inspector Treadles, for instance. But I'm all right. How can I not be, in the company of handsome old men?"

"Huh," he said again, at her use of the plural noun, and kissed her.

"My dear, I'm back!" Mrs. Watson called out.

She pushed open the door to the parlor only to see Miss Holmes step back from the embrace of an older gentleman.

A choked sound emerged from Mrs. Watson's throat. Before she could comprehend what was happening, the older gentleman half bowed and said, "Good afternoon, ma'am."

He spoke in Lord Ingram's voice. Mrs. Watson gasped again. She rushed forward, took him by the shoulders, and peered at his face.

The previous autumn, in experimenting with various makeup techniques that would result in a better disguise, she'd discovered that bits of crumpled tissue paper could be used to simulate wrinkles, when brushed over with a formulation made by Miss Longstead.

Miss Longstead, not resting on her laurels, made further modifications and came up with a new solution that could be layered onto the face in sufficient thickness to alter the shape of the nose or the height of the cheekbones. Which was what Lord Ingram had done, in addition to a sharp-tipped beard that suggested a different jaw structure from his own.

"My goodness, I couldn't tell that it was you!" Mrs. Watson marveled.

Lord Ingram kissed her on both cheeks. "You should have seen me in Paris," he said wryly. "My disguise there was exceptional."

The food Miss Charlotte ordered came, and they sat down around the tea table. Mrs. Watson had little idea what she was eating. She barely even kicked herself for walking in on the young lovers. As soon as Lord Ingram had received an account of the meetings with Lord Bancroft and Mrs. Claiborne, she set down her silverware.

"My dear boy, do you think it's remotely possible that your brother would do so much, including taking Miss Bernadine hostage, merely because he's concerned for a henchman?"

Miss Charlotte, who was more interested in the small sandwiches that had come with the tea service, had given her dinner to Lord Ingram. He sliced a spear of asparagus into several smaller morsels and looked up with a frown. "The answer should be no. But I'm not the best person, ma'am, to give you that emphatic no you were looking for. I—I still think that under the right circumstances, my brother might do someone a great favor."

Mrs. Watson's heart ached. She herself despised Lord Bancroft with a great purity, but for Lord Ingram, it could not be so simple. She pushed aside her plate altogether. "You're thinking of the drawing lessons he gave you when you were younger?"

Lord Ingram's three brothers were all much older than he. He got on the best with Lord Remington, the next youngest. The current duke, the eldest, had always been too much of a second father—and far sterner than the old duke had ever been. And Lord Bancroft, that cold fish, had never been anyone's favorite.

But Lord Bancroft, confined to the family estate for long stretches in his youth because the old duke didn't want him out and about being profligate, had occasionally taken his baby brother under his wing.

Mrs. Watson, then the widowed old duke's mistress, had spent a fair amount of time at Eastleigh Park. Lord Ingram used to show her his latest sketches and illustrations, pointing out where Lord Bancroft's comments and examples had improved his technique and composition.

And of course it had been Lord Bancroft who had advised him to take up drawing in the first place, or at least drafting, to become a better archaeologist.

"I know the logical conclusion is that Bancroft was simply bored at Eastleigh Park," said Lord Ingram, "and not that he was invested in me or my hobbies. One could even make the argument that he decided to be nice to me because someday I might inherit my godfather's fortune.

"I would not dispute those theories. But it remains that I benefited greatly from the drawing lessons he gave me. And so, despite what he did later, I do not consider it out of the realm of possibility that he could do something nice for Underwood."

Mrs. Watson touched him on the shoulder. Lord Bancroft did not deserve such tender opinions, but she could not fault Lord Ingram for seeing the best in him—it was what she admired so much about the dear young man.

He smiled at her. But when he glanced at Miss Charlotte, his eyes were troubled. "That said, do I believe that my brother is acting out of the pure goodness of his heart? No. In the search for Underwood, there must be either a gain he cannot pass up or a loss he must prevent."

"What kind of gain? What kind of loss?" asked Mrs. Watson, both afraid and desperate to know.

He, too, set down his knife and fork. "The greatest gain, at this point, is his freedom. If there is a plot to spring him from Ravensmere, and Underwood happens to be the linchpin of the entire plan, then of course a missing Underwood must be found, or at least accounted for. As for the greatest loss, that would be his life. But do you see his life being in immediate danger, Holmes?"

Miss Charlotte took a piece of the fillet of sole that he had scarcely touched. "If my lord Bancroft doesn't have his talisman of compromising royal letters, then maybe he ought to worry about his safety. But have you heard from anyone that those letters have exchanged hands?"

Lord Ingram shook his head. "No, and I don't think he would have entrusted something that crucial to Underwood. Now it's possible that Underwood knows where his money is—the money that the crown has been trying to recover. If Underwood's disappearance means Bancroft no longer has his money, then finding Underwood also becomes a priority."

He looked back at Mrs. Watson. "You're disappointed, ma'am, because we have no definite answers?"

Mrs. Watson sighed inwardly. "I should be more accustomed to uncertainties, at this point. Yet because Lord Bancroft is someone we all know, I want a surer grasp on the situation."

"If it makes you feel any better, when Holmes investigated the death at Stern Hollow, she did not eliminate me from consideration—not right away, in any case. By comparison, none of us knows Bancroft *that* well, so how can we say with any confidence his exact purpose?"

Miss Holmes had just served herself a scoop of berry fool. She did not dig into the fruit-swirled custard right away but glanced at Lord Ingram's plate. "You haven't eaten much."

He smiled at her warmly, but with more than a trace of fatigue. "I'm still thinking about the situation in Paris. But don't worry. Tomorrow I'll be back in Stern Hollow, and Cummings will feed me properly."

To maintain his convalescent façade, he needed to make an appearance at home once in a while.

Miss Charlotte settled a hand briefly on his elbow. "Very well, then. Make sure you feast on the morrow."

Then she turned to Mrs. Watson. "Have you made any progress, ma'am, in the search of Mr. Underwood's boxers?"

—�֍—

At quarter past two in the morning, the heat of summertime Provence had at last become gentler, like that of an oven that had baked its last loaf hours ago.

The man who lay crouched atop the roof, however, still perspired—not so much from the heat as from the height of the damned roof. He was five stories up and had absolutely no assurance that he wouldn't slip off.

An upper-story window of the house across the street was still lit. All the other residents of the elegant boulevard had gone to bed, but this one still lingered, unable or unwilling to sleep.

Occasionally, the man on the roof thought he could make out a silhouette moving about behind the curtain.

He pulled the slingshot in his hand. The Cours Mirabeau was famous for its proportions: The town houses that lined its sides were exactly as tall as the boulevard itself was wide. He had practiced the parabolic trajectory needed for a pinecone to cover the one hundred forty feet across and knock very gently into the lit window, so gently that the sound would not be heard in any other rooms.

His first shot went wide. He swore, loaded the slingshot with another pinecone, and forced himself to wait until his pulse and breaths both slowed.

He let go. The pinecone sailing toward the window. Thankfully, the light emanating from behind the curtain was enough to show the change in the pinecone's trajectory—it bounced off the window at an oblique angle.

His heart raced again, this time from relief.

In the end, it took ten attempts to hit the window seven times. At least he hoped it was seven times. The last one could have fallen a hairbreadth short or struck the pane just as its trajectory became spent.

He counted it as a success because his instincts deemed it so. In any case, in the morning there would be a small notice in the local paper—a paper known to be delivered to the house. And the notice would state, in code known only to a few, *Seven*.

The occupant of the room should understand. Or at least he would understand in a day or two, if he paid attention.

The light behind the window extinguished.

The man on the roof remained in place.

In a nearby street, a bakery was now lit, the *boulanger* busy at work. By the time the first loaves had been shaped and set to rise again, the man was long gone.

Ten

The house Mrs. Watson had hired in Paris was situated some seven or eight miles outside the center of the city, in a leafy little community on the Rive Droite of the Seine. A honey-colored villa with a large veranda, it perched right on the bank and enjoyed a wide, panoramic view.

In happier days, Penelope Redmayne had brought her friends and classmates to the house on many a Sunday afternoon to row on the river, stroll along the embankment, or picnic in an open field. A gaggle of young people frolicking around a picnic blanket very much resembled an Impressionist tableau, all blue sky, tall grass, and luminous faces.

Even now the area was lovely, full of the warmth and verdure of summer. Which made the ordeal feel even more like a nightmare, in which everything seemed normal except for a single horrifying change.

Penelope did her best to muster a smile for the hard-faced man who opened the door. *"Bonjour, monsieur. I've come with your provisions."*

The man squatted down to examine the shopping baskets on the portico. He tapped the baguettes and squeezed the vegetables, the leg of ham, and even the already scaled and gutted fish wrapped in paper. She could only be thankful he handled the eggs and the strawberry tarts with greater care.

"You have no cheese here," he said with something close to dismay as he straightened. "Bring a Camembert next time. And a good Gruyère, some chèvre, and as much Époisses as you can carry."

"I will deliver all that this afternoon." Penelope decided she might as well be shameless in currying favors. "Anything else you'd like, monsieur? Beefsteak, lobsters, ice cream? There's a good wine merchant who is—"

"We do not drink while working," said the man flatly.

"No, of course not." She smiled again. "May I go inside now?"

The man glanced behind him. He must have received permission, for he stepped back and let her pass. The woman mercenary patted her down, then escorted her deeper into the house.

She tried to tell herself that her errand was not terribly dangerous: She was not there to secretly reconnoiter or to mount a rescue. But she *was* dealing with armed individuals, and she did not possess great faith in the agreement Miss Charlotte had brokered with Lord Bancroft.

Before she entered Miss Bernadine's room, she took a moment to collect herself, so that she would not infect Miss Bernadine with her anxiety.

Inside the room, Miss Bernadine spun her rack of spools. In a peaceful mood, she set one or two spools in motion at a time and put her palm against the revolving spools to feel the friction on her skin. But now a dozen spools spun wildly. Miss Bernadine kept accelerating them, only to knock them against one another in a series of grating *clacks* to force them to stop.

Mademoiselle Robineau, a woman of fifty with fully grey hair and a kind face, shook her head. "Ah, *la pauvre*. She's been like this since she woke up. Last night, too. She misses her walk."

For most of her life, ever since her parents realized that she was not going to be a normal child, Miss Bernadine had been kept in her room. Her infrequent transits elsewhere had proved difficult, as she balked at stairs.

Miss Charlotte, always willing to try new things, asked Mrs. Watson to put Miss Bernadine in a ground-floor room when Mrs.

Watson moved her household to Paris this past February. Without the obstacle of the stairs, Miss Bernadine proved perfectly amenable to walking outside her room for some time every day. After they'd made a ramp with wooden planks, she even went into the garden, where she'd sit contentedly for a while, cranking a reel that had been detached from a fishing rod.

But now she was confined indefinitely to her room.

Miss Bernadine grunted a few times and once again set all the spools to spin, rows upon rows of agitation.

Her appetite, according to Mademoiselle Robineau, was still not good, but no worse than it had been since the mercenaries took over. This was the best news Penelope could report to London: that things hadn't taken a drastic turn for the worse.

She asked after Mademoiselle Robineau herself. The nurse waved off her concern. "Don't you worry about me, mademoiselle. I lived through the Siege of Paris. A few criminals don't scare me."

The other members of the staff, she said, were also carrying on as best as they could, including Mr. Mears, a captive in his own room.

A knock came. "That's long enough," said the woman mercenary.

Penelope glanced at the clock—exactly half an hour had passed. She'd been allowed the minimum stipulated in the agreement and not a minute more.

She stepped into the hall. A loud peal came from the front door. "Who's that?" the woman asked Penelope, suspicion in her voice.

"I haven't the slightest idea," answered Penelope in all honesty.

The bell clanged again, followed by a boisterous voice. "Anyone home? Open the door! Come quickly, Aunt Watson. Let's do a *bisou-bisou* and then I must be off to Paris. Paris proper, that is. You lied in your letter—this isn't Paris at all! There isn't a single café concert nearby!"

Who was the clown? Wait, *Aunt* Watson?

The man who had let Penelope in earlier appeared just as perplexed. He peered out of a narrow window. "Looks like an English toff."

The unannounced caller certainly sounded like an English toff.

A fist pounded upon the door—a big, meaty fist, by the solid *whomps* it produced. "Come, come, Aunt Watson. I won't be young forever, so I must make hay while my youth shines. You can come with, if you promise to behave. Not sure I trust your promise, though, you naughty old gal."

Penelope's eyes almost fell out of their sockets. Aunt Jo had not deliberately concealed her past from Penelope, so Penelope had always known about her days in the theater and her protectors. But she'd never heard anyone refer openly to the woman who raised her as "you naughty old gal," let alone someone who was obviously around Penelope's age.

The mercenary by the door yanked it open, but before he could ask questions, a big blond Adonis pushed past him and said, "Quick, my man, bring in my luggage. I'll just say hello to Aunt Watson and be gone."

The mercenary was not about to do his bidding until he saw the carriage full of young men on the circular drive outside, one of whom, a native speaker of French, demanded to know what was taking so long.

"*Une minute. Je reviens!*" called the man to his mates in an Englishman's standard public school French.

He turned around, his attention settling on Penelope. "Why, hello! You must be Miss Redmayne. You probably don't remember me, but I'm Bobby Fontainebleu, and my father courted Aunt Watson for a while about fifteen, sixteen years ago."

The surname rang a bell. Aunt Jo had indeed taken a lover at some point after the duke, her last protector, had passed away, but before she'd married Dr. Watson.

"I was all set to have her as my wonderful stepmamma, but she married someone else and broke my heart," continued young Fontainebleu, whipping off his hat and using it to fan himself. "All the same, we kept in touch. And when she said she was in Paris, I knew I must come and stay with her for a few days. Anyway, I sent a cable about a week ago. Did it go astray?"

Don't worry, Miss Charlotte had said to Penelope, just before she began her most recent return journey to England. *I'll think of something. I won't let you shoulder this problem alone.*

Had she sent young Fontainebleu?

Penelope glanced at the silver salver on the console table near the door, which usually held correspondence but was now completely empty. "I'm—I'm sure I don't know anything about your telegram, sir, but it's been a bit of a madhouse here. Aunt Jo had to go back to London all of a sudden and—"

"What? She's not here?"

"No—"

"Well, then, I'd better not let my friends wait. We've a whole day planned in Paris. Don't expect me back before three in the morning, and don't expect me sober. You and I will catch up when I wake up tomorrow. *À demain, ma cherie.*"

He turned to leave, only to turn around and kiss her on the cheeks, an astonishingly correct French *la bise* in a whiff of bay rum aftershave. And then he, a tall, broadly built man, somehow flounced out to the waiting vehicle, which then raced off toward the excitement of Paris proper.

Leaving Penelope—and the mercenaries, too—to gape at the disappearing carriage in slack-jawed amazement.

Mrs. Watson was ready for a stiff drink.

To be sure, since yesterday afternoon she had been inside more pubs than she cared to count. But she'd stuck to either soda water or ginger ale—and not too much of either to avoid visiting the water closet more frequently than necessary.

"Cheer up, this might be the one," said Lawson.

Her groom and coachman looked nothing like his usual self. Instead, he was now a man of humble birth who had become well-heeled late in life and didn't want to waste a single moment not being nouveau riche and self-indulgent.

His jacket had too many gold buttons. He wore not one but three watch fobs. And a golden serpent wrapped around his walking stick, its head curving to form the handle.

Mrs. Watson stared at the snake's green eyes and massaged her temple. "I hope you're right, old boy. I do hope so."

They'd ferreted out and visited just about every boxing gymnasium in and near New Cross, in southeast London. But they had to use an oblique approach—*Lord Bancroft thinks that a blatant search might set the crown on your trail*, Miss Charlotte had said. And Lawson's story of having heard about a trio of good boxers who had lost their sponsor hadn't yielded the results they sought.

At the last place they tried, however, the pub owner, his brow furrowed with effort, had said that he recalled being told something similar when he visited his brother in Smithfield.

Think we were at a place called—blast it, can't remember the name. But I remember the sign over the door. It's a whale with a great big pointy horn.

Don't know about that, but there's a whale that's got a long tusk, Lawson had answered cautiously. *A narwhal.*

Must be that then.

Smithfield, part of central London, was a good six miles northwest of New Cross. In this densely populated city, six miles might as well be six countries in terms of distance and character.

But in Smithfield their luck improved. A description of the unusual sign quickly produced directions to the Unicorn of the Sea, with the comment, *Always thought that was a fancy-looking sea lion. A tusked whale, eh? Blimey.*

And now they were standing outside the Unicorn of the Sea. The painter of the sign had clearly never seen a stuffed narwhal at the Museum of Natural History, let alone a real one. A fancy-looking sea lion—it was swaddled in a scarlet cape—was exactly how Mrs. Watson would have described the image. And the slender tusk wasn't even situated on the sea lion's head, but held in a flipper.

"Remember your promise to me, Harry," she said loudly as Lawson held open the pub's door for her, "no more than half an hour here. There's already been too many smelly old gymnasiums on this trip."

The early rush of workers from the nearby market had left, and the midday customers hadn't arrived yet. There weren't many patrons in the pub, and Mrs. Watson's arrival turned every head. She had on the same elaborate promenade dress she'd worn the summer before, on the day she first spoke to Miss Charlotte. The wide blue silk polonaise, worn over a tiered white underskirt, was perfect for a woman in the role of decorative appendage to a man generous with his money.

A sharp-eyed man of about forty stood behind the bar. They sat down directly in front of him.

He put aside the pint glass he was polishing. "Something to quench your thirst, sir, ma'am?"

"Too early in the day for pints, too late for coffee, and this one," Lawson pointed at Mrs. Watson, "drinks only the best claret."

Mrs. Watson traced the tips of her gloved fingers over the enormous white plume in her hat. "Why, thanks to you, darling."

"That's right." Lawson turned his attention to the man. "This your place then, lad? You ever been at sea?"

The nautical theme proliferated inside the pub, with fishing nets hanging from the rafters, rusty anchors in corners, and fishermen's lanterns on the walls.

"It's been my place these past five years," said the pub owner, "but I bought it from an old sailor."

"And did the old sailor also start a boxing gymnasium?"

The publican smiled slightly. "No, that was me. Got a bit of a bum leg and was never able to box myself, but I've always wanted to be part of it."

Lawson nodded. "I'm luckier than you. I did get to box when I was a lad."

He slapped himself lightly across the chest. "Too bad you never saw me in the ring, Suzie. Deadly I was, I tell you. Deadly."

Mrs. Watson cooed accordingly as the publican looked on in amusement.

"And now that I've made good in my old age," said Lawson, once again addressing the publican, "I'm looking for a few boxers. Saw two I liked in Manchester, but turned out they were sponsored by a friend. And they were the only good ones—the rest were useless.

"So I thought I'd try my luck in London. Look in on a few places with good reputation and see if I see anyone promising. And of course"—he set a sovereign on the bar—"if I get the talent I want, I won't forget the one who made the introduction, Mr. uh—"

"Mowlem is the name, sir." The pub owner took out two glasses, poured a golden liquid inside, and passed one each to Mrs. Watson and Lawson. "And you are—"

"Harold Nelson, lately of Manchester. And this is the missus, of course."

"Of course," said Mowlem, bowing slightly to Mrs. Watson, a respect accorded not to her, per se, but to the shining coin on the bar. "Now, Mr. Nelson, I'm sure you know that sponsors can be a feisty bunch. If I made introductions willy-nilly, I might find myself cornered in my own pub by angry men demanding to know why I helped to poach their boxers.

"However . . ." He drew out the word.

Mrs. Watson tensed but pretended to study her bracelet.

"At the moment," continued the publican, "there are three hardworking young people who have recently lost their sponsor. He hasn't been seen in these parts since October of last year, and their stipends ran out in April."

Mrs. Watson's heart leaped. Could it be—

"If I stopped paying someone four months ago, I wouldn't consider them remotely obliged to me today. And indeed one of the boxers has found a new sponsor. But last I heard, the other two still held out hope that their Mr. Underwood might return."

The sound of that name pulsed in Mrs. Watson's veins, a wild relief. She took a healthy gulp from her glass. West Country scrumpy, going down surprisingly easy.

"That's good intelligence, that," Lawson said heartily. He turned to Mrs. Watson. "See, I told you I had a good feeling about this place."

Mrs. Watson clapped her hands. "I guess now it's just a matter of meeting these young boxers. Is it not, Mr. Mowlem?"

"I haven't seen those two lately," said the publican. "But their friend, the one who already has a new sponsor, will be here tonight for a fight. I believe he wants them to follow his example and jump ship."

"Oh?" said Mrs. Watson. She set an exaggeratedly quizzical fingertip on her chin. "Is he helping his friends out of affection, or is he afraid that this Mr. Underwood might return, and therefore doesn't want to be alone in abandoning him?"

"Could be both."

Lawson narrowed his eyes. "Do *you* expect this Mr. Underwood to come back, Mr. Mowlem?"

The publican picked up another pint glass to polish. "Hard to say. Until the kids' stipends stopped coming, I expected him to turn up any day. But after that, let's just say, now I'd be surprised if he *did* turn up."

"But there's still a chance that he would?"

"Sure." The publican shrugged. "But by this point, if he's a man with any sense of decency, he wouldn't make a fuss. After all, he'd stopped being those kids' sponsor."

Lawson turned to Mrs. Watson again. "Well, what do you say, Suzie dear?"

"I guess you'll need to ask around a bit, won't you, Harry? But I don't mind." Mrs. Watson caressed the plume on her hat again. "It'll give me time to order new hats and shoes to go with my new frocks."

"Ah, I knew you'd never object to a longer stay in London." Lawson downed a finger of scrumpy and asked the publican, "You wouldn't be able to tell us anything about this Mr. Underwood, would you? It sounds as if he must have had a moneyman handling payments to his boxers."

"I believe he did, but that's all I know about that. The kids themselves would know more."

Mrs. Watson slapped her palm down on the bar. "You don't suppose, Mr. Mowlem, that some other boxer or sponsor did Mr. Underwood in, do you? In that case, it might not be wise for us to inquire too closely."

Lawson tapped his fingernails against the side of his glass, making little pings. "You have a point, good woman. But then again, we haven't even met the kids yet. If we don't like the kids, then we're certainly not going to ask more questions about this missing Mr. Underwood."

Mowlem glanced toward the sovereign that still lay on the bar, quietly glistening. "It's odd, Mr. Underwood's disappearance—no doubt about it. But if you'll indulge me for a moment here, Mr. Nelson, I don't think it was connected to boxing. Mr. Underwood wasn't exactly one of us, if you know what I mean. I'm not sure where he hailed from. And while he was most certainly a man you wouldn't want to cross, he didn't grow up in these streets—and maybe not in any kind of streets.

"He liked boxing, but he didn't exactly *associate* with boxing folks— even his kids held themselves a bit apart from the rest of us. He came to fights, but he didn't become friends or enemies with anyone. And if his methods were dirtier than anyone else's—" Here the publican hesitated. "Well, let's just say that when all was well, I didn't hear much about Mr. Underwood, except speculation on where he came from and what he did besides sponsoring boxers."

Mrs. Watson set an elbow on the bar and dropped her chin into her palm. "You've made me curious, Mr. Mowlem. What *did* folks think about where he came from?"

"They thought that maybe he himself wasn't a gentleman but his father was."

"Ah," said Mrs. Watson, elongating the syllable to signal her understanding.

Goodness, they thought him a by-blow.

"He didn't drink, didn't carouse, didn't get into fistfights, didn't look at anyone's lady the wrong way," said Mowlem, a note of genuine wonder in his voice. "I see no reason anyone from hereabouts would want to 'disappear' him."

Mrs. Watson perked up, an affectionately indulged woman who caught something in the conversation and wished to receive a bit of praise for her cleverness. "But you said, Mr. Mowlem, that before this Mr. Underwood vanished, no one had anything particularly evil to say about him. What about afterwards?"

"I hate to say it," said Mowlem, shaking his head, "but lately there have been all kinds of rumors accusing him of cheating and knavery."

Lawson, who had just taken another sip of his scrumpy, set his glass down with a thud. "And you want *us* to step into all that muddy water?"

Mowlem rubbed hard at a spot on the pint glass in his hand before he looked up and met Lawson's eyes. "If you were from London, Mr. Nelson, maybe I'd have second thoughts. But since you're taking the kids to Manchester, you won't have trouble from anyone."

Eleven

When Inspector Treadles handed the Christmas Eve Murder to Charlotte, he had already uncovered some useful information. That Garwood Hall was empty and up for let, for one thing. And, for another, Miss Harcourt's address.

Victor Meadows's sister, Mrs. Harcourt, had passed away. Charlotte wrote her daughter, claimed to be an old acquaintance of Mrs. Meadows's, and requested an audience. That was immediately following her meeting with Inspector Treadles. But even after her return from Paris, having reassured herself that Bernadine and everyone else in Mrs. Watson's household were all right, there was no response from Miss Harcourt.

Last night, however, as soon as Charlotte had said good-bye to Lord Ingram, a telegram from Miss Harcourt landed on her doorstep.

Apologies. Was away and read your note only now. Do not know anyone's current whereabouts but am keen to speak together. Will postpone all other engagements to await your call.

Charlotte would have happily set aside the Christmas Eve Murder for the time being. But in pretending to be Mrs. Meadows's old friend, trying to find her again after many years, she *had* made herself sound most eager. The fictional Mrs. Beaumont would not have turned down Miss Harcourt's invitation, especially now that Miss Harcourt was rearranging her own schedule.

Her reaction surprised Charlotte—she had expected at best a polite tolerance, not this avid interest to meet a murdered uncle's wife's forgotten friend.

She weighed the matter, entrusted the ongoing search for Mr. Underwood's boxing connections entirely to Mrs. Watson and Lawson, and set out by rail early in the morning.

Miss Harcourt lived in Oxfordshire, at the edge of the Cotswolds. Unlike the modern mishmash that was Garwood Hall, Trilby Park had been built in the heyday of neoclassicism, with an exterior that was severely symmetrical, almost humorless.

Miss Harcourt's carriage had picked up Charlotte from the railway station. Miss Harcourt herself was waiting by the wide granite steps at the front of the manor as the vehicle rolled to a stop.

She pumped Charlotte's hand with both of her own. "Oh, Mrs. Beaumont, I'm so glad you're here. Do please come in!"

Her Wedgwood blue drawing room felt comfortably worn. Not threadbare or ill maintained, simply a little faded with the passage of time.

Miss Harcourt, if one judged her by appearance alone, was also slightly faded. At thirty years of age, she had faint lines on her forehead and at the corners of her eyes, and a few grey strands in her light brown hair. But she walked fast—she'd bounced up the steps—gesticulated expansively, and peppered Charlotte with questions about Mrs. Beaumont's life, her curiosity benign and lively.

If anything, Miss Harcourt had understated her keenness to speak to Mrs. Meadows's long-lost friend.

After a cup of tea, Charlotte ventured to ask, pointing at the garden outside the windows, whether they could chat while taking a stroll outside. "I've been on a great many railway journeys of late and am growing terribly stiff. Given that I must still return to London by rail today . . ."

When she was younger, whole days on end of sitting—or lying on a chaise—exacted no toll at all. Now if her bottom remained glued to chairs for such Homeric durations her back protested. And Mrs. Watson, always one to encourage movement, had warned her that the stiffness would only worsen with age.

"Oh, absolutely." Miss Harcourt immediately led the way. "I prefer the outdoors. In fact, as a part of my grand tour, I plan to stay awhile in Southern California. I've heard that it has marvelously agreeable weather and one can be outside most of the year without being too cold, too hot, or too drenched."

As it turned out, Miss Harcourt was days away from beginning that globe-spanning voyage, the first leg of which would see her visit Madeira, the Canary Islands, and the Azores.

Charlotte had met her share of heiresses. Often they carried an unhappy tension within: They were raised to believe in the superiority of their bloodlines—a massive fortune must be a sign of God's favor—only to be regarded as lowly upstarts when they were thrust into the thick of Society. And for all the wealth they would inherit, they often had little say in the most pivotal decisions of their young lives.

But Miss Harcourt had endured no ambitious parents forcing her to marry a resentful peer. She'd never even partaken in a London Season. Instead, she'd invested in an education for herself and then cared for her mother.

"In the final months of my mother's life, we spoke quite a bit of my aunt Meadows," she said. "In fact, that's part of the reason I'm going on this rather intimidating voyage. Cousin Miriam—that's what I called Aunt Meadows's sister—she once said that someday they were going to see the whole world. I would dearly love for them to be doing just that right now—and for me to run into them along the way."

They were walking between two tall hedges—the garden boasted a hedge maze. And the wistfulness in Miss Harcourt's voice made Charlotte wonder whether her dealings with Mrs. Meadows hadn't been somewhat one-sided.

"All I know is that Mrs. Meadows stayed in Manchester for a year or two after she was widowed. She left no forwarding address?"

"No." Instead of tassels, the edge of Miss Harcourt's parasol had been trimmed with strings of clear glass beads. She raised a hand and filliped one such string. "Nor had she breathed a word to us beforehand."

Aha, so the Harcourt ladies had indeed been the more fervent ones in their friendship with Mrs. Meadows.

Charlotte told Miss Harcourt the story of how her younger self, lonely and homesick in Australia, had exchanged letters with a young Angelica Tipton for two years. "My letters spilled on for pages and pages, but hers were always short and to the point."

That regular correspondence ended abruptly.

"I found out later it was around the time of her wedding that Angelica stopped writing. My mother cautioned me against reading anything sinister into it, but I was never able to feel completely at ease about her marriage. She was only sixteen, and it followed so closely on the heel of her parents' bankruptcy and deaths."

The path turned. They had reached the center of the maze. In the small clearing, a stone nymph danced in a fountain, water pouring from the vase she held aloft.

"Even my mother didn't know much about the state of her marriage—she wasn't close to her brothers," said Miss Harcourt. "But my aunt Meadows was thought of as a dutiful wife who managed her household well and rendered onto her husband all due deference. And we never heard about my uncle Victor not treating her well or anything of the sort."

She looked contemplative. "He was eighteen years her senior. But age difference aside, theirs was a domestic arrangement that attracted little attention. And knowing Aunt Meadows, it feels . . . deliberate. There was always something unknowable about her, do you not think, Mrs. Beaumont?"

Miss Harcourt would have been all of seven when Victor Meadows had married his young wife, and fifteen at the time of his murder. If even her mother hadn't known much about the state of the Meadowses' marriage, then there was no point for Charlotte to press further on the topic.

Charlotte made a show of twirling her parasol and thinking. "Yes, I do believe you're right, Miss Harcourt. She listened far more than she spoke, and even when she spoke, it was rarely of herself."

"Yes, that was exactly how I remembered her," concurred Miss Harcourt.

The maze path turned again. Now their shadows were in front of them, small, stubby shapes surrounded by more nimbus-like shadows cast by the lace parasols.

"My mother always felt curious about her," continued Miss Harcourt. "After Uncle Victor died, Aunt Meadows lived in Manchester for a while and our family, too, because Mother had to look after the factories. During that time, Mother called on her regularly, often with me tagging along. And most of our visits consisted of Mother and me blathering on and on about this and that, and my aunt Meadows listening with a nunlike concentration."

"Did she never say *anything* about herself then?"

"She was more likely to say something about Cousin Miriam. Cousin Miriam was very active and curious, so we heard tales about her spraining her foot trying to teach herself ballet and such.

"But even though Aunt Meadows didn't like to talk about herself, I never received the impression that she found us trying," Miss Harcourt went on. "She was curious about Mother's work running the factories. And she always made sure to tell us how much Cousin Miriam enjoyed our visits. Which was why her disappearance dumbfounded us so—and baffles me to this day."

Their shadows disappeared—a tall plume of a cumulus had eclipsed the sun. Charlotte turned to Miss Harcourt. "Can you tell me exactly what happened?"

Miss Harcourt looked at the darkening sky and collapsed her parasol, its trimming beads clinking pleasantly. "For Cousin Miriam's twelfth birthday, we called on them with presents. As Mother had just then learned how to use a camera, she also photographed the two sisters together.

"When the photograph was developed, we used the opportunity for another visit. But when we reached their hired house, Aunt Meadows and Cousin Miriam were gone, and a for-let sign had been put up. When we found the estate agent, he said the house was vacated a fortnight earlier—mere days after the birthday visit—and the departing tenants had left no forwarding addresses.

"Mother spoke to two women who had been Aunt Meadows's neighbors when Uncle Victor had been alive. They called on her occasionally, but it was from Mother that they first learned Aunt Meadows had moved away. She then managed to track down a few distant cousins of Aunt Meadows's, but they hadn't heard from her since before her marriage.

"The photograph of the two sisters together, which we weren't able to give to them, found a place on our mantelpiece for a time— for as long as Mother's search continued. We used to stand together and look at it. And then one day the photograph disappeared. Mother said that it felt wrong to keep staring at Aunt Meadows, when it was obvious she didn't want to see us again."

A stiff breeze blew. The fringes on Charlotte's parasol streamed horizontally. "I was seventeen then, and took the snubbing personally. Aunt Meadows was like the *Mona Lisa*, smiling yet inscrutable. We crowded near her not because we wished to be kind to someone less fortunate but because she was this beautiful mystery and we, her gauche admirers, longed to bask in her enigmatic allure.

"I'd been angry, but when the photograph disappeared and Mother said aloud what we'd both been thinking, I was crushed. Perhaps that's how a rejected suitor feels—all that fervor and adoration marked undeliverable and returned to sender."

This disclosure was not meant for Charlotte Holmes. Even Mrs. Watson, before whom everyone opened up like steamed clams, might not have elicited as deep a confession. These words were meant only for Mrs. Beaumont, a fellow devotee who had been ejected from Mrs.

Meadows's orbit just as unceremoniously—and who understood Miss Harcourt's distress and bewilderment.

They walked silently for some time before Charlotte asked, "Would it be possible for me to see this photograph? I should dearly love to see her all grown up."

"I would love to show it to you. In fact, I long to see it myself and started looking for it as soon as I received your note. But it was put away so many years ago and—"

Another gust of wind blew, and with it came large raindrops. Charlotte swung aside her parasol and looked up just as a small deluge came down, heavy and cool on her face, while the sun emerged at the same time.

She and Miss Harcourt stared at each other for a moment.

"This way!" cried Miss Harcourt. "There's a covered swing!"

They were shaking out their drenched parasols—at least parasols could not develop pneumonia—when Miss Harcourt's servants sprinted over with raincoats, umbrellas, and towels.

After inquiring into Charlotte's preference, Miss Harcourt asked the staff to return to the house with the soaked parasols but leave behind the extra umbrellas that they had brought, along with the flask of whisky that the housekeeper had thrust into one footman's hand.

The sun shone fiercely. The rain came down just as fiercely. Charlotte drank a small draught from the flask and offered in return a ginger-studded biscuit from her reticule—after having known real hunger the summer before, she never went anywhere these days without a supply of foodstuff.

The biscuits were the last of what remained of Lord Ingram's hamper, now that most of its vast contents had been donated to Mrs. Watson's staff in Paris. Miss Harcourt was eating solemnly when she broke out laughing. "My goodness, I don't remember the last time I was caught in the rain."

"I don't mind this sort of being caught in the rain," murmured Charlotte, "with shelter almost immediately at hand, and people to see to our comfort within seconds."

Miss Harcourt laughed again. "True, this is a very pleasant way to be caught in the rain."

Threads of rain shone white and silver in the brilliant sunlight—and then in the next minute dwindled to almost nothing, except for a steady *drip-drip* from some nearby trees.

In the new silence, Charlotte gauged that the time had come. "Miss Harcourt, do you think my Angelica had anything to do with her husband's murder?"

Miss Harcourt, who had been brushing crumbs from her fingertips, stilled.

"Over the years, I've always worried about her, especially after I learned about her parents' bankruptcy," said Charlotte, her tone urgent. "She was a young girl left alone and destitute, with the care of a sister barely out of infancy. Maybe she married a man more than twice her age out of something other than desperation, but I'm no longer an adolescent romantic who can convince myself of that.

"And his death was so gruesome. If someone had shot him, perhaps I wouldn't have been so perturbed, but I went to Manchester and found articles in the newspaper archives and—" She took a deep, audible breath. "I hope I don't sound a complete ghoul, but I've been terrified ever since that Angelica—Mrs. Meadows—that—"

Miss Harcourt placed a finger before her own lips.

Charlotte hushed accordingly.

"If she did it, then it must have been for a good reason." Miss Harcourt's voice was low and equally urgent. "And if she did it, she's been able to keep herself free all these years. Let's not accidentally shatter the safeguards she may have put into place for her well-being."

So Miss Harcourt *had* given the matter plenty of thought. Charlotte dropped her voice, too. "No, never."

The errant rain cloud had moved on; the entire garden glistened under the midday sun. Miss Harcourt looked all around them before she spoke again. "The good news is that my mother didn't think Aunt Meadows did it. The bad news is my uncle Ephraim also disappeared, sometime after my aunt Meadows. Taken together, that wouldn't look good—if anyone were still looking into the murder, that is."

Inspector Brighton had looked into the case. Charlotte was looking into the case. And an ambitious young detective sergeant might receive the full dossier from Scotland Yard in the near future.

Charlotte gripped the handkerchief that she had been using as a napkin. "Surely you aren't implying that . . ."

That Mrs. Meadows and Ephraim Meadows, her brother-in-law, had been in collusion?

"Not only do I not want to imply it, I do not even wish to think about it." Miss Harcourt downed another draught of whisky and scooted a few inches closer to Charlotte on the covered swing. "But Mrs. Beaumont, do you remember what I said about my mother taking away the photograph from our mantelpiece?"

"Yes?"

"We didn't talk about my aunt Meadows for years upon years. It was only in the final months of my mother's life that Aunt Meadows came up again as a topic of conversation. That was the first time Mother told me the reason she removed the picture: She found out from my uncle Victor's solicitors that before my aunt Meadows left for parts unknown, she'd informed them that she had remarried and would no longer be collecting the annualized dower that had been set out in my uncle Victor's will."

Charlotte sucked in a loud breath.

"That was when Mother became convinced that Aunt Meadows really wanted absolutely nothing to do with us. Why else would she have not breathed a word of something as significant as her remarriage? At the time, Mother happened to be extremely busy with the factories—and with me about to leave for Girton College—so it was some time before she realized that my uncle Ephraim hadn't either called or written for a while.

"As he usually called or wrote to ask for money, at first she was simply glad not to have his news. But when more time passed and she still received no new entreaties, she began to find it incomprehensible."

"No!" Charlotte leaped up from the swing. Her abrupt motion caused a metallic squeak. "My friend would never have married such a leech."

Miss Harcourt rose, too. She had in hand an umbrella that the servants had brought and tapped its tip against the flagstone clearing on which the covered swing sat. "I don't believe so either, and neither did Mother—her dower would have been too moderate for him, and his character too deficient for her. And that she refused further dower? Without a doubt, her bridegroom could not have been a man who had never seen a farthing he didn't try to put into his own pocket."

Miss Harcourt exhaled. "What worried Mother more was that they might have committed the crime together."

"I'd rather that she did the killing herself, if it had to be her!" Charlotte cried softly.

At her minor outburst, Miss Harcourt, who had been frowning and tight-jawed, blinked—and burst out laughing, "I'm sorry." She quickly gathered herself and apologized. "I'm not sure what made me laugh—I just did."

"It's this ridiculous murder," said Charlotte. "It makes one conjure up too many awful theories. If we can't find something to laugh at once in a while, we'd all be like a cat on a hot bakestone."

"True. And anyway, I was trying to reassure you that neither my uncle Ephraim nor my aunt Meadows had the least reason to kill my uncle Victor—they both became worse off as a result of his death, and they both knew ahead of time that, for them, his will would not prove a lucrative document."

"But still it begs the question." Miss Harcourt looked up, but there was no rainbow in the sky. "Why did they both drop off the face of the earth?"

Charlotte sighed. "And in the end, whom did she marry?"

Twelve

$\diamond$

Miss Charlotte returned to London in time to join Mrs. Watson and Lawson at the Unicorn of the Sea for the evening's pugilistic matches.

Mowlem, the publican, introduced them to Johnny E., the boxer who had left Mr. Underwood for greener pastures—and the greener pastures himself, a nervous-looking grocer named Gore.

It took little time to learn that Gore was a novice sponsor, Johnny E. being his very first boxer. And while Mowlem had reassured him that the rich Mr. Nelson from Manchester was interested only in Johnny E.'s friends, not Johnny E. himself, he still fretted about his new investment.

Lawson promptly took Gore aside for a chat. Johnny E., small, whipcord lean, his wary eyes set in an incongruously boyish face, darted a quick glance to where his new sponsor had been cordially abducted, then across the table at Mrs. Watson, attired as if she were on her way to the opera: glittering opera hood, satin opera cloak, sixteen-button kidskin opera gloves, all in a luxurious midnight blue and as thoroughly out of place in the tavern as a ballerina would have been at a Maypole dance.

If it weren't for her, Miss Charlotte—in masculine disguise as Herrinmore, the parvenu Mr. Nelson's bookish-looking general dogsbody—would have been the one standing out like a sore thumb in a crowd of working-class men drinking ale, eating whelks, and happily anticipating bouts of violence to come—no one present, however, matched the description Mrs. Claiborne had given of the scarred man who had quarreled with Mr. Underwood at her villa.

The boxer studied Miss Charlotte more closely, even though Mrs. Watson was confident that she herself was at once the most outlandish and most beautiful person inside these walls. Was it a survivor's instinct that had him focus greater attention on the more dangerous individual, even if she presented herself as a harmless minion?

He returned his gaze to the bowl of peanuts on the table that he had been shelling since he sat down.

"Shall we order something to eat?" asked Mrs. Watson.

Johnny E. looked up. "Yes, for after the match, please."

His voice, so young. Mrs. Watson realized that she wasn't looking at a man with a boyish face but a boy with eyes too old for his no-more-than-nineteen summers.

The slightly singsongy quality of his speech, his blue-black hair, dark lugubrious eyes, and bronze complexion that she had assumed to have been tanned due to outdoor work—had the boy, in fact, been baptized as Giovanni?

Miss Charlotte, upon hearing Johnny E.'s affirmative answer to Mrs. Watson's question about food, had leaped up to order at the bar. Now she returned and sat down heavily. "The kitchen will have two rump steak pies packed up for you. Chips, too. And a boiled pudding."

Johnny E. nodded. And then, perhaps coming to the conclusion that by accepting the bribe, he must now give something in return, he said, "You want me to tell you about Mumble and Jessie?"

"We can judge them for ourselves. It's your Mr. Underwood that we need to know about," said Mrs. Watson. "I understand you were the first boxer he took on?"

Johnny E. nodded again, somewhat unwillingly.

"But you were also the first to leave him?"

The boy shifted but answered flatly, "I've a sick mother and three younger siblings. They need to eat."

Poverty was written all over him, from his too-slight frame to the atlas of patches on his jacket, little fiefdoms of careful fabric matching and even more meticulous needlework on a garment that could very well predate his birth.

"Do you believe that he's dead?"

"Don't know." As if sensing that it might be an insufficient answer, he shelled another peanut and added, "Sometimes people get in trouble and have to go where nobody can find them."

"Do you know where he might have gone?"

"No. He never told us anything about himself."

His reticence was not something Mrs. Watson had encountered a great deal in her life. In fact, her usual problem was how to extricate herself from those who couldn't stop unburdening themselves on her, pouring out torrents of headaches and heartaches.

"Did you try to search for him?" she tried again.

He shook his head, an outright no.

"Why not? Was he not good to you?"

A burst of laughter came from near the door of the pub. They all glanced in that direction. It was a table full of burly men; an especially large specimen with a tattoo on his neck pointed at them.

At Johnny E.

Johnny E. only shelled another peanut. He collected a handful of shelled peanuts and ate one. "Mr. Underwood was good to me—he bought me my first pair of decent shoes. But I don't have time to wait for him or look for him. I'm lucky if I have two more years in the ring before nobody wants to see me fight anymore."

How well Mrs. Watson understood that feeling of pressure, of valuable time leaking away unstoppably. A man's athletic career might be as brief as a pretty girl's stint on the stage, and his future almost as uncertain. "You aren't worried about Mr. Underwood coming back and being displeased with you?"

Johnny E. began peeling peanuts again, the already shelled and uneaten peanuts in his palm having disappeared. Into a pocket? "What was I supposed to do, let my sister go hungry or stop buying medicine for my mother?"

"What about your two mates? You said you can't afford to wait for Mr. Underwood. What about them?"

"Mumble and Jessie? They *are* looking for him."

"Have they found out anything?"

"Nothing much. They spoke to his accountant and said the accountant didn't know anything either."

Someone brayed with laughter again, the shrillness of the sound overriding the general din of the pub. It was Mr. Gore the grocer, and he stopped as abruptly as if someone had stuffed a sock in his mouth, to stare in amazed dismay at the man with the neck tattoo.

"Do you know where this accountant is?"

"Somewhere in the City of London. Mumble and Jessie know the exact address. Do you need to talk to the accountant?"

"You never know. Sometimes an accountant knows more about a man than his wife does."

"Well," said Johnny E., his expression almost as blank as Miss Charlotte's usual countenance, "I wouldn't know about that."

Oh, this child.

Mrs. Watson girded herself for more teeth-pulling. "So Mumble and Jessie, even though they haven't found out much, are still carrying on with their search?"

"That's right."

"What propels that search? Affection or some other reason?"

"They don't need money as much as I do. And—" He glanced at his new sponsor, who now looked as if he needed Lawson's support to stay upright. "I'm not sure someone like Mr. Gore would have taken them on, even if they were willing to go with him—not that he was enthusiastic about me either."

He meant that his new sponsor, the grocer, hadn't been too happy about associating with an Italian.

"What makes Mumble and Jessie more difficult to place?"

Johnny E. looked toward the door, as if he hoped someone might show up. "Well, Jessie is a girl—some sponsors don't want girls, and Jessie doesn't want anything to do with most of the rest. And Mumble, you might as well know this now, Mumble is Gypsy. Or maybe half-Gypsy, but he looks all of it."

—⚹—

Lawson brought Mr. Gore the grocer back just then and told Johnny it was time to prepare for his fight.

The boxer and his sponsor departed, but a good quarter hour passed before Lawson escorted the women down to a surprisingly large basement. The place must have been where a former publican had once made his own ale. But more and more pubs these days were supplied by large breweries, which negated the need for brewing equipment on-site.

Close to a hundred spectators crowded around the ringed platform, and more were coming in—still no badly scarred man. The place began to smell of too many bodies crammed too close. Mrs. Watson's heart jammed her airways once she saw that Johnny would be fighting the man with the neck tattoo, who had five inches and ten times that many pounds on him.

The boxers entered the ring. A shirtless Johnny looked even scrawnier—hardly any muscles separated his skin from his skeleton—while his opponent was a fortress of brawn.

A bell rang, and the bare-knuckle match began.

The big man grinned, launched himself at Johnny, and knocked him to the ropes with a single blow. Mrs. Watson flinched.

Cheers erupted. Boos, too.

Were the spectators booing because they might lose their wagers or because they'd heard rumors about Mr. Underwood having used unscrupulous means to secure victories for his boxers?

The big man pursued Johnny to the ropes and punched at his face. Johnny sidestepped the attack, pivoted with remarkable speed, and while the man was still turning around, landed an uppercut to his jaw.

Lawson bellowed in approval. Mrs. Watson did not cheer; she only dreaded the next blow that would land on Johnny.

Vaguely she remembered that in her salad days she'd attended boxing matches on the arm of a protector and relished the bouts with a gleeful bloodlust. Now every time the big man's fists connected with Johnny, even if Johnny successfully parried the blow, she felt her skin abrade, her skeleton rattle apart. Every time Johnny managed to punch his opponent, however, she was sure that it could do no more harm than a baby waving its tiny hands in the air.

"He's no natural pugilist," said Miss Charlotte in Herrinmore's voice and accent.

"But what a fighter," answered Lawson.

There was no beauty to his style, only a spectacular endurance for pain, a willpower that Mrs. Watson would have termed desperation if it didn't also have a certain inexorability to it.

It was as if Johnny decided that he was going to outlast his opponent, and that was that.

By the end of the fight, both of his nostrils had to be plugged with cotton to stop his nosebleed, he had a nasty cut to his right cheek, and his lips, too, were swollen and bleeding, but he was still standing whereas his much more formidable-looking adversary was on the floor.

Even those who had booed him in the beginning clapped, almost as overwhelmed as the defeated man, still wheezing and gasping inside the ring.

Minutes after his victory, with the next match beginning, Johnny was already dressed and walking out, stopping only to collect the supper that Miss Charlotte had ordered, in the now largely empty taproom.

"Not staying to watch the other fights?" Lawson caught up with him, Mrs. Watson and Miss Charlotte trailing a few steps behind.

"My shift in the morning starts at six." He no longer had cotton in his nose but still sounded heavily congested.

"Let me send you home in my carriage then."

Johnny gave them a suspicious look, but the lure of an earlier bedtime overrode his reservations. "All right."

He gave an address near Saffron Hill, less than half a mile north of where they were.

"You fought well," said Lawson once the carriage was on its way. "If your friends are as good, I'll be impressed."

Johnny, who had been studying the slender, bracketed vase that held a stem of pink hydrangea, glanced at him and said, "They're better."

"Even the girl?" Mrs. Watson exclaimed.

"Jessie is fierce—I wouldn't want to go up against her. And Mumble, he can tell what a man is going to do in the ring before the man has worked it out for himself."

Lawson nodded with a credible look of satisfaction. Johnny's face, which had remained wooden even when battered by large fists, crumpled for a moment.

Mrs. Watson's heart clenched. This child, who was responsible for a family of five and probably had no time between work and training for his boxing matches—was it possible that Mumble and Jessie were his only friends?

"If they come to Manchester," she said impulsively, "they'll like it. I'll look after them, I promise. And you can write to one another and stay in touch. It costs only a penny to send a letter."

"People like me don't write—and we don't have friends in faraway places. When they leave, they might as well be dead to me." Johnny turned his battered face back to the vase. "But I'll take you to see them tomorrow."

The next evening, the two women picked up Johnny, who worked as a bricklayer by day, from a surprisingly fashionable address not far from their hotel, where a row of shops had been torn down to make room for a new department store that was just beginning to take shape.

Before the boy emerged, ready to leave, Mrs. Watson and Miss Charlotte, who was once again disguised as Herrinmore, the nonexistent Mr. Nelson's lackey, managed to speak to the foreman for a good quarter hour, largely due to the strength of Mrs. Watson's smiles and the splendor of her lilac promenade gown.

Sherlock Holmes and company said nothing about boxing but

passed themselves off as representatives of a certain ladies' charity, making sure that the recipients of their largesse were working hard and looking after their families instead of squandering donated funds on drinking and gambling.

The foreman was obliging. "Ah, Johnny Esposito, good boy, that one, doesn't say much, works fast, and builds walls better than bricklayers twice his age. You almost can't tell he's an Italian."

Or rather, he used a casual pejorative for an Italian. Mrs. Watson was fiercely glad that Johnny wasn't within earshot, even if he must have already heard too many such insults in his young life.

She had braced herself for the olfactory assault of sharing close quarters with a man who had been working outside all day, but Johnny had scrubbed himself and changed into patched but clean clothes. A trace of perspiration still clung to him, mixed with the scent of soap powder—the smell of honest labor.

"The foreman doesn't mind your face like this, Mr. Esposito?" asked Miss Charlotte once they were in the carriage, sounding like a clergyman's son who had gone to a second-tier boarding school.

There hadn't been enough time for the cuts and bruises from the night before to fade.

Johnny shrugged. "I told him my old man gave me a belting, and he thought it was funny."

Mrs. Watson didn't think it was funny at all. Had his late father beaten him? Had he protected his mother and his younger siblings from the man's wrath? Was that how he had acquired his remarkable capacity for pain?

"Long day for you?" she asked. The mother hen in her wished she could fold him under her wing and keep him warm and safe.

Johnny shrugged. "Same as every other day."

Twelve long hours per shift.

He seemed to approach life as he approached boxing in the ring, with a numb endurance. Did he not want anything besides keeping his family alive?

Their destination wasn't another gymnasium but a small meeting hall that had been hired for the evening. Chairs had been pushed to the walls, and two pairs of boxers were in the middle of sparring. Mrs. Watson's gaze was immediately drawn to two young women, one in a tennis costume, the other in a blouse and a billowy pair of bloomers.

Both were tall, both had wide eyes and high cheekbones, both wore boxing gloves and moved fast on their feet, but it was immediately clear that one was largely defending and the other hard on the offensive.

"Come on, don't just block. Land a blow for once!" cried the young woman in bloomers.

"Is that Jessie?" Mrs. Watson murmured.

"That's Jessie," replied Johnny.

"I'll try that as soon as your fists stop flying thick as a blizzard!" retorted the other young woman, whom Johnny identified as a Miss Greengard.

Miss Greengard, despite not being anywhere as good as Jessie, was athletic and spirited. And when Jessie slowed down for a moment, her gloved fist jabbed at Jessie's jaw. Jessie blocked it easily, but the attack earned Miss Greengard an earnest "good try."

Her brother Mr. Greengard, on the other hand, seemed fundamentally ill at ease in a face-to-face conflict. Nevertheless he fought on, his teeth gritted, his features scrunched together in a perpetual grimace.

"Remember your feet," said Mumble, a slender, dark-haired young man whose complexion and features reminded Mrs. Watson of the handsome population of Punjab and Rajasthan. "Relax your shoulders. Good, just like that."

He did not mumble at all but spoke with a case of near overenunciation, his voice surprisingly deep for one so young.

"Who are the Greengards?" asked Miss Charlotte.

"Rich people," said Johnny simply.

He was studying the two young men. Mumble did seem to know

exactly what his opponent meant to do next. And there was not only intelligence to his boxing but elegance, too: He moved with the deadly agility of a shark.

Miss Charlotte's gaze flickered between Johnny and Mumble. Mrs. Watson noticed that Johnny wasn't studying both the male boxers but only his friend Mumble.

"And how did the rich Greengards come to Mumble and Jessie for tutoring?" she asked.

"They came to a fight night—Miss Greengard was having trouble finding a female instructor. At the time, Mr. Underwood had only me. But after he took on Jessie and Mumble, he tracked down Miss Greengard and asked if she still needed a woman for sparring. She said yes and Mr. Underwood put her together with Jessie. And then her brother decided that he liked Mumble better than his own instructor."

Miss Charlotte hooked a thumb on the fob chain of her watch. "Is this why Mumble and Jessie aren't as desperate to find another sponsor? Because they still have the Greengards as a source of income?"

"The Greengards don't live in London year-round. But then again, Mumble and Jessie don't need money the way I do."

Mrs. Watson cast another glance at Johnny; he was again looking at Mumble.

But not for long, as the practice session finished before another ten minutes had passed—apparently the rich young people had an evening function to attend and must head home and get ready.

Once they had left, Johnny presented his friends, Jessica Ferguson and Absalom Waters, whose faces were still slightly damp from a quick washing-up, to the visitors. Miss Charlotte, after a few compliments on their dexterity as boxers, invited everyone for supper at a nearby hotel.

When they were shown into the private dining room, the boxers looked around at the silver-blue wallpaper and the large plaster medallion on the ceiling, full of swirls and curlicues. Jessie appeared pleased by the thorough prettiness of the décor, Johnny discomfited, and Mumble curious but dispassionate.

Mrs. Watson's attention was ensnared for a moment by a brooch that Jessie wore as a hair ornament: a memorial brooch, made of loops of laminated hair that simulated the shape of a flower. The strands used in the brooch were almost the exact same auburn as Jessie's own hair, pulled back into a large bun at her nape.

"My employer extends his apologies," said Miss Charlotte after the company had taken seats at a table that easily accommodated twelve. "He had to go back to Manchester earlier today for business. In the meanwhile, I am to squire his beautiful lady about London and look deeper into the matter of your sponsor."

Johnny and Jessie both glanced at Mumble, who, after a moment, said, "If you'll pardon me for the observation, sir, ma'am, you seem more interested in Mr. Underwood than you are in us."

Mrs. Watson's heart plowed into her sternum, but Miss Charlotte only smiled. "Very astute of you, Mr. Waters. You see, my employer, Mr. Nelson, is the only one who can assess your merit as boxers. I cannot do that, so my responsibility is to make sure that should he take you on, he would be, in fact, acquiring assets and not liabilities.

"To assess the quality of an investment, it is best to learn as much about it as possible. For example, we know that you, Miss Ferguson, are an assistant cook at a tea shop, and that you, Mr. Waters, work as a bookbinder's apprentice. The bookbinder is extremely pleased with your pursuit of excellence and your appetite for knowledge, Mr. Waters. The owner of the tea shop is stingier with her praise, but even she had to admit she couldn't find much to fault in Miss Ferguson's work."

Johnny shot to his feet, his face ashen. "I didn't tell them anything about you other than that you're good boxers!"

He was speaking to Mumble. Mumble looked him over for a second, then calmly gestured for him to sit down. Johnny opened his mouth as if he wanted to further defend himself, but complied.

"Indeed," said Miss Charlotte, "Mr. Esposito has been most

discreet in his dealings with us. But none of what I said about you was terribly difficult to find out."

Mrs. Watson, in fact, had been the one to ferret out everything today. She'd spoken to the two young people's employers even as they were in the back working, without the bookbinder or the teahouse owner realizing that she'd sought information on a specific person at the establishment.

"So you see," continued Miss Charlotte in her role as the quietly shrewd Herrinmore, "even though I cannot vouch for your ability as boxers, I can gauge your reliability as individuals—and you are good people to have. About Mr. Underwood, however, I have been unable to gather anything concrete. No one seems to know what he did—or even where he lived. I found a single address, a flat, but the owner said he moved out years ago and left no forwarding address. And that during the five years he lived there, he always paid rent three months at a time in advance, therefore the landlord never had reason to demand letters of character."

"So you are looking for letters of character for Mr. Underwood?" asked Jessie. When not shouting in the middle of a bout, her voice was soothing—dulcet, almost.

Both Jessie and Mumble turned toward Johnny. There was nothing accusatory in their gaze, but Johnny still squirmed. "I already told them yesterday that he was good to us, to all three of us," he said, again speaking to Mumble.

"I think," said Mumble, "that our hosts wish to hear specifics."

Johnny's jaw moved. He stared at the finger bowl in front of him. "I don't know that I'd have been able to keep my family alive if it hadn't been for Mr. Underwood. Winter before last, both my mamma and my little sister fell ill. He raised my stipend so we could move to a better place, somewhere not so damp and cold. And they got better almost right away."

Guilt. The boy had tried hard to come across as uncaring, but in truth he was racked by guilt.

"Mr. Underwood raised Jessie's and my stipends, too," added Mumble, "just to be fair, even though we weren't in dire straits."

All that Mrs. Watson had known about Mr. Underwood was that he had been a trusted and loyal lieutenant to Lord Bancroft. A more complex picture was emerging from those who knew him in different capacities. He appeared to have been a good mate to Mrs. Claiborne, suspicions of another woman notwithstanding; he certainly seemed to have been an exceptional sponsor to these three young people.

"All I know is that he never touched me. And he never commented on me except as a boxer," said Jessie. "He never told me that I ought to be a different sort of woman inside or outside the ring. Never said anything about how I looked or how he'd like me to look. I know it may not seem like much, but you wouldn't believe the things a woman hears in a gymnasium, especially on a fight night."

Mr. Underwood, not only shrewd and capable but also principled and kind?

Could a kind man have served as henchman to Lord Bancroft all these years? Mrs. Watson was unclear on everything Lord Bancroft had done, but he had very clearly orchestrated the murder of one completely innocent bystander, so that he could have a body to use to frame Lord Ingram. And given his fastidious nature, Mrs. Watson would be surprised if he hadn't delegated the deed to Mr. Underwood.

How, then, did one reconcile Mr. Underwood, the cold-blooded killer, with Mr. Underwood, the softhearted sponsor?

Not to mention Mr. Underwood, the probably devoted lover?

Their waiter came into the dining room; Miss Charlotte ordered for the table. She then said to Mumble and Jessie, "So the two of you want, as much as possible, to stand by Mr. Underwood?"

Mumble and Jessie exchanged a look—and nodded.

Johnny, who had just then looked up, bent his face to the table again.

Miss Charlotte continued her questioning of his friends. "I understand you've been searching for him. Have you found anything?"

"We spoke to Mr. Constable, his accountant," answered Mumble, the obvious leader of the trio. "The ledgers and records looked shipshape. But Mr. Constable also didn't know any more about Mr. Underwood than we did. And the only address he had was of Mr. Underwood's old flat, the one he moved out of a while ago."

"When did you speak to Mr. Constable?"

"You mean, specifically to ask about Mr. Underwood? It was after Mr. Constable told us that he had given us the last installment of our stipend, and that there would be no more unless he heard from Mr. Underwood again."

"I believe your stipends ran out in April?"

"Yes, but it came as such a shock to us—I'm not sure why, but it did—that it took some time before we recovered enough to even think about asking questions."

The boy was skilled at answering questions without giving concrete particulars—he had yet to provide a date, or even a time frame, for this meeting with Mr. Underwood's accountant. And he managed to do so without looking calculating.

Mrs. Watson wondered how hard Miss Charlotte needed to press him for the specifics. But Miss Charlotte abandoned that line of questioning altogether.

"Have you ever heard that Mr. Underwood had a mistress?" she asked instead. "This might be the most interesting rumor I've chanced upon about Mr. Underwood since I started asking—that he kept a mistress in St. John's Wood."

Jessie and Mumble again glanced at each other. Then Mumble's gaze settled on Johnny. Mrs. Watson couldn't be sure whether he was expecting the latter to give an answer or instructing him to.

"I always assumed he had a family somewhere," said Johnny, after a glimpse at Mumble. "But he never brought a woman to the gymnasium—or anywhere I've ever seen him."

Mumble picked up his glass of water and drank, indicating that he had nothing to add. Jessie, after a moment, did the same.

And Miss Charlotte failed to pursue this line of questioning, too, but cheerfully welcomed the waiter who returned with their soup, and encouraged everyone to enjoy the repast.

Johnny ate with the speed and efficiency of someone who had lived too long not knowing where his next meal would be coming from. Jessie also had a healthy appetite and consumed more pudding than Miss Charlotte, a sight Mrs. Watson did not witness often. Mumble, more restrained in his dining, carried on a conversation with Miss Charlotte concerning, of all things, the mystery of where eels originated.

Unlike Jessie, who retained a slight Scottish lilt to her speech, the Romani—or perhaps half-Romani—Mumble spoke with an accent that made it difficult to pin down his geographical or class origin. He hadn't been educated at a public school like Eton or Harrow, of that much Mrs. Watson could be certain. Otherwise, even someone of her sensitive ears couldn't glean much more about him from his consonants and vowels.

His table manners were also excellent. Jessie, too, seemed familiar with the veritable parade of silverware on the table, though she waited to see which dining implement Mumble selected, before she made the same selection. Johnny, on the other hand, made Mrs. Watson think of a schoolgirl abruptly thrust into the midst of a London Season, with no preparation other than a hasty skimming of *Debrett's*.

At the end of supper, Miss Charlotte offered to send the boxers home, and they all, to a one, declined firmly. The young people left on foot; the consulting detectives climbed into their carriage.

As the vehicle pulled away from the curb, Mrs. Watson exhaled. "They are pleasant enough company, Mr. Underwood's boxers. But this evening wasn't exactly the most productive use of our time, was it, when we still have so much to do?"

"I'm afraid I must disagree vociferously, ma'am," murmured Miss Charlotte. "This has, in fact, been a most illuminating evening."

Mrs. Watson stared at the girl—the carriage lanterns cast just enough light to make out the gleam in her eyes. Then she looked out the rear window at the boxers on the curb, walking shoulder to shoulder, their eyes fixed on the carriage.

"How? How was this meeting illuminating?"

Miss Charlotte smiled very slightly. "Because now I know who searched Mrs. Claiborne's villa shortly before I did: Mumble and Jessie."

Thirteen

Mrs. Watson stood at the back door of Mrs. Claiborne's hired town house and rang the bell again.

Still no response.

She'd sent a message the night before, informing Mrs. Claiborne of her intention to call. Mrs. Claiborne should have been anxiously waiting for any news that might shed light on Mr. Underwood's fate.

But even if Mrs. Watson's letter had gone astray, she would still have expected Mrs. Claiborne to be home. After all, this was a woman who, out of fear, kept her drapes drawn all day and no longer answered her front door.

Mrs. Watson rang the doorbell one more time, pulling on the cord repeatedly. But after the clamor of the bell died down, the house remained resolutely silent.

Where had Mrs. Claiborne gone? And what had motivated her departure, when she had seemed so determined to hide in her shelter either until Mr. Underwood came for her or until she learned that he never would?

The sea was a brilliant, almost tropical blue, the sky dotted with fat puffs—another idyllic day on the English Riviera.

Lord Ingram walked along the gently curving beach, the tip of his walking stick sinking into soft sand. The sun shone warmly on his shoulders, the breeze soft yet cool. He could drop to his stomach and fall asleep this instant, but that he would do on the train instead, in an hour. For now, he quickened his pace and did his best to look brisk and energetic.

Two women, each holding a lacy white parasol, ambled toward him from the opposite direction. Beyond them stretched slopes dotted with holiday villas, a postcard-perfect view. One of the women spied him and waved eagerly. He raised his hand in salute.

"Mrs. Calder, Miss Dearborn, how do you do?" he said with grave courtesy when the other party drew closer.

The silver-haired Mrs. Calder grinned. "Oh, but we haven't seen you for some time, have we, Mr. Faraday? It must have been a good ten days. Don't you think so, Miss Dearborn?"

The woman she addressed as Miss Dearborn nodded. "I do believe you're right, Mrs. Calder. You have a wonderful memory for such things."

She had a pleasant face and becoming manners, Miss Dearborn. Before this, Lord Ingram had known her as Norbert, lady's maid to Holmes's irascible mother and also, in secret, an agent of the crown who worked for his brother Remington.

He turned and strolled with the women. "Have you been well, Mrs. Calder? Has the area continued to agree with you?"

"Oh, it agrees with me splendidly, my dear Mr. Faraday. We visited Dartmouth, a most appealing town—and Paignton again, too, you know how I adore Paignton. Miss Dearborn and I hosted a mother and her two daughters for tea three days ago and had a roaring game of cribbage going afterwards. Yesterday we found a charming little bookshop on our walk. And, of course, one runs into handsome young men here and there, too."

Mrs. Calder winked. Lord Ingram looked more or less the same as he had when he'd met Holmes last, not a day under sixty. But to Mrs. Calder, well north of eighty, he was indeed a young man still.

He chatted another ten minutes with Mrs. Calder before he took his leave. As he straightened from his bow, Norbert, who had been largely silent, tapped her fingertips three times against the shaft of her parasol. *All is well.*

He wished the women a good day and left Norbert to her task.

———✳︎———

Mr. Constable, Mr. Underwood's accountant, received Charlotte in his spartan office with a pained smile. "If you don't mind my saying so, Mr. Herrinmore, you're the fourth party I've received, inquiring after Mr. Underwood."

Charlotte, disguised yet again as Mr. Nelson's underling, adjusted her weight in the uncomfortable chair, the edges of which dug into the backs of her legs. "Let me guess. The first party must have been late last year, most likely in November. The other two, including a visit from Mr. Underwood's boxers, would have been more recent."

"Why, yes." Mr. Constable took a moment to contain his surprise. "But no matter how many inquiries are raised, my knowledge of and involvement with Mr. Underwood remain limited. This portfolio contains the entirety of his transactions with this firm."

Charlotte had been contemplating a break-in at the accountant's office in order to see the transactions Mr. Underwood had routed through him—that is, until she'd learned that Mumble and Jessie were allowed to inspect those ledgers.

Still, Mr. Constable's ready compliance was a little too . . . compliant. Charlotte glanced at the large brown paper envelope in the accountant's hands and gauged that her question would not make it disappear. "I am very much looking forward to reviewing the transactions, sir. I will admit, however, a certain surprise that I am granted this privilege."

Mr. Constable unwound the twine that held the envelope together. "Believe me, Mr. Herrinmore, I am even more astonished than you. But Mr. Underwood's instruction, from the very beginning, was that the accounts should be open to anyone who wished to scrutinize them."

So Mr. Underwood very much did *not* want his sponsorship of those young people to be viewed as a secret?

"Well, whatever his reasons, I'm glad of it," said Charlotte. "Ready when you are, Mr. Constable."

The accountant pointed at a date from the spring of 1884—more than three years ago—written in ink on the corner of the envelope. "That would be the first time Mr. Underwood called on me and explained what he wished to do. I didn't see him for some time after that, until he came in again with the first installment of funds."

He pulled out a ledger from the envelope and flipped it open. "You'll see the sum recorded here."

Six months passed between the first time and the second time Mr. Underwood came in to discuss business.

Mr. Constable then took out several small envelopes from the larger envelope and opened the first one, marked 1884. "This is the receipt for that first sum—you see my signature. A duplicate was given to Mr. Underwood. Here's his acknowledgment of my fees, which are also reflected in the ledger. With that subtracted, we arrive at the amount to be distributed. So I began distribution, leading to signed receipts from Mr. Giovanni Esposito for each of the two remaining months of the year."

He collected all the slips of paper, returned them to the 1884 envelope, and then opened the next one, marked 1885. "A new sum was wired by postal order. No signature from Mr. Underwood this time, but the postal order itself, specifying the fees to be paid to the firm and the amount to be subsequently distributed, is attached. Again, I signed for the amount due me. Here is one month's receipt signed by Mr. Esposito and from then on, every month, receipts from all three of the boxers."

So Mumble and Jessie joined the group in February 1885.

Mr. Constable laid out more receipts and referenced them back to the ledger. It was as Mumble had said, everything shipshape. Whenever a signature was missing, reasons and reasonable substitutes were supplied, such as the cables that came along with the wired sums that served as Mr. Underwood's directive on how the money ought to be apportioned, and Jessie's signature for Mumble's stipend, the one time he had to work late and could not go to the Unicorn of the Sea to receive it in person.

"Every penny was signed and accounted for, up to the very end," said Mr. Constable, not without a trace of pride.

"Excellent record-keeping," Charlotte concurred. "If you don't mind, I'm curious to know whether this is all the work you've done for Mr. Underwood. Has he ever entrusted you with other tasks?"

The accountant scooped up the contents of the last small envelope and slotted everything back into the portfolio. "None whatsoever. I broached it with him once, when I saw him at the Unicorn of the Sea. He answered firmly that he did not require other services, and I did not raise the topic again."

"So he didn't ask you to direct funds to any other recipients?"

"No, indeed." Having tidied his desk, Mr. Constable patted the rather thin portfolio with the satisfaction of one who loved order. He looked up at Charlotte, his plain face serious and earnest. "I'm not sure how I can make this clearer, Mr. Herrinmore, but I have shown you the entire extent of my business dealings with Mr. Underwood. I was willing to participate in his other ventures—provided they were reasonable and legitimate—but my participation was not needed, much to my disappointment at the time. Now, however, I'm grateful that he did not entrust me with more, given all the questions I've had to field."

If Mr. Underwood did not use an intermediary to pay Mrs. Claiborne but instead footed her household expenses, etc., directly, then did that lend more credence, the possibility of the other woman notwithstanding, to Mrs. Claiborne's account of the two as a close and loving couple?

But she was not going to get an answer to that question here. Charlotte shifted topics. "Mr. Constable, what do you think of Mr. Underwood as a man?"

"Well, his boxers are decent and hardworking, no doubt about that." The accountant's forehead furrowed. "Mr. Underwood himself— I'm a little less sure. I mean, as a client he was above reproach—until recently he sent money when he promised to and was courteous and reasonable in all ways. But other than that, he was a complete mystery."

Mr. Underwood did seem to become more of a puzzle the more Charlotte pursued his disappearance: The knowledge she'd acquired arrived in disjointed pieces, and a partially filled-in picture with key sections missing raised more questions than a completely blank canvas.

"Do you by any chance remember what exactly Mr. Underwood said when he came in for the first time, in terms of what he wanted you to do?"

"From memory, not quite, but I keep a record of my meetings with clients and prospective clients. Let me find that particular entry."

Mr. Constable went to a locked cabinet and brought back a large notebook with 1884 embossed in gold on the cover. "Aha, here it is. 'Mr. William Underwood. Declined to give occupation and source of income. Stated only that he aimed to transfer funds to Mr. Giovanni Esposito, apprentice bricklayer, but not until further notice. In addition, he instructed that minutes of meetings and any future transactions be open to inspection by one and all.'"

Could Mr. Underwood have anticipated that so many parties would wish to plumb the depth of these accounts?

"Do you recall whether he mentioned the sponsorship of a boxer?" Charlotte asked. In the brief entry, there was no reference to the Unicorn of the Sea. Or to boxing.

"I would say no—something like that I'd have noted. I remember being surprised when we met the next time and he specified that Johnny was a boxer. Let me see."

He flipped some pages. "Yes, indeed, in my minutes on our next meeting, I wrote that 'Mr. Underwood informed me that Mr. Giovanni Esposito is a boxer he has decided to sponsor.' I even jotted down at the bottom that I felt 'trepidatious about the prospect of dealing with boxers. The reputation of the group as a whole is hardly sterling.'"

He gave a self-deprecating grin. "Obviously I overcame my qualms."

"Would you mind reading me the entries from the other times Mr. Underwood called on you?"

Mr. Constable obliged. But those offered nothing of interest. Each time Mr. Underwood came in with money, signed his name in the ledger, commended Mr. Constable on his excellent work, and left.

There was something entirely self-contained about Mr. Underwood's venture into boxing. The night before, Mumble had commented incisively that they seemed more interested in Mr. Underwood than in his boxers. By the same token it could be said that Mr. Underwood appeared more interested in his boxers than in boxing as a sport.

"I have one last request, if you will humor me. I'd like to know about the parties that inquired after Mr. Underwood. If I can find them, perhaps they might have something to tell me."

Mr. Constable hesitated.

Charlotte added, "And no need to tell me anything about the first party. I assume they came at the behest of the crown."

The accountant stared at her for a moment, his fingertips scratching against the leather binding of the notebook. "All right, then. I won't say anything about them. I'm sure, Mr. Herrinmore, you also wouldn't wish me to divulge the specifics of *our* conversation."

"To the contrary, sir," Charlotte said generously, "I shall have no quarrels with your disclosure to all and sundry that Edmond Herrinmore, on behalf of Mr. Harold Nelson of Manchester, has inquired after Mr. Underwood's dealings with you, in order to ascertain whether he is likely to return and make trouble for Mr. Nelson, if the latter were to take Mr. Underwood's former boxers under his wing.

"However, I do understand your hesitation, and I commend you for your scruples. Shall we do it another way? Let me tell you my conjecture. If I'm wrong, please say so. But if I'm right, you need say nothing."

Before the startled accountant could object, she said, "The first party, which came late last year, represented the crown—and we need say no more about them. The second party, I am guessing, consisted of a woman who claimed to be Mr. Underwood's fiancée.

"She was beautiful and distressed. Perhaps she was interested in your records on the boxers' stipends and perhaps she wasn't. But the main objective of her visit was not that. Instead, she was terribly interested in whether you had directed payment to another woman on Mr. Underwood's behalf."

"You know Mrs. Anderson?" Mr. Constable blurted out.

Mrs. Anderson? Was she the other woman—or Mrs. Claiborne under a different guise?

"Was she a brunette who spoke with a French accent?"

"Not at all. She was fair-haired and spoke the Queen's English."

"Indeed."

"She—" Mr. Constable stopped himself, as if remembering that he had just been praised for his discretion.

"I imagine she came not too recently," said Charlotte, "but also not too long ago. Let's say, sometime between when Mr. Underwood's money ran out in April and the middle of June."

Which would have been roughly six weeks ago, around the time Mrs. Claiborne had to decamp from the villa to the much more cramped town house.

"How—how do you know all this? She came at the beginning of June," said Mr. Constable, once again forgetting to cleave to a professional tight-lippedness.

Charlotte ignored his question—her deductions had the greatest impact when they were shrouded in mystery. "I already know that Mr. Waters and Miss Ferguson called on you, so naturally they must form the third party who came before me. I take it they came very recently, within the past ten days—perhaps even within this past week."

"True, on Monday."

Five days ago then. "And were they, like me, interested in prior parties who had inquired about Mr. Underwood?"

"Why, they—" Mr. Constable started. He stood the notebook

still in his hand on its bottom edge and tapped it several times against the surface of his desk. "I'm afraid I cannot and should not say anything more on the matter."

Charlotte nodded gravely. "Again, I commend you on your circumspection, Mr. Constable. You wouldn't happen to have the address for either this Mrs. Anderson or the boxers, would you?"

Mr. Constable exhaled. "I cannot help you with that at all, Mr. Herrinmore. Both parties declined to leave addresses."

Charlotte could imagine Mumble and Jessie learning about the existence of a woman in Mr. Underwood's life from the insufficiently guarded accountant. But assuming this Mrs. Anderson was indeed Mrs. Claiborne in disguise, how had they obtained her address if she hadn't given it here?

She rose. "I thank you for your patience and generosity, Mr. Constable. You have been most helpful."

Mr. Constable winced.

Fourteen

After she left Mr. Constable's office, Charlotte could not find Mumble or Jessie. Jessie had already left for the day, having taken an earlier shift to help with the tea shop's baking—the proprietress didn't trust bread from nearby bakeries not to be adulterated with alum, chalk, or plaster of paris. And the bookbinding shop where Mumble worked as an apprentice was closed for the Jewish Sabbath.

Charlotte did, however, manage to locate Johnny at his construction site. The day was overcast and relatively cool, not bad for working outside. And Johnny had already made substantial progress on the wall he was building. He was climbing down the scaffolding as she arrived.

"May I have the pleasure of buying you your luncheon, Mr. Esposito?"

"I brought my lunch, and I'd best eat it. But if you're in a generous mood, Mr. Herrinmore," answered Johnny, rinsing the mortar from his hands, "I wouldn't mind having something to take back to the family."

Charlotte promptly crossed the busy intersection and bought a trio of grilled sausages and a ham pie from a street vendor. When she came back, Johnny had laid out his lunch on a plank set upon two stacks of bricks. His meal consisted of a single sandwich, which looked substantial at first glance, but on closer examination turned out to be only two slabs of bread with an almost invisible layer of butter in between.

Johnny stared at the glistening, faintly blistered sausages she set down before him. "Thank you. My family will enjoy these."

"These aren't for your family—I'll buy some for them later. These are for you, for lunch. A man who works all day ought to have more than bread for lunch."

Johnny, for whom pride must be an unattainable luxury, offered no protests. He thanked "Mr. Herrinmore" and tucked into the bounty. And only after he'd polished off everything Charlotte had bought did he pause to say, "Today it isn't only bread. There's butter and a bit of sheep's trotter inside, too. Plenty enough to get me through the rest of the day."

He asked for so little, this young man.

Or maybe it was more accurate to say that he was accustomed to almost nothing and expected even that to be taken away.

"I was looking for your friends, Mumble and Jessie. I might have bought them luncheon if I'd found them, but I didn't."

"Guess it's my lucky day then." Johnny pinched a bite from his sandwich. "They weren't at work?"

"No. Do you know where they live?"

He shook his head.

"I thought you all were good friends."

He chewed without speaking. All around them, workers carted squeaky wheelbarrows back and forth. Sandwich board men trundled by, advertising custard powders and shoe polish. A bobby blew his whistle on the next street, shouting for a pair of unruly drivers to behave themselves.

Just as Charlotte thought Johnny wasn't going to answer her, he said, "We are—we *are* all friends."

His tone, both hesitant and emphatic, as if he'd just come to that conclusion himself . . .

"Last year Jessie baked a beautiful cake for my mamma's birthday.

It was decorated like a garden, with roses and tulips made from marzipan—all because Mamma told her that she wished she had a garden.

"Mumble . . ." He touched the inside of his bare forearm, still splattered with bits of mortar, as if at a sudden recollection. "After Mr. Underwood became my sponsor, I put my brothers back into school. But it was hard—they were behind all the other pupils. When Mumble came along, I asked if he could help them. He reads a book a day, Mumble—the bookbinder has rooms full of books at home and loans them to him by the boxful. And he's good with numbers, too, from looking after the shop's accounts. So Mumble came on Saturday evenings for a full year to catch them up.

"And every time he came, Jessie sent along baked goods from the tea shop. They said those were stale buns and biscuits that Mrs. Hatfield let Jessie have for next to nothing, but they tasted perfectly fresh to me, and I don't think Mrs. Hatfield is all that generous."

He took another bite from his brick of a sandwich. After three sausages and a ham pie, and a sizable supper the previous evening, Charlotte doubted that his stomach wanted more food. But he ate with the same doggedness with which he'd endured—and overcome—the boxing match.

"Yes, we are friends," he repeated, "even if I don't know where they live."

His voice fell. "Even if they won't let me do anything for them in return."

A street musician began playing nearby, a violin rendition of Pachelbel's Canon in D Major.

Johnny listened for some time and said, rather savagely, "Mumble plays much better."

Mumble, Charlotte was beginning to think, could do no wrong in this young man's eyes.

"Do they live together, Mumble and Jessie?"

"I think so, but don't get the wrong idea. They're foster siblings—they grew up together."

The thought that someone might get the wrong idea about Mumble and Jessie seemed to bother him—and Charlotte didn't think his anxiety was on Jessie's behalf. "How long have you known them?"

"Two and a half years—since the beginning of '85."

Which accorded with Mr. Constable's records and receipts.

"When did you start boxing?"

"The year before I met them."

"To help your family? You don't seem interested in boxing for its own sake."

"I hate it." He drank from a dented canteen whose strap had been mended in two places. "After my old man died, we couldn't make ends meet, not even with me and my two brothers all working. Someone said that I was a scrappy bugger and ought to try boxing. So I did. Guess that was a good idea."

"Who said that?"

"Not sure. Some bum tried to steal my bread and ran away after I punched him. A bystander said it, I think. Gave me a two-bit bob and told me that at the Unicorn of the Sea, if I could prove myself I might just get a sponsor and wouldn't have to scrap for bread anymore."

Some fifteen feet away, a workman, probably freshly returned from luncheon, began breaking rocks with an awl and a hammer. In the greater din, Charlotte considered Johnny's answer. "What did this man look like?"

Johnny shrugged again. "The bum I fought ran off, but not before he left me with a pair of black eyes. I could barely see. All I remember is that the fellow who made the suggestion had a thick cockney accent."

"When did your father pass away, if you don't mind me asking?"

"March of 1884. March twentieth."

"And how much time after his death did this incident take place? This near robbery that led to the comment that began your boxing career?"

"Must have been two months afterwards? Yes, end of May." Johnny, finished with his sandwich, sighed in relief and downed the rest of the water in his canteen. "It was the day before my little sister's birthday, and I remember thinking that I couldn't let her go hungry on her birthday."

Mr. Underwood first visited Mr. Constable the accountant that April, a full month before the idea of becoming a boxer had even taken hold in Giovanni Esposito's head.

"Did you go to the Unicorn soon afterwards?"

"As soon as my black eyes faded, I went and took a look. But then I had to convince my mother that it wasn't the worst idea since the creation of man. And she'd have held out for longer, if we weren't running out of money."

He glanced at her, a flicker of worry in those dark pupils.

Perhaps he wasn't as taciturn as he'd made himself out to be. Perhaps he needed only encouragement from someone he trusted, even a little, to talk at length.

"But of course your mother has had no cause to regret her decision," she said.

"Actually, she regretted it almost as soon as she gave me permission, because someone sent her five quid in the mail, someone who said that he was an old friend of my father's, wanting to do something decent for his widow and children. She always said it was an angel who sent it, because the men my father ran around with were no better than him. They took money from babes' mouths to buy drink, and none of them would have given a single thought—let alone a sou—to some dead fool's widow and children."

Mysterious aid, eh? "Did you ever find out the identity of this angel?"

"No." Johnny dusted off his hands. "Five pounds was a huge sum, but between rent, food, and my mother's medicine, even with those five pounds, we'd have barely lasted through autumn. Winter would have been even more expensive, with coal to buy."

He sighed. "Mr. Underwood became my sponsor in the nick of time."

No indeed. Mr. Underwood took his time and became your sponsor at a moment of *his* choosing.

"Forgive my curiosity, Mr. Esposito, but how did your father die?"

Johnny rose. "We're not entirely sure, but most likely he got drunk, fell, and hit the back of his head on the curb. His body was discovered only the next morning."

"He fell *backward*?"

Charlotte didn't have a great deal of experience with drunks, but the world would have far fewer sots if falling straight back was the usual mode of succumbing to an alcoholic stupor.

Johnny balled up the wrapping papers from his luncheon and lobbed the entire thing neatly into the nearest rubbish bin. He glanced at Charlotte, looking only a little bitter. "Have I ever mentioned that not long before my old man died, my mother became convinced he'd soon abandon us? I saw it in his eyes, too—he'd had enough. He was giving her less and less money and drinking more and more. And what he didn't spend on drink, he kept in a pouch under a floorboard."

He wiped a sleeve across his face. "I didn't care how he died. All I cared was that we could at last use that money to buy some food. That for once, my little sister wouldn't go to bed hungry."

— ✴ —

Dear Miss Holmes and Mrs. Hudson,

Unfortunately, I had to abandon my hired town house for a "bolt-hole" that Mr. ~~Under~~ Overhill had prepared for me as a last resort. Please forgive me for not divulging its address——Mr. Overhill forbade that strictly.

It may not be a good idea for me to go to your hotel in person. But I'm desperate for help. May I propose a meeting at ~~Pettifer's Hotel~~?

Yours truly,
~~Marie Claiborne~~

P.S. I'm sorry for scratching out the proposed location. Mr. Overhill once mentioned that, in the course of his work, sometimes the most crucial information is sent separately from the rest. I will do that instead.

P.P.S. In that case I had better cover over my own name, too.

P.P.P.S. But if the wrong party gets their hands on this letter, they will know then to watch out for the next one from me. I really have no idea what I am doing, do I? Nevertheless, I must proceed.

Dear Miss Holmes and Mrs. Hudson,

This is that separate missive.

I anxiously await you four o'clock this afternoon at Pettifer's Hotel. Ask for Mrs. Overhill.

Yours truly,
Mrs. Overhill

—※—

Mrs. Watson took three different hansom cabs. After she alit from each, she made sure to disappear for a few minutes, either by using the carriage lane behind a row of houses to emerge onto a different street, or by going into an establishment from the front and leaving via a service door.

What had happened? One moment they were speaking to some young people who boxed to supplement their income, the next Mrs. Claiborne had become frightened enough to flee.

Perhaps Mrs. Claiborne had been in no immediate danger and merely overreacted. Still, Mrs. Watson's own heart raced. The temperature hovered steadily in the mid-sixties, yet she perspired. As she finally approached Pettifer's Hotel, she felt as if she were only marginally tethered to this reality of an ordinary summer day, with pedestrians all around her, umbrellas hooked over elbows, hurrying toward their own destinations.

The hotel was the kind favored by solidly respectable country squires. Mrs. Watson, in a discreet grey velvet walking dress and an even more restrained toque that featured barely any trimming, could have blended into the wallpaper in the foyer.

There was indeed a private room reserved by a Mrs. Overhill. Mrs. Watson was quickly shown into a genteel, old-fashioned space, but it was empty. No sign of Mrs. Claiborne.

Mrs. Watson glanced at the clock on the mantelpiece. Despite the labyrinthine route she'd taken, she had arrived a good quarter hour ahead of the appointment. She ordered the full tea service to arrive at four sharp, and asked the server to find out when Mrs. Claiborne had asked for the private room.

There was a post office not far from the hotel, and it was possible that Mrs. Claiborne had reserved the room after she had posted her letters to Miss Charlotte and Mrs. "Hudson."

And then what? Had she gone back to the "bolt-hole" she'd mentioned? And there waited anxiously for time to pass, pacing back and forth in a bare, airless space?

The server returned at exactly four o'clock with tea, a plate of sandwiches, a plate of sliced Battenberg cake, and the intelligence that the room had been reserved in the morning.

Mrs. Claiborne herself, however, did not arrive at the stroke of the hour.

Mrs. Watson did not expect strict punctuality—times like these called for careful reconnaissance, not a rushed entrance. But when another ten minutes passed and still Mrs. Claiborne did not appear, she could no longer remain seated. She went to the window to look down to the street below, then to the door to listen for footsteps outside. Once she opened the door with hope, only to see a party being led to the room next door; another time it turned out to be a laden food trolley being pushed down the corridor.

Ten more minutes passed. Mrs. Watson, on her feet, her hands braced against the top of a chair, tried to breathe deeply and not imagine the beautiful Mrs. Claiborne in mortal peril.

Or herself, in the midst of a trap.

The door opened. Mrs. Watson gasped, but the young woman walking in, dressed unobtrusively in a light brown jacket-and-skirt set, was not Mrs. Claiborne, only Miss Charlotte.

"I saw the note you left in our hotel suite," said she. "I take it Mrs. Claiborne has not come yet?"

Mrs. Watson gave a tight shake of her head. "I've been here since quarter to four."

"Let me make some inquiries," said Miss Charlotte, and left the room.

When she returned, the tea Mrs. Watson had poured for her had already cooled to room temperature, but the results of her investigation were even more tepid: No reception clerk or server had seen anyone of Mrs. Claiborne's description this afternoon.

To distract herself, Mrs. Watson requested an account of Miss Charlotte's day—and had to ask the dear girl to repeat herself several times because her concentration kept slipping.

Time froze, the second hand taking an eon to complete a journey around the clock face. And yet time also surged, like floodwater bursting forth: Every time Mrs. Watson looked up, another ten or fifteen minutes would have passed, with Mrs. Claiborne neither honoring the appointment she herself had set nor delivering any excuses for her failure to attend.

At quarter to six, a server came in. With many apologies, she informed them that the next party who had reserved the private room would be arriving soon.

Mrs. Watson's head throbbed. The slow progression of their hackney, caught in the usual congested evening traffic, did not help matters: It gave her too much time to examine the tide of pedestrians for a sign of Mrs. Claiborne, while wondering whether the latter was even now headed to the hotel from some other direction.

She forced herself to think of the bigger picture. "What if Lord Bancroft was wrong in his assessment that Mr. Underwood's personal enemies were responsible for his disappearance? What if it *was* about the work they did for the crown and the secrets they'd sold against the crown's interest? And what if Mrs. Claiborne wasn't as ignorant concerning these men's work as she claimed to be? She could very well be in as much danger as Mr. Underwood."

But before Miss Charlotte could respond, an even wilder possibility struck Mrs. Watson. "What if I'm worried over nothing? What if Mrs. Claiborne and Mr. Underwood are in this together, the two of them? Maybe this whole thing is simply Mr. Underwood wishing to get away from Lord Bancroft without making the latter suspicious that he'd been abandoned. Maybe this song and dance that Mrs. Claiborne has put on is all so that she, too, could disappear without anyone thinking that she orchestrated it herself."

A placid Miss Charlotte nodded. "There is merit in that notion."

Mrs. Watson did not typically comment on Miss Charlotte's implementation of fashion; Miss Charlotte returned that courtesy by not evaluating Mrs. Watson's every speculation concerning their investigations. Therefore, if she stated outright that a concept had merit, then it had merit.

Mrs. Watson's heart fluttered—there was nothing better than a compliment from an expert. "In that case, I have an even more outlandish idea. What if the depth of Mrs. Claiborne's knowledge concerning Mr. Underwood's secrets isn't the only thing Mrs. Claiborne lied to us about? She was Lord Bancroft's mistress, after all. What if the love affair with Mr. Underwood had been by her design—or Lord Bancroft's?"

"You mean, she might have seduced Mr. Underwood very artfully while making him believe the entire time that he'd been the one in pursuit?" murmured Miss Charlotte.

"Precisely. And it was not for romance or even curiosity but at Lord Bancroft's behest, so he could keep a better eye on his chief lieutenant."

"Diabolical," pronounced Miss Charlotte. "Not to mention, that would go a good way toward explaining why Mrs. Claiborne, of all people, undertook *conjugal* visits to Lord Bancroft."

They had not asked that question of Mrs. Claiborne—it would have been far too indelicate—but Mrs. Watson had not failed to notice the downright peculiar arrangement.

Maybe they only exchanged information chastely during those

conjugal visits. But if Mrs. Claiborne was truly, at heart, the old-fashioned woman she claimed to be, one who longed for nothing so much as married bliss, then it would have been wiser not to spend time alone with Lord Bancroft.

Unless it had been Mr. Underwood's idea and he trusted his fiancée completely.

Even so, Mrs. Watson wouldn't put it past Lord Bancroft to take advantage of a beautiful woman. Out of his rampant self-regard, he might not force Mrs. Claiborne into anything, but he could very well make advances and *not* take kindly to rejections.

Mrs. Watson rubbed her temples. Too many thoughts collided inside her skull; her head pounded like a drum. "Now I don't know whether I ought to be sympathetic toward her or extremely wary of her."

The slowly fading light of the day limned Miss Charlotte's soft features, a profile worthy of a cameo brooch. "We can be both, my dear Mrs. Watson," she said quietly. "We can be both."

The decrepit-looking woman shuffled down the steps carrying a large bucket of water. At the bottom of the steps was a short, narrow corridor with six padlocked doors, three on the left, three on the right.

On the floor beside each door—except one—was a wooden tray that could slide in and out of a narrow opening in the door. At the sound of the old woman's approach, five trays slid out, each holding an empty wooden water bowl and an empty wooden food bowl, with a wooden spoon inside.

With a groan, the old woman bent down and retrieved the food bowls. Those were hers to wash. But really, did a dungeon need clean bowls?

Once she had stacked the bowls and the spoons, she ladled fresh water into the water bowls.

"*Bonjour, madame,*" said the voice of a young man from behind the last door on the right. "*Vous avez l'heure?*"

The old woman did not have a watch on her, but even if she did, she wouldn't tell him the time. What good was knowing that for a prisoner? He only asked so that they would strike up a conversation, however short.

And she had been warned against speaking to the prisoners. She did not want to be let go from her position. She brought water and food. She emptied a few piss buckets. There were far more difficult ways to make a living.

The young man switched to a different language, presumably still asking about time.

She continued to ignore him. Eventually he quieted.

The old woman proceeded to the first door on the left. This one didn't have anyone inside but led down to a cellar. She'd heard that sometimes old wines fetched exorbitant prices, a mountain of gold.

But she had better not think about gold that did not belong to her. That way lay dismissal.

The old woman placed the used bowls and utensils into her now-empty water bucket, slowly climbed up the stairs, and locked the heavy door behind her.

Fifteen

I t's so much warmer here than in Paris," said Miss Redmayne.

The sun was behind rooftops, sinking toward the horizon. But stored heat from cobblestone streets, which had baked all day, rose and swirled.

Livia sweltered.

No one loved heat more than she did. But after Bernadine became Lord Bancroft's hostage, Provence's high register on the mercury began to make her feel parched. Fevered, at times.

She had been astonished to receive Miss Redmayne's cable, informing her that she would venture south on Le Train Bleu, the express service that linked Paris and the Côte d'Azur. Except instead of going all the way to Nice, she would get off at Marseille and take another train to come to Aix-en-Provence.

Livia was thrilled to learn from Miss Redmayne that Lord Ingram wasn't really injured after all. The two young women commiserated over their worries for everyone. And Livia couldn't be more grateful that with everything else Miss Redmayne had to look after, she'd found the time to travel seventeen hours by rail to Aix-en-Provence, so that Livia could have a detailed account of what was going on in Paris.

But this couldn't be the sole reason for Miss Redmayne's long journey, simply to reassure Livia that everything had been done for

Bernadine, up to and including the presence of the mysterious young Fontainebleu.

And when Miss Redmayne suggested that they dine at a place she had heard about, somewhere off the beaten path, Livia became even more convinced that she was up to something.

Miss Redmayne's venue of choice took them north of the Cours Mirabeau, on streets that after a while acquired a noticeable upward slant. They found themselves in a small square where, turning around, they beheld the entire town spread out beneath them, all tall trees and ochre roofs, bathed in sunset.

Miss Redmayne asked her way to a tiny restaurant where the wife cooked, the husband served, and there were all of six tables, arranged in a little courtyard that had lanterns hung in the trees.

And there, waiting for them, was a man Livia immediately recognized. Forêt, the butler at the Parisian *hôtel particulier* that had hosted Sherlock Holmes and company when they had been in France last December to burgle Château Vaudrieu.

But Miss Redmayne introduced Forêt as Lieutenant Atwood. Livia shook his hand in astonishment. He smiled and told her that he was related to Lord Ingram on his mother's side and that he was pleased to offer his assistance to their endeavor in Aix-en-Provence.

No explanation was given for his former identity as a very French, albeit very good, butler.

They drank a young red wine and ate grilled aubergines, stuffed tomatoes, and chicken that had been braised with rosemary, olives, and anchovies. Lieutenant Atwood, who was apparently stationed in India, of all places, offered anecdotes of life on the Subcontinent. Miss Redmayne found some humorous incidents from her time as a medical student that would not turn anyone's stomach. And Livia, after listening without quite understanding what was happening—or why—for a solid quarter hour, eventually joined in and gave what she thought to be a rather rousing account of her voyages this past summer, especially that of the tackling of a murderer aboard the RMS *Provence*.

The night cooled enough to become pleasantly breezy. The stars were out; the lanterns in the trees twinkled. The entire courtyard hummed with conversation and laughter. Livia, slightly inebriated, her stomach uncharacteristically full of cake and ice cream at the end of the meal, thought it one of the most delightful evenings she'd ever spent.

But she still had no idea why they'd met Lieutenant Atwood.

And she said so to Miss Redmayne as they stood on the railway platform, waiting for the train that would take Miss Redmayne back to Marseille, where she would catch the northbound express service to Paris at half past midnight.

Miss Redmayne glanced at the gate of the platform, outside which Lieutenant Atwood waited to escort Livia to her hotel. "He is in charge of operations in Aix-en-Provence, and Miss Charlotte had a note she wanted me to give to him."

A note so important that Miss Redmayne had come all this way . . .

Mr. Marbleton. Did Livia dare let herself believe that Mr. Marbleton was really here, that every day she passed underneath his window?

Without quite meaning to, Livia threw her arms around Miss Redmayne. "Thank you for coming. Thank you for all your help!"

Miss Redmayne hugged her back fiercely. "It will be all right, Miss Olivia. You'll see. Everything will be all right."

―❊―

Mrs. Claiborne's town house, while cooler at night, remained completely airless. Charlotte fanned herself with a small notepad that Lord Ingram had brought. Her lover, meanwhile, bent over the typewriter in the house's small study, scanning the row of keys in the light of a pocket lantern.

She loved observing him in a state of concentration. When they'd been children spending summer afternoons together at his minor digs—or to be completely accurate, when he had been excavating and she had been his uninvited guest—she used to look up from the book she was reading and watch him brush away encrusted dirt from all kinds of artefacts.

And then her gaze would travel to the forearms exposed by his rolled-up sleeves, the triangle of skin at the open collar of his shirt, and then back to his very serious, almost frowning face, this boy who radiated a palpable appeal she couldn't quite understand but responded to in all-too-visceral a fashion.

For years she waited for that fascination to go away. Spending time alongside him, propositioning him when she'd been just a bit short of seventeen, even their long, fruitful correspondence—she did everything to gratify herself, but also in the logical expectation that familiarity would eventually lead, if not to outright contempt, as in the case of her parents, then at least to tedium.

Little could she have predicted that sometimes familiarity led to a more profound appreciation, or that their friendship would prove to be one of the great anchors of her life.

She studied his profile, something that at last she no longer needed to do surreptitiously. He was not in disguise, the contours of his young visage bold and sharp-hewn. Over the summer, his hair had grown longer and brushed over his collar in a way that made her want to place her hand at his nape to tickle the center of her palm.

"We are alone in a dark house, and we are not doing anything scandalous," she murmured. "I am consternated."

Her lover glanced at her, set down his pocket lantern, pulled her to him, and kissed her—but only a skimming of the tip of his tongue against hers. Then he pulled back and said, "Why consign scandalous acts to the dark? They can and should be committed in good light."

Charlotte batted her eyelashes. "Is that a promise, Ash?"

He smiled, his teeth a flash of excellent enamel. "That, Holmes, is practically a threat."

Charlotte smiled, then shook her head. She wouldn't call it an empty threat, but given how infrequently they had been in the same place at the same time of late, and how much of that precious little time had been consumed by non-amatory concerns . . .

"And you are right," said he, bent over the typewriter again. "This is the device that produced the notes Bancroft sent you."

It made sense that Mrs. Claiborne had been the one to type up Lord Bancroft's letters, as she had been the one to visit him at Ravensmere, and prisoners there were typically not allowed to communicate with the outside world.

Like Mrs. Watson, Charlotte did not trust Mrs. Claiborne entirely—or much at all. But if Mrs. Claiborne had lied about her flight, at least she hadn't made the elementary mistake of still lurking about in the same house.

They had found an unmade bed in her boudoir, a half-finished glass of water on the nightstand, and half a bag of provisions in the kitchen—all consistent with a hasty, unplanned departure. And other than the attic and the coal cellar, all the other interior doors had been unlocked, which had made the search relatively straightforward— and Lord Ingram had made short work of the few padlocks.

Mrs. Claiborne was not here. And neither was Mr. Underwood, dead or alive.

"Shall we go then?" asked her lover.

They still had other places they needed to be.

On their way out, the final lines of his prewritten letter came to mind. Or maybe they'd never decamped but remained like a trio of country cousins in the recesses of a ballroom, awkwardly yet patiently waiting for the more prominent guests to leave so that they might have a chance to at last pay their respects to the host.

The man stared at the closing door.

The painting was finished some time ago, and he suspected that she knew it.

Where did that leave him then?

She had felt his astonishment and hers as a single reverberation. His, because he realized what it could be read as; hers, that it had come so early in a reunion.

Their circumstances dictated that they spent far more time apart than together. Upon partings that preceded long separations, they had made various confessions and pledges. But by tacit agreement, their subsequent letters never referred to those words of commitment. Then, after weeks or months apart, when they met again in person, that tacit agreement somehow held, a garment for their sentiments, so that they did not need to bare too often the naked heart.

But this had been an instance of exposed emotions on his part, when hers still had on not only corset and combination but a full promenade gown and a pair of gloves besides.

Perhaps he had felt mortified to be unshielded. She could not quite explain it, but she had been almost as self-conscious about her state of emotional overdress, her desire to shed a few layers running smack into her inexperience at this kind of disrobing.

She did not do that here either but asked a lesser question. "You haven't said much about your Society summer."

As little as a year ago, he had been dead set on maintaining the outward appearance of a man who had achieved all the mandated markers of manhood—marriage, children, property, and the respect of his peers. Now, even if his personal popularity had not diminished, he was in the curious and uncomfortable position of being a divorced man, one who had no intention to marry again.

He set his hand on the small of her back to steer her away from the sharp corners of a console table. "It's odd, I will not deny that. But . . . in a way it's not as discomfiting as I thought it would be. You know what I'm sometimes reminded of?"

"What?" She was genuinely curious.

"You. Or perhaps I should say, your life after you were expelled from Society. At the time, when you ran away, it seemed to me that your life had ended. That nothing could possibly go right for you ever again. But I was proved remarkably wrong. Being outside the confines of the Upper Ten Thousand had a salutary effect on you; you became happier and more fulfilled than you could have been otherwise."

He stopped; they'd reached the back door. "I wasn't ostracized by my peers to anywhere near the same extent. But still, because of your example, I wasn't as bewildered as I would have been. I have something to look forward to: Perhaps I will thrive as a divorced man, as you have as a no-longer-eligible woman."

She gazed up at this man she knew so well yet still found so engaging. Before he could open the door to peek outside, she pulled him close for another kiss, this one long and passionate—because it was easier to kiss than to find words for things she could not yet define. "To cement our lamentable new tradition of not doing anything scandalous in the dark."

Mrs. Watson buttered her breakfast roll mechanically. She hadn't slept too badly, but doubts and concerns about Mrs. Claiborne had returned the moment she'd opened her eyes. The one she worried about the most, of course, was Miss Charlotte, working for an enemy who didn't mean her well.

The private entrance's doorbell rang.

Mrs. Watson shot to her feet. Could it be Mrs. Claiborne?

But the young woman who stood outside, in her modest Sunday best, was only about sixteen, plain and rather squarely built, hardly the ravishing Mrs. Claiborne.

"Are you Mrs. Hudson, ma'am?"

Mrs. Watson hesitated. "Yes?"

The girl curtsied. "My name is Sally Tompkins. And I work in the kitchen at Pettifer's Hotel. Yesterday afternoon I was standing outside and this fancy-looking lady came up to me and told me to give this letter to you."

Mrs. Watson sucked in a breath. "You'd best come in then."

By the time tea arrived, Mrs. Watson already knew how long Sally Tompkins had worked at the hotel, where she lived, and her general family situation. It seemed that the girl was who she said she was, a kitchen maid, but Mrs. Watson would personally verify that with the hotel later.

"Tell me how you came to have this letter."

The sealed envelope in Mrs. Watson's hand was made of cheap brown paper, already wrinkled from time spent in Sally Tompkins's pocket. *To Miss Holmes and Mrs. Hudson* was written in black ink on the front of the envelope.

The girl sat with her bottom barely on the chair, holding the cup and saucer Mrs. Watson had offered her with both hands. "Like I said, mum, I was standing outside for a bit—the kitchen was hot and I was feeling faintish. The lady ran up. She had a funny accent and talked fast. She said that she was supposed to meet you inside the hotel but she couldn't anymore, and it was really important that you had this letter.

"And then she ran off, speedy as the Scotch Special Express, before I could tell her that we kitchen maids aren't allowed in the front of the hotel—or to speak to guests.

"All the rest of my shift I thought about it. She gave me a whole crown, and I didn't want to take that much money from someone and not do what they asked. So when my shift was over, I asked one of the waitresses if anyone in the private dining rooms waited for someone who didn't show up.

"The one I asked was the one who waited on you, and she knew that you'd left your address with the reception in case anyone could tell you anything. She got that address for me, so I thought I'd best come, mum, and give this to you before church."

Mrs. Watson urged the girl to have a slice of cake and at last opened the envelope.

Dear Miss Holmes and Mrs. Hudson,

I hope this note will prove to be an unnecessary precaution. But just in case . . .

If you have come to Pettifer's at all, you must have received word I had sent earlier. At the time, I dared not set down the reason for my secrecy, lest my missives were intercepted by the wrong parties. Applying that logic here, I ought not write too much either. But I am confused and need your sage advice.

So here it is: I felt the need to leave the town house because I found it under surveillance last night. I believe there were two of them, one man and one woman.

And if all they had done was watch the house, it would still have been all right. But they approached the back door. By the service stairs Mr. Underwood had hidden a rifle. In my fright, I grabbed it.

I listened, my heart pounding, for the door to be breached. When I heard nothing, I slipped to the window and to my surprise saw the would-be intruders running away. Perhaps they had heard me loading my firearm. I could not tell—my blood pounded in my ears just then.

They must be young for they were fast and agile as they leaped over the low wall of the small rear garden. But come to think of it, maybe they were not a man and a woman—the night was too dark for me to make them out clearly. It was only that I had seen a man and a woman observing the house recently, sometimes together, sometimes singly, and immediately decided that it must have been the same two people.

I could be grossly overreacting. I do not know. I wish Mr. Underwood were here to advise me.

I cannot tell you how I long to hear your words of counsel.

> *Yours,*
> *Mrs. ~~Claiborne~~ Overhill*

Miss Charlotte appeared then, clad in a cream-colored dressing gown embroidered with poppies and buttercups. She wore a large cap to cover her short hair, but her face still looked splotchy from all the beard-gluing of late.

"My dear!" exclaimed Mrs. Watson. Her partner had scarcely slept—she'd returned from her night's work just as Mrs. Watson had woken up in the morning.

"Good morning, ma'am," she said, her voice sludgy, her eyes barely open.

To Sally Tompkins, who had leaped out of her chair to curtsy, she nodded and gestured for the girl to sit down again. And then she extended her hand for the letter.

Mrs. Watson waited for her to read the letter twice. It was how Miss Charlotte took in important information—one quick perusal, followed by a more meticulous study.

After she was finished with the letter, Miss Charlotte appeared slightly more awake. "Miss Tompkins, is that correct?"

Sally Tompkins rose to her feet again. "Yes, mum."

Miss Charlotte poured herself a cup of tea and took a sip. "Did the woman who entrusted this letter to you give you a name?"

"No, mum. She didn't tell me her name. But I found out later, from my friend the waitress, that it was a Mrs. Overhill who didn't show up."

"What did the woman look like?"

"She was awful pretty—brown hair, blue eyes, nice figure."

That sounded exactly like Mrs. Claiborne. Mrs. Watson glanced at Miss Charlotte, who again looked as if she could fall back asleep at any moment. But that did not stop her from continuing with her questions. "Do you remember what she was wearing?"

"I do, mum, something beautiful. It was a traveling costume, I think. Grey broadcloth with a few blue braids."

"That does sound nice," said Miss Charlotte, who never wore such understated outfits unless she was in disguise. "And did she tell you the reason she couldn't come into the hotel?"

"She didn't, mum."

"Do you recall what she said exactly?"

Sally Tompkins nodded eagerly. "She said, 'My dear, I have a great big favor to ask. Will you take this letter and give it to the ladies who are waiting inside for me? And this is for you.' And then she gave me the letter and a crown and ran off."

"She really ran? She sprinted?"

Sally Tompkins again nodded in complete certainty. "She picked up her skirts—I saw her stockings. She ran so fast she didn't even hear me trying to tell her that I wasn't allowed inside the dining rooms."

"Did she look afraid?"

The question stumped Sally Tompkins. But after thinking about it for some time, her brow furrowed, she shook her head. "She sounded out of breath the entire time she was talking to me. I'd have said that she was in a huge hurry, rather than afraid. But me mum always says I hardly ever know what's going on. Maybe she *was* afraid and I was too busy looking at her fancy handbag to notice."

Miss Charlotte smiled a little, her lips dry and pale. "Or maybe you are right and she was only in a great big hurry."

———※———

Miss Charlotte's conjecture was contradicted by the arrival of Mrs. Claiborne's next letter, this time by post.

Dear Miss Holmes and Mrs. Hudson,

My deepest apologies! I feel wretched for not keeping to our appointment, but I also feel, well, competent—almost—for the course of action I did take.

This morning, after I proposed our meeting, I felt better for having done something. As I headed out in the afternoon, my spirits further buoyed—I was sure you would be able to help me.

But upon approaching the hotel, who should I spy but the man and the woman I had seen loitering outside the town house!

I felt dizzy and nauseous. But I kept moving and soon found myself in the alley behind the hotel. A girl in an apron stood there. I accosted her and begged her to give you the letter I'd prepared ahead of time.

And then I hopped in a hansom cab and shouted to be taken to the nearest railway station.

I have not wanted to leave London. Despite what I said about the smell of perfume on Mr. Underwood and the possibility he might have already absconded with someone else, deep in my heart I still believe him nearby, trying to resolve things in a manner that would allow us to have a wonderful future.

But now I am on a train rumbling toward Dover.

Once I finish this letter, I will get off at the next station and post it. But after that, ought I find a railway inn and sleep on the matter? Or should I proceed to the end of the line and buy a passage overseas?

I seem to have the vague notion that with postal orders one can purchase small notices in the papers from anywhere in the world. Which means that no matter where I end up, I can still inform Mr. Underwood of my whereabouts, in the code he taught me, a code he'd devised himself. And he can then find me.

If, that is, he still wants to——and still can.

Again, my apologies for the inconvenience I might have caused you. I beg your forgiveness.

Yours,
Mrs. Overhill

P.S. I remembered to sign my alias, but upon rereading the letter I noticed at least two instances where I used Mr. Underwood's actual name. But I am too weary now for corrections——and goodness, I might have erred similarly in a previous letter, too. If I am but a fly caught in an invisible net, my every movement watched, then let me not make any more futile attempts to be clever or oblique.

Sixteen

The bookbinding shop where Mumble worked had a bow window that displayed beautifully bound ledgers, journals, and books of private correspondence. Behind the proudly exhibited wares, a curtain had been drawn shut.

But apparently, to customers in the know, this Sunday closure was incomplete. Charlotte watched from a nearby lamppost as a refined-looking elderly couple rang the bell and were admitted. They emerged a few minutes later, the husband carrying a pair of packages.

Mumble, holding open the door, half bowed as they departed.

He spied Charlotte, dressed as Mr. Herrinmore, standing across the street. Without any notable reaction, almost without hesitation, he continued to hold the door open.

Charlotte crossed the street. "How do you do, Mr. Waters?"

"I can't complain. Yourself, Mr. Herrinmore?"

"Other than that I am working on a Sunday, no complaints either." She smiled. "May I have a moment of your time?"

Mumble inclined his head. "After you, Mr. Herrinmore."

Just enough daylight filtered into the interior for Charlotte to make out the display of stationery to one side and the locked cabinets to the other side, glass panes reflecting darkly, obscuring the tomes and assorted objects they housed—the bookbinder also had a good reputation as an antiquarian trader.

Mumble took her into a workroom at the back of the shop. Here it was much brighter, curtains open, lamps lit. At the center of the space was a large table on which lay several oddly shaped, milky-white sheets—calf vellum, cut as book covers.

Mumble donned a long dark apron and stationed himself before a smaller raised table on which another piece of vellum, this one perfectly rectangular in shape, had been spread and pinned on a frame. He picked up a metal container and applied a thin uniform layer of something translucent and sticky-looking to the vellum—a glue meant to neutralize the lime that had been used in dressing the skin, most likely.

"It is a beautiful craft, bookbinding, but one that is likely to become less and less in demand in our mechanical age," commented Charlotte.

"That it is a beautiful craft is enough reason to learn. Mr. Rosenblatt wasn't always a bookbinder, and I need not always be one," said Mumble without looking up. "Do you have more questions about Mr. Underwood, Mr. Herrinmore?"

"I do."

Mumble continued his work, sizing the vellum in gentle yet swift strokes. "I hope you won't mind, but I am not convinced that you are who you say you are. Or perhaps I should say, I have never believed that a rich man from Manchester is interested in Jessie and myself as boxers."

Charlotte smiled slightly. Excellent timing—she was about to drop that façade, too. "Highly astute of you, Mr. Waters. You are correct that Mr. Nelson is no Manchester man of business but a friend who was kind enough to lend his help to my investigation."

She handed him a calling card for E. E. Herrinmore, private investigator.

Mumble set down his brush, wiped his hands on a rag, took the card from Charlotte, and studied it. "A private investigator. Like Sherlock Holmes?"

Charlotte did not bat an eyelash. "I wouldn't presume to compare myself to the great consulting detective. But his work has created a certain demand that he cannot fulfill by himself, especially now that he is overseas for his health."

Mumble pocketed the card, picked up the frame of vellum, and examined it under a lamp. "What are you investigating, exactly, Mr. Herrinmore?"

"I've been tasked to find Mr. Underwood—or to discover what has befallen him, if he is no longer among the living—by someone who has known him for over thirty years and is deeply invested in his welfare."

Mumble, satisfied with the vellum, put it to dry on a rack that held several similar frames. Then he took another frame of vellum from the bottom of the rack and set it on the raised worktable. "I believe Mr. Mowlem at the Unicorn already told you that Mr. Underwood didn't mingle with the boxing crowd. If you're looking for clues to his disappearance, you're looking in the wrong place."

"Is that why you and Miss Ferguson are so interested in Mr. Underwood's dwellings? You suspect that he has been hiding at home?"

Mumble, about to set a long ruler against the top of this new sheet of vellum, stilled. "What do you mean, Mr. Herrinmore?"

"I visited the villa belonging to Mr. Underwood's mistress. It has sat unoccupied for some weeks but has been recently searched. The intruder—or intruders, most likely—left behind no hints to their identity inside the house, but in the garden, I found this."

"This" was a strand of reddish-brown hair that had been varnished and made into a small loop, the ends of the loop held together by silver fastener.

"It seems that an errant twig caught on some sort of head cover— a black knitted cap, I would venture, judging by the trace of yarn left behind on the twig. The tip of the twig further snagged on a piece of mourning jewelry underneath the cap. And in the ensuing struggle for the wearer of the cap to free everything, this insignificant loop of hair was left behind."

Charlotte held it up. "Imagine my surprise when I saw Miss Ferguson sporting an ornament made of small loops of hair just like this two nights ago, when I first laid eyes on her."

Mumble turned and looked directly at Charlotte. "Thank you for not saying anything at the time. Johnny isn't involved in this—nor does he have any need to be. Jessie and I were looking for Mr. Underwood, not he."

Charlotte inclined her head in acknowledgment of his expression of gratitude. "I believe that Mr. Esposito is not involved in your efforts. However, you and Miss Ferguson, you last saw Mr. Underwood in autumn. Your stipend ran out this April. Yet you sought him not last year, nor in April.

"You visited both his mistress's villa and his accountant's office toward the beginning of the week—and you were at his mistress's new place even more recently, if certain reports are to be believed. I'm curious as to why you've been so interested in Mr. Underwood of late."

The apprentice took a pencil, leveled the ruler with the top of the new sheet of vellum, and began to mark a row of equidistant dots. "I could ask the same of you, Mr. Herrinmore. The party that engaged you, the one who was so interested in Mr. Underwood's welfare, why did that person wait until now to act?"

"That person has been and remains in considerable difficulty. Communication between them had been sporadic for some time. It was only lately that Mr. Underwood's lady was able to convey the news that he was missing."

Mumble, now marking dots on the bottom of the vellum, glanced up, his gaze dark and unreadable. "And why did Mr. Underwood's lady wait so long to do that conveying?"

Sharp boy. "She claimed that although she hadn't seen him in six weeks, communications from him did not cease altogether until slightly less than three weeks ago. And he was, until then, most reliable at dispatching news of his well-being."

Charlotte took off the spectacles she wore for the role and polished them with her handkerchief. "That's my reason for not inquiring into his disappearance earlier. What about you? What has made you into an ardent housebreaker these last few days?"

Mumble began to connect the dots on the vellum, dividing it into thin segments. "Mr. Herrinmore, I am Roma. What makes you think I would admit to any charges that might get me dragged to the nearest police station to answer questions?"

His reaction was not unanticipated. "Let's find some less sensitive topics of discussion then. I was given the addresses to those two places in St. John's Wood. How do you know about them?"

"Maybe Mr. Underwood told me about them."

"Even the second one, which was acquired long after he disappeared from view?"

"Sponsors have mysterious ways."

He was neither nervous nor hostile but simply less than forthcoming—Charlotte suspected that he would have been even less cooperative had she not found that loop of hair from Jessie's ornament. She tried a different tack. "Have you ever seen his mistress?"

Mumble lifted the vellum and began cutting along the lines he had drawn. "I once saw a hackney stop in front of Johnny's place. The cabbie accepted a large basket from the passenger and carried it to Johnny's front door. By the time someone answered the door, the carriage was already driving away, but I happened to be standing near the window and saw a woman look out from the carriage."

"What did she look like?"

"Dark hair. Good-looking. In her thirties."

Charlotte nodded. "What are the vellum ribbons you're cutting for?"

"To use as lacing to strengthen a large book's spine."

"And were you and Miss Ferguson at or near Pettifer's Hotel yesterday afternoon?"

"We passed in front of it. The hotel recently began to acquire bread from the tea shop where Jessie works. Since we were already out and about, she wanted to show me the fancy place that is now serving bread she helped to bake."

"And afterwards, did you go back to either of the mistress's places again?"

"I shall not dignify that with an answer, Mr. Herrinmore."

"Very well, Mr. Waters." Charlotte set her spectacles back on her nose. "I'll leave you to your work and show myself out."

He rose. "I'll need to latch the door after you."

As he opened the front door to let her out, he said, "I still don't believe you, Mr. Herrinmore. You are not who you say you are. And I very much doubt that the one who sent you is in fact a friend of Mr. Underwood's."

Charlotte looked back. "That is an odd sentiment to express, Mr. Waters. Are *you* searching for Mr. Underwood as a friend?"

Mumble blinked.

Charlotte marched away.

———※———

At various points in the excavation process, the woman had been the kicker, the bagger, and the trammer. The kicker, lying on a plank slanted at a forty-five-degree angle, drove a kicking iron into the clay ahead with their feet; the bagger swept up the loosened material into bags; the trammer then placed the bags onto a cart that rode on wooden rails placed on the floor of the tunnel, and pushed the cart out until it reached a point where the displaced earth could be removed and disposed of.

Every single position entailed cramped and laborious work, all undertaken under complete silence, whenever possible. At the end of every shift, measurements were taken and retaken. Were they still on the predetermined path? Had there been any deviation? Success depended on absolute accuracy; anything less would see them emerge in the wrong place.

Wrong and deadly.

That hour of reckoning was drawing nigh. They had finished the slanting upward portion of the excavation and were now digging straight up.

Most of the digging had been done by the day crew—the din of a busy thoroughfare allowed them to advance faster, rougher. But now they worked at night, in the hope that their destination would be as empty as possible.

Her hands perspired inside her gloves. Her shoulders ached. And her neck felt like a stem that had been twisted this way and that once too often, barely able to hold up her head in this space that forced her to work at a contorted angle.

The candle near her feet flickered. She almost wished it would go out—that would force them to leave. But no, the candle burned on, its flame feeble yet steady.

She lifted her trowel. Dirt fell. The bagger swept everything up soundlessly. She took another breath. The candle must be lying. The air must be oxygen-deficient. Why else would she feel light-headed—surely not from fear alone?

In the silence, the noise of metal on stone was an explosion. She stilled. The bagger emitted a soft gasp.

So soon—too soon. She was not ready. But they had reached the very lowest level of the structure they had been aiming for.

It was as simple as that.

—⁂—

"My dear, do you remember a time when you broke into places—or attempted to, at least—and I merely stayed home and fretted?" whispered Mrs. Watson. "Now look at me."

It was almost exactly a year ago that Miss Charlotte performed her first feat of breaking and entering—which had gone none too well. Afterward she'd had to endure a lecture from Mrs. Watson concerning risks that one ought not to take.

Tonight, the two women had been lounging in the parlor of their hotel suite, having a cup of tea before bed, when Miss Charlotte had risen and ambled to the window. "A fog has rolled in."

Mrs. Watson sat up straighter. "And?"

"And I've been asking myself why Mumble and Jessie were so interested in Mrs. Claiborne's houses. At first I only wondered what they might know that we don't, and then it occurred to me—"

She turned around. "Ma'am, where do you suppose Mr. Underwood would be safest now, if he were still in London?"

Mrs. Watson stared at the girl a moment. "You mean, at one of Mrs. Claiborne's houses?"

"To be sure there could still be other parties looking for Mr. Underwood, but two seems about the right number. We represent Lord Bancroft, and Mumble and Jessie, possibly an enemy of his. And if both parties have already searched these houses from top to bottom—"

Mrs. Watson was on her feet. "Then the houses become, for the moment at least, ideal shelters for Mr. Underwood!"

"I was planning to test that hypothesis later, in a few days, but"— Miss Charlotte gestured toward the obscured street outside the window—"a fog has rolled in."

And there was no better time for breaking and entering than under a thick blanket of London fog.

So here they were. They had already been to the villa, where they'd found no trace of Mr. Underwood. This made Mrs. Watson more nervous about the town house. Since they still had the key for the villa, their entry had been technically legal. At the town house, however, Miss Charlotte had picked the locks to the mews and the back door.

Mrs. Watson's derringer was in her pocket. In her hand she clutched her favorite weighted umbrella, almost as slender as a walking stick. If Mr. Underwood wasn't at the villa, then there was a greater chance he was here instead.

They went through the entire house, from the attic to the basement. And the only thing Miss Charlotte could be sure hadn't been there earlier was a handful of advertisements and circulars that had been pushed through the mail slot on the front door.

"If Mumble and Jessie have been here, they have been very careful and disturbed nothing," said Miss Charlotte, her expression pensive.

Mrs. Watson was disappointed that they hadn't uncovered anything, but she was also, deep down, relieved. Mr. Underwood was a man who did not want to be found, and she was not confident they could have left the house unscathed if he had been on hand.

"But there is one place we haven't looked at yet," added Miss Charlotte.

That place was the coal cellar.

The town house, as was often the case, had a set of stairs beside the front door, leading down to the basement service entrance. The space was enclosed by a wrought iron fence. From the service door, the cellar was directly opposite on the other side of the enclosed space, its interior entirely under the street.

Fog swirled damply around Mrs. Watson's face. The vapors smelled of rotten eggs and standing water that had started to scum over. She waved a hand in front of herself and whispered, "But surely Mr. Underwood couldn't stay in *there*."

It was a dark, unfinished space with no ventilation. If Mr. Underwood was running for his life and had police dogs chasing after him, then perhaps the coal cellar might not be the worst place to hide until the coast cleared. But was he facing that kind of danger?

Miss Charlotte went to work on the padlock. But only a moment later, she straightened. "The lock is jammed. It looks as if a key was broken off inside."

Mrs. Watson's blood pulsed. "And that wasn't the case last night?"

"No. Last night Lord Ingram picked this lock in less time than it would have taken me to eat a biscuit."

"What do we do?"

"I suppose we could drop matches from the hatch on the pavement, but the hatch would not be easy to lift up."

Coal cellars under the street usually had an opening on top for replenishing coal, but the hole was blocked by a heavy metal cover that fitted exactly flush to the opening and exactly flush to the street, which was highly challenging to remove if one didn't already have access to the coal cellar underneath.

"Let's find Lawson," suggested Miss Charlotte.

Lawson had driven them to St. John's Wood and parked several streets away. They found him exactly where they had left him. Alas, he didn't have bolt cutters, but in the boot of the carriage he did have screwdrivers.

Back at the town house, Miss Charlotte set to work, loosening the hasp on the coal cellar door. It took some time, as the screws had rusted in place. But as soon as she had detached the hasp from the doorframe, the padlock became merely a decoration.

Mrs. Watson's heart thundered. Miss Charlotte had investigated a number of unnatural deaths. Yet somehow, in all this time, Mrs. Watson had never seen the remains of a victim, let alone discovered one.

And she did not want to. Incoherently, she prayed that the jammed lock had resulted from a simple lock-picking accident.

Miss Charlotte pulled open the door and shone her pocket lantern into the stygian interior.

"Do you see anything?" Mrs. Watson barely got the words out.

Miss Charlotte did not answer but struck a match and tossed it inside.

Mrs. Watson stopped breathing.

There, against the far wall of the largely empty coal cellar, lay a roll of carpet.

Mrs. Claiborne? Surely not! Mrs. Watson tried to remind herself that she didn't believe Mrs. Claiborne entirely, not even above half.

And yet . . .

Had the hapless girl been caught just when she was beginning to feel safe? But who wanted *her* dead?

Miss Charlotte stepped into the cellar, her footsteps gritty upon the few inches of coal remaining on the floor. Reflexively, Mrs. Watson followed, almost not feeling the chunks of fossil fuel poking into the soles of her shoes.

Maybe she was being far too morbid. Maybe there was no cadaver here at all, merely some loot that had been conveniently stashed away. Maybe—

The carpet had already unrolled somewhat in transit. Miss Charlotte pulled at the edge still caught under the weight of whatever it hid.

The edge did not budge. Miss Charlotte yanked again, again it did not budge.

Mrs. Watson bit the inside of her lip, set down the pocket lantern she held, and joined Miss Charlotte. They each took one side of the carpet edge and pulled.

The carpet edge gave and flapped back.

And Mrs. Watson was looking not at a lovely young woman, taken before her time, but a middle-aged man she'd never seen before, his eyes open, his lips slack, a look of sorrow and regret on his grey lifeless face.

In horror, she looked toward Miss Charlotte, who murmured, "I see we've found Mr. Underwood."

Seventeen

Chief Inspector Talbot was silent for some time. "Miss Holmes, I find your account questionable. It seems much more likely that you were coerced into cooperating with Lord Bancroft. What did he do? Did he, for example, threaten the safety of your sister Miss Bernadine Holmes?"

Treadles, who had been writing furiously to record the interview, nearly tore through the page with the steel nib of his fountain pen. He looked up at Miss Holmes. She had told him that she and Lord Ingram had anticipated problems. Was this the problem that they had anticipated? But if she had been prepared, how had the situation turned so unwieldy?

She got up and rang for a pitcher of lemonade. Then she sat down and adjusted her cuffs. Her sleeves were three-quarter length, the cuffs trimmed with large, dusky pink rosettes. "Chief Inspector, I may be a fallen woman in the eyes of the world, exiled to a scabrous wilderness, but I am not without friends. What makes you think that if my sister was in danger I couldn't have mounted a rescue?"

"So did you?" Talbot sounded genuinely curious.

Their hostess—and chief suspect—smiled slightly. "Has anyone ever told you, Chief Inspector, that after Lord Bancroft was confined to Ravensmere, Lord Ingram sent him wine and dessert on multiple occasions, knowing that his brother was a gourmet whose palate was tormented by the indifferent cuisine at that genteel prison?"

The digression caught Treadles by surprise; even Chief Inspector Talbot seemed unsure how to respond. His thumb traveled up and down along the handle of his teacup. "No, I have not been made aware of that."

"You can find out easily enough from the records at Ravensmere. If Lord Ingram can extend such grace to a brother who nearly caused him grievous harm, why should I not bestir myself a little when the same brother feared for his life?"

But had Lord Ingram been, in truth, offering grace to Lord Bancroft? To the recipient, the very desirable wine and dessert could have been a boon, a moment of joy in the dreariest stretch of his life. But it could also have been a taunt, the brevity of that intense sumptuousness a harsh light on the intolerable mediocrity of everything else he would have to choke down for months to come.

"You need not dig for more sinister reasons for my cooperation, Chief Inspector," continued Miss Holmes. "And if you must, you may attribute it to a woman's concern for her lover. The feelings between the Ashburton brothers are complicated, but I'm sure Lord Ingram would take solace in the fact that I tried to help Lord Bancroft, even if I wasn't successful."

Chief Inspector Talbot set down his teacup and tented his fingertips together. "Very well. So you agreed to aid Lord Bancroft. Please continue."

Treadles didn't know whether he ought to relax a little or brace himself for worse to come. He tried to concentrate on his note-taking.

"Lord Bancroft's greatest need was to reestablish contact with Mr. Underwood, his chief lieutenant. But Mr. Underwood, according to his mistress, was missing," said Miss Holmes. "Lord Bancroft told me that Mr. Underwood was a boxing aficionado, and that I might find his whereabouts if I spoke to those he knew in that context.

"And that was what I set out to do. I found the gymnasium where Mr. Underwood's boxers had trained. I spoke to the boxers. I spoke to the accountant via whom he paid the boxers. But their knowledge of him was strictly limited to the role he played in their lives. They didn't know his origins, his livelihood, or even his address—except for the accountant, I suppose, who was supplied with an outmoded one.

"In this regard, my efforts, though conscientious, amounted to an unqualified failure. I never saw hide or hair of Mr. Underwood, dead or alive."

"What about his mistress?"

Treadles's stomach twisted.

With an apologetic look in his direction, Miss Holmes said, "Mrs. Claiborne? Yes, we did find her."

Eighteen

Charlotte stood by the manor at Ravensmere, looking at the back wall of the garden. Elsewhere the garden wall was seven feet high, but behind the manor, its height rose to a solid eleven feet.

She turned around and studied the iron bars outside the windows. The bars were each half an inch thick, spaced three inches apart. Unlike prison bars, installed directly into the masonry of the window opening, here at least some thought had been given to appearance. At each window, the bars bowed out and formed a decorative grille that was bolted at its four corners into the exterior of the manor.

"What brought you here today, Miss Holmes?" came Lord Bancroft's voice.

He wore the same unfortunate orange-brown suit—or perhaps a different one cut in the exact same fashion—and he did not appear remotely pleased to see her.

But he did extend his arm, and after a moment she placed her gloved hand on his sleeve. They strolled around the periphery of the small side garden in which more privileged prisoners were allowed to take their daily exercise.

"I found Mr. Underwood and he is dead," she murmured, once the guards were far away enough.

Lord Bancroft's hand balled into a fist—so forcefully that the leather of his glove rasped. "How?"

"Shot in the back. I found him in the coal cellar of Mrs. Claiborne's new place. I would say that at the time he'd been dead less than twenty-four hours—a closer estimate is beyond my expertise."

"He was killed there?"

"I do not think so. We found no sign of a struggle and no indication that bloodstains and such had been wiped away."

Lord Bancroft was silent for some time. "No condolences?"

Charlotte glanced at her adversary. His skin was papery; thin blue veins showed at his temples. "Are you saddened by his passing, my lord, or only inconvenienced?"

His expression turned frosty. "My lieutenant is dead. I hope you have not come to gloat over my misfortune."

"I have come because I have completed my assignment: I have found Mr. Underwood. It is time you removed your mercenaries from Mrs. Watson's house in Paris."

Lord Bancroft stared straight ahead. "Your task was to find him, if he was alive, and if he was no more, to find out what happened to him. I need to know who killed him and why—and then we will discuss the situation in Paris."

Charlotte looked up—but from under her parasol, there was no sky. "You do not wish for the police to handle the matter?"

"No."

"What about his body then?"

"If you've seen all you need, then you need no longer concern yourself with it."

Unlike Mrs. Watson, Charlotte had not repeatedly expressed her gladness that she had refused to marry Lord Bancroft. But she was. Oh, how she was.

She inclined her head. "I take my leave of you, my lord."

"How do I know that you did not, in fact, kill Mr. Underwood?" He spat out the question as she turned away.

She glanced over her shoulder. "How do I know *you* did not have him killed, my lord?"

Lord Bancroft's jaw worked. "So I was in a position to get rid of one of the very few people I trusted?"

"And I am in a position to deliberately prolong my sister's tenure as your hostage? If you don't have other instructions, my lord, I will be on my way."

———◆———

Mrs. Watson kept rearranging the display on the mantelpiece. The figurine, the glass box, the vase with the peacock feather—she went on changing their order, left to right, right to center, switching the two on the outside, then switching them back again.

The memory of Mr. Underwood's pale, lifeless face against the dark blue pile of the carpet beneath him, the smell of coal dust and the beginning of putrefaction, the trembling in her arms as she and Miss Charlotte pushed him over, so that the girl could get a good look at where he had been shot.

He had been running away was all that Mrs. Watson had been able to think. Then and now. *He had been running away.*

From whom? And how safe were any of them, just when they believed themselves meticulously careful and properly safeguarded?

At the sound of a key turning in the street entrance, she rushed into the vestibule to embrace Miss Charlotte.

When she let go, the young woman, uncharacteristically enough, took her arm as they walked into the parlor together. "Are you all right, ma'am?"

Mrs. Watson exhaled. "Not entirely, I'm afraid. But I shall be better once we're out of this pickle. Once we're safer."

Miss Charlotte did not say anything, but unpinned her plain toque from her head.

Mrs. Watson knew then her trip to Ravensmere had not yielded any hoped-for results. Not that she'd hoped for anything, really, but still, Mrs. Watson's ire rose. "He won't do the honorable thing, will he? The bastard!"

This was strong language for Mrs. Watson. Strong language for anyone.

Miss Charlotte did not bother to pass judgment. "I might need to talk to Mumble and Jessie again. And it would be good if Mrs. Claiborne surfaced. How did your inquiries go, ma'am?"

"The villa is indeed under Mrs. Claiborne's name. But interestingly enough, it was never in Lord Bancroft's name. Before the deed changed hands three years ago, it was owned by an old widow who left it to a charity in her will. The charity sold it after her passing. There is no record on who leased it from the old widow earlier, so there is nothing to trace the house to Lord Bancroft."

More indication that Lord Bancroft had known even then that if anyone scrutinized his finances, it would become apparent that he had too much income.

"As for the town house in which Mrs. Claiborne received us, it is leased to a Mr. Overhill, of course. Three months of rent paid ahead of time."

Miss Charlotte took off her wig and dug her fingertips into her scalp.

"It does make sense, not to use either her own or Mr. Underwood's name on the lease," continued Mrs. Watson, "if they wanted to keep her new location hush-hush. And it also makes sense, I suppose, that Lord Bancroft kept his name out of any documents to do with the villa, if he didn't want the crown to notice the extent of his personal assets."

With Lord Ingram's hamper of foodstuff on a diplomatic tour in Paris—perhaps having already perished in the line of duty—Mrs. Watson had acquired a few tins of biscuits. Miss Charlotte opened a tin on the sideboard and took one out.

But she only held it. The sight made Mrs. Watson uneasy. She was much more accustomed to the girl eating and thinking at the same time, not staring through a perfectly good disk of butter, sugar, and flour.

"Do you think we can find Mrs. Claiborne, given that we know she stopped to post a letter in Sittingbourne?" she asked.

They had mounted a similar search in Cornwall earlier this year. Well, perhaps not entirely similar, but they had prowled a number of railway stations up and down a branch line and eventually found a carriage they had been looking for. Except this time they weren't looking for a carriage, liable to be parked for hours, even days, in the same place. But a person—a person in hiding, no less.

Miss Charlotte shook her head. Her face, reflected in the mirror above the sideboard, was grave, almost grim. "I'm not sure we should pursue Mrs. Claiborne's whereabouts. We know now that Mr. Underwood was in real danger, and it behooves us to think twice before running the risk of bringing those who might wish to harm Mrs. Claiborne to her doorstep."

A year ago, when Miss Charlotte had been new to both detection and the greater dangers of the world, she had inadvertently brought a tail to her half brother's doorstep.

Mrs. Watson immediately nodded in accord and regretted that she'd made the suggestion without thinking the matter through.

"But that isn't the only reason I am unlikely to search for her," said Miss Charlotte's reflection in the mirror. "She could have had something to do with Mr. Underwood's death."

Mrs. Watson, who had just opened a biscuit tin herself, snapped the lid shut again. She was still not accustomed to think of a pretty, seemingly helpless woman as a perpetrator. "Right," she mumbled. "There's that also."

"And—" Miss Charlotte began, but she was interrupted by someone at the street entrance.

The lively knocks were followed by a woman's happy voice. "Mrs. Beaumont, are you home? It's Miss Harcourt!"

———❊———

It took Mrs. Watson a moment to remember Miss Harcourt. The Christmas Eve Murder. The victim's niece.

"Shall we pretend that no one is home?" whispered Mrs. Watson to Miss Charlotte.

The latter glanced at the clock. "We can receive her, but I'll need to change my clothes and hair to look older."

The Mrs. Beaumont who had visited Miss Harcourt in Oxfordshire had been a woman in her mid-thirties, her age set to be a few years younger than Mrs. Meadows's so that Miss Charlotte, who had learned a great deal from Mrs. Watson, could embody her without resorting to heavy makeup or prosthetics.

"All right," said Mrs. Watson. "I'll let her in and tell her you'll be back soon."

Miss Harcourt, instead of feeling disappointed that Mrs. Beaumont hadn't come back yet, was delighted to be admitted. "It's much too forward for me to call without prior notice, but I happened to be due in London anyway, and I really wished to see Mrs. Beaumont!"

Mrs. Watson, having in short order taken on the identity of Mrs. Beaumont's companion, rang for tea and explained that she'd have traveled with Mrs. Beaumont to Miss Harcourt's estate the other day had Mrs. Beaumont not given her leave to visit some elderly relatives.

After a while, their topic turned to Mrs. Meadows, the vanished widow who had long fascinated the Harcourt women.

Mrs. Watson decided she might as well give in to her nosiness. "Thanks to Mrs. Beaumont, I have now become highly intrigued by Mrs. Meadows. Mrs. Beaumont has fretted over whether her friend was satisfied with her marriage—whether she loved her husband. But do you think, Miss Harcourt, that Mr. Victor Meadows loved his wife?"

Miss Harcourt's countenance lost some of its native cheer. She glanced in the direction of the street entrance and said quickly, "Because of Mrs. Beaumont's recent visit, I went into the box of diaries my mother had left behind and found something I didn't know existed—a notebook in which she kept a record of everything having to do with the murder."

"Oh my," murmured Mrs. Watson.

"She was most knowledgeable about the murder, my mother," said

Miss Harcourt. "In fact, she used to wonder why the police inspector didn't investigate her more thoroughly, as she was the only one who benefited from it.

"But I digress. The final entry in the notebook came five years after the murder, when my mother was getting ready to sell the factories she'd inherited from my uncle Victor. She had to spend a great deal of time sorting through years of paperwork related to the business and, in that effort, came across evidence that my uncle Victor might have been in part responsible for Mrs. Meadows's father's bankruptcy."

Mrs. Watson covered the lower half of her face with both hands. The possibility had occurred to her and to Miss Charlotte, but it would have been staggering to Mrs. Beaumont's companion.

"I was appalled," continued Miss Harcourt, her voice tight. "But the evidence was inconclusive, and I really shouldn't have said anything—in fact, I mean to keep it from Mrs. Beaumont. She adored Mrs. Meadows."

"Oh, my dear, but you adored her, too."

"I know." Miss Harcourt gripped her hands together. "Which is why I'm desperately hoping for that not to have been true but only another theory born of my mother's fertile imagination."

Mrs. Watson removed her hands from her face only to gasp aloud. "But—but wouldn't that undermine the premise that Mrs. Meadows had no reason to kill her husband?"

"That was my first thought, too, but my mother wrote that she didn't believe Mrs. Meadows would have known it. After all, my uncle Victor had no reason to ever tell her, if he'd indeed committed such an insidious act."

"Oh, that poor woman."

"I know," said Miss Harcourt quietly. "She deserved better. She deserved so much better."

Mrs. Watson didn't say anything—it always saddened her when women had scant control over their lives. Gradually the silence turned heavier.

The sound came of a key being inserted into the street entrance.

"Oh, that must be Mrs. Beaumont," cried Mrs. Watson in relief.

Miss Harcourt shot her a beseeching look. Mrs. Watson nodded—were this real life, she absolutely would have kept the worst news from Mrs. Beaumont.

But the older, rounder version of Miss Charlotte who walked in needed no such protection. "Why, Miss Harcourt," she exclaimed. "What a wonderful surprise!"

Miss Harcourt leaped up. "I did want it to be a surprise for you, Mrs. Beaumont. Guess what? I found the photograph!"

Miss Charlotte hopped in place. "May I see it? May I?"

Miss Harcourt extracted an envelope from her handbag and tilted it. A photograph slid into her palm. She studied it for a moment. "Pictures can be such lifeless things, everybody all stiff and clench-jawed. But not this one—it captured the essence of my aunt Meadows. Not just her beauty but her strength of will."

She chuckled, a sound at once amused and nostalgic. "Enough strength of will to keep my mother at bay. Believe me, no one else was ever able to resist her offers of friendship."

Miss Charlotte, in her guise as Mrs. Beaumont, eagerly accepted the photograph. Mrs. Watson looked down into her tea. The romantic in her still hadn't given up and was spinning ever battier possibilities. Perhaps Victor Meadows had been awful but Ephraim Meadows only pretended to be? Perhaps he and Mrs. Meadows had indeed eloped and found happiness together somewhere far away.

"How beautiful she had become," murmured Miss Charlotte. "Would you like to see my friend and her sister, Miss Wicks?"

Mrs. Watson, still caught in her own reveries of a good life for Mrs. Meadows, almost didn't recognize the name she and Miss Charlotte had decided for her twenty minutes ago. "Oh, yes, of course."

The image had been taken in an ordinary parlor. Everything was tinted reddish-brown. It was hard to tell the colors of wallpaper and upholstery; they could have been blue and white or green and yellow. But the woman in the image seemed to be covered in black crepe, even though, according to Miss Harcourt, enough time had passed that she no longer needed to wear full mourning.

She was beautiful indeed, sitting at an angle to the camera, looking not at it but straight ahead. Her three-quarter profile could have served as that of Diana the huntress's—her beauty was not delicate or seductive but cool and angular, meant to be captured in marble.

Mrs. Watson goggled. And then she goggled at the girl beside Mrs. Meadows. Unlike her sister's carven stillness, Miriam looked as if she were on the verge of jumping up from the settee to twirl in the center of the parlor, a girl full of irrepressible verve and energy.

"I also found a photograph from her wedding, of the entire wedding party," said Miss Harcourt.

She handed over another photograph and helpfully pointed out the unsmiling bridegroom, his fleshy, beady-eyed brother, and her own very handsome parents. Mrs. Meadows looked so impossibly young, and Miriam, held by a seven-year-old Miss Harcourt, a dumpling of a toddler.

Miss Charlotte looked again at the photograph of just the sisters, taken ten years later. "I do wonder," she said wistfully, "what has become of them."

Mrs. Watson stared down at her hands, for fear that the shock and grief on her face would otherwise be all too evident.

She recognized both sisters. Miriam was now dead, murdered in her prime, and Mrs. Meadows was no longer beautiful, her face ruined by life.

"I keep imagining running into my aunt Meadows somewhere," said Miss Harcourt equally wistfully. "I wonder whether she'll recognize me. I know I'll recognize her."

Oh, you would not, thought Mrs. Watson. *You would not.*

Mrs. Watson displayed her usual quick recovery. She praised Mrs. Meadows's beauty *and* the late Mrs. Harcourt's skill as a photographer. And then, in that discreet manner of ladies' companions, she mentioned an upcoming appointment.

Miss Harcourt got the point and started to take her leave. Charlotte, as Mrs. Beaumont, bemoaned the fact that rendezvous with solicitors had been the bane of her existence of late. But what could she do when there was her aunt's estate to be disposed of?

As the door closed behind Miss Harcourt, Mrs. Watson spun around, her hand clutched around her throat. "I have *always* wondered about that woman."

For eight Seasons, Charlotte had been simply another eligible young lady on the London Marriage Mart, albeit one with a reputation for eccentricity.

Unbeknownst to most people, she had been waiting for the arrival of her twenty-fifth birthday. Her father, Sir Henry, had promised her that should she turn twenty-five and still prefer to become the headmistress of a girls' school rather than a gentleman's wife, he would sponsor the education and training necessary for her to embark on that path to independence.

But Sir Henry had reneged on his word. And Charlotte, in an attempt to retain some control over her destiny, had made an unfortunate error in judgment that had resulted in her expulsion from Society.

Before her parents could escort her back to the country, there to lock her up for the rest of her life, she ran away from home. Life was not friendly to a young woman with no particular skills and very little money, but her worst moment had come at the hands of a mother-and-daughter pair of beggars.

The mother, blinded in one eye, an empty husk of a woman, had evoked in Charlotte such a stab of compassion that she'd given her child a sixpenny bit *and* her luncheon. Only to later realize that the child beggar had stolen the one-pound note Charlotte had stowed in a hidden pocket, reducing her already-meager reserves by a whopping 40 percent.

The incident had so shaken Charlotte that she had experienced an uncharacteristic surge of panic when she had come across the woman again a few months later.

But by then, she had been doing well as Sherlock Holmes, consulting detective. And the woman, going by the name of Mrs. Winnie Farr, had been desperately seeking to find her sister.

At the time, Lord Ingram had been the lead suspect in the death of his wife. Charlotte, investigating the case on his behalf, discovered that Lord Bancroft had attempted to frame him, using a body that bore a certain resemblance to Lady Ingram's.

And the body had belonged to Mimi Duffin, Mrs. Farr's sister, who had been of a similar height and build to Lady Ingram, with brunette hair and a very similar beauty mark by the corner of her lips. But because her face had otherwise looked nothing like Lady Ingram's, her head had been bashed in, her features rendered unrecognizable except for the crucial mole.

Charlotte, as Sherrinford Holmes, had traveled with Mrs. Farr to identify the body. Mrs. Farr had barely spoken that entire day. Her face, a face that should have been immortalized on a coin, had seemed to be made of wood instead, wood that could only withstand so much wind and storm before cracking and crumbling altogether.

And that devastated, street-roughened woman had once been the genteel and beautiful Mrs. Meadows. Throughout the tumultuous changes in her life, the only constant had been the sister she had raised. Yet that sister she had kept safe all these years had met a violent end just so Lord Bancroft could mount his pernicious stratagems.

"Well, now we've found our vanished Mrs. Meadows." Mrs. Watson paced back and forth, fanning herself vigorously. The painted lovers on her blue silk fan flirted on in a blur of powdered wigs and beribboned pannier dress. "I hate to say this, but that woman is certainly capable of killing a man who had wronged her."

"We have *not* found our vanished Mrs. Meadows," replied Charlotte slowly. "She wrote to Sherlock Holmes from a poste restante address."

A poste restante address was not a residential address but the location of a post office where letters were held and called for.

Mrs. Watson massaged her forehead. "You'd think I'd remember—I was the one who wrote back to her."

"But she also took her worries about her sister to Scotland Yard. There she spoke to our friend Sergeant MacDonald. Perhaps he would have a better address for us."

Mrs. Watson stopped moving; even the lovers on her fan seemed to have pulled apart. "My goodness, what if you run into Inspector Treadles at the Yard and he asks you whether you've made any progress on the case he gave you to investigate?"

"I will tell him the truth: that Mrs. Meadows is the same Mrs. Farr who tried and failed to obtain help from the police concerning her missing sister."

"But what will happen to Mrs. Farr?"

"There is no more evidence against her now than there was fifteen years ago. A woman whose husband died an unnatural death is perfectly at liberty to move to London and become poorer."

Mrs. Watson snapped her fan shut. "Very well, then. Let me locate the letters that we received from her."

The dear lady kept excellent records of all the correspondence Sherlock Holmes had ever received in her house near Regent's Park.

They were putting on their hats and reaching for their parasols when Mrs. Watson suddenly gripped Charlotte by the arm. "I forgot to tell you this, my dear. When Miss Harcourt and I spoke, she said that there was a chance Victor Meadows had deliberately bankrupted Mrs. Meadows's family so that she would have no choice but to marry him.

"Lord Bancroft and Mr. Underwood were responsible for Mimi Duffin's death, were they not? If the woman Mrs. Farr had once been killed her husband for his nonlethal treachery, what are the chances that she hasn't been seeking, all this while, to avenge her sister's murder?"

Wordlessly Charlotte pulled on her gloves. With the photograph Mrs. Harcourt had taken all those years ago, had they, in fact, discovered the identity of Mr. Underwood's killer?

Mrs. Farr, Mrs. Meadows—Charlotte still had trouble thinking of the two as the same person. The Christmas Eve Murder had seemed so remote in both time and effect, a purely intellectual exercise.

No longer. Now everything could hinge upon it.

Nineteen

Mimi Duffin, the Cousin Miriam whom the Harcourt ladies had once pampered with presents, had been a postcard girl at the time of her death: She'd posed in various stages of undress, and her images had been printed on postcards and disseminated as pornography.

Scotland Yard, therefore, had not taken her disappearance seriously. An anxious Mrs. Farr had visited repeatedly. Those visits had not led to an investigation but left multiple forms filled out and filed away.

The always helpful Sergeant MacDonald, after a quick search, produced two addresses for Charlotte. The first led her to a chemist's in Lambeth, south of the river, where her inquiries about Mrs. Farr were met with a blank stare by the young clerk manning the counter. The second was Mimi Duffin's lodging house in Bermondsey, farther to the east, an even shabbier district than the already-hardscrabble Lambeth.

To reach the address, Charlotte's hansom cab drove past streets characterized not so much by crime and vice, or even poverty, but by listlessness: fruits wilting on the carts of the few mongers still on the pavement, maids fanning themselves on the front steps of little draper shops, pubs and taverns open and occupied but their mirrors dim, their patrons as silent and joyless as mourners at a funeral.

At the lodging house, every effort had been made to keep the place clean and cheerful. But windows had to be open in summer, and the breeze brought in an unmistakable whiff of a tannery not too far away, and perhaps even of remnants of horses being boiled down for glue.

Charlotte, calling on the landlady, pretended to be Mimi Duffin's long-lost friend and acted appropriately shocked and grieved when she was told that Mimi Duffin had passed away the year before.

Mrs. Earp, the landlady who apparently knew nothing about Mimi Duffin's scandalous occupation, was obliging. But as Mimi Duffin had lived there for scant weeks before she died, Mrs. Earp could offer Charlotte nothing of note except her previous address.

Which led Charlotte back to Lambeth, near Lambeth Palace, the seat of the Archbishop of Canterbury. From the window of *this* landlady's parlor, one could glimpse not only the gardens of Lambeth Palace but the Palace of Westminster across the river, a mere quarter mile away.

It was a superior place, not only to Mrs. Earp's humble, if diligently maintained, abode in Bermondsey but also to the boarding-house Charlotte had stayed at for a while, in a lesser part of Lambeth, before Mrs. Watson had taken her in.

However, Mrs. Osborne, the superior place's very superior land-lady, was not pleased to field inquiries about Mimi Duffin. "Yes, she lived here for three years. And true, she paid her rent on time, got on well with my other guests, and made no trouble. But I cannot help but feel grievously injured that while she lived under my roof, she conducted herself in an extremely regrettable manner. Miss Duffin, I'm sorry to say, was no lady at all."

Mrs. Farr, too, did not escape her wrath.

"Well, Mrs. Beaumont, I don't know why you'd want to know about her sister. I am not saying Mrs. Farr did anything as appalling as Miss Duffin, but she brooked no criticism of her dreadful sister, when she ought to have been horrified and outraged. I cannot help but think that she gave her tacit approval, and I cannot countenance that at all."

Mrs. Osborne went on, but besides her indignation, Charlotte could glean little else.

She did manage to get in a question, as she was taking her leave, about Mimi Duffin's final resting place.

"I wouldn't have any idea about that," huffed Mrs. Osborne. "Why would I?"

"Then do you mind very much if I inquired of some of your lodgers if they might know?" Charlotte put on her most beseeching look. "Perhaps from tomorrow on I'll endeavor to forget her, but she was kind to me when we were little and I'll find it hard to forgive myself if I leave England again without at least leaving a few flowers by her headstone. Please, Mrs. Osborne. She's already dead. She can't embarrass you or this very excellent establishment again. Please let me have that."

---　❊　---

Worn down by Charlotte's entreaties, Mrs. Osborne allowed Charlotte to speak to a lodger named Mrs. Lane. Mrs. Lane was perhaps a little younger than Charlotte, a widow who'd lost her husband before she turned twenty. She had worked as a pottery painter for the Doulton factory but was now an artistic designer for the company and sometimes did her sketching from home.

Unlike the cramped single room Charlotte had barely been able to afford when she'd been first cast out of Society and had to fend for herself on her own, Mrs. Lane's room was large enough to be partitioned into several areas with screens. On her ceiling and walls she had installed hooks and loops through which wound swaths of gauzy fabric in mint green and sky blue. The crisscrossing undulating yardage of tulle and voile reminded Charlotte of waves in a warm shallow sea.

And if Miss Harcourt had been happy to see Charlotte, then Mrs. Lane was thrilled.

"You knew Miss Duffin as a child? Oh, how wonderful that must have been for you. I miss her. I really do. She made everything lively and fun—and goodness knows that for women like us, who must labor for our own support and worry about rainy days to come, the days aren't always lively or fun.

"She was also a marvelous friend," Mrs. Lane gushed on. "When she came to tea in my room, she always brought things I loved but wouldn't have bought for myself. Oh, let me show you!"

She jumped up and brought back a novelty biscuit tin that looked like a penguin. "Is it not adorable?"

"It is extremely adorable," Charlotte concurred.

"I would have been more than satisfied with a friend who gave me gifts, but Mimi listened, too. I cannot tell you how dull my life is, Mrs. Beaumont. I work, and on Sundays I go to church—there is little else. And yet if I should fall ill, I could quickly deplete my savings and lose this monotonous stability that is the envy of so many others."

She caressed the penguin tin's printed-on beak. Tin and woman seemed to share an identical expression, that of melancholy leavened by a hint of hope.

"In front of most people, I only dare admit how fortunate I am to be able to support myself. But Mimi understood both how penned in I felt and how afraid I was of losing what little I'd achieved. And the strange thing was, after I griped to her about everything that was wrong with my life, I always ended up feeling much better. I'd notice how pretty my room was or how I only needed to save a few more pennies to afford a seaside holiday."

She set down the tin, went to the mantelpiece, and came back with a small framed photograph. "This was us, in Brighton. Mimi and I went together last summer. We ate ice cream, walked on the pier, and she told me that before she died, she meant to visit every continent on Earth."

The two young women, caught by the camera, looked solemn. But there was a spark in their eyes, and an energy to their posture.

Charlotte gave the photograph back to Mrs. Lane, who trailed a fingertip across the top edge of the frame. "When she talked about traveling around the world, not only did I believe that she would do it, I believed that I, too, might go with her, if only for a small portion.

"Maybe Mrs. Osborne was right; maybe Mimi did corrupt the world with her postcards. But in what little time I knew her, she made my life far more beautiful than it would have been otherwise."

Her eyes gleamed with tears. She turned to the side and wiped them away. "I'm sorry. You wanted to know about Mimi, and I've only talked about myself."

"I couldn't have asked for a better account of her life," said Charlotte truthfully. "To hear her remembered like this, and loved like this."

Mrs. Lane took out a handkerchief and dabbed some more at the corners of her eyes. Then she picked up the penguin tin, opened it, and showed Charlotte three paste hairpins inside.

Taking a butterfly-shaped hairpin in her hand, she turned it slowly. "These were also gifts from her—and I happened to be wearing this one the day I learned that she was about to be expelled from our lodging house. I didn't know anything about those postcards before then. Afterwards, I visited her once at her new place.

"Her sister was just leaving—that was the first time I met Mrs. Farr—and Mimi was in a mood. She railed against Mrs. Farr and said that she was too obdurate, and too antiquated in her opinions. She said she hated that Mrs. Farr would not leave her alone to lead her own life."

So Mrs. Farr berated her sister in private but refused to let her be berated by the Mrs. Osbornes of the world?

"And then she wept," continued Mrs. Lane. She now had a different hairpin in hand, this one studded with green paste jewels, resembling a leaf. "I was flabbergasted by her tears, but she sobbed that she was a terrible person for saying such things about someone who had not only sacrificed endlessly for her but was a literal angel, an angel who managed to bring up half a dozen street urchins and even adopted one of them.

"'I just don't know why we can't get along anymore,' she said to me. 'Everything I want to do is wrong in her eyes, and everything she does is controlling and interfering. We love each other so, but we can't be in the same room these days without getting into a huge quarrel. I'm exhausted just thinking about her. And I hate that.'"

Mrs. Lane fell silent—and carefully jabbed the sharp end of the leaf pin into the palm of her opposite hand, as if trying to gauge how much pressure she could apply before she caused pain to herself. And then, very gently, she placed the hairpin back in the penguin tin.

"I went to Mimi's funeral last year. I was devastated by her death, and I was only more devastated for Mrs. Farr. She didn't shed a single tear, but every time I looked at her, I would start crying again. Even now when I think back to that day, I can feel the force of her grief— and beneath that, the burn of her anger."

———— ❊ ————

Mrs. Lane accompanied Charlotte to a large cemetery, where Mimi Duffin was buried in a quiet corner. Charlotte placed a bouquet of roses on her simple grave, next to the handful of wildflowers already there.

On the headstone were engraved her name and the dates that spanned her all-too-brief life. Underneath those, the words *Gone, but not forgotten.*

And underneath that, *Vengeance is mine; I will repay.*

Mimi Duffin, in the full bloom of life, would not have bought herself a headstone. The words, then, represented not her own sentiments but those of Mrs. Farr: She would see to it that justice would be done.

Had she already succeeded? Was that why Mr. Underwood was dead?

In its consideration of Lord Bancroft's crimes, the crown had given barely a thought to Mimi Duffin's brutal murder, except to order Charlotte's silence on the matter. There was never any chance that he would stand trial for such a trivial crime. After all, the crown could not afford for his threats to be made good and the indiscretions of a certain royal exposed to the public.

Charlotte, on the day she had traveled with Mrs. Farr to identify Mimi Duffin's body, had to tell her that this limited success was all that Sherlock Holmes could deliver. That there was too little to go on for a full investigation into the identity of Mimi Duffin's killers.

In the face of Mrs. Farr's despair, it had taken every ounce of Charlotte's inborn talent for dissemblance to lie convincingly, not to give away the fact that she knew exactly who had killed Mimi Duffin and for exactly what despicable reason.

"I would like to call on Mimi's sister, if I could," she said. "I remember her from all those years ago. And even then she was extremely protective of Mimi. I don't know if she can bear yet another condolence call, but I feel I ought to do something. Send a note, at least."

Mrs. Lane set a fabric rosette on the gravestone. "I know what you mean. I accidentally ran into her one day, right here. We both came with flowers for Mimi. At the time she wasn't in the mood for prolonged conversation, but she was kind and told me that if I ever needed any help, I could send word to her via Kramer and Carnahan on Badger Lane."

And Kramer and Carnahan on Badger Lane happened to be the chemist's shop that Charlotte had visited earlier, where the clerk had known nothing about Mrs. Farr.

Twenty

Livia had thought that she wouldn't be able to get much out of Lieutenant Atwood, the man in charge of operations in Aix-en-Provence. To her surprise, he had been quite forthcoming and even invited her to visit their headquarters, situated almost directly across the street from the house belonging to Moriarty.

They were in a large drawing room that faced the Cours Mirabeau, its walls covered with academy-style paintings of peasant girls who somehow maintained spotless feet and milky complexions.

"Did you enjoy your outing, Miss Holmes?"

The day before, Livia had visited Mount Sainte-Victoire in order to appear more like a real tourist.

"I did—I always relish the outdoors. What about you, sir—have you had any chance to visit the surrounding countryside?"

Immediately she realized she'd asked a silly question. He couldn't possibly have had the time.

"Actually, I have," said Lieutenant Atwood, setting down his coffee. "We visited a quarry and bought some tools shortly after we arrived in Aix. The quarry was halfway to the Luberon and made for an agreeable excursion."

Quarry tools. Were they working with stones or—

"Surely—surely you're not digging a tunnel."

He smiled, white teeth against suntanned skin. "Of course not, Miss Holmes."

He seemed sincere, but she had no idea how to gauge his cordial denial.

"It's for storming Moriarty's house," he added, "if it came to that."

She had imagined an invasion with guns drawn, but not one that involved chisels and splitters.

Lieutenant Atwood smiled again and pointed at Moriarty's house across the Cours Mirabeau, bathed in afternoon light. "There is a window on one of the upper floors that remains lit longer than anyone else's."

The very one that she always glanced up at when she walked past the house.

"Recently the occupant of the room began to move the curtain at night in such a way that we can only interpret as sending messages via Morse code."

Livia's heart thumped. "What messages?"

"So far, it's always been the same message. *Be careful.*"

"That's it?"

"That's it. Repeated as many times as the number of pinecones I toss on the window."

Livia swallowed. "And will you be very careful?"

Lieutenant Atwood picked up a small olive oil cake, supposedly a specialty of the region, and said, "Rest assured. We're not planning to do anything dangerous at all."

Penelope stopped in her tracks.

What was that smell inside Aunt Jo's house? And what was going on in the *salle de séjour* to the side of the entry?

Fontainebleu, the young man who claimed to be the son of one of Aunt Jo's lovers, sprawled sideways in a padded chair. He was dressed in only his shirtsleeves, a lit cigar clamped between his teeth, a handful of cards held facedown on his chest. A glass of whisky and a mostly empty coffee cup sat on the table before him. Also on the table, a small gleaming pile of napoleons.

"Why, hullo," she said.

She hadn't seen him since the day he'd arrived like a speeding bullet and then ricocheted off just as abruptly. Not that he hadn't returned to the house periodically from his merrymaking. Once, when she asked, a mercenary said he was sleeping. And on a different occasion, she was told he was bathing.

"Why, hullo yourself," he said. "But shhhh, don't talk anymore, or my friend here will blame his loss on you."

He yawned and addressed the man across the small table from him. "*Patron*, are you playing cards or reading my fortune? Hurry up."

"One second," answered the leader of the mercenaries, whom Livia had termed Number One. He looked to be agonizing over his cards.

Fontainebleu yawned again. "It's been your turn for five minutes, and if you don't put down a card in the next ten seconds I am going to pull one from your hand."

Penelope glanced at Mercenary Number Two, the one who had opened the door for her. "Is Monsieur Fontainebleu a good card player?"

Number Two shook his head decisively. "He's terrible, but sometimes his luck is good. I won forty napoleons from him, but then lost everything, plus another fifteen napoleons."

All at once cards were being slapped down on the table one after another. And Number One cried in jubilation. "Yes, yes, thank God!"

"Did he win?"

"He recouped his losses," said Number Two, looking envious. "The next hand he might win."

But the opportunity was denied Number One. Fontainebleu stretched and tottered out of the chair. "Time for bed."

It was six o'clock in the afternoon.

"Will you play after you get up?" Number Two asked eagerly, as Fontainebleu staggered up the staircase.

"No, I'm going out tonight. It will be smashing fun." He turned around, leaning on the banister. "And you ought to be ashamed of yourselves. My aunt Watson hired you to look after her house in her absence, not for you to gamble with any riffraff that walks in from the street."

And with that, he resumed his ascent.

By the time Charlotte said good-bye to Mrs. Lane and scribbled a note to the chemist's shop—she might as well follow Mrs. Farr's instruction to Mrs. Lane and "send word"—the day was growing late, and the city had become congested.

Before her hackney turned onto the street where the Treadleses lived, she had already spotted the family carriage driving away. It took some spirited chasing and a great deal of shouting to attract the coachman's attention. Fortunately, the coachman recognized Charlotte: She had spoken to him on Sherlock Holmes's behalf the previous winter, when his master's fate had hung in the balance.

Inspector Treadles had already alit when Charlotte finally caught up. She swung herself up directly into his carriage. "I understand you have a train to catch, Inspector, and no time to lose?"

The alarmed policeman nevertheless followed her into the vehicle with alacrity.

As soon as the door closed, even before the carriage rejoined the tide of traffic, Charlotte said, "Concerning the case you gave me, Inspector, I have spoken to Miss Harcourt, Victor Meadows's niece. And she has found an old photograph of Mrs. Meadows for me. It so happens that we are both acquainted with her."

She handed over the photograph, which Miss Harcourt had said she could keep, as in happier days multiple prints had been made.

Inspector Treadles stared at the image, then at Charlotte. "Are you sure I know this—"

He looked down yet again. "My goodness, could it possibly be Mrs. Farr, the one who wanted the Yard to look into her sister's disappearance? And is that the sister beside her?"

"Correct on both accounts."

Inspector Treadles spent another minute scrutinizing the photograph, looking only more stunned. And then his expression grew sober. "I think back to my conduct at the time with much self-reproach. I'd told Mrs. Farr quite blithely that her sister must have disappeared on a lark, based on little more than my disinclination to believe a troublesome woman. But Mimi Duffin *was* killed—by a jealous lover, it was said, but I don't recall that anyone was ever charged for the crime."

Inspector Treadles, alongside Chief Inspector Fowler, had investigated the murder at Stern Hollow. Yet even he didn't know that Lord Bancroft had been the initial instigator of the crime, the one who had first put a female body in the estate's ice well to frame Lord Ingram.

He gave the photograph back to Charlotte, his brow furrowed. "What happened to the former Mrs. Meadows and her sister? They weren't extravagantly provided for, but there was enough of a dower, wasn't there?"

"Enough if one was willing to make some economies," said Charlotte. "But about two years after Victor Meadows's death, Mrs. Meadows and her sister disappeared from Manchester. According to Miss Harcourt, her mother, the late Mrs. Harcourt, found out from Victor Meadows's lawyers that Mrs. Meadows had married again and would no longer receive the dower."

"You think she married to her economic disadvantage this time around?"

"I was inclined to consider that likely, because Mrs. Farr has a child. But according to Mimi Duffin's friend, whom I met this afternoon, the child was adopted. In any case, Mrs. Watson should have already visited Somerset House this afternoon to check marriage records."

Inspector Treadles picked up the newspaper on the carriage seat next to him and tapped the rolled-up column against his palm. "After I learned about Mimi Duffin's death, I looked a little into Mrs. Farr. She is no ordinary woman. She isn't part of London's underworld, per se, but she exists on the edge of it. And she has a network of . . . scouts, let's say, who keep her supplied with valuable information."

Unfortunately, Mimi Duffin had known how to evade that network and had kept Lord Bancroft's identity a secret from her sister until it was too late.

"She has stayed far away from the gaze of the police by being muted about her work, and I've heard rumors that she developed that network by helping people in need, especially women and children," continued Inspector Treadles. "Still, any good senior barrister can make the case that she has the cunning and the mental fortitude to carry out a murder."

He shook his head. "Miss Holmes, perhaps it would be best if we pursued this case no further. I doubt that Mrs. Farr would wish her past revealed, and she might not appreciate being approached by someone with that dangerous knowledge."

"I agree," said Charlotte.

It would indeed be wiser if she stopped. But did she have a choice in the matter?

She looked outside the window. Until last year, she'd never spent an August in London—the end of July had always marked her family's migration to the seaside or the countryside. Mrs. Farr would have been about the same age as Charlotte when she'd abandoned the familiar rhythms of a Manchester woman of means for a very different life in the poorer districts of London.

Except she'd had a young sister to look after and no friends on a par with Lord Ingram and Mrs. Watson to cushion her fall.

Charlotte realized she had been quiet for some time. She had finished her report, but she and Inspector Treadles were not on such close terms that she could simply indulge herself in silence.

"Are you headed to a riveting case, Inspector?" she asked.

This was small talk for her, though he might not consider his case to be an idle topic.

"A baffling one, to be sure," answered the policeman. He did not sound reluctant to speak of his work. "A lone woman arrived in a small community and was killed almost right away."

A lone woman?

"Where is this small community, Inspector, if you don't mind my curiosity?"

Perhaps he heard the sudden interest in her voice, for he studied her, a little taken aback. "Near a village called Feynham, not far from the Swale."

That was only a little farther from Sittingbourne, where Mrs. Claiborne's last letter had been postmarked.

"Is there any chance that the case happened extremely recently, as in the woman only arrived in the area two nights ago?"

Inspector Treadles's brows leaped up. "Correct. She arrived in the area exactly two nights ago, took the house yesterday, and the body was discovered this morning."

"Did she tell anyone local that she was from somewhere *other* than London?"

Inspector Treadles leaned forward. "This can't be a matter of deduction. You have someone specific in mind, don't you, Miss Holmes?"

"I'm afraid I do. She is in her early thirties, beautiful, well-dressed, speaks with a slight French accent—and used a name that wasn't her own. Something along the lines of Mrs. Overhill?"

Inspector Treadles sucked in a breath.

Charlotte sighed. "Inspector, I'm afraid I shall have to go with you."

Twenty-one

M iss Holmes, of course, could not accompany Treadles as a
woman without darkening his reputation or hindering his investigation. Instead, she took the earliest train the next morning and
arrived as the rotund, bespectacled, and very professional-looking
Mr. Adams. Odd—Treadles had been under the impression that the
great detective and her associates typically used the name Hudson
when they wanted a casual alias. It was as if she didn't want anyone
to know that Sherlock Holmes was involved.

"I have engaged Mr. Adams to take photographs for the case,"
said Treadles to Sergeant Burr, the local police officer assigned to assist him.

His conscience prickled at the deception. But compared to the
violent internal struggle he'd experienced concerning her presence at
Stern Hollow, this was only a twinge.

The use of photography in police work being spotty and very
much at the individual investigator's discretion, the presence of a photographer greatly impressed Sergeant Burr. "A pictorial record of
crimes. At least she was beautiful, Mrs. Overhill. Imagine some poor
future bobby coming across a picture of old Mr. Tavis after he'd been
stabbed seven times. Or the sight of Squire Gibbons's favorite greyhound skinned and strung up on his front gate."

Treadles occasionally imagined retiring to the country someday. The skinned greyhound gave him pause.

Miss Holmes, in her guise, questioned Sergeant Burr eagerly about the poor dog and the just as brutally done-in Mr. Tavis, details of which the sergeant was more than happy to provide as they drove to the scene of the murder.

"But in those cases, gruesome as they were, there was hardly any mystery," said Sergeant Burr. "We knew the culprits, and we knew the causes. Mrs. Overhill's case makes me scratch my head."

"I understand she spent a night at the railway inn in Sitting-bourne?" asked Treadles.

He glanced at Miss Holmes. She had said only that she happened to be in the midst of another inquiry and the victim's description matched that of a witness known to have left London under less-than-ideal circumstances. He hadn't asked for more information beyond that—he had received the impression that a fuller picture would not have been forthcoming.

What was she investigating? And was it related to the trouble she and Lord Ingram had expected?

"That's right," answered Sergeant Burr. "At the inn in Sitting-bourne Mrs. Overhill saw the house being advertised. She visited the place the next day, and liked it enough that she paid for two weeks and took the key right away.

"Mrs. Staples, the caretaker's wife, was instructed not to enter the house to clean except every three days. It was only because provisions Mrs. Overhill had ordered were delivered to the caretaker's cottage that she decided to go over to the house. When no one answered her knocks, she let herself in. That was how she found Mrs. Overhill dead."

Miss Holmes nodded gravely and made all the appropriate noises of sorrow and dismay.

They were driving through some rather featureless countryside, but even featureless countryside was fresh, green countryside. Due to Kent's relative proximity to London, the land was becoming more and more desirable as residential plots.

The scene of the murder was a former farmhouse bought by town dwellers and remade as a rustic villa. It was hired out most of the year, with the owners descending only at Christmas and Easter, according to the sergeant.

They looked around the grounds first and found little of note, besides a largeish fishpond that had acquired a landscaped border in the renovation. The sergeant then unlocked the front door and ushered them inside.

The inside of the villa was decorated like a hunting lodge, with wood-paneled walls, stuffed animal heads, and even a few hunting horns set on stands. The air smelled of floor polish, which must have been applied liberally when the previous guests had left.

Their footsteps echoed on the floor as they marched toward the back of the house, where the parlor was located. Presumably the parlor gave onto the pond, but all the windows were shuttered, all the curtains drawn. The sergeant lit two lanterns; their light shone on leather-upholstered sofas and tapestries that depicted medieval woodlands.

"I read in a circular from Scotland Yard that we ought to leave crime scenes as undisturbed as possible until expert detectives arrive. I tried to do exactly that," said the sergeant. "'Course we've had to move the body, but other than that, Inspector, I haven't touched a thing. Mrs. Staples said she also didn't touch anything—not in here, at least. But it's a shame about the rug."

A large zebra-skin rug near the center of the parlor was now grotesquely bloodstained.

"Mrs. Overhill lay facedown on the rug, shot three times in the back," said the sergeant, rather reluctantly.

"Shot in the back," mused Inspector Treadles. "Does that mean she was headed to the sideboard to fetch some whisky?"

The sergeant looked thunderstruck. "Is that possible? I thought that she was fleeing her attacker."

"That is, of course, also a possibility."

The sergeant scratched his beard. "Then again, there were no signs of forced entry on either the front or the back door. 'Course the assailant could have turned threatening after he was admitted to the house . . . No, then she would have been running out of the parlor, wouldn't she, rather than toward the wall?"

He looked back at Inspector Treadles. "So she turned away to fetch some whisky. Does that mean the murderer was sitting right there in that chair? I can't believe it. She let this person in, offered hospitality, and was killed for her trouble."

"It happens more often than I would like to acknowledge," said Treadles, "people murdered by those they trust."

Sergeant Burr grimaced. "And she let him in at night, too. When I got here, the candles were all burned down to stubs because no one had snuffed them out.

"Yes, it must have been at night." The sergeant nodded to himself. "Otherwise, three shots—the caretakers should have heard those. But that night, after the Stapleses made sure that indeed she wanted neither cooking nor attendance, they took themselves to visit their daughter in the next village."

"Did anyone come through the area during that time?" asked Treadles.

"I inquired as soon as I left here yesterday, Inspector. Neither the ticket agent, the station master, nor the shopkeepers on the high street could recall seeing any new faces in the last few days.

"And there's another odd thing. She had only one small valise and no other luggage, according to the estate agent. But we can't even find that. I can only assume the murderer took it. Earlier, when I thought she was shot in the back because she was fleeing, I could have theorized that this was a robbery gone wrong. But if she was going to offer the murderer a glass of whisky, then I'm at a loss as to why he also robbed her."

Treadles looked toward Charlotte Holmes. She had one arm across her chest—on her false paunch, in truth; her chin rested against the knuckles of her other hand.

"Let me take a look at the curtains and the windows," Treadles suggested. "And then we can let in some light and Mr. Adams can take photographs."

"Mr. Adams" wasted no time setting up the camera. She pulled the shutter, then expertly swapped in a new plate and recorded another image.

"Very advanced policework, this is," said the sergeant, full of admiration.

"And if in this country we ever take up photographing inmates, as they now do in France, I'd never run out of work," said Mr. Adams cheerfully.

———※———

They toured the rest of the house, spoke to the caretakers, who could tell them little, and then traveled to the constabulary to view the body.

Mr. Adams winced as soon as "he" saw the victim. "What a pity."

Treadles had noticed that when playing characters, Miss Holmes was far more expressive. In person, not a single muscle on her face would have moved.

"Yes, a pity indeed," he echoed.

But neither the victim's unpeaceful expression nor the three bullet holes in her back told them anything about why she had been killed— that is, they did not greatly increase Treadles's knowledge. What Miss Holmes gleaned, she kept to herself.

She took more pictures, then Sergeant Burr presented the scant items the victim left behind. Treadles opened a golden locket. Only one side of the locket held a picture, an image of a shy but happy-looking Mrs. Claiborne, captured some years ago.

Miss Holmes caught Treadles's attention, pointed at the locket, and then pointed to herself.

Before he could ask why, Sergeant Burr handed him a mono-grammed handkerchief. "We call her Mrs. Overhill because that's the name she gave to the estate agent. But her initials say *MGC*. And look here, Inspector."

He brought them the dress that the victim had been wearing when she'd been shot. At the hem was sewn a small label that read *Claiborne, 2 Prince's Grove Close.*

It was not uncommon for a household that sent out its washing to attach such labels to the clothes, so that the laundress would know which garments belonged to which client.

"Would this be an Exeter address? She told the estate agent she was from Exeter."

Treadles might not know every street in London, but he knew that there was a Prince's Grove Close in St. John's Wood.

"We will find out," he said. "Now, Sergeant, before you pack everything away, I should like to send the locket with Mr. Adams back to Scotland Yard. The photograph inside might help in finding out the victim's true identity."

"Certainly, Inspector. Anything to advance the investigation."

Sergeant Burr placed the locket in an envelope, asked Treadles to sign a register for the loan of the item, and then gave the envelope to Miss Holmes.

"Thank you, Sergeant," she said. "And thank you, Inspector, for the trust you have placed in me. Now may I have a word with you before I leave?"

Treadles thought she would impart some wisdom concerning the murder at hand, but she said only, when they were out of the hearing range of others, "I would recommend that you take your time with this case, Inspector, and not return to London too soon."

Twenty-two

THE INTERROGATION

M rs. Claiborne? Yes, we did find her," said Miss Charlotte
Holmes, "thanks to Inspector Treadles."

His own name sounded like a cannon shot in Treadles's ear. A
spate of cannon shots.

"I met with Mrs. Claiborne once and then couldn't locate her
again," continued Miss Holmes. "Since her protector, Mr. Underwood, was missing, it made sense to check with the police about her.
So I asked Inspector Treadles whether he had come across any cases
with victims that matched her description.

"It so happened that at that moment Inspector Treadles was on
his way to the railway station to investigate a murder near a village
called Feynham, outside Sittingbourne. He had read the summary
sent in by the local constabulary and knew that though the victim
called herself Mrs. Overhill, the laundry tag on her dress named her
as a Claiborne."

Treadles tried not to breathe too audibly, when he wanted to collapse to the floor, clutching at his chest in relief. Thank goodness he
had confessed the matter as soon as he'd met with Chief Inspector
Talbot today.

Still, the retired officer's glance in his direction felt like a shower of needles. "When was that, Inspector?" asked the chief inspector, when he knew the answer very well.

"Four days ago, sir," answered Treadles. Did his voice squeak?

Three days ago, after they'd inspected Mrs. Claiborne's body, Miss Holmes had advised him to remain longer in Kent, if he could. She had given no reason, but he had taken her counsel to heart and dragged out the investigation.

The dredging of the fishpond he had ordered yesterday had produced Mrs. Claiborne's valise, much to the admiration of the local constables. Even if that discovery put him no closer to solving the murder, his prolonged stay in Kent meant that he did not have anything to do with Charlotte Holmes immediately before she became a murder suspect.

Was that why she had advised him to do so?

Chief Inspector Talbot regarded Treadles another moment, then turned his attention back to their main suspect. "Miss Holmes, three days ago, you went to see Lord Bancroft."

"That is correct. I informed him that Mrs. Claiborne was dead."

"And what was his reaction?"

"He did not particularly care."

"Why did you not simply send a note, Miss Holmes? Surely an investigator of your caliber must have known that the news would not have mattered greatly to Lord Bancroft."

Treadles would have squirmed, but Miss Holmes remained perfectly still. "It seemed the courteous thing to do at the time."

"The day before that, the logs at Ravensmere recorded another visit by you. What was the reason for *that* visit?"

"To keep his lordship abreast on my investigation."

"According to you, you never unearthed anything significant concerning Mr. Underwood's whereabouts. Such a nullity of success required a trip in person to present to Lord Bancroft?"

It did look questionable, so many visits against her insistence that she had managed to do very little for Lord Bancroft.

"When no results can be shown," said Miss Holmes gravely, "it becomes even more important to let the client know that every effort has been expended."

She would have made a terrific charlatan, the thought occurred to Treadles.

Chief Inspector Talbot was apparently impervious to charlatans. "Miss Holmes, all those trips to see Lord Bancroft for no reason, were you in fact there to study the configuration of Ravensmere?"

"Should I take any interest in that?"

"If you wish to better break him out of that prison."

"And why should I do that, I who am no friend of his?"

"Because he would be that much easier to kill, away from Ravensmere." Talbot smiled. "Where were you last night, Miss Holmes?"

Treadles broke into a sweat, even though he'd been waiting for that question.

"Chief Inspector—"

"I would caution you to speak the truth, Miss Holmes," said her adversary, his soft words falling like hammers upon Treadles's hearing. "I have enough evidence to arrest you, and culprits have been tried and convicted on less. Now think carefully, Miss Holmes. Where were you last night?"

Twenty-three

Returning from Sittingbourne, Charlotte changed trains and headed again to Ravensmere.

This time, Lord Bancroft was already in the small side garden. At her approach, he tossed down the magazine in his hand.

Charlotte glanced at the magazine, a recent issue of *Cornhill*. "I hope you have sufficient reading material, my lord?"

"Hardly. I've already read this one three times," he said impatiently. "Why have you come again, Miss Holmes?"

Charlotte, still dressed as a man, thrust a hand into the pocket of her jacket, leaving her thumb hooked over the double-welt opening. "I have further bad news: Mrs. Claiborne is also dead."

Unlike the strong reaction he showed for Mr. Underwood, Lord Bancroft barely frowned. "She was irrelevant."

Charlotte was hard-pressed to argue with that, at least from his point of view. If Mrs. Claiborne had mattered, it had been only to Mr. Underwood, who could no longer care about such things. And she couldn't have been Lord Bancroft's sole means of getting messages into the hands of his minions.

"On your way out, you might as well instruct the gate to remove her name from the list of permitted visitors," said Lord Bancroft dismissively.

She knew him to be an unfeeling person; still, this was a strikingly callous response to the violent death of a woman who had shared his bed for years. But Charlotte made sure to relay his request to the guards at the gate.

"Ah, that's a shame," said one guard. "Such a beautiful woman, Mrs. Claiborne. Any reason we're taking her off the list?"

"His lordship didn't say, save that she would not come again."

The guard kept shaking his head. "I should have had a better look at her three weeks ago, if I knew she wasn't going to come around again."

"Well, good sir," said Charlotte, "this is your lucky day, as I happen to have a photograph of Mrs. Claiborne with me. Can't compare to having her in front of you, but still, here's another look for you."

The guard eagerly accepted the locket. He smacked his lips. "Ah, what a beauty. So generous with her smiles, too. I shall miss those smiles. I shall."

⸻※⸻

The previous evening, before Holmes had sent a note to the chemist's shop that seemed to have some connection to Mrs. Farr, she had first telephoned Lord Ingram. Lord Ingram, unable to get away just then, had dispatched someone else to watch over the chemist's shop.

The agent had returned a few hours later and shamefacedly reported that while he had seen a young man come to pick up a message from the shop well after the shop had closed for the evening, he had not been able to follow the man for more than ten minutes before the man had turned a corner and disappeared into the night.

Lord Ingram had decided to replicate the experiment the next day. He wrote another note, in a decent imitation of Holmes's hand, and dropped the message in the post. Postal delivery was remarkably frequent and swift in London—friends living in different districts could exchange correspondences several times in a day.

Experience indicated that he had two hours or so before his letter arrived at the chemist's. He used that time to walk around the neighborhood, familiarizing himself with its alleys and back ways, before he started to patrol the chemist's street up and down as a sandwich board man.

The community was far from wealthy, but it was composed of artisans, shop clerks, and others of modest but steady income. The street, one of the busiest in the area, made for a reasonable market for makers of cleaning soap, tinned goods, and such.

His simple disguise allowed him to loiter in plain sight but also to occasionally sit down with a small beer to quench his thirst as the day grew increasingly warm.

What he feared was not the heat but that given the special relationship between the chemist's shop and Mrs. Farr, whoever came to take messages during the day might do so from the back door. So from time to time he crouched down near the mouth of the alley behind the shop, a biscuit in hand, with the air of a weary man stealing a moment of rest.

Except he didn't need to pretend about being a weary man. He saw it in the mirror daily. That same fatigue was etched on Holmes's face, too. Neither of them had slept much since she returned to England; a state of ill rest had not resulted from anything scandalous, or even remotely pleasurable.

And he missed his children fiercely. He knew they were having an excellent time with their beloved cousins, under the careful eye of both their governess and his sister-in-law. Still, he worried that the protective shield he held out before them was cracked and falling apart.

He had no idea how much of that anxiety stemmed from his personal circumstances, and how much was simply a by-product of parenthood. He wished there was time to sit down and talk with Mrs. Watson about how best to raise his children. He also wanted to reread the letter that he often carried with him these days, a recent one from Holmes.

I don't believe that anything anyone says can alleviate your concerns, Ash, because yours are issues for which there are no perfect or even neat solutions. Miss Lucinda and Master Carlisle are children of divorced parents, and at some point, they will face prevailing attitudes.

But it is worth pointing out that they are extremely fortunate children. They are healthy, comfortably off, and cherished. No one can guarantee anyone's happiness or success in life, but the effort everyone around them has put into that endeavor—what Livia wouldn't have given to have been raised by you and Miss Potter. (Or even Lady Ingram, for that matter. I think Livia would not have minded a lioness of a mother who swooped in once in a while.)

Holmes did not excel at consoling people. But it was precisely due to this minor characteristic of hers that he found so much encouragement in her words. If she called his children extremely fortunate, then they must be, in some way.

He took a bite of a plum that he'd bought off a costermonger, and was just about to take a sip from his canteen when a short squat man marched past him, not from the alley but on the street. And in his hand was a mourning envelope.

Lord Ingram had used a mourning envelope, with a distinctive black border, in the hope that he might better see the note change hands from outside the chemist's. But he would also gladly accept being lucky in ways he had not anticipated.

He slowly stood up, waited another second, then stepped into the street himself.

❧

It was past four o'clock in the afternoon when Charlotte arrived at the bookbinder's shop, looking for Mumble.

She was met by the bookbinder himself, Mr. Rosenblatt, a slightly stooped, gentle-looking man. After she introduced herself and stated her purpose, he said, "Young Waters left early today, Mr. Herrinmore. Someone in his family isn't well."

She raised a brow. "I thought Mr. Waters was an orphan."

Johnny had said that Mumble and Jessie had grown up as foster siblings, not that either's parents had fostered the other.

Mr. Rosenblatt ran a wheeled embosser down the side of an already-bound leather volume, completing a rectangular frame on the cover. "Orphans can form families, Mr. Herrinmore. Young Waters and his foster sister are as much siblings as any two people born of the same parents."

"It's not Miss Ferguson who is unwell, is it?"

"Oh no. She's fine. Strong as an ox, that one."

The spine of the book he was working on showed a sharp crisscross pattern underneath—Charlotte recalled the vellum strips Mumble had been cutting the other day.

"You wouldn't happen to have Mumble's address, would you, Mr. Rosenblatt?"

The bookbinder, now rolling a different embossing wheel, shook his head. "I do not."

Charlotte did not believe him, but she could hardly tell him that she suspected him of dishonesty. "Do you expect him back to-morrow?"

"I am not sure," he said rather sadly. His embossing wheel traveled with the swift alignment of a beam of light, leaving behind a trail of delicately intertwined vines on the brown leather. "The patient he would be looking after is suffering from something serious."

Charlotte's eyebrow shot up again. "You have very liberal policies, Mr. Rosenblatt, to permit your apprentice to come and go at his convenience."

"My son is no more, and my grandson is too young. Young Waters works here as a favor to me, not the other way around," said the bookbinder rather cryptically.

Charlotte hesitated a moment. "In that case, would you tell him that I would like to see him, soon as could be. Here's my address, and there's a half sovereign in it for Mr. Waters should he come to see me."

She would have preferred to speak to Mumble without giving him her current address, but needs must.

After she secured the bookbinder's promise that he would pass on the message, Charlotte remained in the shop another quarter hour and bargained over a slender penannular silver brooch. It was likely Viking in origin, close to a thousand years old and nearly unscratched, with tiny but exquisite brambled terminals on its incomplete ring.

A nice little present for her lover.

"You have an excellent eye, Mr. Herrinmore," said Mr. Rosenblatt as he wrapped her purchase.

Lord Ingram was the expert; Charlotte merely benefited from her proximity to him.

"Thank you," she said.

As she slipped the package into the inside pocket of her day coat, her fingertips touched the envelope that held Mrs. Claiborne's locket, which she had planned to show to Mumble.

She extracted the locket, opened it, and handed it to Mr. Rosenblatt. "By the way, sir, have you ever seen this woman?"

Mr. Rosenblatt put on his glasses and squinted at the small photograph. "Why, yes. She came into the shop about a month ago, not once but twice. We don't receive much patronage from young ladies, or from young people at all. A beautiful young woman stood out."

"Did she ask after Mumble?"

"Not in the very least," said the bookbinder with great certainty. "On her first visit, she inquired into wedding stationery, and I told her that unfortunately we would not be able to assist her with bespoke invitations. She came back a few days later and said that she planned to ask all her guests for handwritten good wishes and could I help her turn the collection into a bound volume. To that I said yes—if she brought the pages, we could make an exceptionally handsome book."

He shrugged. "But then I never saw her again."

———※———

Earlier, Charlotte had decided against going to the tea shop where Jessie worked: Not only would she arrive too late to catch Jessie, but she was still dressed as a man, and a man hanging about asking for

Jessie would not have pleased the proprietress, who seemed to be the sort to implement strict rules concerning her female employees.

But after Mr. Rosenblatt's disclosure, she changed her mind.

In décor and general atmosphere, Mrs. Hatfield's tea shop was not very different from the many tearooms that had sprung up in recent years: clean, cozy places that smelled of sugar crust and baked fruit and catered to a female clientele, offering them a safe, welcoming place to dine in public.

But men, as it turned out, enjoyed tea shops, too. They did not always wish to deal with the noise and drunkenness of a pub or a tavern when all they wanted was a decent meal at a decent price.

Mrs. Hatfield's tea shop, therefore, did not turn away male patronage, but had a reserved section to one side, with an older waitress who had salt-and-pepper hair. As soon as Charlotte showed her Mrs. Claiborne's picture, she said, "Oh, I remember her. Mind you, sir, we have a great many pretty ladies that come in, but she was just lovely. I saw her only that once, but I think, from talking to the girl who served her, that it wasn't her first time as a patron."

Since Mrs. Hatfield would frown upon waitresses not assigned to the gentlemen's section sidling over to chat with one, Charlotte passed a coin into the older server's hand and asked her to speak to the one who had waited on Mrs. Claiborne.

The senior waitress came back some minutes later and reported that Mrs. Claiborne had heard about the reputation the tea shop enjoyed for its unadulterated breads, and so the server who attended to her had proudly boasted about how even fancy hotels were coming to them now, to order rolls and whatnot for their fancy tables.

"Did she ever ask about anyone working here?"

"Pauline didn't say. And why would such a fancy lady know any of us? Even Mrs. Hatfield isn't grand enough for her, if you ask me. But Pauline did say that the second time she came in she wanted to know which hotels ordered rolls from us and how the rolls were delivered."

"And Miss Pauline knew that?"

"Oh, we all know. That would be the Dolphin's Crown, the Round Oaks, and Pettifer's. And we have a girl with a truly strong back. She's the one who does the deliveries."

Pettifer's was the hotel where Mrs. Claiborne had asked to meet with Charlotte and Mrs. Watson, and where she had claimed to run into the young man and the young woman who had tried to break into her town house.

What were the chances that she *didn't* know, when she proposed the meeting, that Jessie, on behalf of the tea shop, was a frequent visitor to the hotel?

Lord Ingram returned to the hotel as Holmes and Mrs. Watson were sitting down to a simple supper. Mrs. Watson leaped up to embrace him. To his surprise, Holmes did likewise. Not that she never did, but certainly not in front of others—and so casually, too.

He was slightly embarrassed and exceptionally gratified.

Mrs. Watson, hiding her own surprise, pressed a plate of food into his hands, and told him what they had found out this day.

"You see, my lord," she said as she sawed at her beefsteak, "Mrs. Claiborne told us a pack of lies about being ignorant of Mr. Underwood's boxers. She even knew where Mumble and Jessie worked."

"I caught Johnny just before he left work," added Holmes. "Interestingly enough, neither he nor the construction foreman recognized her—though to be sure a month ago Johnny was working at a different site. After that I went to the Unicorn of the Sea. Mr. Mowlem, the publican, also said that he was sure he'd never seen her in his life."

She turned her face to the side and yawned into her hand before digging into a jacket potato. He, too, felt like falling face-first into his plate.

Only Mrs. Watson still had the nervous energy to ruminate on the investigation. "All the lies would have made me cross with her, were she not already dead. What was she thinking, really, to allow someone into her parlor while she was on the run—very possibly in the middle of the night?"

Holmes sprinkled salt and pepper on her potato. "Perhaps she opened the door to Mr. Underwood?"

"But he was dead!" exclaimed Mrs. Watson.

Even Lord Ingram was taken aback by the idea. He took a bite of his sandwich and glanced at Holmes.

"We don't know Mr. Underwood's precise time of death," said Holmes. "Or that of Mrs. Claiborne's."

"But why would he wish to kill her?" Mrs. Watson demanded to know.

Holmes shrugged. "Maybe he finally learned that she'd been holding conjugal meetings with Lord Bancroft?"

After all, those had taken place only after Mr. Underwood could no longer spend time at home regularly.

Mrs. Watson was incredulous. "Then who killed him afterwards? Lord Bancroft, to avenge his former mistress?"

Holmes took a sip of water. "My lord Bancroft was quick to declare his former mistress utterly irrelevant when I conveyed news of her demise."

"Then what? Mrs. Claiborne killed Mr. Underwood, and Lord Bancroft killed her for Mr. Underwood?"

"This is a more believable version. If Lord Bancroft is willing to kidnap my sister to force me to help him locate Mr. Underwood, then presumably he would also be angry enough at whomever killed him to take vengeance."

"Does he have the manpower to do something like that?" asked Lord Ingram. "It would require him to have had Mrs. Claiborne followed, wouldn't it? And if he'd already deemed her irrelevant, then why would he squander such resources on her?"

Mrs. Watson rubbed her forehead, then she shot to her feet.

"Good gracious, my lord, do you remember that when Miss Charlotte visited the accountant, she learned that there had been a Mrs. Anderson who had asked about Mr. Underwood?"

She turned to Holmes. "Do you think, Miss Charlotte, that we haven't been dealing with Mrs. Claiborne at all but with the other woman?"

━━━ ❈ ━━━

"Ash, are you thinking longingly of spending some time in Stern Hollow, with your 'broken' limb propped up, so that you don't need to do anything at all from sunrise to sunset?"

Supper was finished and Lord Ingram had a rare few hours before he had to head out again. He had chosen to spend the time in bed with Holmes. But much as she had lamented earlier, they lay fully clothed, the sides of their heads touching, both half-asleep.

At her slow, slightly slurred question, he chuckled sleepily. "You're speaking of yourself, Holmes, with your feet on an ottoman and a plate of cake by your side. *I* would like to do some riding, which alas I cannot at Stern Hollow, not as long as I'm still supposed to be recovering from my 'accident.'"

She chortled and then said, after a moment of silence, "We're almost done with all our preparations. Can you believe that?"

"No, I cannot believe it. My eyes tell me I've crossed off almost every item on my original task list, but every day I come up with more things to check and to do."

Because he could not accept that they could ever be adequately prepared.

"What if we manage to come out of this in one piece?"

He opened his eyes. "Do you remember the gate at Stern Hollow that gave me so much trouble?"

She turned onto her stomach and propped herself up on her elbows. "The one near the little cottage for your children? The remote wooden one for which you had to replace fifty feet of estate boundary and then design a new wrought iron gate yourself? The gate you never saw that ended up taking three weeks of your time?"

Holmes remembered everything one ever told her—even things one didn't remember ever telling her. Therefore, she had to recollect that the subject of the gate had come up while he was being treated as a murder suspect, in answer to a question Chief Inspector Fowler had asked him about whether he enjoyed looking after his estate, acknowledged by all and sundry to be one of the fairest in the land, something worth cherishing.

But his answer, at the time, had been one of disillusionment. Not with Stern Hollow in particular but with his life in general. He had been foundering. The life he'd thought he wanted—and achieved—had turned out to be a mirage. And he had been going through the motions, fulfilling his obligations without knowing what to do next, when what he had thought to be the perfect path had led him straight over a cliff.

"I've seen the new gate a few times since, actually, since it's rather close to the little cottage. And I've come to realize that I like it very well. It's handsome and sturdy, and it opens and closes smoothly—it's everything a gate ought to be."

She listened attentively, no longer looking sleepy at all.

"So I've been thinking of late that if only troublesome gates were my biggest problems, I would be a very happy man indeed."

Because he had found out, as she had, that sometimes one discovered a new world beyond the precipice, beyond the plunge. He was relieved to be divorced, relieved not to have to keep up appearances, relieved that he needed never again measure himself against any sort of perceived perfection.

He no longer felt tied down by his estate, because it was never the estate that had tied him down but his own unachievable expectations. Now he looked forward to his daily life—to the peace and quiet of Stern Hollow, the laughter and chatter of his children, and letters from Holmes several times a week, compact, reassuring little envelopes in his breast pocket.

And he looked forward equally to the less quotidian experiences.

"I'm glad you like the gate," she murmured. "I've seen the gate, and it is a worthy gate indeed."

—⋇—

Her lover slept soundly, the travel alarm clock on the nightstand set to wake him up in an hour and a half.

Charlotte placed a hand on his sternum and felt the warm cambric of his shirt, the steady rise and fall of his chest with every breath. He had done so much. In the past few days, in addition to all his other tasks, he had searched deep into various archives for her and taken another trip to Torquay to make sure that old Mrs. Calder was still happy as a clam on her seaside holiday.

The man stared at the closing door.

The painting was finished some time ago, and he suspected that she knew it.

Where did that leave him then?

She knew now how the story ought to go—how their story ought to go.

But . . . later.

Now he needed his sleep—and so did she.

———❈———

Lord Ingram, of course, had not come back to the hotel merely to dine and to rest for a few hours. He gave Charlotte an address, the place to which he had followed the man who had picked up the second letter from the chemist's shop.

Charlotte, disguised as an old woman, reached the house midmorning the next day—she would have liked for it to be earlier, but other than milk deliveries and emergencies, people did not show up in front of one another's doors at the crack of dawn.

The street was overpopulated—as was so much of London. The houses, worn but not yet dilapidated, were packed cheek to jowl, lines of washing flapping in the breeze. It was the kind of neighborhood where most everyone went to work, including the older children. As Charlotte walked by, only a pair of five- or six-year-old boys peered at her from the dirt they were digging up in someone's tiny front garden.

As expected, her knocks at the door produced no reply. She proceeded to the next house down the street and then the next, until a frail-looking old woman holding a toddler girl answered the door.

"Do pardon me, missus," said Charlotte. "I'm mighty sorry to bother you, I am. But I'm looking for Mrs. Trimmer. She used to live in number 17 over there."

Lord Ingram, who never settled for being merely competent, had found out, via London's municipal records, the identity of the house's owner: Robert Epping, hansom cab driver by profession. As this was not terribly helpful, he further discovered the house mentioned in the annals of the city as the site of a neighborly spat eight years ago, with the resident at the time named as Mrs. L. Trimmer, fifty-six years of age.

"Oh, but you're awful late, missus," said the old woman. "Mrs. Trimmer passed away two years ago."

"Dear me. I had no idea, and me living only five miles away! The poor dear—I hope her passing was easy."

"It was, thank goodness. She developed pneumonia and went speedy quick."

Charlotte bemoaned the abrupt volatility of life for a minute, and then, "Do you think, missus, whoever is living there right now— would they let me in to take a look at the front room where Mrs. Trimmer and I used to sit and chat?"

"I don't see why not, except they are such busy people and hardly ever home."

Charlotte made a wary face. "I do hope they're not pretending to be working but whiling away the day in taverns and gambling houses. I had a nephew like that, and it was terrible for my sister."

"Oh no, no worries on that. At number 17 they are excellent young people. You won't find harder workers or better neighbors than Mumble and Jessie, you won't, missus."

Twenty-four

M umble and Jessie.

Charlotte was not particularly surprised. The two young boxers, with their midnight surveillance and their likely breaking and entering, had already made it clear that their interest in their late sponsor far exceeded what would be considered normal.

It made sense that they were investigating for Mrs. Farr, who had loved her sister fiercely and had been consumed with grief and anger.

Vengeance is mine; I will repay.

Charlotte, as Sherrinford Holmes, had disclosed to Mrs. Farr the reason Mimi Duffin had been murdered—she bore a resemblance to someone else—but not the identity of the party responsible for her death. Even Inspector Treadles had not known the truth. How, then, had Mrs. Farr learned who had killed her sister?

Had she found a circuitous route to the truth?

It was not impossible. She could have gleaned from the papers that at the time Sherlock Holmes had been assisting with the investigation at Stern Hollow, home of one Lord Ingram Ashburton. But reporters had been given an extremely redacted version of events, and Lord Bancroft's name never once came up. With such scant information, could she have inferred the significance of this brother who had retired from public life shortly thereafter?

And even if Mrs. Farr, ill-informed on the inner complexities of the case, had been able to make that spectacular leap of logic, how would she have found out that Mr. Underwood had worked for Lord Bancroft? Lord Bancroft's had been a shadowy role, and Mr. Underwood, officially at least, hadn't even belonged to the same ministry.

Yet Mumble and Jessie, after quietly carrying on with their lives after Mr. Underwood's disappearance, had suddenly become extremely interested in his whereabouts.

What had caused this volte-face? And had they killed Mr. Underwood, at Mrs. Farr's behest, to avenge Mimi Duffin?

The thought jarred, given the praise the young people had heaped on Mr. Underwood. Charlotte rarely shied away from jarring possibilities, but this one raised a thorny question.

Lord Bancroft had demanded to know who killed Mr. Underwood and why. But if it was indeed Mumble, Jessie, and ultimately Mrs. Farr who were responsible for Mr. Underwood's death, could Charlotte simply hand over their names—and their fate—to that man?

But if she didn't, then what about Bernadine?

—✳—

Mumble was not at work this day, but Jessie was. Charlotte, having visited the tea shop earlier in her old-woman disguise, returned shortly before four as herself, bought a few things, and exited in time to see Jessie leave from the alley in the back, a shopping basket in hand, and merge into the crowd of pedestrians.

The girl walked almost faster than an omnibus. Charlotte had not imagined, at the beginning of her career, that stamina would be such an important part of her work. Thankfully, she had become a fitter and stronger woman during the past year *and* she had invested in first-rate walking boots.

She was almost beginning to suspect that perhaps Miss Jessica Ferguson took no precautions about being followed when Jessie stopped at a cheesemonger's shop. That gave Charlotte time to slip into a nearby alley and reemerge with the feathers on her hat removed, a dingy shawl covering much of her jacket, and her rather stuffed handbag turned inside out and, with some folds released, transformed into a large shopping bag.

Jessie exited the cheesemonger's with a round of hard cheese. She stuck it inside her shopping basket and looked about casually, as if deciding where to go next. Charlotte, bent over to examine a coster-monger's selection of wilted lettuces, saw out of the corner of her eye that Jessie continued down the street.

Two intersections later Jessie disappeared into a bakery. This gave Charlotte pause. Mrs. Hatfield was not generous, but according to the talkative waitress who had served Charlotte today, the proprie-tress did give reasonable discounts to her employees on her increas-ingly famous unadulterated breads. Therefore it made no sense for Jessie to visit another bakery on her way home.

Charlotte estimated where the back door of the bakery might be located, turned onto the intersecting street, and slipped behind an advertising column. There she dropped her shawl and her small toque into her bag and put on a long apron and a starched cap. Then she rounded to the other side of the advertising column to study all the handbills stuck to it, as if she were a serving maid stealing a moment of leisure.

She had her back to the street, but from the reflection of a nearby window, she caught sight of Jessie inching toward the opening of the back alley. Jessie turned left and hurried, heading west when earlier she'd been headed south. But then she turned left once more and was again going in her original direction, except on a different street.

She turned back to look a time or two. But Charlotte, now di-vested of the apron and holding out a large umbrella—it had conve-niently begun to rain—blended into an entire pavement of foot traffic, a veritable river of black umbrellas.

Jessie did not go home or into the chemist's, even though she passed close to both. Instead, she veered a few streets farther west and let herself into a house that had a pocket-sized yet deeply utilized front garden. Trellises placed all around the periphery supported peas, beans, and aubergine. A variety of herbs crowded a small raised bed to one side. To the other side, chard, chicory, and radishes grew in their own minuscule plots.

Not too far away, Charlotte found a school of industrial and commercial art and engaged the gregarious gate guard in a conversation about what sort of students were admitted to the school and where they could reasonably be expected to find posts after finishing their curriculum.

She was beginning to wonder how else she could linger nearby when Jessie emerged and solved the problem for her. Jessie went directly home. Charlotte, having followed in her wake, strolled around her neighborhood for some time, enough to assure herself that fifteen minutes later Jessie was still home, her person visible from the open window, wiping down walls and furniture in the front room.

Charlotte headed for the house Jessie had visited.

Her knock was answered more swiftly than she'd anticipated.

"I was wondering when you'd remember your shawl, Jes——"

The woman who opened the door had one eye that was milky and blind, the other a deep periwinkle blue. Mrs. Farr.

Her welcoming expression congealed into wariness. "Who are you?"

She looked much frailer than Charlotte remembered, as if she'd been gravely ill and lingered at death's door a good long while and was only now slowly recovering. Her voice was scratchy, her hair thin, her stark black dress loose and shapeless around her frame.

Yet at the sight of a stranger on her doorstep, her gaze sharpened into a dagger. The beautiful mystique that had so struck the Harcourt mother and daughter was nowhere in evidence, only the stone-hard defenses of a survivor facing fresh danger.

Before Charlotte could introduce herself, Mrs. Farr's eyes narrowed—the misfortune that had taken the sight of her left eye had not affected the muscles that controlled the movements of her eyelids. "Where have I seen you before?"

Charlotte shoved back an irrational surge of fear. "You first saw me near the General Post Office last summer. I was wearing a jacket-and-skirt set in blue twill. You had a little girl with you, and I was so moved by your plight I gave her more money than I should, as well as my luncheon. But for my trouble, your daughter took the pound note I had in my pocket."

Mrs. Farr frowned. "And you're here for that pound?"

Charlotte moved past her into the foyer and closed the front door. Now she spoke with Sherrinford Holmes's voice—or, as close as she could get to his slightly garbled enunciation without an orthodontic device in her mouth. "No need. I had my purser charge you an extra pound when I investigated your sister's disappearance last autumn."

"That was you?" Mrs. Farr's voice now sounded like a saw dragged across a brick.

Charlotte had been highly helpful to her as Sherrinford Holmes—and highly solicitous. But there was no acknowledgment of any kind in Mrs. Farr's question, only a heightened distrust.

"I am a woman of many faces—for work, that is."

"What do you want?"

"Shall we discuss it over tea, like civilized people?" said Charlotte, wading deeper into the house.

Mrs. Farr's parlor was cramped with a great many mismatched chairs. The floor sagged underfoot. The wallpaper's pattern was hardly discernible. The place was clean, and more or less tidy, but it was clear that the hostess gave few thoughts to how her house might appear to a caller.

"Recently I've been working on a private inquiry concerning the unsolved murder of one Mr. Victor Meadows," said Charlotte, from the middle of the room.

Mrs. Farr had been standing by the parlor door, watching Charlotte. At her late husband's name, a great rigidity took hold of her, as if she stared not at Charlotte but directly into the eyes of a basilisk.

"I see you recognize that name, Mrs. Farr," Charlotte murmured. "I am on calling terms with Miss Harcourt, your niece by marriage.

Her mother, Mrs. Harcourt, is no more. But thanks to a photograph she took many years ago, I was able to recognize you and Miss Duffin."

Mrs. Farr did not speak. She did not even seem to breathe.

Charlotte dug deep into her shopping bag and extricated a brown paper package of baked goods. On the rickety round table next to the fireplace, the tea things that had been there for Jessie's visit hadn't been removed yet. She refilled the kettle from a nearby pitcher of water and placed it to boil on a spirit lamp. By the time Mrs. Farr shuffled into the parlor, Charlotte had already set out the lemon biscuits and sliced pound cake she'd purchased from Mrs. Hatfield's tea shop earlier in the afternoon.

"What do you want?" asked Mrs. Farr once again, this time more insistently.

Her voice remained raspy, but her accent had changed, the roughness of the streets dropping away to a polish acquired by elocution exercises overseen by a strict governess.

Charlotte seated herself. "I am not entirely certain. The Christmas Eve Murder, you see, could very well be subject to a new investigation.

"Looking at the case, it may not be difficult for someone to make the argument that you committed the murder and were let off the hook because the investigating officer did not want a beautiful young woman to hang."

Mrs. Farr gave a lopsided, rictus-like smile. "The poor inspector. What did he do to deserve this?"

A sarcastic reply.

"I am also interested in that," said Charlotte. "In the meanwhile, I have some guesses about what happened that fateful Christmas Eve. As so much remains unknown, my guesses necessarily rest on a number of assumptions.

"First I assume that the police inspector assigned to the case was a capable investigator. The report he authored was clear and cogent— I can infer from that only a high degree of professional proficiency.

"Next I assume that the attachment Mrs. Harcourt felt toward you was genuine. Judging by the open, indeed eager, manner with which Miss Harcourt speaks of you, and the unrestricted discussion she and her mother had held on the murder over the years, I would have to conclude that either the late Mrs. Harcourt had a completely clear conscience with regard to you, Mrs. Farr, or that she was the most devious liar and criminal I've ever had the misfortune of coming across."

Mrs. Farr's lips twitched, as if amused by the idea of her late sister-in-law as an arrant evildoer.

"For the moment, I choose the former interpretation: Mrs. Harcourt felt free to discuss the murder not out of a culprit-at-large's desire to gloat but because she was riveted. And because she was anxious for you after your disappearance from Manchester.

"With those two assumptions in place, we can begin to consider an intriguing observation Mrs. Harcourt made to her daughter: that she herself, by all means a suitable main suspect, received little attention from the police.

"If we accept that as an expression of genuine bafflement, and if we accept the premise of the detective inspector's general competence, then we cannot consider it an oversight on his part. I posit that he showed scant interest in Mrs. Harcourt because he already knew she was not guilty, which implies that he knew who *was* guilty."

"But if he knew who committed the murder, why did he make no arrest?"

Mrs. Farr, recovered from her initial shock, had taken a seat across the tea table from Charlotte. Her question sounded casual, that of a politely interested bystander.

The kettle burbled and steamed. Charlotte warmed the teapot, which she'd emptied earlier, then set fresh tea to steep. A pedestrian walking by the house would have paid little heed to this most ordinary tableau, two women at tea, gossiping about neighbors and the price of milk.

"I cannot speak in absolutes," Charlotte carried on, "but it is quite possible that you murdered Mr. Victor Meadows, your late husband."

Mrs. Farr crossed her arms over her chest. "His bedroom was locked from the inside, both doors."

"True, but *when* were they locked? The maid who came to relight the fire in the morning hadn't expected to encounter a blocked entry. And judging by the evidence you gave, you also found it unusual that the connecting door between the master's and the mistress's bedrooms was barred on your husband's side.

"An argument could be made that a disgruntled rabble-rouser from the factories entered the bedroom from the window—in his stockinged feet, as he left no prints—and proceeded to lock the doors from inside to prevent any disruption to his deadly work.

"But it is just as likely that the murderer entered Mr. Meadows's typically unbarred bedroom from inside the house. And then, wishing to give the impression that someone not of the house had taken his life, locked the doors and opened a window."

"And then leaped to the ground?"

"And then walked across the architrave. The distance is only fifteen feet or so. The architrave is three inches wide at the top. A daring and dexterous individual can manage the trek without the aid of the climbing vines that covered the wall. With the vines, a determined soul, even one lacking all training and experience, can make it to the nearest window, which happened to be yours."

"You think that so easy? You think you can manage to move fifteen feet on a ledge narrower than the width of your hand, in the dark, in the cold, without falling off?"

"Only at the height of desperation would I attempt such a thing. And I would more likely than not plummet to the ground. But then again, I have always enjoyed cake a little more than is good for me," said Charlotte, biting into a slice of surprisingly well-made pound cake, moist and crumbly.

"But that *I* am doomed to fail does not mean someone else could not have succeeded at the same endeavor. Let's suppose that I were built more favorably for such trials. Since I'd have decided, beforehand, that I wanted the murder to appear to have been committed by outsiders, hopefully I'd have also thought of other difficulties that might arise.

"The murder weapon, for one thing. The most likely weapon would be Mr. Meadows's own shaving blade, a sharp implement close at hand. After the deed was done, most of the blood could have been wiped off on the already blood-soaked bedcover. And then the murderer could have given the razor blade a wash in the en-suite bath.

"The house is no longer so new. But at the time it was built, it boasted of every modern convenience, including plumbed washbasins. Good plumbing, too—I tested it myself when I visited. The water came nice and quiet, without the kind of rattling of the pipes that happens in some houses.

"The now thoroughly clean shaving blade could have been dried and placed in its customary spot, looking as if it had never been disturbed since the last time the master had need of its sharp edge.

"As for the murderer's clothes—frankly, I would have taken off my clothes to do the deed. The way the killing was carried out, with the bedcover between the blade and the murderer, there wouldn't have been much blood on the killer in the first place besides on the dominant hand.

"With the murder weapon put away, and blood on skin washed off, the murderer could now lock the doors and brave the journey of fifteen feet on the architrave—with some clothes on, if that was deemed necessary."

Mrs. Farr made a derisive snort. "You make it sound so easy."

"I certainly do not mean to diminish the forethought in the planning or the audacity of the deed itself. But so far, what I have narrated is a perfect crime. And a perfect crime would not do."

Did she observe a darkening of Mrs. Farr's countenance?

"Where did it go wrong? The ladder that had been moved from its customary spot near the gardener's hut and left on the ground? The murderer had moved it, but never intended to use it—once it was brought in the morning to climb into the locked bedroom, who could tell that it *hadn't* been used the night before?

"But no, the detective inspector wouldn't have been there to see you move the ladder—and no one else mentioned such a thing in their testimony. So it wasn't that.

"What gave you away probably had something to do with the most puzzling aspect of this otherwise simple case—your late husband's absolute docility. Granted, he was sleeping, but his throat wasn't cut as such. Whoever killed him first pulled up the duvet so that it not only thoroughly covered his throat but stretched a foot beyond the top of his head. And then the killer had to put his or her hand under the cover and find Mr. Meadows's neck. And only then, carefully place the blade.

"Not to mention, given his position on the bed and the direction his throat was cut, the killer must have practically straddled him. I am a sound sleeper, but with so much fuss, even I would have opened my eyes to see what was going on.

"But Mr. Meadows slept on soundly. Too soundly. Which makes me suspect that he had been given a narcotic substance. And that could be verified by chemical analysis. Or, even if it could not be, most laymen would not know. The threat of exposure might be enough for the truth to emerge."

A muscle twitched in Mrs. Farr's jaw.

Charlotte poured two cups of tea and placed one in front of her. "What do you think of the scenario I've illustrated? Does it fit the general contour of events as you recall?"

"I've listened to you long enough, Miss Holmes."

"Indeed, you have been very patient, Mrs. Farr. Do you not have rebuttals for me? Are my assumptions unable to support my conclusions? Or are there facts that I am entirely unaware of that would change the complexion of the case? Milk or sugar, by the way?"

Mrs. Farr ignored her attempt at hospitality. "You should go."

"I will," Charlotte promised calmly, adding two lumps of sugar and a good pour of milk into her own tea. "But I'd like to know what happened to your brother-in-law, Mr. Ephraim Meadows. The way you disappeared from Manchester, without a word to anyone, it makes me think that you were trying to escape extortion. Did he blackmail you? And did you, in the end, find a way to make him stop?"

"I never saw Mr. Ephraim Meadows after my husband's funeral, Miss Holmes," said Mrs. Farr flatly. "And I have no idea what happened to him."

"Is that so?"

Charlotte took a sip of her tea. Alas, Mrs. Farr took as little interest in her tea as she did in her décor—Charlotte suspected that the flavorlessness of the brew was caused by secondhand tea leaves, collected and peddled by servants from wealthier households.

"That is so." Mrs. Farr pushed her own teacup aside. "And I do not care about either your investigation or the official reinvestigation, should that ever take place. There was no evidence to incriminate anyone then, and there is no evidence now. Without evidence, nothing will happen. Therefore, will you go?"

—❖—

A little girl entered the parlor.

She seemed disappointed to see Charlotte but looked toward Mrs. Farr, as if waiting for introductions. When none proved to be forthcoming, she said, a little hesitantly, "Mama, did Jessie come?"

"Yes, and she already left."

"Oh," said the girl in a small voice.

"But Mumble will be here later. And Caro, too. Now be a good girl and go read in your room. If you can understand the new story all by yourself, I'll have Caro make some sherbet for you."

The girl's face lit with anticipation. "All right."

Charlotte smiled at little Eliza, who had, once upon a time, robbed her blind. "She's grown taller," she said after the girl left the parlor.

The patience and tenderness that had come into Mrs. Farr's countenance at the sight of her adopted child fled at Charlotte's words. But Charlotte did not allow her to make yet another attempt at eviction.

"To be perfectly honest, Mrs. Farr, I also don't care about the Christmas Eve Murder, for the exact same reasons you listed. As you were a former client, I merely consider it an obligation to caution you of potential trouble on the horizon. But that's not the only reason why I have called on you today, not even the primary one.

"You see, around the time I was asked to look into your late husband's death, I also accepted another commission, to investigate the disappearance of one Mr. William Underwood."

Mrs. Farr's eyelids twitched, but she said nothing.

"Lord Bancroft Ashburton, Mr. Underwood's former superior and the one who asked me to inquire into the matter, suggested that perhaps Mr. Underwood's ties to boxing had turned out to be troublesome. As I had no other clues, I started by finding his protégés, two of whom are apparently closely connected to you.

"Mumble and Jessie have been described to me as foster siblings. Were you their foster mother, Mrs. Farr?"

Mrs. Farr still said nothing.

"I will take your silence as a non-denial then." Charlotte took a sip of her tea—she had decided to think of it as sweetened water, a decent enough beverage for a woman who had walked many miles this day. "It soon came to my attention that Mumble and Jessie had been at the villa where Mr. Underwood and his mistress once resided. The mistress moved to a town house about six weeks ago. There is a strong suggestion that Mumble and Jessie were also at the town house in recent days.

"And that is a dangerous position for these two foster children of yours. He is Roma—it is almost assured that any hint of misdeed on his part would become guilt itself. Jessie's situation is not much better. She is an orphaned girl who boxes. A woman with a propensity toward violence? Who knows what else she would be capable of? Criminality would be the easiest assumption."

Mrs. Farr's jaw clenched.

"Why are you so interested in Mr. Underwood, Mrs. Farr, to an extent that you have steered these otherwise promising young people onto a path of potential ruin?"

"That is none of your business."

"Indeed not. But I admire their dedication to you and do not wish to see their future thrown away for an old woman's whim."

Mrs. Farr's fingers dug into the armrests of her chair.

Somewhere outside the parlor, footsteps sounded on a creaky staircase, followed by a whispered conversation, which sounded like someone trying to convince Eliza to go back upstairs and resume her reading.

"However," Charlotte carried on, "if you think I am trying to put a stop to your madness, you are mistaken. I'm here to tell you that Mumble and Jessie are in far greater trouble than you can imagine. The woman whose houses they broke into to search for clues to Mr. Underwood's whereabouts has been found dead, shot three times in the back. Mr. Underwood, too, is dead."

The whispers outside the parlor stopped.

"I don't believe you," said Mrs. Farr.

"You don't need to believe me," said Charlotte, "but that will not change the facts. Mr. Underwood is no more, and whatever you wanted of him—unless Mumble and Jessie killed him—"

Mrs. Farr slammed her hand down on the table. "Of course they didn't!"

The tea service rattled. Charlotte drained her sugared and milk-cloudy hot water. "That aside, whatever you wanted from Mr. Underwood, you will never have it now. Best tell Mumble and Jessie to leave London for a while, if you still care about them."

Twenty-five

C harlotte stood outside the street entrance of her hotel suite, Mrs. Watson's parting words still echoing in her ears.

Be careful, the dear lady had said. These days, they were always saying that to each other.

Charlotte looked around and made a left turn. Several streets away she got in a hansom cab and asked to be taken to Great Russell Street.

The most notable landmark in that part of the town was the British Museum. At this time of the night, even with the establishment's extended summer schedule, the last museumgoer had departed hours ago.

Despite streetlamps and lights that illuminated the façade of the museum, the area was shadowy and starkly empty. The houses that surrounded the great institution stood as silent as stone sentries around a mausoleum, all shut doors and blind windows: It was late enough in summer that those headed for the country had already departed and those remaining in London had gone to bed at a reasonable hour.

Charlotte marched past the museum's front gate, swinging her cane a little. She turned right, then turned right again. Behind the museum it was even quieter. Her footsteps echoed. The tapping of her cane on the pavement, inaudible in the rush of the day, boomed in the nocturnal silence, loud as a door slamming.

She barely saw the shadow swim toward her on the ground. Spinning around, she lifted her weighted cane just in time to intercept a strike of her attacker's umbrella. The clash was muted by the umbrella's neatly rolled canopy, only a dull *thump* that barely rippled the air.

The impact, however, jolted Charlotte's shoulder. She had not neglected her *canne de combat* practice with Mrs. Watson; still, it felt as if her cane had met with a sledgehammer. She stumbled backward. Her attacker's umbrella swooped down almost before she could parry again.

The cane had a steel core—yet it seemed to have cracked upon this second strike. Charlotte gave more ground and ducked her attacker's next swing to the side. She attempted a whack at the attacker's shoulder blade, but the attacker spun around and smashed the umbrella toward Charlotte's shin.

Charlotte hopped off the pavement into the street. Like a jungle cat, her attacker pounced. Back Charlotte went, step by step. She panted. Her arm hurt. The cane was now the weight of an anvil. She barely avoided tripping over the curb on the other side of the street.

She tried to at least pivot, so she could retreat along the length of the street, but her attacker boxed her in, forcing her toward the wrought iron fence of a mansion, at which point there would be no further retreat.

Hurry, hurry!

She blocked the next onslaught inches from her nose. Dear God, she really liked her nose.

Hurry!

She slashed outward, but her attacker was the superior combatant, and the dreaded fence was now directly against her back.

"Stop and step away, Miss Ferguson. I have Mr. Waters," said Lord Ingram.

The attacker froze. Charlotte wasted no time in striking her across the shoulder and scurrying away.

Lord Ingram stood on the other side of the street, the granite hulk of the British Museum behind him. He held a limp, masked Mumble, his hands and feet bound.

Jessie, her hand clamped over where Charlotte had thwacked her, hissed, "Don't you dare hurt him."

"Oh, I dare," replied Lord Ingram, his tone glacial. "Drop your weapon. On your knees, and put your hands where I can see them."

———— ✤ ————

"It is preferable, of course, not to be a damsel in distress in need of saving," said Charlotte to Lord Ingram. "But once in a while, a stylish rescue is quite refreshing."

She held Mumble by the latter's inert feet, while her lover walked backward, gripping the young boxer under his arms. He snorted. "In what way was this a rescue?"

True, the whole thing had been a ploy, using Charlotte to lure Mumble and Jessie into an attempted kidnapping. A few paces before her, a young man Lord Ingram had brought along carried Jessie on his back, with Mrs. Watson beside him, keeping an eye on the girl.

Mumble had been unconscious because the "mask" over his face had been a cloth doused with chloroform. Jessie, after being bound hand and foot, had also been subjected to the same treatment. But she was still struggling, albeit weakly.

"It was a rescue in that I was overawed and would have been hurt had my inauspicious struggle against Miss Ferguson gone on for much longer." Charlotte smiled at her lover. "You were very convincing as a knight in shining armor."

He glanced down at himself. He was dressed much like a London cabbie, his jacket ill-fitting, a hole in his hat, his electroplated watch fob scabbing and peeling. "Thank you, Holmes. I'm never happier than when I'm being a knight in shining armor."

He was jesting, but it also happened to be God's own truth.

"I can't always promise you quests as glamorous as tonight's—watch out for the curb!—oh, please excuse me."

She'd dropped one of Mumble's feet and had to bend down to pick it up before they could continue.

"I, too, could do with a few less glamorous tasks," murmured Lord Ingram.

They loaded Mumble and Jessie into the vehicle they'd brought. Lawson had already located the carriage waiting for Mumble and Jessie several streets away. Lord Ingram informed the driver that if Mrs. Farr wanted to see her foster children again, she had better come right away to the house where she had first met Sherrinford Holmes and bring her houseguest—and only her houseguest—along.

Mrs. Watson's house near Regent's Park and 18 Upper Baker Street, her property that served as Sherlock Holmes's office, were both available. But those were addresses known to their enemies, and they hadn't wanted to take chances. So Lord Ingram had volunteered a place he had quietly bought earlier in the year, a house in St. John's Wood that Sherlock Holmes and company had once hired for an investigation.

More memorably, it was the first place outside Stern Hollow where Lord Ingram and Charlotte had made love. Less memorably, they had not done so in this particular room.

The rest of the house was staid enough. The parlor immediately next, all dark blue wallpaper and rose damask upholstery, was the very exemplar of respectable décor. Yet this—Charlotte could think of it only as a boudoir—featured an enormous divan piled high with cushions and decorative pillows, enclosed by a diaphanous rose-colored canopy.

Mumble and Jessie currently occupied this heavenly divan.

"I like this place," Charlotte said to her lover.

"I knew you would."

"Are you embarrassed to own it?"

"Not as much as I thought I would be."

She chortled. She wanted to say something more to him, but Mrs. Watson called from the next room, "They're here!"

The dear lady ran down, the late Dr. Watson's service revolver in hand, to reinforce Lawson, in case Mrs. Farr tried anything unwise—or brought a larger contingent than Lawson could handle.

Charlotte left Lord Ingram to keep an eye on Mumble and Jessie and reached the ground floor as two visitors were admitted to the house, Mrs. Farr and a woman with a scarf pulled across her face.

Charlotte nodded at a stony-looking Mrs. Farr. Then she addressed the veiled woman. "My deepest condolences, Mrs. Claiborne."

The autumn before, when Holmes and Mrs. Watson—and even the Marbleton siblings—had met Mrs. Farr, Lord Ingram had been stuck at Stern Hollow, facing a murder investigation. He had, therefore, only seen her image in the photograph taken by Mrs. Harcourt.

Holmes had told him, emphatically, that she no longer looked anything like her old self. But such was the power of first impression that he couldn't help staring at the ravage writ large on her face, her once stately beauty now only bent lines and tattered angles.

Had she paid any attention, she might have taken offense at his involuntary reaction—even though he quickly remastered himself. But she rushed to her comatose foster children and didn't give him a second glance.

She didn't hasten to feel their foreheads or check their pupils, but bent over the side of the divan and gazed upon their features, as if they were sleeping infants and she the mother who had prayed long and hopelessly for their arrival, her tenderness completely at odds with her otherwise harsh aura.

"As you can see, not a scratch on them," said Holmes, who had come to stand beside Lord Ingram.

At her words, Mrs. Farr stiffened. She touched Mumble and Jessie briefly on their faces and walked out of the boudoir. Holmes, with a similarly brief touch on Lord Ingram's arm, followed. Mrs. Watson, after serving coffee to their guests, came in and took up a spot at the foot of the divan.

Lord Ingram moved a few feet to his right so that he straddled the doorway and could keep an eye on both their captives and the newcomers in the parlor.

He had seen the counterfeit Mrs. Claiborne's photograph in the locket. The real Mrs. Claiborne was in her mid, rather than early, thirties and, despite her currently splotchy face and swollen eyes, possibly even more ravishing.

When Mrs. Farr took a seat next to her, Lord Ingram realized with no small shock that the two black-clad women were, in fact, not that far apart in age, Mrs. Farr being only a few years older. Yet she could have passed for Mrs. Claiborne's stern, gaunt-looking aunt.

His chest constricted at the cost of her survival.

Holmes sat down with her profile to him. She had donned men's attire tonight, not those suits tailored for a sizable paunch, nor the form-revealing jacket and trousers she had sported once to practice *canne de combat* with him—which had been very distracting—but loose-fitting garments that managed to obscure most of her curves while retaining some sense of structure and style.

"My apologies," said Holmes to Mrs. Claiborne, "for breaking the news of Mr. Underwood's passing in so abrupt a manner. But I had to break it to you."

"It—it could not be helped. It would have been the worst news no matter how it was delivered," replied Mrs. Claiborne.

She managed to have barely any accent and yet sound smoothly and indubitably French.

"I believe you can see it now, too, Mrs. Farr, why I had to go into your house. Before Mr. Underwood entrusted Mrs. Claiborne to your care, he must have cautioned her against saying anything, anything at all, that could put her—or you, for that matter—in danger's way."

Mrs. Farr gave no sign of any such understanding. In fact, she gave no sign that she'd heard Holmes.

Mrs. Claiborne, despite her grief, was at least able to concentrate on the conversation. "But how did you know that I was there, Miss Holmes, at Mrs. Farr's, when even she didn't know, until mere days ago, that Mr. Underwood had any knowledge of Miss Mimi Duffin's death?"

"We were engaged by Lord Bancroft Ashburton to look into Mr. Underwood's disappearance."

The mention of his brother's name was a barbed pang in Lord Ingram's chest. Sometimes he felt nothing toward Bancroft. And sometimes there was anger enough to burn, confusion enough to drown.

As if sensing his agitation, Mrs. Watson glanced at him. He gave her a small smile. She smiled back, then went to take Jessie's wrist to check the girl's pulse.

"Lord Bancroft provided us, essentially, only two pieces of information," continued Holmes. "One, that Mr. Underwood had connections with boxing, and two, his mistress's address. I take it you know of this counterfeit Mrs. Claiborne?"

The real Mrs. Claiborne nodded.

"When we met her, the counterfeit Mrs. Claiborne spoke more prettily and for longer than Lord Bancroft did, but in the end probably told us even less. One detail that stood out was her mention of the scent of perfume on Mr. Underwood's person, a scent that she herself did not use."

"What?" Mrs. Claiborne cried softly.

"Something else that we found strange was that she had called on Lord Bancroft regularly, under the guise of conjugal visits."

"What?" Mrs. Claiborne's voice now rose half an octave. "That is a despicable claim. I never visited Lord Bancroft at Ravensmere. I haven't seen him since the day we parted ways."

Mrs. Watson, now checking Mumble's pulse, exhaled, as if relieved by Mrs. Claiborne's declaration, even though she already knew it was a different woman who went to see Bancroft.

"Rest assured, I believe you—the guard at Ravensmere recognized the counterfeit version. I only bring it up because the initiative she displayed in visiting a former protector did not accord with the image she presented of a woman who was maladroit at mistressing and who longed for nothing more than the simplicity and security of married life."

"Is that so?" the real Mrs. Claiborne murmured. "I did long for companionship that wasn't based on buying and selling, but I had no idea I was so inept at my own line of work."

She hadn't touched her coffee; Holmes poured her a glass of water. Lord Ingram wondered why in the world he had believed, when they were children, that Holmes wouldn't know how to look after others—was it because she had never been interested in catering to his every whim?

"Due to these incongruities," said Holmes, "and because everything we know about the counterfeit Mrs. Claiborne came from the counterfeit Mrs. Claiborne herself, we did not place our entire faith in what she said. But when I examined the locket that was found with her body, it began to appear far more likely that something had been fabricated entirely: The locket was too new and handled too little."

"I would not have worn a locket—it's practically an invitation for people to wonder who matters enough for you to keep their image near your heart," said the real Mrs. Claiborne quietly. "My photograph of Mr. Underwood is in the handle of my hairbrush, and his of me is inside the back of his watch. We decided that no one would be looking too closely at those items."

In the boudoir, Mrs. Watson shook her head. She was near enough that Lord Ingram reached out and held her hand. She smiled rather tremulously at him, raised their combined hands, and rubbed the side of his palm against her cheek before letting go to straighten the pillow under Mumble's head.

Holmes tucked a strand of hair behind her ear. Now that Lord

Ingram was accustomed to how her short hair framed her features, he wondered that more women hadn't adopted the style.

"Because of these inconsistencies presented by the counterfeit Mrs. Claiborne," said she, "I was at a bit of a loss. If the woman who had introduced herself to us as Mrs. Claiborne wasn't in fact Mrs. Claiborne, who could verify that? Mr. Underwood? The servants that the real Mrs. Claiborne had already dismissed a while ago—records of whom had disappeared from the domestic offices at the villa? And it was possible, indeed even likely, that the counterfeit Mrs. Claiborne had brought up a second woman in Mr. Underwood's life just so that if her house of cards started to fall down, she could always claim that in fact she was Mrs. Anderson, who really truly had Mr. Underwood's affection.

"The bigger question, however, was, if she was not the real Mrs. Claiborne, then what had happened to the real Mrs. Claiborne? She could have died; she could have fled the country; she could have left Mr. Underwood for less perilous pastures—and I had no evidence for any of it.

"But when I learned of the close ties between Mrs. Farr and Mumble and Jessie, a new likelihood arose. Assuming that Mr. Underwood knew himself to be in danger, assuming that he was terrified for Mrs. Claiborne's safety, too, and assuming that—if it had so happened—they had missed the best opportunity to send her abroad, where could he trust her to be safe? And who could he trust not to betray her—and him?"

Tears rolled down Mrs. Claiborne's face. Belatedly she reached for her handkerchief and wiped the moisture away. Mrs. Farr remained unresponsive, as if what was going on in the parlor had nothing to do with her—except, after a while, in an abrupt motion, she glanced toward the boudoir. Mrs. Watson, who could not have seen that look, nevertheless took a handkerchief and patted Jessie's slightly perspiring forehead.

Holmes was the calm center of the maelstrom. As a boy Lord Ingram had found her calmness unnerving, but now he understood that it was not an absence of feelings but more an unruffled acceptance of other people's emotions. "Would you say, Mrs. Claiborne, that before Mr. Underwood took on Mr. Waters and Miss Ferguson, he investigated them thoroughly?"

"Yes. He wanted only the best companions for Johnny."

"And in that process, he learned that Mr. Waters and Miss Ferguson had been fostered by Mrs. Farr. He subsequently learned that among a certain subset of the population, Mrs. Farr is known to provide temporary refuge to those in dire straits, especially women and children. Am I still correct?"

"Yes."

"But he went one step further, didn't he? To ensure that you had Mrs. Farr's personal attention, when you met her, he had you give her a letter. The gist of the letter promised that crucial information concerning Miss Mimi Duffin's murder would be revealed to Mrs. Farr if she kept you away from all unfriendly gazes."

Mrs. Claiborne nodded, even as another tear dropped down her face. Lord Ingram took a shaky breath. Sometimes people failed because they hadn't prepared adequately. But no one could say that Mr. Underwood hadn't done everything possible. And yet in the end, that still hadn't been enough.

He, Holmes, and everyone—they, too, were doing everything possible. But what if their preparations still fell short? What if Destiny had its thumb on the scale and they could only ever toil in futility?

"Of course, upon reading this letter," continued Holmes, "Mrs. Farr immediately questioned you. But you weren't able to tell her anything—because you sincerely knew nothing, because Mr. Underwood forbade you to mention either himself or Lord Bancroft, or both. In any case, Mrs. Farr, whose desire for vengeance burned harsher with each passing day, had to wait, as you did, for Mr. Underwood to return and fulfill his promise.

"But then something made you defy Mr. Underwood's strictures and confide in Mrs. Farr, at least to the identity of the letter writer."

Mrs. Claiborne tucked away her handkerchief and glanced at Mrs. Farr. Lord Ingram was wary of Mrs. Farr, but in Mrs. Claiborne's gaze there was no fear, only admiration and sorrow.

"My birthday was ten days ago," she answered. "Mr. Underwood had told me that if by then I still hadn't heard from him, I should go to Southampton and use the passage we'd bought for Freetown. But I couldn't simply go. What if he needed help?

"I knew I'd only make a muck of things if I went about looking for him, but Mrs. Farr was no ordinary woman, and she was clearly prepared to go to great lengths to avenge her late sister. So I told her that Mr. Underwood had been the one who sent the letter; Mr. Underwood, well-known to Mrs. Farr's foster children.

"As it turned out, Mrs. Farr had not allowed his sponsorship of her foster children without first looking into *his* background. She had managed to learn that he worked for the crown, in a capacity that ordinary subjects were not to know. And that had seemed respectable enough for her. She did fret that his house—mine, that is—seemed a bit too grand, which she knew because she had Mumble follow him home once or twice. But she approved of how he treated Johnny, and felt that he did want the best for his boxers."

An unhappy presentiment came over Lord Ingram: He had an idea now how Bancroft had found Mimi Duffin.

"Mrs. Farr," Holmes asked, "Mr. Waters said he saw Mrs. Claiborne once, when she delivered something to Mr. Esposito's house on Mr. Underwood's behalf. He never identified Mrs. Claiborne to you?"

Mrs. Farr's only response was to rise out of her chair and head for the boudoir. Lord Ingram stepped back to allow her inside. She drew up short at the sight of Mrs. Watson gently prying Jessie's braid from underneath her shoulder, so the girl wouldn't yank on her own scalp if she were to roll on her side. But when Mrs. Watson looked up uncertainly, Mrs. Farr sat down on the floor beside the divan and placed a hand on Mumble's knee.

In the parlor, as it became apparent that Mrs. Farr would not return immediately, Mrs. Claiborne cleared her throat and replied for her. "Mr. Waters and Miss Ferguson were not involved in how I sought and found refuge with Mrs. Farr. And after I moved into Mrs. Farr's house, I made sure to always remain in my room when she had visitors. But this time I was trying to keep young Eliza focused on her reading and chased her down the stairs when she wriggled too much . . ."

Holmes nodded. "So Mrs. Farr set things into motion to look for Mr. Underwood. But alas, it was too late."

"You are absolutely certain, Miss Holmes, that he is no more?" Mrs. Claiborne managed.

"I saw his body with my own eyes, I'm afraid," said Holmes with that same calm authority.

Mrs. Claiborne's lips quivered, but she accepted that as the final truth.

"Mr. Underwood's death, among other things, led me to call on Mrs. Farr," continued Holmes. "And Mrs. Farr, who initially was only too happy to eject me from her house, realized after my departure that perhaps I could be a source of intelligence concerning her sister's murder."

Without turning around, she added, "All you had to do was ask, Mrs. Farr. Perhaps you've become accustomed to harsher methods, but really, there was no need to kidnap me. No need to put your devoted foster children in harm's way."

In the boudoir, Mrs. Farr flinched, as if Charlotte had struck her. Her hand, on Mumble's knee, trembled.

Mrs. Watson, who had been watching her closely, hesitated a moment, then rounded the divan and touched her on the shoulder.

Mrs. Farr jerked. Mrs. Watson yanked her hand back. But she set her jaw and settled her hand on Mrs. Farr's shoulder again. This time, Mrs. Farr only removed her hand from Mumble's knee and gripped the counterpane.

"Mrs. Farr, do you still wish to know what happened to Miss Mimi Duffin," came Holmes's voice from the parlor, "and who was ultimately responsible for her murder?"

A teardrop fell from Mrs. Farr's blind eye. Her mouth opened, but no words emerged. Mrs. Watson glanced at Lord Ingram and then took Mrs. Farr's arm and helped her get up.

Together they trudged back into the parlor.

Twenty-six

Lord Ingram still wondered how his brother had turned into some-one who ordered the killing of others with little compunction.

Many of his most beloved childhood treasures had been presents from Bancroft. The windup toy soldiers that marched in formation, the marble chess set with figurines in correct medieval garb, the ex-pansive train set that, over time, had grown to the size of an entire room.

The terrible thing about being in Bancroft's orbit was that he wasn't always or even consistently evil. When it was convenient to him, he was perfectly capable of giving time, attention, and gifts, making one feel valued—loved, sometimes.

But individuals who stood in his way, or who could be sacrificed to achieve a greater goal, found themselves eliminated without a sec-ond thought—including those who had once been the recipients of his time, attention, and gifts.

Mrs. Watson, always sensitive to the moods of others, glanced at Lord Ingram several times while Holmes chronicled the events that led to Mimi Duffin's death. Holmes did not mention Moriarty by name, but spared very little else, including Bancroft's betrayal of his official duty.

Lord Ingram wished he could stop feeling this scalding shame on his brother's behalf. Perhaps his robust sense of shame was what separated him from Bancroft. But in the meanwhile, it was excruciating to be anywhere near Mrs. Farr, who'd had to bear the human cost of Bancroft's schemes.

Holmes had relayed the vow of vengeance on Mimi Duffin's tombstone. Yet instead of blazing with fury at the end of Holmes's concise account, Mrs. Farr seemed to shrink further into despair.

"So . . ." she said, her voice so low it could barely be heard, "my Miriam died to provide a corpse. Yet in the end, her body wasn't even used in the intended manner but was thrown away as rubbish because someone substituted a better body?"

"Unfortunately, yes."

She turned, very slowly, toward Mrs. Claiborne. "And your Mr. Underwood participated in this butchery?"

Her words were not spoken with menace, only a great weariness, yet Mrs. Claiborne blenched.

"He would never have done anything like that!" she cried. And then she looked to Holmes, as if Holmes were Solomon himself, able to settle any disputes. "*Would* he?"

The anguish in her voice—did anyone truly dare to confront the possibility that a beloved someone could be a monster?

Holmes, her calm unwavering, asked, "What manner of man would you say he was, Mrs. Claiborne?"

Mrs. Claiborne was taken aback by the question. "I don't know how much my opinion will count, since I desperately do not want him to have had anything to do with Miss Duffin's death . . . But since you asked, Mr. Underwood is—was an excellent man."

After this initial appraisal, her voice grew a little steadier. "He was loyal and took his responsibilities seriously. But he was also kind—and not only to me. He was kind insofar as kindness was possible. I would have a remarkably difficult time believing him of senseless killing—and if you do manage to convince me, I shall be completely devastated."

Holmes turned to Mrs. Farr. "Your foster children gave good reports on Mr. Underwood, I believe?"

To Lord Ingram's surprise, after a moment of silence Mrs. Farr nodded.

"Did Mr. Underwood ever tell you anything about Giovanni Esposito, the first boxer he took on?"

This question was for Mrs. Claiborne, who leaped to it. "Yes, he accidentally ran over Johnny's father when he was chasing down suspected foreign agents for Lord Bancroft. He couldn't stop in the heat of the chase but went back as soon as possible and then did everything in his power to make sure that the man's family was taken care of.

"He always felt guilty about it, even though it was the senior Mr. Esposito who had stumbled drunkenly into the street. Mrs. Esposito even told him that her husband would have left them if he hadn't died, and still Mr. Underwood never forgave himself."

On the divan, Jessie gave a slight jerk. She turned still again, but it would not be long now before the effects of the chloroform wore off.

In the parlor, Holmes had more questions. "It might appear that Mr. Underwood took on Miss Ferguson and Mr. Waters because he wanted to give Johnny companions who were even more despised by the general public?"

Something that was almost amusement curved Mrs. Claiborne's lips. "I wouldn't put it quite that way. He wanted Johnny to have friends—the boy worked constantly and had few solaces in life. But he didn't want random lads who'd mock Johnny for being poor, foreign, and Catholic. He liked how Mumble and Jessie looked out for each other and how well they managed their lives. He thought Johnny would feel safe and happy with them, and he was right." She turned to Mrs. Farr. "Mr. Underwood told me that Johnny is never happier than when he is with your foster children."

Mrs. Farr's right hand closed into a fist.

Holmes rose and came to Lord Ingram. He thought she had some information to impart, but she only stood beside him and addressed the parlor. "I used to think Mr. Underwood heavily involved in Miss Mimi Duffin's death, but now I'm less certain."

Mrs. Claiborne, who had at last picked up the glass of water

Holmes had poured for her, clutched it with both hands and stared at Holmes.

"Here's what I think might have happened. Lord Bancroft told Mr. Underwood that he was looking for a dark-haired young woman with a beauty mark at the corner of her lips—and who had allowed risqué images of herself to be captured for public consumption. In hindsight, we can pinpoint Lord Bancroft's purposes—the physical resemblance to make this woman a better duplicate for Lady Ingram, the profession so that when she went missing, her family, having likely already disowned her, would not mount a search. But Mr. Underwood did not have such foreknowledge to guide him.

"Mr. Constable, the accountant who dispensed funds to the boxers for Mr. Underwood, had instruction from Mr. Underwood that his transactions could be inspected by anyone who wished to do so.

"Mumble and Jessie took advantage of that, and so did I. But given that the stipulation was handed down long before Mr. Underwood took on Mumble and Jessie, he did not have them in mind—or me for that matter. Who did he think would want to see those accounts then?"

"Lord Bancroft," murmured Mrs. Claiborne.

"Indeed," agreed Holmes. "It's possible that while they continued to work well together, the trust between them, or at least that Mr. Underwood felt for Lord Bancroft, had corroded somewhat: He believed Lord Bancroft might check on his personal pursuits, and he did not want to be seen as hiding anything.

"By the same token, Lord Bancroft might have grown increasingly suspicious of Mr. Underwood for the exact reason others came to love and depend on him: his scruples. As Lord Bancroft's ventures sailed further and further from the shores of acceptability, a lieutenant who was fundamentally decent and principled became less and less of an asset.

"Most likely, then, Lord Bancroft concealed what he truly intended with that dark-haired woman with a beauty mark—and declared his reasons private.

"Mr. Underwood, having looked into Mumble's and Jessie's backgrounds, happened to know that Mrs. Farr's sister suited Lord Bancroft's needs. Mrs. Claiborne, did he ever ask you, explicitly, whether Lord Bancroft had any unusual proclivities?"

Mrs. Claiborne set down her water glass with an audible *thunk*. "My goodness, he did, somewhere in the middle of last year. He rarely asked about my years with Lord Bancroft—or about Lord Bancroft himself—and then, out of the blue, a question like that.

"He told me that Lord Bancroft was looking for a woman of certain attributes. He didn't say what those attributes were—the word *postcard* never crossed his lips—only that he wanted to make sure that if he did find such a woman for Lord Bancroft, it wouldn't lead to anything intolerable for her.

"Once I was assured that he wasn't faultfinding *me*, I told him that Lord Bancroft was a rather inconsiderate lover, but not a cruel or bizarre one." With a hesitant glance in Mrs. Farr's direction, Mrs. Claiborne added, "Miss Holmes, you think Mr. Underwood asked the question for Miss Mimi Duffin's sake?"

"I do," concurred Holmes. "If Mr. Underwood was assured that Lord Bancroft would not mistreat a lover, and if he had no reason to believe that Lord Bancroft wanted a postcard girl for anything other than personal titillation, then he likely informed Lord Bancroft of Miss Mimi Duffin's existence.

"When he learned of the horrifying truth, it was too late. Soon after that, he had to go on the run himself. If not, today he might very well be trying to make it up to you, Mrs. Farr, the way he was trying to make it up to Johnny and his family."

———※———

Mrs. Farr stared at nothing in particular.

"Miss Ferguson and Mr. Waters are waking up," said Lord Ingram.

Mrs. Farr shot up and had to steady herself on an armrest before she charged into the boudoir. Mrs. Watson had half a mind to follow her. But as Mrs. Farr probably preferred some privacy, Mrs. Watson remained in the corner chair where she had been seated since she walked Mrs. Farr back into the parlor.

Miss Charlotte left Lord Ingram's side and retook her own seat. While Mrs. Farr whispered to her foster children, Miss Charlotte addressed Mrs. Claiborne: "Madame, I believe you already know who killed Mr. Underwood?"

The Frenchwoman shuddered.

"When did Mr. Underwood begin to change his mind about Lord Bancroft?" continued Miss Charlotte.

Mrs. Claiborne gripped the engagement ring on her left hand, her lover's token of devotion and commitment. "That happened before Mr. Underwood became my protector, I think, but I didn't perceive it right away. My first inkling came when he said that at least on the night he ran over the senior Mr. Esposito, he'd been doing something genuinely important, but he wasn't so sure about his assignments since then.

"At the time I thought he meant that he'd received mundane, tedious tasks. Until he started to talk about Lord Bancroft. I already mentioned that Lord Bancroft rarely came up as a topic of conversation between us, as he was awkwardly both my former paramour and Mr. Underwood's then still-current superior.

"Yet Mr. Underwood abruptly began to share his recollections of Lord Bancroft—and he did so compulsively. Lord Bancroft plucking him out of obscurity to become his right-hand man. Lord Bancroft enabling him to leave service altogether. Without Lord Bancroft, he would not have achieved a similar level of financial security. Without Lord Bancroft, he would never have met me.

"After a while I realized that these paeans of praise were not expressions of faith and gratitude but manifestations of fear: His faith and gratitude were fading and must be bolstered with recitations of old favors."

Mrs. Claiborne rubbed her thumb over the old-mine-cut sapphire on her ring. "I let go of most of my staff when I accepted him as a protector, so I had some light housework every day. He used to dust and polish alongside me and frankly did everything better, thanks to his training in the Duke of Wycliffe's household when he was young.

"I loved those moments—I'd never had a protector who was also something of a partner. When the work was done, we would sit down at the piano and I would teach him how to play.

"Around the time he began to forcibly recall all the ways in which Lord Bancroft had been a positive influence in his life, he started doing heavier and heavier work around the house, tasks I usually left for the charwoman who still came in a few times a week. He would haul coal, shine grates, scrub and polish floors, even in the attic. It was as if he was trying to exhaust himself—or to remain occupied with something, anything.

"And instead of playing music, sometimes he would simply sit on the piano bench and stare at the keys. One day he smashed his fist into the keys and made such a ruckus that I very nearly dropped the book I was pretending to read. After that, he never spoke again of the Lord Bancroft of yesteryear, the one to whom he owed eternal allegiance.

"Not long after that, Lord Bancroft lost his favor with the crown. Before he went into hiding himself, Mr. Underwood sat me down and told me that Lord Bancroft had sold state secrets. But even then he couldn't bring himself to say anything about Mimi Duffin. It's only now, knowing everything I do, that I can look back and see that he'd smashed the piano and stopped talking about Lord Bancroft right around the time Miss Duffin went missing."

"Why didn't the two of you leave the country after Lord Bancroft was arrested?" asked Mrs. Watson.

It was the most useless question and certain to be painful, but for once Mrs. Watson couldn't help herself. These two lovers' failure to escape to a new life saddened and frightened her in equal measure. It made the world seem too cruel, too indifferent.

Mrs. Claiborne gazed down at the engagement ring on her hand that would now never nestle against a wedding ring. "If Lord Bancroft hadn't been caught soon after Miss Duffin's murder, if he'd killed her and blithely went on to sell more state secrets and perhaps arrange for other innocent people's deaths in cold blood, I believe Mr. Underwood would have found a way to take me and leave.

"But Lord Bancroft had been brought low. He was born a lordship, he'd risen high on his own merit in service to the crown, and now, all of a sudden, he was a prisoner. Mr. Underwood was loyal to a fault; he could not find it in himself to abandon Lord Bancroft right when he had been toppled off his pedestal.

"Another reason it wasn't so easy for him to flee to the other side of the world was that Lord Bancroft had entrusted him with two keys. He'd never been told what the keys were for or where the locks they would open were located, only that he should guard the keys with his life. Mr. Underwood could not pass the keys to anyone else. But had he absconded with them, he would have ensured retribution from Lord Bancroft."

Mrs. Watson's heart thrashed—did the keys lead to Lord Bancroft's ill-begotten gains? Miss Charlotte listened with the guileless expression of someone who had never schemed to rob Lord Bancroft of his unlawful proceeds.

Mrs. Claiborne sighed. "Around April of this year, Mr. Underwood was told to hand over one of the keys to a stranger at a pub just shy of East London. This worried him greatly. He believed the keys opened safe-deposit boxes and the contents of those boxes must be highly valuable. That Lord Bancroft was willing to give up half of his greatest treasures meant that he was planning something. Or rather, that something had already been planned and would soon be carried out.

"Also, he worried because he considered his—and my—safety linked to his possession of the keys. With one key left, he felt we were only half as safe.

"Six—no, seven weeks ago he received further instruction: I was to move out of the villa. I didn't object to that. Though the house was in my name, I hadn't bought it, and I'd only ever considered myself Lord Bancroft's tenant, subject to eviction at any moment." So much for the scar-faced man Mrs. Watson had been on the lookout for. Lies, all lies.

"But the strange thing was that this woman, Mrs. Kirby, came. She said she was sent by Lord Bancroft and asked me all sorts of intimate questions about myself and Mr. Underwood. When Mr. Underwood learned of this, he told me that he'd been cautioned to stay out of sight—not that he wasn't already—but to stay out of sight in such a manner that no one could find him. I believe it had been strongly suggested that he ought to vacate London for the time being.

"So there I was, staying in a flat near Victoria Street, with no idea what was going on. One day Mr. Underwood came and said I had to leave immediately. He had a hackney waiting. We got in and he confided that he was in trouble. He'd found out that Lord Bancroft's recent shenanigans were meant to entrap someone. He wanted to warn that someone but believed that his efforts had been discovered. And now Lord Bancroft had asked for the other key.

"Once Lord Bancroft had the other key, Mr. Underwood would become disposable. But if he didn't give it, he was afraid that Lord Bancroft would use me to threaten him. So he had to get me to safety. And safety, as I later learned, meant Mrs. Farr's house."

She flicked the corners of her eyes with her fingertips. "Mrs. Farr did keep me safe. But Mr. Underwood . . . there was no one left to save *him*."

Twenty-seven

Mumble and Jessie were now awake enough to leave. As Lord Ingram and Miss Charlotte helped them out, with Mrs. Farr hovering close, Mrs. Claiborne took Mrs. Watson aside.

"I'm a little worried for Mrs. Farr," she said. "After she learned that Mr. Underwood knew something of her sister's death, she became excitable and impatient. She had her foster children over frequently—not just Mumble and Jessie but that young man—"

She tilted her chin at the hackney and the cabbie who had taken Miss Charlotte's message to Mrs. Farr and then brought back Mrs. Farr and Mrs. Claiborne—Mrs. Watson would guess him to be Robert Epping, the man who, on paper at least, owned the house in which Mumble and Jessie lived. "And also a young woman who owns a bakery. They were discussing things and making plans at all hours of the day. But tonight, after news came that you had Mumble and Jessie, it was as if something inside Mrs. Farr collapsed."

Mrs. Watson knew what she meant. Even on the night Mrs. Farr had learned of her sister's death, she had not appeared so overwhelmed.

So broken down.

"And you must be careful, too," continued Mrs. Claiborne. "You and Miss Holmes and everyone else here tonight. I believe that you are the ones Lord Bancroft wanted to entrap—the ones Mr. Underwood wanted to warn. Please . . ."

Please don't let anything happen to you, not when Mr. Underwood lost his life trying to save yours.

Mrs. Claiborne did not finish her sentence. She only nodded at Mrs. Watson and hurried to join Mrs. Farr and her foster children in the hackney.

Mrs. Watson exhaled. Of course they were the ones Lord Bancroft meant to entrap. They hadn't always been 100 percent sure what roles Mr. Underwood and Mrs. Claiborne—real and sham—played in the scheme, but about Lord Bancroft's malice there had never been any doubt.

Mrs. Watson, Miss Charlotte, and Lord Ingram returned to the parlor. Miss Charlotte yawned. Mrs. Watson's mind still raced, even though her eyes felt gritty and her head woolly.

"My lord," said Miss Charlotte, rubbing her arm that had been sorely tried in combat with Jessie, "we didn't have time to discuss this earlier, but you showed the counterfeit Mrs. Claiborne's picture to your liaison inside De Lacey Industries?"

The dear young man had been keeping strange hours of late. Perhaps for that reason, tonight he looked no worse for wear, clear-eyed and alert. "I did. The counterfeit Mrs. Claiborne—what did the real Mrs. Claiborne call her? Mrs. Kirby? She had been seen there."

De Lacey Industries belonged to Moriarty's organization. Mrs. Watson sucked in a breath. "So Lord Bancroft really did form an alliance with Moriarty. But if he must blame someone for his downfall, Moriarty was almost as much at fault as Miss Charlotte here."

"Holmes, however, would never seek to cultivate my brother," said Lord Ingram, gathering up used cups and plates from the tea table. "But Moriarty must look upon a disgraced Bancroft as someone potentially useful, a wellspring of highly sensitive intelligence, if nothing else."

"Does that mean the men holding Miss Bernadine and my staff hostage are Moriarty's minions?"

Lord Ingram, carrying the dishes on a tray, walked toward the door. "I'm inclined to agree with your initial assessment that they are mercenaries. Moriarty and his lieutenants have had to rely on mercenaries of late, since they themselves are short of personnel."

Miss Charlotte held the door for him to walk through.

"But mercenaries must be expensive," said Mrs. Watson. "Will Lord Bancroft have to become Moriarty's minion, too, to pay him back? I hardly think he'd subject himself to the sort of control Moriarty likes to exert over his underlings."

"Nor do I," answered the great detective. "Which means Lord Bancroft would have needed to put up something valuable in exchange for Moriarty's help. One moment, please."

She, too, left the parlor and came back a minute later with a photograph.

"Do you remember, ma'am, the cache of photographic plates we took from Château Vaudrieu?"

In an effort to save Mrs. Watson's old friend—and former lover— the Maharani of Ajmer from blackmail, Sherlock Holmes and company had inadvertently burgled none other than Moriarty's stronghold outside Paris. Mrs. Watson had never examined the loot in detail, but she knew that Miss Charlotte had gone through all the photographic plates to make sure that there had been nothing incriminating concerning the maharani or her family members in those images.

"Lord Bancroft was captured in one of those photographs. I don't think he was the intended subject of the photograph—which was a group of men I didn't recognize—but he'd been caught in the periphery."

Miss Charlotte handed the photograph to Mrs. Watson. The picture was barely half the size of Mrs. Watson's palm. And there he was, a miniature Lord Bancroft, seated on the terrace of a café, one ankle on his knee.

"By the time I came across this, Lord Bancroft was already confined to Ravensmere. All the same, I alerted Lord Ingram to the existence of the photograph, and he took a look before he committed our entire cache to a safe-deposit box in Paris."

Miss Charlotte now handed another photograph to Mrs. Watson, this one much larger.

"Why, it's the exact same place!" exclaimed Mrs. Watson.

Except this photograph had been taken from a higher vantage point, and there was a milliner's next to the café, rather than a tobacconist's.

"Being better traveled than I, his lordship immediately recognized the place in the photograph as Bruges. And in January of this year, he traveled there and took this second photograph from a nearby hotel.

"Lord Bancroft, on the other hand, is not much of a traveler. I believe he undertook a standard grand tour in his youth, but did not stray much from these shores in recent years. It's quite possible he went to Bruges to conduct some of the illicit business that led to his downfall.

"But our dear lord Ingram, being the enterprising gentleman he is, walked around the district in Bruges, located several financial institutions, and inquired at each about the hiring of safe-deposit boxes. One bank didn't offer such services, but the other two did.

"And as he never ceases to amaze us, he broke into the bank managers' offices, checked the records, and found one box leased to a name that he recognized. Not Lord Bancroft's own, of course, but an alias he had used in his youth, when he didn't want his father to find out that he had opened a line of credit at an expensive establishment."

Mrs. Watson's jaw hung open. "So you know what the crown has failed to find out. You know where Lord Bancroft's ill-begotten gains are."

"But we don't have the key to it," said Lord Ingram, back from the kitchen in the basement and still drying his hands with a handkerchief. "And the bank's strong room is highly secured, with a steel door that's quite beyond my lock-picking skills."

"Which is really too bad. Had we known then what troubles he would create for us, we'd have dug a tunnel under and picked the box clean," said Miss Charlotte, rather savagely for her.

"And now Moriarty has the loot," lamented Mrs. Watson.

Certainly they hadn't found anything remotely resembling a key on Mr. Underwood.

"Well, I don't think that money was ever meant to be ours," said Miss Charlotte. "But it's a shame I can't show these photographs to Lord Bancroft and taunt him that we already have his hoard."

"Without showing the photographs, you can still hint that to Bancroft," said Lord Ingram. "That thought should make Bancroft lose sleep, especially if he has already promised the money to Moriarty."

That prospect made Mrs. Watson lie down with a smile on her face.

She slept until about eight. Lord Ingram had already left. She and Miss Charlotte dressed and returned to their hotel to wash and change. When they arrived, however, they found that an urgent telegram had come overnight from Paris.

Penelope had been barred from visiting Miss Bernadine the previous evening. Even young Fontainebleu had been kicked out. And they had been told in no uncertain terms that they would not be allowed back inside again.

There was also a typed, unsigned message, which could only have come from Lord Bancroft: If they wanted to see Miss Bernadine alive and well again, they must assist in his escape from Ravensmere.

Tonight.

Twenty-eight

The estate at Ravensmere had a ten-foot-high outer wall running around its entire periphery. Within those boundaries, there was a solid secondary wall topped with glass shards that secured the large French garden. Near the manor itself, the garden was divided yet again by a wrought iron fence across its entire width, which made for three sets of obstacles altogether if one approached from the front.

But from the back one did not need to deal with the wrought iron fence, only the two sets of walls.

Bancroft's instructions were specific. Sherlock Holmes and company were to provide him passage over those two walls and transportation to a spot of his choosing—and they were to be ready at quarter past one in the morning.

There was no surveillance beyond the outermost wall, so they put up a ladder. Lord Ingram, his back laden, climbed up and waited, his hands tight on the ladder's side rails.

"Nice, isn't it?" said Bancroft, barely twenty years of age. He had been handsomer then, and laughed more.

"It's wonderful!" exclaimed a seven-year-old Lord Ingram, his heart bursting with pride and happiness as he beheld the model railway that took up an entire dining table. "I don't think I'll ever love anything more. Thank you, Bancroft!"

"Of course. Anything for my little brother."

He closed his eyes and listened.

There were three guards patrolling the grounds, one within the wrought iron fence, one in the French garden, and a third between the two sets of walls.

The heavy footfalls of the third guard thumped past after fifteen minutes. Lord Ingram had walked along the peripheries outside the walls and estimated that at the guard's current speed, it would take him thirty minutes to come back to the same spot. He let three minutes pass, then carefully lowered himself to the ground on the other side of the wall.

In the wide corridor between the two walls, there was only short grass. He crossed to the second wall, helped by the darkness of an overcast night.

Here his task became trickier. On the other side of the wall was the manor. The guard in the area immediately outside the manor had the least ground to cover. He made a round every five or six minutes, and would hear any loud noises.

The guard trundled past. Lord Ingram unfastened the items on his back and imitated a nightingale's warble. No replies came, but shortly after the guard went by again, he heard a soft *thud*. He made the nightingale call again and this time, after fifteen seconds, an answering call came from almost directly opposite him on the other side of the wall.

He tossed a thick mat above the embedded glass shards atop the wall and threw over a rope ladder. Immediately the ladder tautened and pulled. A darker shadow appeared atop the wall. Bancroft.

As soon as Bancroft lowered himself to the ground, Lord Ingram retracted the rope ladder and yanked down the mat. Without a word, they marched to the outer wall. Bancroft sounded out of breath, his footsteps uneven, but he kept up.

When they reached the spot where Lord Ingram had entered Ravensmere, he again tossed the rope ladder over. On the other side, Holmes's and Mrs. Watson's combined weight would anchor it.

The brothers scaled the wall, Lord Ingram last, gathering up the rope ladder as he stood atop the other ladder before descending to the ground.

Mrs. Watson, who held the ladder, hugged him briefly. Could she feel his heart pounding? Inside Ravensmere he had felt strangely nerveless. But now that Bancroft was free, he was sick to his stomach.

Holmes took the rope ladder from him, Mrs. Watson the mat; he hefted up the ladder. They were about to depart when Bancroft whispered, "Give me all your firearms."

They glanced at one another and submitted four pieces, one revolver apiece from Lord Ingram and Mrs. Watson, and one derringer apiece from Mrs. Watson and Holmes.

Holmes began walking. Everyone else followed in single file, with Bancroft bringing up the rear, a revolver in each hand. Lord Ingram, directly in front of Bancroft, felt the presence of those revolvers, their muzzles a pair of metallic eyes boring into his back.

——— ❉ ———

They walked for more than a mile before they arrived at a cabin in a clearing by a stream. Lawson was there, waiting, a pair of lanterns next to him. "Ma'am, Miss Holmes—"

Bancroft preempted him. "Where is the balm I asked you to bring?"

Mrs. Watson handed him a tin, thoughtfully opening the lid as she did so.

"I'll need some whisky, too."

Mrs. Watson gave him a flask, again with its lid removed. Bancroft took two large draughts, then removed his gloves and dabbed the balm on his hands, hissing in pain as he did so.

Holmes had told Lord Ingram that Bancroft looked different. He did. The shadowy light illuminated a bitter old man.

"Your change of clothes and shoes are inside the cabin," Holmes told him. "There are sandwiches, too, if you need sustenance."

"We will leave as soon as I change."

Lawson had the carriage ready. Bancroft emerged from the cabin a few minutes later, clad in a country squire's summer tweed and boater hat, the small satchel of extra clothes and essentials they had prepared for him in his hand.

The sandwiches, on the other hand, had been left behind in the cabin. Bancroft had not become less suspicious with captivity, but really, he was suspecting all the wrong things.

Holmes, who had not wasted a single crumb since her outcast days, packed up the sandwiches in a small basket.

"Well," she said to Bancroft, her tone uninflected, "good-bye and good luck in your freedom."

"But it's not time for good-byes yet."

"Oh? But you asked to be dropped off at the abbey, and Lawson here will do just that."

"And you, Mrs. Watson, and my brother will accompany me. Otherwise, how can I be sure you will not go back to Ravensmere to let them know where I am headed?"

Lord Ingram's heart thudded again, a slow, difficult motion smothered by the despair in his chest. Why could this not be good-bye? Why couldn't freedom be enough for his brother?

"Very well," said Holmes. "We will come with you."

Lawson drove carefully in the pitch-black night. They had five miles to cover, and it took close to an hour.

As they approached the ruined abbey, birds startled into flight, their wings thrashing loudly. Owls hooted. In the deeper recesses of the derelict edifice, other creatures shuffled and slithered.

The moon came out from behind the clouds as Bancroft leaped off the carriage. He had been silent since they left the cabin and had looked out the window in tense watchfulness. Now, as he stretched and loosened his limbs, for the first time he seemed genuinely excited by the end of his incarceration.

Are you interested only in the things of long-dead people, Ash? What about those long-dead people themselves—ever think about them?

That, too, had been in summer. Bancroft had been in his mid-twenties, and they had been walking across a moonlit glade that twinkled with fireflies.

Pain stole upon Lord Ingram like a mist, hazy yet all-enveloping.

"How does it feel, little brother, that you of all people had to break me out of captivity?"

His words pierced Lord Ingram like a knife of ice. "Now that you're here, I assume good-byes can commence?"

"Not yet. I am ever so slightly early to my rendezvous, so you might as well remain my companions a little longer." Bancroft spun around slowly, the revolvers he had taken from Lord Ingram and Mrs. Watson in his hands. "Well, have you no questions for me, Miss Holmes?"

Holmes, just then alighting from the carriage, thought about it. "Hydrochloric acid?"

"You mean, how I managed to remove the iron cage from my window. Why, yes, young lady."

"So for all that you gave me a veritable dissertation on how impregnable Ravensmere was, you long ago pinpointed the one great weakness in its security: If you could remove the bars on the windows, then there would be very little to prevent you from a quick dash to the outer walls."

Bancroft chortled. "Worked that out finally, did you?"

At the smugness in his tone, Lord Ingram's hand closed into a fist. "How did you obtain hydrochloric acid in Ravensmere?"

"Simple. The charwoman needed money and could be bought. And she's been there so long the guards no longer bother to check her basket anymore. Even if they noticed something, they would have assumed that it was a bottle of booze she was smuggling in for someone."

Holmes rubbed her lower back. "I'm assuming Mr. Underwood did not participate in any of this? Remarkable how much you were able to accomplish without him, my lord. You really didn't need him after all."

"He was disposable, like everyone else."

"Such as Mrs. Kirby, the counterfeit Mrs. Claiborne?"

Bancroft raised a brow. "So you found her out? Well, women are especially disposable."

Lord Ingram forced his breaths to remain even. He had never met Mimi Duffin or Constantina Greville, the *other* woman killed so that there would be a corpse that could pass for his then wife, but their fate would always haunt him.

"I feel bad for her," said Holmes quietly. "I feel worse for Mr. Underwood, since there were indications that he died trying to warn me."

"The wages of disloyalty. I would have suffered him to live after we caught him, but he tried to escape. And those mercenaries guarding him had no understanding of subtlety."

"Would you really have suffered him to live—or did you merely not want to deal with his corpse for a while? After all, in this weather, a body would not keep very well, and one thrown away willy-nilly would quickly end up in police custody. You knew that I would not have neglected to check new unclaimed bodies that came in."

Bancroft sniffed but made no reply.

"Did it displease you when I stumbled upon his body?"

"Sometimes the meddlesome are unaccountably lucky. His body would have been in that coal cellar mere hours before being removed. But you had to happen upon it."

She shook her head slowly. "You invited me to ask questions, my lord, but now that I ask questions, you don't seem too pleased."

Lord Ingram almost chortled aloud. Bancroft invited questions because he wished to gloat, but the questions Holmes asked were hardly conducive to that.

"In that case, I might as well eat a sandwich. Are you sure you still don't want any?" She sat down on a large round stone and held out the basket toward Bancroft.

"I am sure," he said frostily.

"And you, my lord Ingram, anything for you?"

Lord Ingram's stomach was wound tight. Still, he walked toward her. "What do you have?"

"Cheese sandwiches and butter-and-jam sandwiches."

"I'll take a cheese sandwich."

She gave him a paper package. He opened the package and sniffed the salty sharpness of cheddar. It was nice, sitting shoulder to shoulder with her in the moonlight, sandwich in hand, as if they were a pair of children who had run away from home—but not too far—for a nighttime adventure.

She didn't eat her sandwich but only drank from her canteen. "Mrs. Watson? Lawson?"

They declined. Lawson remained by the side of the carriage; Mrs. Watson stood close to him.

Bancroft resumed his ambling. At one point he ventured a few steps into the ruins and set a hand on a still-standing arch. He even hummed for a while. As time passed, however, he fell silent.

"Are you still early for your rendezvous?" Holmes asked, after another quarter hour.

The night had become cool, the spill of moonlight on blades of grass white as frost.

Bancroft did not answer.

"Or is the party you are meeting running late?" Holmes continued, perfectly—or perhaps deliberately—oblivious to the irritation Bancroft radiated.

"Things don't always run according to schedule."

"*We* managed despite the very short notice, Mrs. Watson, Lord Ingram, Lawson, and I," said Holmes. "Those tardy folks, were they the ones originally entrusted with your escape from Ravensmere?"

Bancroft sounded as if he spoke through clenched teeth. "They have, by and large, already fulfilled their end of the bargain."

"Only to abandon you in the middle of nowhere?"

Lord Ingram wanted to laugh at the frustration on Bancroft's face, but he didn't dare. He didn't dare tempt Fate by laughing too early.

They could still show up, the people Bancroft was waiting for. And if they did, then Sherlock Holmes and company would be in greater trouble than even Holmes's cleverness could handle.

"I wonder what has delayed them, your allies," murmured Holmes. "I wonder."

Twenty-nine

A FEW HOURS AGO

D e Lacey, Moriarty's chief lieutenant in Britain, was uneasy.
Since he'd joined De Lacey Industries, there had been three
other de Laceys, each a wilier, more capable man than he, and each
had met an unnatural demise. So the former Timmy Ruston dared
not be too comfortable in his new identity, his new authority, or his
new surroundings.

A man of extremely moderate ambitions, he believed in sticking to one's primary proficiency. In the case of De Lacey Industries, it meant doing what they'd always done, what they'd proved
beyond a shadow of a doubt to be good at: the fleecing of other en-
terprises.

But forces beyond his control always pushed new and uncertain
tasks on him. Case in point, Lord Bancroft Ashburton.

De Lacey did not want to traffic in state secrets. But Moriarty,
referred to by his subordinates as Mr. Baxter, much as Timmy Ruston was de Lacey, hankered for state secrets as opium addicts needed
their next puff. For months, Mrs. Kirby, the woman he'd sent to ne-
gotiate with Lord Bancroft, had prowled in and out of de Lacey's
fiefdom, treating it quite as her own.

When Moriarty and Lord Bancroft had at last settled on the

terms of their agreement, de Lacey had almost laughed to learn that Lord Bancroft had wanted a disposable woman agent and Mr. Baxter had said why not sacrifice Kirby the negotiator—neither had any use for her afterward.

But the pleasure de Lacey took in her misfortune was quickly displaced by fear. She might have been annoying, but had she been any less capable or less loyal than he?

What, in the end, would be his fate?

At least Mr. Baxter had been pleased about Lord Bancroft's partial surrender.

De Lacey, who had to do the actual work of arranging for Lord Bancroft's escape, was less pleased. His lordship had devised a plan he proclaimed to be foolproof, not realizing that de Lacey wasn't worried about fools but gods.

The gods punished hubris.

He'd learned the word from Mr. Baxter. Immediately after Mr. Baxter had executed a previous de Lacey at a company soiree, he'd said, "The man had too much hubris. And too much hubris displeases the gods."

Yet men like Mr. Baxter and Lord Bancroft feared no gods.

But that was because the gods had not yet acted.

Charlotte Holmes, of course, wasn't a god. But to de Lacey, she was a countervailing force, a reminder from the gods to the Mr. Baxters and the Lord Bancrofts of the world not to go too far.

One ought to leave some people alone. A woman who managed to escape Mr. Baxter's trap unscathed—and who now had Lord Remington Ashburton's protection—ranked high among "some people."

Of course, de Lacey, with his sheer mediocrity, could not make the great men around him understand that. But at least his own part in all this was coming to an end. Tonight, in fact. He didn't mind in the least the request to pick Lord Bancroft up from the abandoned old abbey a day or two early. The soonest over, the best.

He planned to arrive at the abandoned abbey fashionably late, at quarter to four in the morning. Which meant he needed to reach De

Lacey Industries by quarter past eleven, to load the body into a second vehicle.

For the sake of comity and politesse—the vocabulary he'd acquired since he'd first met Mr. Baxter!—he'd acceded to Lord Bancroft's request to hold Underwood's body. But after tonight, it didn't need to stay hidden anymore. Might as well get rid of it at the ruins. It would bother no one there and might even provide sustenance to carrion eaters.

His brougham stopped. De Lacey, who had dozed off a little, if with worrying thoughts crowding the landscape of his head like so many uncounted sheep, opened his eyes and glanced at his watch. Perfect timing.

His coachman opened the door. But instead of standing back respectfully to let him descend, the man leaned into the vehicle and whispered urgently, "Mr. de Lacey, something ain't right! Men are coming out from the front door."

A jolt went through de Lacey. "What do you mean?"

He pulled aside the carriage curtain. Across the street, there were indeed men exiting the wide-open front door of De Lacey Industries. Moreover, there were several police vans piled helter-skelter in the street, with uniformed men milling about.

De Lacey, having been a petty criminal in his youth, had a healthy fear of the police, especially a uniformed bobby wielding a nightstick. But Mr. Baxter was a criminal of a different order of magnitude, the kind who never had to deal with the law. And De Lacey Industries, on the outside at least, was a legitimate business with legitimate assets generating legitimate profits.

De Lacey swallowed his instinctive trepidation, leaped out of the brougham, and charged toward his fiefdom.

He was stopped at the door by an owlish-looking man. "Mr. de Lacey, I presume? You quite resemble your photograph in the foyer."

De Lacey regarded the man warily. "And you are?"

"Chief Inspector Fowler of Scotland Yard. How do you do, Mr. de Lacey?"

Fowler. De Lacey remembered that name. The one who had investigated the murder at Stern Hollow last year and mistakenly arrested Lord Ingram.

Chief Inspector Fowler, however, did not look like a man with an egg on his face. Instead, he seemed to be someone who had single-handedly found all the eggs at Easter and could barely restrain himself from outright gloating.

"If I may ask, what are you doing here, Chief Inspector?"

Only as de Lacey barked the question did he notice that the policeman's attire was mud-stained. An effort had been made to brush away the splotches, but still, now that he paid attention . . . why in the world would anyone who hadn't been crawling around a pig farm have this much mud on his person?

"I am, of course, investigating a serious crime, which then turned out to be a number of serious crimes, Mr. de Lacey, all on the very premises of De Lacey Industries, if you can believe that."

De Lacey was so staggered he barely heard the alarm clanging in the back of his head. "Chief Inspector, I have no idea of what you speak. This is a most respectable establishment, and there are no crimes of any kind taking place either on these premises or in any activities connected with the running of De Lacey Industries."

"Oh, I certainly *thought* this a most respectable establishment, but I'm afraid I've had my mind changed for me tonight." The policeman wagged a finger. "What kind of respectable establishment, Mr. de Lacey, would dig a tunnel from its wine cellar to the strong room of the City and Suburban Bank, where there sit thirty thousand pounds' worth of napoleons borrowed from the Banque de France?"

If the policeman had told him that he was the long-lost tenth child of Queen Victoria and her prince consort, he could not have been more dumbfounded. What tunnel? What bank? He vaguely recalled that there was a bank on a parallel street, but the business of De Lacey Industries was not bank-robbing. There weren't even any plans to rob banks, let alone tunnels already dug from the cellar.

Wait, the cellar? The *wine* cellar?

Officially, there was no wine cellar. Because the wine cellar was beneath the subbasement, and the very respectable De Lacey Industries, officially, at least, had no subbasement!

But—but—

De Lacey stared some more at the mud stains on the policeman's clothes. If there had really been a tunnel running from De Lacey Industries to the branch of City and Suburban Bank on the next street, and Chief Inspector Fowler had crawled through that tunnel and reached the wine cellar, then he would have come out of the wine cellar—never mind how he managed that with the wine cellar padlocked from the outside—directly into the subbasement.

And in the subbasement—

"As if it is not egregious enough that you have done that," continued Fowler, "what should I discover when I came up, but *prisoners* in your lower basement? Six individuals held against their will, some for months."

"There—there must have been some mistake. There—"

Dear God, *six individuals held against their will*, did the policeman say? *Six?* But there had been only five prisoners in the subbasement.

"Oh, believe me, Mr. de Lacey, there was no mistake. I, as well as my men, even two directors of the City and Suburban Bank, can bear witness to that in court."

Perhaps this was not real. Perhaps he was in fact being driven to the ruined abbey and suffering from a nightmare featuring an abundance of horrors well beyond what his own limited mind could have conjured.

"And guess what we found in addition to those prisoners held against their will? A dead body kept on ice, a man who had been shot in the back."

Fowler's words still ringing in de Lacey's head, he saw two uniformed men carry out a stretcher. Under the sheet lay no doubt the late Mr. Underwood, now no longer to be breakfast for crows and vultures.

Behind them, four men and two women slowly shuffled out of De

Lacey Industries. One of the women saw de Lacey and flashed a sardonic smile, as if to say, *Your turn, you knobstick.*

And the other woman—he felt faint. The other woman was *Lady Ingram*, who had been at large since last autumn and never found, let alone brought to him for incarceration.

"Chief Inspector," he said hoarsely, "I'm afraid there has been a horrible mix-up. There have never been any dead bodies at De Lacey Industries, any prisoners, or any tunnels."

"Well, Mr. de Lacey, I came via the tunnel, so most assuredly there is a tunnel. The prisoners that I and a dozen men of sound mind freed from the subbasement were certainly there, and they told me not only that you were the one who personally brought them their food every day, but that for months on end, they'd heard digging crews come down to work at night. And that they heard you, swearing profusely, drag something heavy into the subbasement—and then brought in chunks of ice, too, which caused the temperature in the subbasement to drop."

Fowler smiled, now no longer trying to stop himself from gloating. "Mr. de Lacey, for all those reasons and more, I am placing you under arrest."

Thirty

By the Ruined Abbey

It was quarter past four. The very first suggestion of light glimmered along the eastern edge of the sky.

Charlotte's eyes were dry and the back of her head ached. But for someone who did not enjoy staying up late, her mind felt unusually sharp. Nimble, even. Her bottom, however, was numb from sitting on the cold rock. Lord Ingram had got up ten minutes ago to stretch his legs and now stood next to Mrs. Watson. Charlotte rose to her feet and shifted her weight around.

At her motion, Lord Bancroft, who had been staring at the dirt lane from which no cavalry had ridden to his rescue, wheeled around. "You did this, didn't you, Charlotte Holmes?"

They'd been in place almost an hour. Either Moriarty had abandoned him or something had happened.

Charlotte took a step back—she did not want to be any closer to Lord Bancroft. "Sir, you pay me a great compliment. But please remember, until a fortnight ago I was in Paris, minding my own business. And since then I've been running around London looking for Mr. Underwood and his murderer. You think that in my few minutes of spare time I could have managed to sunder your alliance with Moriarty?"

Lord Bancroft pointed an accusatory revolver muzzle. "You were up to something before that. In your note to me you said that you happened to already be in England because Ash broke his limb."

The revolver now jabbed in Lord Ingram's direction. "There is nothing the matter with Ash. He lied about it so you could come back to England."

"He did indeed lie about that, but it was only so that he could see me." She turned toward her lover, her voice gentle. "And you would not do such rash, childish things anymore, would you, Ash?"

Lord Ingram lowered his face and appeared commensurately contrite. "No, Holmes. I won't make you worry ever again."

She sighed. "You didn't make me worry. I guessed that you simply missed me too much. But poor Mrs. Watson, how she imagined all the worst."

"Oh, Miss Charlotte," piped up Mrs. Watson from beside the carriage, "don't give the poor boy a hard time. He was fine. We are fine. Everyone will be fine."

"Oh, I don't think so," growled Lord Bancroft.

"Wherever you were planning to go, my lord, Lawson can still drive you," said Charlotte soothingly. "And if you need some money until you can sort things out with Moriarty, there is twenty pounds in the satchel in usable denominations."

"I meant, I do not believe *you* will be fine." Lord Bancroft ground out the words.

Charlotte took another step back. "Still trying to hold on to your bargain with Moriarty even after he has abandoned you?"

"He did not abandon me—his men have been delayed. And yes, I will still uphold the bargain."

"What did you promise to do for him?"

The question came from Lord Ingram, his voice heavy.

There was almost enough light to make out the sneer on Lord Bancroft's face. "I promised him that your Holmes would no longer be a nuisance to him—or to me, for that matter."

And there it was finally his intention in the open, the last shred of pretense ripped away.

"It made sense, your bargain, given the agreement that now exists between myself and Lord Remington," mused Charlotte. "Moriarty would be wary of harming me himself, lest Remington's reprisal did more damage to his organization than what benefit he could reap by eliminating me as a potential threat. You, on the other hand, are not afraid of similar reprisals from your brother."

"Exactly. Given all that, why shouldn't I fulfill my bargain honorably and be rid of the person who robbed me of everything?"

Charlotte did not bother to explain that he had been the one who had destroyed his career and his standing: Lord Bancroft and his ilk blame only others, never themselves.

"Because you have bargained with a highly unsuitable party," she said instead. "Have you forgotten Moriarty's interference in the Stern Hollow case? Sherlock Holmes was but an investigator doing what investigators are paid to do, but Moriarty's involvement was entirely malicious, meant only to hasten your downfall."

Lord Bancroft was silent.

"I see you have not forgotten. How could you? Had you been looking for an ally and promised *me* that, in our shared enmity, together we would vanquish Moriarty, now you might already be on a luxury steamer, headed for your new life."

"And you would have had me as an ally?"

"Ash would have been the first person to tell you that my morality is quite flexible. Instead of holding my sister hostage, had you set three thousand pounds in front of me, I'd have broken you out of Ravensmere."

"You?" Lord Bancroft snorted. "Don't flatter yourself, Miss Holmes. You might be able to dig up some facts and make some deductions, but I wouldn't put any program that requires intricate planning and coordination into your hands."

This hardly corresponded with his earlier accusation that she'd been the one behind de Lacey's nonappearance, but Charlotte was pleased. She would be even more pleased if Moriarty believed likewise. What greater advantage could she enjoy than a consistent underestimation on the part of her sworn enemies?

"Oh, how did Moriarty obtain the hydrochloric acid then? How did he even think to employ such a method?"

"He didn't. The plan was of my design."

"I had no idea you were an expert in industrial chemistry. One moment, did you happen to come across the article in the April issue of *Cornhill Magazine?*"

"How did you—" Lord Bancroft's voice had turned sharp. And then his tone relaxed. "Of course, you read everything."

"I must admit, I thought it an interesting article, but nothing else," said Charlotte evenly, happy to play the role of a woman who was a little cleverer than the rest of her sex but posed no threat to the cerebral powerhouse that was Lord Bancroft Ashburton.

She felt no need to let him know that the copy of *Cornhill* that he had read was part of a minuscule print run carried out especially for his benefit, with the insertion of an article on hydrochloric acid that did not appear anywhere else. The laboratory mentioned in the article, located in the Berkshire countryside, had been supplied with the massively corrosive substance by none other than Miss Longstead, who had written Charlotte the moment two of the four bottles especially placed there had been pilfered.

"I still maintain, however," continued Charlotte, "that I could have helped you better, had you been able to see that."

"No, Charlotte Holmes. You were never any help to anyone. You make people's lives more dangerous, more complicated. I would be doing everyone a favor—"

He pointed the revolver in his left hand at her.

"I won't let you hurt her!" cried Lord Ingram.

But he could not move closer to Charlotte. His brother raised the revolver in his right hand, too, aimed at him. In the clearing before the ruined abbey, there was nothing to hide behind. The sun, minutes from rising, provided enough illumination for an expert marksman such as Lord Bancroft.

"And how will you protect her?" he scoffed. "With your broad, manly chest against the firepower of two revolvers? Don't be a fool, Ash. Stay where you are."

Instinctively Charlotte reached into her pocket, but her derringer had already been confiscated by Lord Bancroft outside the walls of Ravensmere. She swallowed. "You may hold overwhelming firepower, but you're still outnumbered, my lord."

"By those standing too far to tackle me in any significant manner before I fill them with lead? Pathetic."

She reasoned with him. "But who else will help you get to where you want to go?"

"Your horse and carriage are still here—I can drive myself. Then again, I need not shoot everyone. I can kill you and still retain compliance from the rest, unless you forget that your sister is still in the hands of my men."

She had never considered him a good enough man not to use her sister against her. All the same, she had hoped that Bernadine would be left alone.

The suffering of others meant nothing to him.

"Right, my sister," she said, her voice turning cold. "Let's set aside your most recent pronouncement that I could not coordinate something as intricate as your unauthorized release from Ravensmere. Instead, let's go back to an earlier moment, when you accused me of having obstructed Mr. de Lacey's arrival by nefarious means. Why would you think, my lord, that someone who can throw de Lacey's night into disarray would find it particularly difficult to liberate a house guarded by all of four mercenaries?"

—⚜—

AIX-EN-PROVENCE, FRANCE

More than anything else, Konstantin Meier wished to impress Mr. Baxter.

Tonight was to be his chance. He'd got rid of the stupid Frenchman who had been appointed to oversee things in Aix—nobody would know that the man *didn't* die in a drunken brawl. Nothing else stood in the way of Konstantin Meier taking all the credit for the success of the operation.

After all, the entire thing was as simple as could be.

He had a man in the house on the Cours Mirabeau, and there were those who wished to rescue this man. They moved into the house diagonally across weeks ago and had been busy as ants, making preparations.

And counting down.

They'd lobbed pinecones at the house, one fewer pinecone each day. They'd run small notices in the papers, both local and Parisian, the coded number featured in the adverts decreasing likewise. And this morning—yesterday morning, given that it was now well past midnight—the small notice had simply said, *Tonight.*

So tonight Konstantin Meier had invited the local *chef policier* and a half dozen of his men. For them, he had laid out an enormous spread of cheese, sausage, bread, and fruits, along with five whole tarts from a nearby bakery.

But with almost all the food gone, and the flow of wine stopped after each man had had a few glasses, the Provençal policemen had grown impatient.

"Are you sure that there are criminals intending to steal from you?"

Konstantin Meier smiled carefully. "Would I be wasting your time and my money if that isn't the case?"

"It's past four o'clock in the morning," the police chief pointed out.

"Maybe they are waiting for the darkest hours before dawn."

The police chief shrugged, clearly not convinced. *"Eh bien*, we wait some more then—and you had better be right."

Konstantin Meier left the room and found the actor in the passage. "What are you doing here? Go back upstairs. Walk some more right behind the curtain. Make sure your silhouette can be seen."

"I'm hungry. I've been up all night."

"Then go to the kitchen, eat something, take the two roast chickens to the policemen, and *go back up!"*

"All right, all right," the actor grumbled.

Konstantin Meier tried to calm himself. It was all straightforward. Someone had been troublesome for Mr. Baxter. That someone was in England—and would be punished there. But here, in Aix-en-Provence, they had a great many of her helpers, ready to storm this house to steal someone called Stephen Marbleton.

And when they did so, they would all be arrested for breaking and entering and sent to French prisons.

An excellent plan.

He hoped those two chickens would be enough to make the policemen stay until that glorious moment.

That is, if only the fools from across the street would come!

And if they didn't, then by God, after breakfast he was going to march across the Cours Mirabeau and demand to know why they— why they hadn't—

Except . . . how did one go about demanding, of complete strangers, why they had absolutely failed to trespass and commit grand larceny?

THE OUTSKIRTS OF PARIS

"Clu-cluck-cluck-cluck. Mooooooo. Cluck-cluck," called the woman mercenary.

"Baa. Baaaaaa," answered Mercenary Number Two, seated next to her.

This barnyard conversation had gone on for at least half an hour; Penelope barely heard it anymore. Her attention was on Number

Three, who was sliding down the banister again, for what must be the hundredth time. Not far from the staircase stood Number One, who had plucked a feather duster bare. He tossed all the feathers up and blew on them to keep them airborne, bending lower and lower until his face was nearly on the floor. Then he collected all the feathers and tirelessly started the process anew.

"*Ooh la la, quel chaos,*" said Madame Gascoigne, their Belgian cook, beside her, slipping back into her native French. "What did you say it was called again, mademoiselle, what young Monsieur Fontainebleu snuck into my hand before he was evicted?"

"Devil's snare. It's a plant from the same family as belladonna, but its toxins are deliriants. When Virginia was still a colony, soldiers in Jamestown ate the plants as greens and ended up acting like monkeys or running about naked for days on end."

"Nobody had better run about naked in this house," said Madame Gascoigne darkly. "Certainly not this unprepossessing lot."

Penelope laughed, the first truly lighthearted emotion she'd felt in days.

The mercenaries had been more careful in the beginning and supervised the preparation of every meal. But after a week in the house without so much as a stomachache, they had relaxed. After ten days, they barely bothered sticking their heads into the kitchen unless it was to ask what delicious dishes Madame Gascoigne would be serving up next.

And tonight, she had put on a scrumptious late repast at ten, and by midnight Number One was crouched at the foot of the newel post, barking.

The women of the staff waited some more time before they signaled Penelope, via a lantern in the window, that she could now come back into the house.

She had to tiptoe around the three male mercenaries on all fours in the entry, sniffing one another's behinds. Mr. Mears, released from his room, made himself presentable and immediately left to alert the police.

Knocks came at the front door. Penelope and Madame Gascoigne both froze. But it was only Mr. Mears, returning with the gendarmes.

"Oh, messieurs, thank goodness you're here!" Penelope cried, throwing herself at the nearest officer. "You cannot believe the terror we have lived through. These three men and one woman *invaded* our home. They barged in and demanded twenty-five thousand francs.

"But my aunt who owns the house is in England right now, and I couldn't come up with that sort of money. So they settled in, these dreadful malefactors. We scarcely dared draw breaths around them.

"Then a few hours ago, they became like this."

She swept her arm toward the delirious mercenaries. The officer—and his men—stared in fascination.

"At first we became even more frightened. But when it seemed that they'd truly lost their minds, our brave butler stole out to inform you of our plight. And thank goodness you're here, gentlemen!"

"Have no fear, mademoiselle, you are safe now," said the officer gallantly. "We will take these lawbreakers away. They have the look of repeat offenders. Perhaps you've heard, mademoiselle, we now have photographic records of our inmate population. Even if they choose to prevaricate, we will be able to identify them quickly—and send them back to prison just as quickly."

—⚹—

Upon Lieutenant Atwood's advice, Livia had left Aix-en-Provence the day before. Her train reached Lyon at ten in the evening, and Paris a little before six in the morning. The sun was up, the day bright but still cool, and Miss Redmayne was there on the platform, waving.

They embraced each other tightly.

"You look like you haven't slept a wink," said Livia. She herself had expected to contend with nerves all night but had instead been lulled into slumber by the motion of the train.

"Only half an hour in the carriage, coming here. But what theater we had last night."

She ushered Livia into the waiting carriage and launched into an account of the spectacle she and Mrs. Watson's staff had witnessed. As she described how the police had to beat Number One to prevent him from removing his trousers right there in the parlor, Livia laughed so hard she had to wipe away tears.

When the carriage pulled up before the house, Livia leaped off almost before it had come to a complete stop. At the door she slowed, shaking her head at herself. Bernadine, not having any social obligations, rarely got up so early.

But she was wrong. Bernadine was up, dressed, and in the garden, walking about, holding on to Mademoiselle Robineau's arm.

To a stranger, Bernadine might appear indifferent to her surroundings. But Livia knew what Bernadine's raised face and half-closed eyes meant. Whether it was the fresh air, the morning sunlight, or the simple freedom of being in the garden, Bernadine was happy.

Livia greeted the nurse and they switched places, so that Bernadine now held on to Livia's arm. She patted her sister's hand. "It's me. I'm back and we're safe."

If only they could have some news from England. If only she knew for sure that Charlotte, Mrs. Watson, Lord Ingram, and Lawson were safe, too.

And Mr. Marbleton, her dear, dear Mr. Marbleton.

Thirty-one

BY THE RUINED ABBEY

The moon hung low, so pale it was almost transparent. The sky, still darkish a minute ago, was now suffused with refracted light, streaks of fiery glow dispelling the gloom of the fading night.

Lord Bancroft stood in the dawn of a new day. Not far to his side, half a wall loomed, its stones cleft and mottled with age.

Did he realize how alone he was? Did he understand that he had step by step, decision by decision, turned allies into strangers and strangers into enemies?

Or was he thinking only of his current difficulties—his next course of action if he could no longer hold Bernadine over them?

He fired four shots in quick succession, two from each revolver in his hand, one projectile each for Charlotte, Lord Ingram, Mrs. Watson, and Lawson.

A scream pierced the air, followed by another shot.

"No!" cried Lord Ingram.

Lord Bancroft's face contorted. Slowly, he looked down at his right side, his arm was still raised and a bullet had entered his torso just below his armpit.

The shot had come from the ruins of the abbey.

He looked around the clearing at his four targets, all still standing, no one injured or bleeding.

He toppled over.

Thirty-two

THE INTERROGATION

N ow think carefully, Miss Holmes. Where were you last night?"
Treadles perspired. If she lied, and if anyone anywhere had
seen her headed in the direction of Ravensmere . . .

He wished he knew what she had been doing the night before, but at
the same time, he was terribly relieved that he had no idea. He would not
have taken the earliest train back to London today had Chief Inspector Fowler not sent an urgent telegram last night, requesting his return.

Except instead of taking part in Fowler's new case, he had been
commandeered by Talbot.

A knock came at the suite's hotel entrance. It was the lemonade
she had ordered an eternity ago.

She poured for everyone. "It's too warm for more tea. A glass of
lemonade is much better."

A cold beverage would have sounded divine a quarter hour ago,
but now he already felt a chill in his stomach, even as his nape continued to grow damper.

Miss Holmes picked up her glass and took a long draught. "Chief
Inspector, do you know a woman named Mrs. Farr?"

Treadles recoiled. He could only hope the horror radiating from
him hadn't raised the temperature in the room several more degrees.

Talbot looked wary, but not concerned. "What makes you think so, Miss Holmes?"

"I recently met a lovely lady by the name of Miss Harcourt, and she related to me the fascinating story of her uncle's unsolved murder. As much as I enjoy being a consulting detective, I am not compelled to solve every mystery I come across. Therefore I only listened and nodded, until she showed me a picture of her slain uncle's wife.

"The image had been taken more than a decade ago, and its subject had undergone a dramatic change in appearance. But still I recognized Mrs. Victor Meadows as not only an acquaintance but a former client—and then I became much more interested. So much so that my partner, Mrs. Watson, and I undertook a visit to Garwood Hall and spoke to the former gardener who climbed in through the window and discovered the body. Mrs. Watson even visited the archives of the *Manchester Guardian*, which is how we learned that you were the investigator for the Christmas Eve Murder."

Treadles breathed again: She was not going to divulge how she truly came to know the case.

"Mrs. Watson also visited the archives of London papers after we came back from Manchester. Here the case barely received two inches of column space. But by searching the indexes for your name in the years before and since, Chief Inspector, she found much laudatory coverage on your skills as an investigator."

Chief Inspector Talbot frowned.

Miss Holmes smiled at Treadles, who hadn't set down a word since she started asking about Mrs. Farr. "Inspector, would you allow a word between myself and the chief inspector?"

For once, Treadles had no desire at all to be a fly on the wall. "With your permission, Chief Inspector?"

When Talbot nodded, he shot out of the hotel suite.

It was only as he stood on the pavement, gulping down London's not-so-fresh air, that he realized that Miss Holmes had taken over the interrogation.

Charlotte studied the man who had given Mrs. Farr a second chance in life. "Chief Inspector, did you ever meet Mrs. Farr again after your inconclusive inquiry at Garwood Hall?"

The policeman held her gaze. "I did. Three years later, in the early months of 1875. I investigated an altercation in Bermondsey that led to several near-fatal injuries, and Mrs. Farr, as she called herself by then, happened to live next door to the residence where the altercation had taken place."

"Miss Harcourt would envy you, Chief Inspector. Ever since Mrs. Farr departed Manchester, she'd hoped to someday run into her aunt again—if only she'd thought to try her chances in London's rougher neighborhoods. Now, if you'll permit me a digression.

"The first time I called on Lord Bancroft at Ravensmere, we met in the garden. And one of his fellow inmates called to me from his room. He was excited to see a woman and eagerly proclaimed his innocence. He had done absolutely nothing, he declared, to merit his imprisonment.

"I did not pay him much mind, until Miss Harcourt showed me a photograph taken at Mrs. Farr's wedding. When she pointed to the picture of Mr. Ephraim Meadows, the victim's half brother, what should I see but a younger, more corpulent version of the 'innocent' man in the window?

"I asked Lord Ingram to look into the matter. It was not easy, but he managed to access certain older files. In July of 1875—that is, a few months after you met Mrs. Farr in London—someone submitted an anonymous tip to just the right person about how much money Mr. Ephraim Meadows had been losing at the gaming tables.

"His wealthy brother, who'd once turned a blind eye to his vices, had been dead for more than three years, and his sister, who'd inherited the brother's fortune, refused to give him a sou. How then was Mr. Ephraim Meadows able to pay his gambling debts? Perhaps someone ought to pay attention to his monthly dinners at Verey's, surely a bit too costly for a middling bureaucrat with no other sources of income?

"Now, Chief Inspector, can you, as an honorable man, deny that you are the one who tipped the crown to the fact that Mr. Ephraim Meadows had been selling low-level secrets to foreign agents?"

Chief Inspector Talbot said nothing.

"And will you deny that your excellent and entirely unwaged work had come about because you realized that Mrs. Farr would not have fallen so low if she hadn't been blackmailed by her brother-in-law?"

The policeman's posture was ramrod straight, his eyes keen and clear. "Is there any point of doubt concerning Mr. Ephraim Meadows's guilt?"

"None whatsoever," Charlotte admitted.

"Then I do not see why it matters whose work put him in Ravensmere, or from what motivation."

Charlotte tapped a fingertip against her chin. "You are right, Chief Inspector, it doesn't matter. Shall we bring Inspector Treadles back in, now that I've wasted enough of your time?"

Thirty-three

Ten hours before the jailbreaking

Charlotte examined her walking dress. Its skirt could be detached and she had brought along a pair of bloomers for the night, for ease of movement. Should everything go well, it would be midmorning tomorrow when she and Mrs. Watson returned to London. By coming back to their hotel in walking dresses, they would appear to have taken a turn in the park—a perfectly salutary activity for a pair of law-abiding ladies.

The bell rang.

Charlotte approached the street entrance. What could it be? Another message from Lord Bancroft? Further news from Paris? As long as something hadn't happened on Miss Moriarty's end . . .

"Who is it?"

"It's me!"

Mrs. Claiborne?

Charlotte opened the door. Mrs. Claiborne had not come alone: Mrs. Farr stood beside her, a patch over her blind eye. Her hair was smoothly chignoned, her dress modest but handsome and well-fitted. Her hat even featured some ribbons and a bow in black velvet.

Charlotte stood aside to let the two black-clad women enter. She was short on time, but Mrs. Farr did not make idle calls.

Indeed, Mrs. Farr wasted no time getting to the point. In fact, they were still in the vestibule, but she advanced no farther. "I've come to apologize, Miss Holmes, for my action last night. And to thank you for your help in finding my sister last year, as I don't believe I said anything to that effect at the time."

Her voice had its usual heaviness, but she spoke without hesitation.

Charlotte was not sure how to respond—she had not expected to see Mrs. Farr again so soon, and she had certainly not expected expressions of either contrition or gratitude.

In the silence came the sound of the hotel entrance of the suite opening and closing and Mrs. Watson's voice, "All right, my dear, let's go. Lord Bancroft's comeuppance will not happen by itself."

———❦———

Mrs. Watson was still kicking herself in the carriage. If only she hadn't said anything about Lord Bancroft's comeuppance!

But she had. Miss Charlotte played a grand chess game, in which every piece had its precise function and movement. The board, on this day at least, did not include Mrs. Farr or Mrs. Claiborne. Yet they were the ones who truly mattered. The ones for whom this was not a contest of strategies but life itself, replete with devastating losses.

Still, they could have denied the women their pleas. But then Mrs. Watson had begun to waver. Seeing her irresolution, Mrs. Claiborne had pressed her point, and Miss Charlotte had sighed and said, "All right, you can come. We'll get you some food and water, but you'll have a very long wait in the middle of nowhere. And you absolutely must not make your presence known, especially after we reach there—probably around three o'clock in the morning—until you hear from me otherwise."

Lawson had been surprised at the number of women he was to drive to the vicinity of Ravensmere, but gamely asked no questions. As the carriage wove through London's busy afternoon traffic, Mrs. Watson cautioned the women several more times that they must remain hidden and not draw any attention to themselves.

And then silence fell.

They were on the northern outskirts of London when Miss Charlotte said, "How are Mumble and Jessie, Mrs. Farr? Are they fully recovered?"

"I hope so. They refused to take more rest. Both went to work," said Mrs. Farr with a sigh. "We were lucky that it was you I sent them to capture—I could have put them in the way of real harm."

She stared down at her hands, clenched in her lap, and then looked up at Miss Charlotte. "You said to me last night that I've become accustomed to harsher methods. You're right. Looking back, it seems I've only ever taken extreme measures."

"Yours has long been a difficult lot," said Miss Charlotte quietly. "Your parents' bankruptcy, their deaths, your distant relations' unwillingness to take in a pair of impecunious girls. At sixteen, for your baby sister's sake, you had to marry a man who was at least partially responsible for your family's downfall."

Mrs. Watson's eyes widened, as did Mrs. Claiborne's. But Mrs. Farr exhibited no surprise.

"You knew?" asked Mrs. Watson.

"Yes, I knew. I overheard my parents' discussions." Mrs. Farr adjusted her black eye patch, the periwinkle blue of her good eye still startling every time Mrs. Watson looked into it. "But it was Mr. Meadows or the poorhouse for Miriam."

She laughed, a soft, bitter sound. "Maybe I should have chosen the poorhouse. Right after Miriam turned ten, he started to talk about sending her to a boarding school. To me that was the sort of place one relegated unwanted girls, but my objections fell on deaf ears. He was determined, and Miriam was excited at the prospect of friends her own age.

"Then, right before we left for Garwood Hall for Christmas, I found a letter in his pocket that declared his intention to more or less sell Miriam to his debtor, who had a penchant for little girls, under the excuse of sending her off to a girls' school after the New Year.

"We could not flee—he was careful never to put any money in my hands. Had I known Mrs. Harcourt better at that time, I'd have sought her help. But there was only one idea in my head, and that was I must kill him, so that he could not do this to Miriam."

She looked weary and hollow.

Mrs. Watson thought of that young woman, on that ice-cold night, struggling across a ledge as narrow as her own feet, with nothing to hold on to except the ivy on the wall that could not have supported her weight.

She had made it back to her room and she had almost carried off the whole enterprise, except . . .

"Did the inspector find the letter?" asked Miss Charlotte.

"In my husband's private safe in our house in Manchester, along with all the jewelry he'd bought so I could look pretty and shiny in front of his friends. The chief inspector also found chloral in the bottle of brandy my husband drank from on Christmas Eve, and I was the only one in the house who used chloral to sleep."

Miss Charlotte glanced outside—they were traveling past a row of factories, spewing black smoke high into the air. "The immediate assumption would be that your beauty and your plight melted the inspector's heart. But I don't believe that was what happened, was it?"

Mrs. Farr's voice turned rueful. "I didn't have the first idea how to use my plight—or my beauty. I only knew that he was the greatest threat I'd ever faced. He seemed implacable, and I did not want to stand trial to defend myself, because then it would become public knowledge what my husband intended, and I couldn't bear for Miriam to find out.

"So I threatened the detective inspector. I said if he charged me, I would tell everyone he fabricated the evidence because I'd rejected his inappropriate advances."

Mrs. Watson grimaced.

"Would you like to learn something about feminine wiles, Mrs. Farr?" said Mrs. Claiborne. "It's not too late, and I'm an expert."

Her unexpected interjection made Mrs. Watson titter. Even Mrs. Farr chortled, a rusty sound.

"But he would have the last laugh. A few years later, I'd lost my eye and was living in the greatest squalor I'd ever known. He saw me like that and demanded to know if this was all I'd made of the second chance he'd given me." Mrs. Farr exhaled. "It was—a most excruciating moment."

A mountainous load of cargo pulled by a pair of dray horses, muscles straining, hooves echoing, teetered past them in the opposite direction.

"Speaking of your presence in London," said Miss Charlotte, "and your departure from Manchester—were you being blackmailed by your brother-in-law?"

Contempt entered Mrs. Farr's countenance. "He knew that Mr. Meadows had bankrupted my family. For years, he'd used that over Mr. Meadows, threatening to tell me if he wasn't given another hundred pounds. Then one day Mr. Meadows said, 'No more,' and he did as he threatened: He told me the truth that I'd known since the very beginning.

"That was just before Christmas dinner. When my husband was found dead, this brother-in-law of mine became absolutely convinced that I'd done it in vengeance for my parents. He held his tongue before the inspector and blackmailed me by post afterward."

"There is one thing I do not understand about the case," said Miss Charlotte. "When you left Manchester, you did so resolutely, telling your husband's estate that you'd married again so that no one would look for you to give you your dower. But why did you wait so long? You would have been in better financial shape had you shaken off your brother-in-law sooner."

Mrs. Farr's jaw moved. "I stayed because I meant to eliminate the man who had wished to purchase my sister. Miriam was safe from him, but what about all the girls who did not have sisters willing to kill for them?"

The carriage drove over a big bump in the road, but Mrs. Farr's words jarred just as much.

"I know—I did say I've only ever resorted to extreme measures, didn't I?" Mrs. Farr smiled in self-mockery. "But the man lived in a great big estate that I couldn't get inside. And then one day he died of undisclosed causes—perhaps someone else had succeeded in ending his life—and I left Manchester within days."

Mrs. Watson couldn't help herself. "I know this is a terrible question, but have you never thought of doing away with Mr. Ephraim Meadows so that you and your sister could have lived in peace in Manchester?"

At her words, Mrs. Farr's hands shook. Mrs. Claiborne rubbed her arm, trying to exert a calming influence.

"I'm sorry!" cried Mrs. Watson.

Mrs. Farr shut her eyes for a moment. "It's all right. I had such episodes often after I killed Mr. Meadows. They went away after some years but returned again after Miriam died.

"It was terrible, cutting his throat. I always knew there would be a high price to pay. My brother-in-law's extortion was but a part of it. My eye. The other difficulties in our first years in London, too.

"I lived looking over my shoulder. I tried to expiate for my great sin by helping as many people as possible. But I always feared that the worst was yet to come. When I found out about Miriam and those postcards, I had a terrible premonition that she'd exposed herself to the evil gaze of the world. The moment I couldn't locate her I knew— I knew that my sins had come home to roost."

"She did not die because of you. She died because of Lord Bancroft," said Mrs. Claiborne, her teeth gritted.

Mrs. Farr, her shaking now under control, nodded at her. Then she looked at Miss Charlotte and Mrs. Watson. "I went wild when I thought I could finally find out who had killed Miriam. But when I learned that you had Mumble and Jessie—

"Miriam was infinitely precious to me. But so are Mumble and Jessie—and everyone else who became my children over the years. If anything had happened to them, I would not have gained Miriam back, I would have only lost Mumble and Jessie."

Her voice broke. "They are such good, devoted children. They deserve everything in the world—except a mad old woman driving them to ruin."

Mrs. Watson's eyes stung with tears. She blinked them back and said, her voice croaking only a little, "Please, Mrs. Farr, I am at least a dozen years senior to you. If you're old, then I must have been born before recorded history."

The mood in the carriage lightened somewhat. The sun shone. The vehicle was now in open country, clacking over a stone bridge that spanned a clear little stream.

"I recently learned something that might be of interest to you, Mrs. Farr," said Miss Charlotte.

And proceeded to tell her that Ephraim Meadows, her onetime tormentor, had spent the past twelve years incarcerated.

Mrs. Farr was silent for a whole minute, then she began to laugh, and laughed so hard she gave herself a side stitch.

"There is an even more interesting part to this," added Miss Charlotte. "Did Chief Inspector Talbot ever learn that Mr. Ephraim Meadows had blackmailed you?"

Mrs. Farr rubbed her side. "Yes, I confessed it—I was desperate for him not to think of me as an irresponsible fool."

"Someone sent in an anonymous tip that led to his arrest. Not long after, Chief Inspector Talbot began to handle an occasional investigation for that particular bureau of the government. I suspect that he had been the one to put Mr. Ephraim Meadows away in the first place."

Mrs. Farr fell silent again. Then, an ineffable sadness came over the proud, dilapidated ruins of her face. "Perhaps that is the great tragedy of my life. Not that I'd encountered my share of terrible people, but that I hadn't known to put my faith in the good ones."

Thirty-four

By the ruined abbey

Bancroft toppled over.

Lord Ingram swore but before he could run toward his brother's crumpled form, Mrs. Watson gripped him by the arm. "Wait. What if he's only pretending to be dead?"

Charlotte would have said the same.

He shook free of Mrs. Watson's grasp and ran, but someone darting out from the ruins of the abbey reached Lord Bancroft first.

Mrs. Farr.

She removed the revolvers from Bancroft's hands and only then felt his neck. "He's dead."

Lord Ingram, kneeling down next to his brother, had his wrist in hand. After a while, he slowly set it down into the grass and covered his eyes with his hand.

Another figure tottered out of the ruins. Mrs. Claiborne, a pistol in hand. "I'm so sorry," she said, her voice shaking. "But when he shot at everyone, I—I'm not even sure what happened—"

She looked around, shook her head, and looked again. "How are you all perfectly fine?"

"Blanks," said Mrs. Watson, putting an arm around her. "The

weapons Lord Bancroft had were all taken from us, and we made sure to load them with only blank cartridges."

Lord Ingram had been so meticulous he had weighed individual bullets for the different firearms, and had a gunsmith insert tiny metal slugs inside the stock of each gun so that they weighed the same as if real cartridges had been used, on the off chance that Bancroft, on picking up a weapon unfamiliar to him, could still detect the eight-to-ten-percent weight differential in the bullets.

And the distance they'd carefully kept from him? Blank cartridges were useless for hitting targets, but had he fired upon them point-blank, the explosion of the gunpowder could still be injurious, possibly fatal.

Lord Ingram shot to his feet. "Holmes, there is going to be trouble for you."

Their plan was never to kill Bancroft, but to deliver him— anonymously, if possible—back to the authorities.

But perfect plans existed only on paper, never in real life. With Lord Bancroft dead, Charlotte, who had visited him frequently of late, would face inquiries.

Lord Ingram was already urging everyone to check that they'd left nothing behind. After he'd ushered them into the carriage, he checked the entire area one more time before climbing inside.

"Mrs. Watson, can you glue a beard on my face?" he asked. "I already told Lawson to drop me off at the nearest railway station."

The safe, he mouthed to Charlotte.

She nodded. "And then please go back to Stern Hollow and 'recuperate.'"

He hesitated a moment. "You're right. Appearances still need to be kept."

"Mrs. Farr"—Charlotte shifted her attention to the next person— "the note you dropped off in the post for your children before you came with us?"

Mrs. Farr had not come for an overnight trip without informing Mumble and Jessie.

"I'll destroy it as soon as I get back," she said.

Charlotte now regarded a paper-white, trembling Mrs. Claiborne. "Accidents happen, Mrs. Claiborne, and yours came about because of an abundance of concern. Lord Bancroft is no more, but it might be safer, all the same, for you to leave the country, as you had originally planned."

"All right." Mrs. Claiborne bit her lower lip. "But what about you, Miss Holmes?"

The locket with the unfortunate Mrs. Kirby's picture inside had already been delivered to Sergeant MacDonald; there were no other loose ends concerning Inspector Treadles to take care of—or none Charlotte could do anything about at the moment. She planned to stop by the counterfeit Mrs. Claiborne's town house and use the typewriter there to fabricate an extra note from Lord Bancroft, a more conciliatory one to aid in the interrogation she was about to face. Then she would go back to her hotel, breakfast, and take a small nap, if possible.

"I will deal with what comes," she said. "I will be fine."

Thirty-five

THE INTERROGATION

"Shall we bring Inspector Treadles back in, now that I've wasted enough of your time?" asked Charlotte of Chief Inspector Talbot.

But instead of alerting Inspector Treadles his presence was required, she added, "One last question, sir, if you don't mind. Why did you help Mrs. Farr in London, even though she threatened you with falsehoods at Garwood Hall?"

The old policeman frowned. Charlotte's deduction of his role in Ephraim Meadows's incarceration at Ravensmere could be attributed to a stroke of luck, but only he and Mrs. Farr had been privy to the threat from Mrs. Farr. That Charlotte knew this meant that she knew everything.

He considered her another moment and sighed. "At Garwood Hall I would have let Mrs. Farr go even if she had not threatened me. She reminded me of my late sister. Most people did not care for my sister, but we, her younger siblings, depended on her wholeheartedly. She lifted us all to secure, respectable livelihoods but died when she was only thirty-one—of professionally acquired syphilis."

This detail he likely would not have shared, were Charlotte not a fallen woman herself.

His expression clouded with grief, then turned sharp with alarm.

"Why all this interest in Mrs. Farr, Miss Holmes? Was she somehow involved in Lord Bancroft's death? Have you been trying to gauge whether I would be lenient toward her again?"

At last, outside the street entrance of the hotel suite came the blessed sound Charlotte had been waiting for, a vehicle reining to a hard stop. She rose, went to the window, and looked out.

When she turned around, she smiled. "No, Inspector, Mrs. Farr was not at all involved in Lord Bancroft's death. And neither am I, of course, as I have been repeatedly trying to tell you."

"Miss Holmes—"

"Even you, Chief Inspector, will very soon no longer be involved."

The retired policeman raised a brow. "What do you mean, Miss Holmes?"

Charlotte returned to her seat and fluffed her skirts. "You will see presently, Chief Inspector."

A light knock came at the street entrance. Inspector Treadles poked in his head. "Do please excuse me, but there is a gentleman who wishes to speak to you, Chief Inspector."

With another nonplussed glance in Charlotte's direction, Chief Inspector Talbot excused himself and followed Inspector Treadles out.

When he came back several minutes later, he had the look of a Middle Ages theologian faced with incontrovertible evidence, for the first time, that the universe did not revolve around Earth.

"You are correct, Miss Holmes, on one thing at least. I am no longer involved in anything having to do with Lord Bancroft's death. My superiors are satisfied that he had been shot by the guards while trying to escape Ravensmere and somehow managed, without outside help and without leaving a trail of blood, to reach a spot six miles away before succumbing to his injury."

He gazed at Charlotte. "My congratulations to you, Miss Holmes."

Charlotte inclined her head. "Thank you, but Chief Inspector, truly no congratulations are needed. As I've said time and again, I had absolutely nothing to do with Lord Bancroft's demise."

Thirty-six

O n the third morning after the jailbreaking, Charlotte and Mrs. Watson arrived in Paris. Livia and Miss Redmayne greeted them with delight and relief, but did not pepper them with questions. The new arrivals visited Bernadine, then spoke with Mrs. Watson's valiant staff, who had acquitted themselves beautifully during the ordeal.

Livia ushered them upstairs to bathe and rest—these overnight trips from London were quite brutal. They woke up at around two, and everyone gathered on the veranda for a late luncheon.

Neither Livia nor Miss Redmayne was acquainted with the scale of the entire operation, though Livia was possibly the most ignorant of everyone, traveling in faraway places while the plan had been laid. She was wondering how long she ought to hold back her curiosity and let Charlotte and Mrs. Watson eat in peace when Miss Redmayne piped up. "I'm dying to know why Lady Ingram was in the papers!"

Mrs. Watson gave her a look. "You mean the former Lady Ingram, my dear."

A divorce was such a rare thing that they were none of them sure how to refer to the woman who was no longer married to Lord Ingram. Well, Charlotte probably knew from some thick, dusty tome on etiquette, but she showed no inclination to change anyone's appellation.

Instead, she spread copious butter on a slice of crusty bread. "Lady Ingram played a most substantial role in this whole affair."

Mrs. Watson, who was not as charitably disposed to Lady Ingram as Charlotte, said, "But if we are to tell the story chronologically, we need to start with Miss Marbleton."

Miss Marbleton was Mr. Marbleton's sister. Toward the end of the previous year, Moriarty had nabbed her parents and her brother. Miss Marbleton, who had remained free, had been desperate to free her family.

"Miss Marbleton, of course, led the digging crew—we none of us had any idea she was so talented at it. But she was the one who pointed out early on," continued Mrs. Watson, "that after Moriarty's trip to England this past February, he left, but she saw no evidence that he took Mr. Marbleton with him."

February was the last time Livia had seen Mr. Marbleton, walking past her in the Reading Room of the British Museum, flanked by a minder on either side.

Charlotte took a sip of her lobster bisque and a bite of her luxuriously buttered bread, and sighed happily—she still looked a bit tired, but at least she relished her meal. "After the events in Cornwall, when I was in hiding—but before I sailed on the *Provence*—I met our brother and Miss Moriarty."

The Holmes sisters had an illegitimate brother named Myron Finch. He and Miss Moriarty, James Moriarty's estranged daughter, were a pair of lovers far more star-crossed than Livia and Mr. Marbleton.

"During our discussion," Charlotte went on, "I relayed Miss Marbleton's speculation that perhaps her brother was still in the country. Miss Moriarty immediately told me about the existence of a dungeon at the headquarters of De Lacey Industries.

"Most people, even those acquainted with what De Lacey Industries actually does, don't know about the subbasement, as it was built before Moriarty became the head of the organization. Once Moriarty took over, he preferred to concentrate his energy on the Continent and chose to detain enemies and traitors at Château Vaudrieu rather than in the more limited cells of De Lacey Industries.

"But in the wake of the internal revolt that dethroned Moriarty for months, perhaps he became less trusting of his people on the Continent. The British branch, on the other hand, had remained loyal throughout.

"That loyalty, coupled with the fact that the dungeon at De Lacey Industries was almost entirely unknown, even to those inside the organization, made it likely that Mr. Marbleton could be held there. But we could not act on mere likelihood. We needed to know for certain."

Miss Redmayne waved her own piece of bread in the air. "And that's where Lady Ingram came in?"

"Right you are," answered Charlotte. "Lady Ingram had been in England for some time before that. She volunteered to infiltrate De Lacey Industries' headquarters because she holds a great grudge against Moriarty, and also because she hoped to render a service to the Marbletons.

"Those who have become Moriarty's foes hold the Marbletons in extraordinary esteem for how long they managed to elude Moriarty's grasp—and how much help they gave to others like themselves. Even though they were now at a temporary disadvantage, Lady Ingram decided that she'd still rather throw in her lot with them, in the hope that after they regained their freedom, they'd take her on as a protégée."

Livia used to wish that Mr. Marbleton could have enjoyed a normal, simple life. Now she was glad that he excelled at living the life that was his.

"But didn't Lady Ingram work for Moriarty for some time?" asked Miss Redmayne, loading a cutlet onto her plate. "Did she worry that she'd be recognized?"

"She met with very few people from De Lacey Industries, and

most of them have since died," said Mrs. Watson. "And we gave her our method of creating wrinkled skin, so she went in disguised as an old woman."

"So if Mrs. Watson hadn't discovered the ingenious method of using crumpled tissue paper, we'd have achieved nothing," said Charlotte.

She set down her soup spoon and clapped. Miss Redmayne and Livia joined in. The veranda rang with applause. Mrs. Watson, who must have received much more thunderous ovations when she'd been onstage, blushed as she stood up and took a bow.

"Now where were we?" said Miss Redmayne, after Mrs. Watson sat down again.

"Lady Ingram infiltrating De Lacey Industries' headquarters," said Livia. She felt tense even though the rescue had been effected days ago. To help with that, she drank from her wineglass. So civilized, a glass of wine with luncheon.

"Lady Ingram started her role as the dungeon helper in March," said Charlotte. "According to her, because the building hadn't been used as a detention center before, and because Moriarty demanded absolute secrecy, de Lacey was reduced to minding the prisoners himself. He desperately wanted to hand the job to someone else, and who better than a deaf-mute crone who also appeared to be illiterate?

"At first he let her into the dungeon himself each time, and watched her as she did her work. After a few weeks passed and nothing untoward happened, he stopped standing over her. Instead, he opened the hidden door to the subbasement, locked her in to do her chores, then let her out sometime later—repeating this process several times a day. This allowed her to verify that not only was Mr. Marbleton there, but also his parents.

"There was one door that de Lacey never opened. Lady Ingram inquired in gestures whether the room needed to be cleaned. He started to tell her about the expensive wines inside before he remembered that she was a deaf-mute and shook his head.

"She picked the padlock on the door one day and saw that de

Lacey had told the truth. Behind the door wasn't an even more secret dungeon but a cellar, albeit not a very well-stocked one, with only a hundred bottles or so in a space that could have easily held thousands. She made sure to report that there were also racks that had once held wine barrels but were now empty and covered with a large tarp."

"So you didn't know about the wine cellar until then?" Livia posed her first question.

"No. But ever since I learned of the dungeon, I'd mulled over digging a tunnel underneath to free Mr. Marbleton. De Lacey still looked in on the cells daily, which made the wine cellar a better spot than anywhere else in the subbasement—even better that a part of it was already under a tarp.

"But that would have been the plan that did the least. We would have put in significant time and treasure, and Moriarty would lose a few prisoners. A few important prisoners, yes, but Moriarty would have been in essentially the same position as before, stung a bit but not materially weakened."

Charlotte glanced at Livia. "I was willing to expend significant time and treasure for Mr. Marbleton. But how best to achieve maximum yield while subjecting everyone on our side to as few dangers as possible?

"By mid-April we'd confirmed Mr. Marbleton's location, and that of the existence of the cellar. A week later came intelligence that Moriarty had moved Mr. Marbleton to a house he owned in Aix-en-Provence. After we double-checked with Lady Ingram and made sure that Mr. Marbleton was still in London, in the subbasement of De Lacey Industries' headquarters, it became obvious that Moriarty was setting a trap for someone, likely me, even though at the time I had not surfaced yet."

Livia's heart thudded, remembering the lovely house she had passed by so many times on the Cours Mirabeau, always peering up with hope.

No effort had been spared in the pretense that they'd pinned all their hope and energy there—the house hired by Lieutenant Atwood and his crew, the excavation equipment, the pinecones and the small notices, Miss Redmayne's visit, and last but not least, Livia's daily walks up and down that thoroughfare.

Mrs. Watson harrumphed. "Instead of dirtying his own hands, Moriarty wanted us to commit the crime of breaking and entering, and for French law enforcement to mete out punishment. What he didn't know was that the same idea also occurred to us."

"Quite right," said Charlotte. "Early in April, Lord Ingram brought me an offer from Lord Remington—the reason I was on the RMS *Provence*. If I succeeded in retrieving a particular dossier, Lord Remington would offer me his protection. But by that time, I was beginning to have an idea of the scale of the operations required to achieve everything I wanted from Mr. Marbleton's rescue. What I needed was more personnel. So I bargained for that in addition.

"Also, once I tallied up everything I planned to do, it became apparent that I could not finance it on my own. I could borrow from Lord Ingram, but what would be the fun in that? There was, however, a source of funding sitting right there if only I could get to it: Lord Bancroft's ill-begotten gains."

Livia sucked in a breath. Charlotte's audacity was making her light-headed.

"Lord Bancroft, though confined, remained a piece on the board. It was a certainty he wanted out of Ravensmere. It was another certainty that Moriarty would have already contacted him, hoping to make him a minion. The only uncertainty was when they would strike that agreement, which I needed to know if I was to properly account for Lord Bancroft's part in the game.

"I performed an experiment. I asked Miss Longstead to write an article about hydrochloric acid. Then I had a special print run done of a magazine Lord Ingram had seen in Lord Bancroft's rooms at Ravensmere, with the insertion of the article.

"This would help Lord Bancroft formulate a straightforward plan that required relatively little assistance from Moriarty, which would give him a stronger bargaining position. And, of course, to give himself an even stronger bargaining position, he would likely propose to help Moriarty get rid of me."

Miss Redmayne's jaw fell. "So everything Lord Bancroft did was what you wanted him to do?"

Mrs. Watson shook her head. "Miss Charlotte simply made it easier for him to do what *he* wanted to do."

Either way, Livia's head spun.

Charlotte used her bread to mop up the remainder of her soup, which Miss Redmayne had told them was perfectly acceptable in France. "But at this point things didn't go as I'd hoped. I'd thought that once Moriarty failed to catch me in Aix-en-Provence *and* saw that Mr. Marbleton had been freed, *then* he'd retaliate by having Lord Bancroft spring another trap for me. But once I received Lord Bancroft's first note, I realized that Moriarty meant to deploy Lord Bancroft at the *same time*, probably because if his plans for Aix-en-Provence succeeded, I would be in a French jail, rather than dead. And also, with me out of the way in England, he might catch more of the people who worked with me.

"This presented problems. It was challenging enough coordinating activities around De Lacey Industries' headquarters and the house in Aix-en-Provence. It would be even more strenuous if I had to do a song and dance for Lord Bancroft at the same time.

"We had to make things happen at our pace, rather than his. That's why we decided that Lord Ingram would pretend to break his limb, so that I would be back in England at a time of my choosing. Then came something else I didn't anticipate: I had *thought* of the possibility someone would take Bernadine hostage, but I hadn't *prepared* for it as I ought to have.

"Yet in the end, the mercenaries in this house did not complicate things too much. In fact, their presence allowed me to dictate the timing of Lord Bancroft's jailbreaking. Miss Redmayne knows all about it."

"That's right." Miss Redmayne beamed. "I smuggled in some chicken blood. Mademoiselle Robineau smeared it on Bernadine and made it seem like she was vomiting blood and suffering from a health crisis. There was a hullabaloo. The mercenaries panicked. They kicked young Fontainebleu out and refused to let me in the next time I came—which gave me a reason to send an urgent telegram to London."

"And which gave *me* a reason to leave London," said Charlotte. "Which, if you're Lord Bancroft, you would not want me to do because to his thinking, I might learn while I was in France that a great many of my cohorts had been arrested in Aix-en-Provence, which would make me unlikely to return to England to do his bidding, which would make his bargain with Moriarty more difficult."

"I *think* I understand most everything," said Livia slowly. "You schemed for everything to happen on the same night, so that Moriarty and Lord Bancroft would not know, until it was too late, that any single piece of their combined plan had suffered a fatal setback. The deliriants Fontainebleu delivered here helped to get rid of the mercenaries. In Aix-en-Provence we made it seem that we had designs on the counterfeit Mr. Marbleton, to keep Moriarty's minions' attention focused squarely there, when everything significant would instead take place in or around London."

"That's more or less what happened," said Charlotte. "You understand everything."

Mrs. Watson adjusted the stems of brilliant sunflowers in a blue vase near her. "Come to think of it, I'm still not quite sure why the counterfeit Mrs. Claiborne died—or why she was going to Mumble's and Jessie's places of employment and all that."

Charlotte served herself some gratinéed leek. "The poor woman. I learned from Inspector Treadles later that all the items inside her recovered valise had been marked with either the real Mrs. Claiborne's name or her initials. She was probably going to leave everything behind in that farmhouse and 'disappear,' not realizing that Lord Bancroft intended to toss a body my way because too much smoke and mirrors would have made me suspicious. And her killer had sunk the valise in a fishpond on the property, because had Mrs. Claiborne truly been on the run, she would not have taken so many things that betrayed her identity.

"As for why she did what she did to call attention to Mumble and Jessie, that was remarkably good strategy on Lord Bancroft's part. Mrs. Farr might not know who had killed her sister, but Lord Bancroft knew very well that I did. He trusted that I would discover the connection between the boxers and Mrs. Farr and suspect Mrs. Farr for Mr. Underwood's disappearance—which, again, would have legitimized Lord Bancroft's 'problem.'"

Miss Redmayne raised her hand. "I want to know about Fontainebleu. Is he one of Lord Remington's agents?"

Livia was also curious—she'd heard a good bit about young Fontainebleu, not only from Miss Redmayne but also from the staff.

"Not quite," answered Charlotte. "He belongs to a different bureau and helped us as a personal favor to Lord Ingram. If you ever see him around London, Miss Redmayne, pretend to have never met him."

"Understood," said Miss Redmayne crisply.

Charlotte, having eaten her vegetables, eyed the platter of desserts with great interest. Livia pushed it closer to her. "There's something I still don't understand. How did you get the crown to call off the investigation into how Lord Bancroft died?"

"Ah," said Charlotte. "Remember his great asset?"

"His money?"

"That is a great asset, but what I meant was the evidence of wrong or scandalous doings he'd collected on various important men, a prominent royal among them. If you're Moriarty, who loves a state secret or any kind of secret, and Lord Bancroft refused to become your minion outright, what then would you demand in return?"

"The letters and whatnot!"

"Mrs. Claiborne mentioned that Mr. Underwood had surrendered one of the keys Lord Bancroft had given him. That would have been the key to that lot. At one point we hoped to steal the letters ourselves, but once Lord Bancroft was shot dead, Lord Ingram sent word as quickly as possible and as high up as possible, alerting the crown that the letters might be found at De Lacey Industries.

"And once the crown had the letters, let's just say that no one was really sad that Lord Bancroft was dead, especially now that the consequences he'd long threatened would not come to pass. What reason did anyone have to further investigate Lord Bancroft's death then?"

Charlotte smiled—at everyone at the table but, Livia felt, at a pile of cream puffs in particular. "We've been lucky, but it's fair to say we've also made our own luck."

Thirty-seven

Johnny stared at the velvet pouch in his hand. It jingled with coins, like something out of a fairy tale.

Ten pounds, that was what Mrs. Claiborne had said.

No, that was only a small portion of what she'd said. What she'd said was, *Mr. Underwood didn't have children of his own. But with the three of you, he came to understand a little bit of fatherhood. He cared a great deal about you and was very proud of your hard work and your beautiful character.*

He never made a will, but I know he would want you to be taken care of, especially you, Mr. Esposito. Before he died, he transferred all his savings to me. On his behalf, I would like to present you with a legacy of five hundred pounds. I hope you will always carry his memory in your heart.

In his youth, Mr. Underwood worked at Eastleigh Park, a great ducal estate. One of the scions of the family, Lord Ingram Ashburton, was saddened to learn of his passing. When he heard that I would be making this bequest to you, he doubled it by putting up five hundred pounds of his own.

He would invest the money for you and pay you ten pounds a month, for the next ten years. At the end of which, you may ask for the remainder in a lump sum, or continue to receive ten pounds a month for as long as the principle lasts. But in any case, you will receive no less than twelve hundred pounds over the next ten years.

Here is the first installment.

And Johnny hadn't heard a word since.

He only gradually became aware of the bustle of the Port of London, the smell of the Thames, the cawing of the gulls wheeling overhead.

"I loved him!" The words left his lips as tears escaped his eyes. He wiped them, the fabric of his sleeves rough on his face. "I loved him."

"He knew. He took such solace in you—in all of you." Mrs. Claiborne sighed. "It's a shame we didn't get to know one another better before this. But I plan to stay in touch with Mrs. Farr, and I hope to have your news from her. Good-bye and good luck."

And then she was walking up the gangway, the last passenger to do so. The ship sailed only minutes later, sliding down the Thames Estuary.

Johnny waved until he couldn't see her anymore, until the ship itself became only a dot on the horizon.

"Better put that in an inside pocket," said Jessie.

Johnny did so. "I'd put it in my shoes if it would fit."

Jessie laughed, the sound as clear as bells.

"You two got something, too, right?"

He knew he'd been singled out, but he also knew that the very kind Mrs. Claiborne wouldn't have forgotten them.

Jessie waved a letter in her hand. "Did you hear nothing at all? We got an invitation to be founding members of the Baker Street Irregulars."

"What is that?"

"Some sort of intelligence-gathering apparatus," answered Jessie. "Should be interesting."

Johnny turned to Mumble. "Do you think so, too?"

Mumble did not answer immediately, which gave Johnny an excuse to stare at his starched collar, immaculate against his golden skin.

"Yes, I do think so. I'm intrigued by the opportunity to work with Sherlock Holmes," said Mumble eventually. "You, Johnny? Any plans for your ten pounds a month?"

Johnny thought of the garden his mother had longed for since they came to Britain. With a hundred twenty pounds a year, he could give her a garden *and* provide his sister with a dowry. His brothers would be educated enough to have professions: Earlier his greatest dream had been that they would man ticket booths at railway stations or, if they were spectacularly lucky, work as guards at the British Museum; but now they could become clerks, even accountants like Mr. Constable.

And he said so, stuttering at the grandeur of his new aspirations.

"No, I meant, what do *you* want to do, Johnny?"

Mumble draped an arm over Johnny's shoulders. Heat suffused Johnny—heat and a happiness so sharp it hurt. What did he want? He wanted this moment to last forever, the weight of ten pounds in his inside pocket, the fullness of hope in his heart, the smile on Jessie's face as she said, "Yes, what do *you* want, Johnny?" and the smell of starch and lavender water on Mumble's clothes.

He wanted Mumble's shirt so he could always remember this day.

The thought startled him so much that he stammered, "I—I—is it too late for me to go back to school?"

He could read—and write if he had to. But he felt downright illiterate next to Mumble, who read a book in less time than other people took to have a meal.

"Possibly," said Mumble. "But I'm willing to hire myself out as a tutor if you are serious about learning."

"You are?"

Chaotic images flashed in Johnny's head, the two of them sitting shoulder to shoulder, heads bent together.

"Of course, but I won't come cheap," said the man who had tutored his brothers for free for a whole year.

Johnny didn't know why, but his cheeks burned—and not in an unpleasant way. "Let me think about it."

"Come on, boys," called Jessie, who was already walking away. "I have to go to work first thing in the morning."

"Coming, madam," answered Mumble, letting go of Johnny and starting after her.

"I like what Mrs. Claiborne said about our character." Jessie turned around and walked backward. "I am going to write it down in my diary."

Johnny hurried to catch up with Mumble. "Nobody has ever said anything to me about my character."

Mumble gave him a sidelong glance. "That's a shame, my friend. Your character—is the most beautiful anything I have ever come across in my life."

———※———

It had been several days, but Miss Harcourt still couldn't believe that her aunt Meadows had called on her at her hotel.

She hadn't recognized the unannounced visitor, but had greeted the woman courteously, thinking she had the wrong door.

The woman, a patch over one eye, had gazed at her and said, "My goodness, for a moment I thought you were your mother."

And Miss Harcourt, in that moment, had realized exactly who she was.

It had been a teary reunion—most of the tears Miss Harcourt's own. For dear Miriam, forever gone. For her aunt Meadows—no, her aunt Farr, who'd had to endure so much. And for gladness, because Aunt Farr was still alive and, after everything, still had hope.

When she had proposed a second meeting, Miss Harcourt had immediately agreed—and half expected that when no one came, she would finally wake up from her exceptional dream.

But no, Aunt Farr had not only come again but brought her adopted daughter.

Miss Harcourt had no desire to marry but adored children. She spent a happy half hour fussing over Eliza, planning a special afternoon tea with the girl.

Afterward, Aunt Farr suggested a walk. The day was overcast, the sky pregnant with rain. But Miss Harcourt loved the outdoors and didn't mind at all.

"Scotland Yard will look into my old case again," said her aunt Farr softly. "It's best that Eliza and I left the country for a while."

Miss Harcourt and her mother had known, from the moment

Aunt Farr disappeared from Manchester, that she had most likely been the one. They simply hadn't known the exact reasons.

"You should come with me—I'm leaving soon, and I can help look after Eliza," she said, not daring to hope. "Except as I mentioned earlier, I'm set to travel slowly, a tour of the world such as Cousin Miriam would have liked."

Aunt Farr had told her never to hesitate to bring up Cousin Miriam: She was not afraid of a pang in her chest at her baby sister's name; she feared only that Miriam, who had so wished to leave a mark on the world, might become forgotten too soon.

"She never did travel as she wished to," murmured Aunt Farr. "And it wasn't because she never made any money but because she couldn't bear to leave me all by myself."

She patted Eliza on the shoulder. "So let's travel slowly. Let's travel for Miriam. It would be good for Eliza to see the world, too. If it's agreeable to you, we will go with you until the west coast of America. I think I mentioned that the two oldest of my foster children have emigrated to Los Angeles. They're doing well and have asked several times for me to join them out there."

She smiled a little. "They said I would have no aches and pains in the Southern California winter."

"I've long wanted to visit California but I never thought—" Miss Harcourt stopped.

"You never thought what?"

Miss Harcourt gathered up her courage. "I never thought that even if we should meet again, you would wish to spend time with me."

Aunt Farr did not answer immediately. She had lost her beauty, but to Miss Harcourt, her magnetism had only intensified, the magnetism of someone who had stared into the abyss and found her way again.

"You and your mother were two of the kindest people I've ever met," she said slowly. "I dared not embrace your friendship at the time; I feared that if your uncle Ephraim ever went public with his allegations, you'd be accused of having aided and abetted me.

"But I've thought often of you over the years. When things were especially bleak, I would remember that little house in Manchester and how glad I always felt when you came to call. Those were some of the happiest hours of my life."

"Mine, too." Tears were once again falling down Miss Harcourt's face. She barely cared. "Mine, too."

Then she did have to use her handkerchief to wipe her face, because without realizing it, she had led them to the London ticket office of the Union Steamship Company, on whose vessel she would begin the first leg of her journey.

"Shall we buy your passages to Madeira?"

Her aunt Farr inhaled deeply and took little Eliza's hand in her own. "Yes, do let us."

❈

Dear Chief Inspector Talbot,

By the time you receive this letter, I will have sailed from Southampton, headed for distant shores.

I write to apologize—and to thank you. I have no excuses to offer for my indefensible action fifteen years ago and can never repay you for your kindness then, and later again in London.

All I can offer is the humble reassurance that I never once took for granted the second chance you gave me.

You, sir, are the greatest benefactor of my life, and I will always remain,

Yours gratefully,
Mrs. Winifred Farr

❈

Livia visited the Jardin des Tuileries each day, even though it necessitated a substantial commute from Mrs. Watson's house much farther down the Seine.

But soon she wouldn't be able to anymore, because soon Mrs. Newell, her dear elderly cousin with whom she'd embarked on this grand voyage, would reach Paris, after a few pleasant weeks at Lake

Como in Italy. And once they were reunited, it would be time to head back to England.

Livia patted the sun-warmed planks of her bench. She and Mr. Marbleton had sat on this very bench last December, when they'd come to Paris as Charlotte's fellow burglars.

On that day she'd told him that she'd finally finished her first Sherlock Holmes story, and he had been delighted for her. Now she was mulling another story, based on recent events, one that had the potential to be quite a crowd-pleaser.

The most ridiculous part of the entire business had to be the way Lord Ingram had obtained old Mrs. Sylvestrina Calder's house.

The tunnel between De Lacey Industries and City and Suburban Bank had, of course, not been dug from the wine cellar at the former but from a house that was located not far from either. Instead of purchasing the house outright, Lord Ingram had opted to make up an entity called the Sylvestrina Society, based on the owner's unusual name.

The Sylvestrina Society was purportedly begun by an extremely wealthy German aristocrat who, having been both proud of and embarrassed by her name, had decided in her will to honor other Sylvestrinas by gifting those her lawyers could find three months at the seaside, all expenses paid, with a weekly stipend besides.

The only significant stipulation was that each recipient must swear to absolute secrecy, lest everyone start naming their daughters Sylvestrina to take advantage of the society's largesse.

Mrs. Calder, after overcoming her initial skepticism, had had the time of her life on the Devon coast, looked after by none other than Norbert, Livia's mother Lady Holmes's former maid and Lord Remington's agent.

Livia's mind buzzed with ideas. Instead of a very rare name, she could make the requirement something like, oh, bright flaming hair. The Red-Headed League. And a red-haired fellow is paid to leave his house so that a tunnel could be dug to the nearest bank.

Yes, that could work. Sherlock Holmes, when consulted, would realize the deceptive nature of the ruse immediately and—

"Excuse me, is this seat taken?" said a soft voice.

Livia turned and saw a woman with a drop-brim hat in a very fashionable dress of printed cotton.

"No, please feel free to sit."

"Thank you."

Livia returned her attention to the statue of Daphne she'd been staring at. Now where was she? Yes, Sherlock Holmes. She ought to find out what the inside of a strong room looked like, so she could write a convincing one. She ought to—

Wait. The woman who had sat down beside her—where had she seen the woman before?

Her head whipped toward the new occupant of the bench, who was twisting her handkerchief in a rather shy manner.

Dear God! Before Sherlock Holmes and company had come to Paris last December, they had met at the house near Portman Square, and a maid who looked somewhat like this woman had opened the door.

Except the maid had been no maid but Mr. Marbleton in disguise!

"Have you been well, Miss Holmes?" said he, his head still bent.

Livia's eyes filled with tears. She looked back at the statue, as if he were but another stranger she'd encountered at the park. "I have been—I have been very well."

She knew, of course, that he had been freed. But no one she knew had witnessed this escape, and the Marbletons had not sent word afterward. It was as if they had disappeared into the ether. As if they had never been there in the first place.

But now he was here.

He was here.

"Have *you* been well?" she managed to ask.

"I am as well at this moment as I have ever been in my entire life."

Was his voice breaking, like hers?

"And now that we've got that out of the way, Miss Holmes, I can no longer keep my impatience at bay. Has your story been published yet?"

Her tears fell. "No, but it will be published in this year's *Beeton's Christmas Annual.* They paid me twenty-five pounds."

"I am beyond happy for you."

"I am beyond happy for you, too."

"Please allow me to apologize for the very ill manner of my speech last December."

She barely remembered now how he had pushed her away, so that she would not realize he had lost his freedom. "You are forgiven, sir."

His handkerchief appeared on her lap. She wiped at her eyes. "Will you disappear again very soon, Mr. Marb—actually, may I call you Stephen?"

He moved so that he sat immediately next to her, their dresses touching. "I thought you'd never ask, dear Livia. Yes, I will disappear for a while. But I will return to your side as soon as possible—I always will."

Thirty-eight

L ivia found Charlotte on the veranda of Mrs. Watson's house, clad in a dress of white-and-gold stripes, watching the Seine flow by.

Livia pulled her baby sister to her feet and hugged her fiercely. "Thank you! Thank you, Charlotte!"

"I enjoy being thanked," said Charlotte after she was let go, "but what does this particular bout of gratitude concern?"

The enormous white-and-gold bow on her bodice had been crushed by the hug. Livia fluffed it up again. "I saw Mr. Marbleton at the *jardin* today."

"How did he look?"

Livia thought for a moment. "Quite pretty. His dress was more fashionable than mine."

This made her laugh. Charlotte smiled, looking at her.

Livia ambled around the veranda and prattled happily for a while about the all-too-brief encounter, and then said, "I can't thank you enough, Charlotte. I know you didn't do it for me—the Marbletons are important in the campaign against Moriarty and—"

Charlotte leaned against the balustrade. "You're wrong."

Livia was taken aback. The Marbletons *weren't* important?

"The Marbletons are crucial allies, and I consider Mr. Marbleton a friend. But throughout the planning and the execution of our entire strategy, you were always foremost in my thoughts, Livia. So yes, I did do it for you."

"But that is—that is—Mr. Marbleton and I might not have a future together."

"No one knows about the future. His freedom has made you happier in the present, and that's good enough for me."

Livia could not speak.

Charlotte came forward and linked their arms together. "Madame Gascoigne reports that there is a little place nearby that does the most magnificent sole meunière. Miss Redmayne is keen to try it and we were only waiting for you to come back."

"Oh, Charlotte!" Livia finally found her voice.

Her sister held her close. "You are the most consequential person in my life, Livia. I would have moved mountains for you. What was a few hundred cubic yards of clay?"

※

Lord Ingram dutifully played the invalid at Stern Hollow for a few days. Then, with a great big plaster cast on his "fractured" limb, he traveled with his children and the Treadleses to the Isles of Scilly, and there played the invalid for another week but enjoyed himself much better.

When Holmes visited him in Bordeaux, at the vineyard he'd inherited from his godfather, another two weeks had passed and he had at last tossed aside all casts and crutches.

When he had collected her from the railway station and brought her to the estate, she surprised him by suggesting a ride around the property—in all the years he'd known her, he'd seen her atop a horse no more than three times. But then again, he had mentioned that he longed to ride, and Holmes remembered everything.

The harvest was in progress. *Vendangeurs*, crouched low, cut grapes from the vines row by row. He led her to a clearing atop a gentle slope, where a picnic had been laid out.

They ate bread and cheese, and drank the vineyard's own wine. It was best known for a heady claret, but it also made a few bottles of crisp white wines that went well with the local cheese.

Afterward, they lay on the picnic blanket and watched clouds drift across a deep blue sky.

"I heard from Miss Longstead a few days ago," declared Holmes. "She and her friend Miss Yates just returned from two weeks in the Highlands. I relayed your invitation to Bordeaux, and she has promised to lay waste to the vineyard's cellar by summer of next year."

"She is welcome to it." He thought of the vineyard's vast cellar, laughed, and set his hands under his head. "All the money has been wired, by the way."

He had been in Bruges. Before Mrs. Claiborne left England, she passed on the key she'd received from Mr. Underwood the last time they had seen each other, the remaining key he had been safeguarding for Bancroft. Key in hand, Lord Ingram had claimed the contents of Bancroft's safe-deposit box, the one containing the latter's ill-begotten gains.

With Remington's permission, Mrs. Claiborne and Mrs. Farr had each received decent compensation, and Holmes, a finder's fee of three thousand pounds.

"Are you all right?" asked Holmes.

Lord Ingram sighed. "The moment he was shot, I felt as if a bullet struck me, too. But I can't say I've missed him much in the days since, except to feel a certain sadness for the young man he had once been."

She placed her hand over his, and they remained for some time without speaking.

"You know," she murmured, "lately I have not been as busy and have started to dabble in erotic fiction again. Would you like to marvel at my latest output?"

He was hot and cold at once. He still grew consternated when he thought of those last three lines he'd added to the story, not only because they'd exposed a state of mind that he hadn't been entirely aware of at the time of their writing, but also because they formed a query, a demand for an answer.

When he was content enough with things as they are.

"Give me a moment to prepare myself for stupefaction," he said lightly.

They both sat up. She waited for him to take a draught of wine directly from the almost empty bottle before she took out a sheet of paper from her handbag and gave it to him. "To review, this is the installment you last added to the story."

Her clothes lay discarded at the foot of the bed. Firelight caressed her smooth, supple skin. She made no attempt to cover herself, though occasionally she adjusted the pillows underneath her head.

He stared at her. His hands were busy, but his feet had been nailed in place since she had removed her garments and lain down on the rumpled bed. Light refracted from the folds of black satin sheets. Her lips were red, her calves shapely.

He swallowed.

His alarm clock clanged. He swore under his breath and silenced it. The woman rose, dressed quickly, came forward, and took her payment from him.

"Thank you," she said softly. "Will the painting be finished soon?"

"Yes, soon," he mumbled.

"Ah, I'm almost sorry," she said as she walked out the door. "Your studio is the only one that's remotely warm in winter."

The man stared at the closing door.

The painting was finished some time ago and he suspected that she knew it. Where did that leave him then?

He scarcely needed the review—every word remained seared in his mind, especially those last three lines. He recorked the bottle and set it aside. "I didn't realize you'd be building upon my little contribution."

"Of course. This then"—she handed him another sheet of paper, her tone matter-of-fact—"is the addition I made."

The inside of his head roared. He took a deep breath.

The door opened again. The woman walked back in.
"Is—is it cold outside?" asked the man hesitantly.
"Very. But I'm not afraid of cold and I have plenty of coal at home."
"Then, have you forgotten something?"
"No. Well, yes. I forgot to tell you that if you'd like, I will be happy to
come by even without the excuse of the painting."

The roar subsided somewhat. This wasn't too bad. Not too bad at all. He could live with this.

But maybe he was also a bit disappointed. Maybe the roar in his head hadn't been only fear screeching but also hope bellowing at the top of its lungs.

"Why is this next section all scratched out?" he heard himself ask, his voice normal enough.

"Because she started to tell him that she was in fact a very young dowager duchess who enjoyed a large dower and was free to take him as a lover, but I decided that was irrelevant to the story."

He chortled. "Still, I must say that the story has progressed in both a logical and satisfactory direction."

"But that's not all. Turn it over."

He did as she asked. "There's more?"

The couple at last tumbling into bed?

On the back of the sheet of paper, it was written, *"I love you,"* *she said. "I have loved and admired you for a long time, and I thought you should* *know."*

The roar came back, loud enough to block out the chatter of *ven-* *dangeurs* down the slope and the grunts of porters who ferried buckets of grapes to waiting drays. "What is this, Holmes?"

"Looks like a declaration of love to me," she said, sounding as if he'd asked her the name of an unfamiliar pastry. *Looks like a profiterole* *to me.*

Under her wide-brimmed hat, her expression was serene, almost blank. He had learned how to read the smallest flickers of reaction on her face, but it was as if he'd suddenly become illiterate again where she was concerned.

"Whose declaration of love?"

Did he force the words past his lips or did the question barrel through all his restraints and hurl itself out there?

"Hers." She pointed at the paper. "And mine."

Inside his mind it was suddenly quiet, so quiet. "You love me?"

She gazed at him, her eyes as deep as the sky. "Yes, I have loved and admired you for a long time. I used to think that you must know it but then I realized that you didn't. You believe that although my friendship is genuine, I sleep with you for novelty and am liable to stop being your lover once that novelty fades."

He raised a hand and cupped her soft cheek. "I don't fear that so much anymore."

"But you're still not sure. I can live with a great deal of uncertainty, but you don't enjoy it nearly as much. So I decided that if it is in my power to make you feel more secure, then I ought to at least try." She placed her hand over his. "I will remain your friend and lover as surely as I will remain Livia's sister."

A whole orchestra dropped into his head, cymbals, strings, acres of brass and woodwind, all surging toward the crescendo of "Ode to Joy." "My God! Do excuse my language—but Miss Olivia is the most consequential person in your life. You're comparing me to her?"

"Yes. That is how important you are to me. I will direct the moving of hundreds of cubic yards of clay for you, too, if I must."

All at once he could read her again. It was not blankness on that beloved face but bone-deep certainty. She was as sure and confident about this as she had ever been about anything in her entire life.

He laughed, his heart so full he could scarcely speak. "I just hope next time I will not need to be in the digging crew again."

"No, for you, I will crawl in that tunnel and dig myself." She looked into her reticule again. "And I have a little present for you, a Viking penannular brooch that—"

He took the reticule from her, tossed it onto the picnic blanket, and kissed her. Later, when they were apart again, he would gaze at the pin, study its every detail, and polish it with the finest, softest cloth. But now he needed no token of love.

Now he needed only her.

ACKNOWLEDGMENTS

At this point, I can copy and paste my acknowledgments from year to year: What remarkable good fortune, that I can count on the same wonderful people, season after season, to help, encourage, and inspire me to do my best work.

Kerry Donovan and the team at Berkley, for their care and dedication.

Kristin Nelson, who worries and strategizes so I don't have to.

Janine Ballard, truly, has there ever been a better critique partner under the sun?

Kate Reading, who makes it really fun to listen to these books, which I need to do to prevent continuity errors.

My family and friends, who have done so much for me.

My brain, still functional. Hallelujah!

And you, if you are reading this, dear friend, thank you. Thank you for everything!

USA Today bestselling author Sherry Thomas is one of the most acclaimed historical fiction authors writing today, winning the RITA Award two years running and appearing on innumerable "Best of the Year" lists, including those of *Publishers Weekly, Kirkus Reviews, Library Journal,* Dear Author, and All About Romance. Her novels include *A Study in Scarlet Women, A Conspiracy in Belgravia, The Hollow of Fear, The Art of Theft,* and *Murder on Cold Street,* the first five books in the Lady Sherlock series; *My Beautiful Enemy;* and *The Luckiest Lady in London.* She lives in Austin, Texas, with her husband and sons.

VISIT SHERRY THOMAS ONLINE

SherryThomas.com

Ready to find
your next great read?

Let us help.

Visit prh.com/nextread

Penguin
Random
House